ALSO BY ROBERTO BOLAÑO

2666

TRANSLATED FROM THE SPANISH BY NATASHA WIMMER

FARRAR, STRAUS AND GIROUX   NEW YORK

66

ROBERTO BOLAÑO

Farrar, Straus and Giroux
18 West 18th Street, New York 10011

Copyright © 2004 by the heirs of Roberto Bolaño
Translation copyright © 2008 by Natasha Wimmer
All rights reserved
Distributed in Canada by Douglas & McIntyre Ltd.
Printed in the United States of America
Originally published in 2004 by Editorial Anagrama, Spain
Published in the United States by Farrar, Straus and Giroux
First American edition, 2008
Published simultaneously as a hardcover and a three-volume slipcased paperback edition

An excerpt from "The Part About the Crimes" first appeared in *Vice*.

"Canto nottorno di un pastore errante dell'Asia," by Giacomo Leopardi, is quoted in Jonathan Galassi's translation.

Library of Congress Cataloging-in-Publication Data
Bolaño, Roberto, 1953–2003.
    [2666. English]
    2666 / Roberto Bolaño ; translated from the Spanish by Natasha Wimmer.
      p.   cm.
    ISBN-13: 978-0-374-10014-8 (hardcover : alk. paper)
    ISBN-10: 0-374-10014-4 (hardcover : alk. paper)
    ISBN-13: 978-0-374-53155-3 (pbk. : alk. paper)
    ISBN-10: 0-374-53155-2 (pbk. : alk. paper)
    I. Wimmer, Natasha.   II. Title.

PQ8098.12.O38A12213 2008
863'.64—dc22

2008018295

Designed by Jonathan D. Lippincott

www.fsgbooks.com

10 9 8 7 6 5 4 3 2 1

This work has been published with a subsidy from the Directorate-General of Books, Archives, and Libraries of the Spanish Ministry of Culture and with assistance from the National Endowment for the Arts in the form of an NEA Translation Grant.

For Alexandra Bolaño and Lautaro Bolaño

An oasis of horror in a desert of boredom.
—Charles Baudelaire

CONTENTS

A NOTE FROM THE AUTHOR'S HEIRS

Realizing that death might be near, Roberto left instructions for his novel 2666 to be published divided into five books corresponding to the five parts of the novel, specifying the order in which they should appear, at what intervals (one per year), and even the price to be negotiated with the publisher. With this decision, communicated days before his death by Roberto himself to Jorge Herralde, Roberto thought he was providing for his children's future.

After his death, and following the reading and study of his work and notes by Ignacio Echevarría (a friend Roberto designated as his literary executor), another consideration of a less practical nature arose: respect for the literary value of the work, which caused us, together with Jorge Herralde, to reverse Roberto's decision and publish 2666 first in full, in a single volume, as he would have done had his illness not taken the gravest course.

THE PART ABOUT THE CRITICS

The first time that Jean-Claude Pelletier read Benno von Archimboldi was Christmas 1980, in Paris, when he was nineteen years old and studying German literature. The book in question was *D'Arsonval*. The young Pelletier didn't realize at the time that the novel was part of a trilogy (made up of the English-themed *The Garden* and the Polish-themed *The Leather Mask*, together with the clearly French-themed *D'Arsonval*), but this ignorance or lapse or bibliographical lacuna, attributable only to his extreme youth, did nothing to diminish the wonder and admiration that the novel stirred in him.

From that day on (or from the early morning hours when he concluded his maiden reading) he became an enthusiastic Archimboldian and set out on a quest to find more works by the author. This was no easy task. Getting hold of books by Benno von Archimboldi in the 1980s, even in Paris, was an effort not lacking in all kinds of difficulties. Almost no reference to Archimboldi could be found in the university's German department. Pelletier's professors had never heard of him. One said he thought he recognized the name. Ten minutes later, to Pelletier's outrage (and horror), he realized that the person his professor had in mind was the Italian painter, regarding whom he soon revealed himself to be equally ignorant.

Pelletier wrote to the Hamburg publishing house that had published *D'Arsonval* and received no response. He also scoured the few German bookstores he could find in Paris. The name Archimboldi appeared in a dictionary of German literature and in a Belgian magazine devoted— whether as a joke or seriously, he never knew—to the literature of Prussia. In 1981, he made a trip to Bavaria with three friends from the German department, and there, in a little bookstore in Munich, on Voralmstrasse, he found two other books: the slim volume titled *Mitzi's Treasure*, less than one hundred pages long, and the aforementioned English novel, *The Garden*.

Reading these two novels only reinforced the opinion he'd already formed of Archimboldi. In 1983, at the age of twenty-two, he undertook the task of translating *D'Arsonval*. No one asked him to do it. At the time, there was no French publishing house interested in publishing the German author with the funny name. Essentially Pelletier set out to translate the book because he liked it, and because he enjoyed the work, although it also occurred to him that he could submit the translation, prefaced with a study of the Archimboldian oeuvre, as his thesis, and—why not?—as the foundation of his future dissertation.

He completed the final draft of the translation in 1984, and a Paris publishing house, after some inconclusive and contradictory readings, accepted it and published Archimboldi. Though the novel seemed destined from the start not to sell more than a thousand copies, the first printing of three thousand was exhausted after a couple of contradictory, positive, even effusive reviews, opening the door for second, third, and fourth printings.

By then Pelletier had read fifteen books by the German writer, translated two others, and was regarded almost universally as the preeminent authority on Benno von Archimboldi across the length and breadth of France.

•

Then Pelletier could think back on the day when he first read Archimboldi, and he saw himself, young and poor, living in a *chambre de bonne*, sharing the sink where he washed his face and brushed his teeth with fifteen other people who lived in the same dark garret, shitting in a horrible and notably unhygienic bathroom that was more like a latrine or cesspit, also shared with the fifteen residents of the garret, some of whom had already returned to the provinces, their respective university degrees in hand, or had moved to slightly more comfortable places in Paris itself, or were still there—just a few of them—vegetating or slowly dying of revulsion.

He saw himself, as we've said, ascetic and hunched over his German dictionaries in the weak light of a single bulb, thin and dogged, as if he were pure will made flesh, bone, and muscle without an ounce of fat, fanatical and bent on success. A rather ordinary picture of a student in the capital, but it worked on him like a drug, a drug that brought him to tears, a drug that (as one sentimental Dutch poet of the nineteenth century had it) opened the floodgates of emotion, as well as the floodgates of something that at first blush resembled self-pity but wasn't (what was it, then? rage? very likely), and made him turn over and over in his mind, not in words but in painful images, the period of his youthful apprenticeship, and after a perhaps pointless long night he was forced to two conclusions: first, that his life as he had lived it so far was over; second, that a brilliant career was opening up before him, and that to maintain its glow he had to persist in his determination, in sole testament to that garret. This seemed easy enough.

•

Jean-Claude Pelletier was born in 1961 and by 1986 he was already a professor of German in Paris. Piero Morini was born in 1956, in a town near Naples, and although he read Benno von Archimboldi for the first time in 1976, or four years before Pelletier, it wasn't until 1988 that he translated his first novel by the German author, *Bifurcaria Bifurcata*, which came and went almost unnoticed in Italian bookstores.

Archimboldi's situation in Italy, it must be said, was very different from his situation in France. For one thing, Morini wasn't his first translator. As it happened, the first novel by Archimboldi to fall into Morini's hands was a translation of *The Leather Mask* done by someone called Colossimo for Einaudi in 1969. In Italy, *The Leather Mask* was followed by *Rivers of Europe* in 1971, *Inheritance* in 1973, and *Railroad Perfection* in 1975; earlier, in 1964, a publishing house in Rome had put out a collection of mostly war stories, titled *The Berlin Underworld*. So it could be said that Archimboldi wasn't a complete unknown in Italy, although one could hardly claim that he was successful, or somewhat successful, or even barely successful. In point of fact, he was an utter failure, an author whose books languished on the dustiest shelves in the stores or were remaindered or forgotten in publishers' warehouses before being pulped.

Morini, of course, was undaunted by the scant interest that Archimboldi's work aroused in the Italian public, and after he translated *Bifur-*

caria Bifurcata he wrote two studies of Archimboldi for journals in Milan and Palermo, one on the role of fate in *Railroad Perfection*, and the other on the various guises of conscience and guilt in *Lethaea*, on the surface an erotic novel, and in *Bitzius*, a novel less than one hundred pages long, similar in some ways to *Mitzi's Treasure*, the book that Pelletier had found in an old Munich bookstore, and that told the story of the life of Albert Bitzius, pastor of Lützelflüh, in the canton of Bern, an author of sermons as well as a writer under the pseudonym Jeremiah Gotthelf. Both pieces were published, and Morini's eloquence or powers of seduction in presenting the figure of Archimboldi overcame all obstacles, and in 1991 a second translation by Piero Morini, this time of *Saint Thomas*, was published in Italy. By then, Morini was teaching German literature at the University of Turin, the doctors had diagnosed him with multiple sclerosis, and he had suffered the strange and spectacular accident that left him permanently wheelchair-bound.

•

Manuel Espinoza came to Archimboldi by a different route. Younger than Morini and Pelletier, Espinoza studied Spanish literature, not German literature, at least for the first two years of his university career, among other sad reasons because he dreamed of being a writer. The only German authors he was (barely) familiar with were three greats: Hölderlin, because at sixteen he thought he was fated to be a poet and he devoured every book of poetry he could find; Goethe, because in his final year of secondary school a teacher with a humorous streak recommended that he read *The Sorrows of Young Werther*, in whose hero he would find a kindred spirit; and Schiller, because he had read one of his plays. Later he would discover the work of a modern author, Jünger, with whom he became acquainted more by osmosis than anything else, since the Madrid writers he admired (and deep down hated bitterly) talked nonstop about Jünger. So it could be said that Espinoza was acquainted with just one German author, and that author was Jünger. At first he thought Jünger's work was magnificent, and since many of the writer's books were translated into Spanish, Espinoza had no trouble finding them and reading them all. He would have preferred it to be less easy. Meanwhile, many of his acquaintances weren't just Jünger devotees; some of them were the author's translators, too, which was something Espinoza cared little about, since the glory he coveted was that of the writer, not the translator.

As the months and years went by, silently and cruelly as is often the case, Espinoza suffered some misfortunes that made him change his thinking. It didn't take him long, for example, to discover that the group of Jüngerians wasn't as Jüngerian as he had thought, being instead, like all literary groups, in thrall to the changing seasons. In the fall, it's true, they were Jüngerians, but in winter they suddenly turned into Barojians and in spring into Orteganites, and in summer they would even leave the bar where they met to go out into the street and intone pastoral verse in honor of Camilo José Cela, something that the young Espinoza, who was fundamentally patriotic, would have been prepared to accept unconditionally if such displays had been embarked on in a fun-loving, carnivalesque spirit, but who could in no way take it all seriously, as did the bogus Jüngerians.

Worse was discovering what the members of the group thought about his own attempts at fiction. Their opinion was so negative that there were times—some nights, for example, when he couldn't sleep—that he began to wonder in all seriousness whether they were making a veiled attempt to get him to go away, stop bothering them, never show his face again.

And even worse was when Jünger showed up in person in Madrid and the group of Jüngerians organized a trip to El Escorial for him (a strange whim of the maestro, visiting El Escorial), and when Espinoza tried to join the excursion, in any capacity whatsoever, he was denied the honor, as if the Jüngerians deemed him unworthy of making up part of the German's *garde du corps*, or as if they feared that he, Espinoza, might embarrass them with some naïve, abstruse remark, although the official explanation given (perhaps dictated by some charitable impulse) was that he didn't speak German and everyone else who was going on the picnic with Jünger did.

•

That was the end of Espinoza's dealings with the Jüngerians. And it was the beginning of his loneliness and a steady stream (or deluge) of resolutions, often contradictory or impossible to keep. These weren't comfortable nights, much less pleasant ones, but Espinoza discovered two things that helped him mightily in the early days: he would never be a fiction writer, and, in his own way, he was brave.

He also discovered that he was bitter and full of resentment, that he oozed resentment, and that he might easily kill someone, anyone, if it would provide a respite from the loneliness and rain and cold of Madrid, but this was a discovery that he preferred to conceal. Instead he concentrated on his realization that he would never be a writer and on making everything he possibly could out of his newly unearthed bravery.

He continued at the university, studying Spanish literature, but at the same time he enrolled in the German department. He slept four or five hours a night and the rest of the time he spent at his desk. Before he finished his degree in German literature he wrote a twenty-page essay on the relationship between Werther and music, which was published in a Madrid literary magazine and a Göttingen university journal. By the time he was twenty-five he had completed both degrees. In 1990, he received his doctorate in German literature with a dissertation on Benno von Archimboldi. A Barcelona publishing house brought it out one year later. By then, Espinoza was a regular at German literature conferences and roundtables. His command of German was, if not excellent, more than passable. He also spoke English and French. Like Morini and Pelletier, he had a good job and a substantial income, and he was respected (to the extent possible) by his students as well as his colleagues. He never translated Archimboldi or any other German author.

•

Besides Archimboldi, there was one thing Morini, Pelletier, and Espinoza had in common. All three had iron wills. Actually, they had one other thing in common, but we'll get to that later.

Liz Norton, on the other hand, wasn't what one would ordinarily call a woman of great drive, which is to say that she didn't draw up long- or medium-term plans and throw herself wholeheartedly into their execution. She had none of the attributes of the ambitious. When she suffered, her pain was clearly visible, and when she was happy, the happiness she felt was contagious. She was incapable of setting herself a goal and striving steadily toward it. At least, no goal was appealing or desirable enough for her to pursue it unreservedly. Used in a personal sense, the phrase "achieve an end" seemed to her a small-minded snare. She preferred the word *life*, and, on rare occasions, *happiness*. If volition is bound to social imperatives, as William James believed, and it's therefore easier to go to war than it is to quit smoking, one could say that Liz Norton was a woman who found it easier to quit smoking than to go to war.

This was something she'd been told once when she was a student, and she loved it, although it didn't make her read William James, then or ever. For her, reading was directly linked to pleasure, not to knowledge or enigmas or constructions or verbal labyrinths, as Morini, Espinoza, and Pelletier believed it to be.

Her discovery of Archimboldi was the least traumatic of all, and the least poetic. During the three months that she lived in Berlin in 1988, when she was twenty, a German friend loaned her a novel by an author she had never heard of. The name puzzled her. How was it possible, she asked her friend, that there could be a German writer with an Italian surname, but with a *von* preceding it, indicating some kind of nobility? Her German friend had no answer. It was probably a pseudonym, he said. And to make things even stranger, he added, masculine proper names ending in vowels were uncommon in Germany. Plenty of feminine proper names ended that way. But certainly not masculine proper names. The novel was *The Blind Woman*, and she liked it, but not so much that it made her go running out to buy everything else that Benno von Archimboldi had ever written.

•

Five months later, back in England again, Liz Norton received a gift in the mail from her German friend. As one might guess, it was another novel by Archimboldi. She read it, liked it, went to her college library to look for more books by the German with the Italian name, and found two: one was the book she had already read in Berlin, and the other was *Bitzius*. Reading the latter really did make her go running out. It was raining in the quadrangle, and the quadrangular sky looked like the grimace of a robot or a god made in our own likeness. The oblique drops of rain slid down the blades of grass in the park, but it would have made no difference if they had slid up. Then the oblique (drops) turned round (drops), swallowed up by the earth underpinning the grass, and the grass and the earth seemed to talk, no, not talk, argue, their incomprehensible words like crystallized spiderwebs or the briefest crystallized vomitings, a barely audible rustling, as if instead of drinking tea that afternoon, Norton had drunk a steaming cup of peyote.

But the truth is that she had only had tea to drink and she felt overwhelmed, as if a voice were repeating a terrible prayer in her ear, the words of which blurred as she walked away from the college, and the rain wetted her gray skirt and bony knees and pretty ankles and little else, because before Liz Norton went running through the park, she hadn't forgotten to pick up 'her umbrella.

•

The first time Pelletier, Morini, Espinoza, and Norton saw each other was at a contemporary German literature conference held in Bremen in 1994. Pelletier and Morini had met before, during the German literature colloquiums held in Leipzig in 1989, when the GDR was in its death throes, and then they saw each other again at the German literature symposium held in Mannheim in December of the same year (a disaster, with bad hotels, bad food, and abysmal organizing). At a modern German literature forum in Zurich in 1990, Pelletier and Morini met Espinoza. Espinoza saw Pelletier again at a twentieth-century German literature congress held in Maastricht in 1991 (Pelletier delivered a paper titled "Heine and Archimboldi: Converging Paths"; Espinoza delivered a paper titled "Ernst Jünger and Benno von Archimboldi: Diverging Paths"), and it could more or less safely be said that from that moment on they not only read each other in the scholarly journals, they became friends, or they struck up something like a friendship. In 1992, Pelletier, Espinoza, and Morini ran into each other again at a German literature seminar in Augsburg. Each was presenting a paper on Archimboldi. For a few months it had been rumored that Benno von Archimboldi himself planned to attend this grand event, which would convene not only the usual Germanists but also a sizable group of German writers and poets, and yet at the crucial moment, two days before the gathering, a telegram was received from Archimboldi's Hamburg publishers tendering his apologies. In every other respect, too, the conference was a failure. In Pelletier's opinion, perhaps the only thing of interest was a lecture given by an old professor from Berlin on the work of Arno Schmidt (here we have a German proper name ending in a vowel), a judgment shared by Espinoza and, to a lesser extent, by Morini.

They spent the free time they had, which was ample, strolling the paltry (in Pelletier's opinion) sites of interest in Augsburg, a city that Espinoza also found paltry, and that Morini found only moderately paltry, but still paltry in the final analysis, while Espinoza and Pelletier took turns pushing the Italian's wheelchair since Morini wasn't in the best of health this time, but rather in paltry health, so that his two friends and colleagues considered that a little bit of fresh air would do him no harm, and in fact might do him good.

Only Pelletier and Espinoza attended the next German literature conference, held in Paris in January 1992. Morini, who had been invited too, was in worse health than usual just then, causing his doctor to advise him, among other things, to avoid even short trips. It wasn't a bad conference, and despite their full schedules, Pelletier and Espinoza found time to eat together at a little restaurant on the Rue Galande, near Saint-Julien-le-Pauvre, where, besides talking about their respective projects and interests, during dessert they speculated about the health (the ill health, the delicate health, the miserable health) of the melancholy Italian, ill health that nevertheless hadn't prevented him from beginning a book on Archimboldi, a book that might be the grand Archimboldian opus, the pilot fish that would swim for a long time beside the great black shark of the German's oeuvre, or so Pelletier explained that Morini had told him on the phone, whether seriously or in jest he wasn't sure. Both Pelletier and Espinoza respected Morini's work, but Pelletier's words (spoken as if from inside an old castle or a dungeon dug under the moat of an old castle) sounded like a threat in the peaceful little restaurant on the Rue Galande and hastened the end of an evening that had begun in an atmosphere of cordiality and contentment.

•

None of this soured Pelletier's and Espinoza's relations with Morini.

The three met again at a German-language literature colloquium held in Bologna in 1993. And all three contributed to Number 46 of the Berlin journal *Literary Studies*, a monograph devoted to the work of Archimboldi. It wasn't the first time they'd contributed to the journal. In Number 44, there'd been a piece by Espinoza on the idea of God in the work of Archimboldi and Unamuno. In Number 38, Morini had published an article on the state of German literature instruction in Italy. And in Number 37, Pelletier had presented an overview of the most important German writers of the twentieth century in France and Europe, a text that incidentally sparked more than one protest and even a couple of scoldings.

But it's Number 46 that matters to us, since not only did it mark the formation of two opposing groups of Archimboldians—Pelletier, Morini, and Espinoza versus Schwarz, Borchmeyer, and Pohl—it also contained

a piece by Liz Norton, incredibly brilliant, according to Pelletier, well argued, acording to Espinoza, interesting, according to Morini, a piece
that aligned itself (and not at anyone's bidding) with the theses of the
three friends, whom it cited on various occasions, demonstrating a thorough knowledge of their studies and monographs published in specialized journals or issued by small presses.

Pelletier thought about writing her a letter, but in the end he didn't.
Espinoza called Pelletier and asked whether it wouldn't be a good idea to
get in touch with her. Unsure, they decided to ask Morini. Morini ab-
stained from comment. All they knew about Liz Norton was that she
taught German literature at a university in London. And that, unlike
them, she wasn't a full professor.

•

The Bremen German literature conference was highly eventful. Pelletier,
backed by Morini and Espinoza, went on the attack like Napoleon at
Jena, assaulting the unsuspecting German Archimboldi scholars, and the
downed flags of Pohl, Schwarz, and Borchmeyer were soon routed to the
cafés and taverns of Bremen. The young German professors participat-
ing in the event were bewildered at first and then took the side of Pelletier and his friends, albeit cautiously. The audience, consisting mostly
of university students who had traveled from Göttingen by train or in
vans, was also won over by Pelletier's fiery and uncompromising interpretations, throwing caution to the winds and enthusiastically yielding to
the festive, Dionysian vision of ultimate carnival (or penultimate carnival) exegesis upheld by Pelletier and Espinoza. Two days later, Schwarz
and his minions counterattacked. They compared Archimboldi to
Heinrich Böll. They spoke of suffering. They compared Archimboldi to
Günter Grass. They spoke of civic duty. Borchmeyer even compared
Archimboldi to Friedrich Dürrenmatt and spoke of humor, which
seemed to Morini the height of gall. Then Liz Norton appeared, heaven-
sent, and demolished the counterattack like a Desaix, like a Lannes, a
blond Amazon who spoke excellent German, if anything too rapidly, and
who expounded on Grimmelshausen and Gryphius and many others, including Theophrastus Bombastus von Hohenheim, better known as
Paracelsus.

•

That same night they ate together in a long, narrow tavern near the river, on a dark street flanked by old Hanseatic buildings, some of which looked like abandoned Nazi offices, a tavern they reached by going down stairs wet from the drizzle.

The place couldn't have been more awful, thought Liz Norton, but the evening was long and agreeable, and the friendliness of Pelletier, Morini, and Espinoza, who weren't standoffish at all, made her feel at ease. Naturally, she was familiar with most of their work, but what surprised her (pleasantly, of course) was that they were familiar with some of hers, too. The conversation proceeded in four stages: first they laughed about the flaying Norton had given Borchmeyer and about Borchmeyer's growing dismay at Norton's increasingly ruthless attacks, then they talked about future conferences, especially a strange one at the University of Minnesota, supposedly to be attended by five hundred professors, translators, and German literature specialists, though Morini had reason to believe the whole thing was a hoax, then they discussed Benno von Archimboldi and his life, about which so little was known. All of them, from Pelletier to Morini (who was talkative that night, though he was usually the quietest), reviewed anecdotes and gossip, compared old, vague information for the umpteenth time, and speculated about the secret of the great writer's whereabouts and life like people endlessly analyzing a favorite movie, and finally, as they walked the wet, bright streets (bright only intermittently, as if Bremen were a machine jolted every so often by brief, powerful electric charges), they talked about themselves.

All four were single and that struck them as an encouraging sign. All four lived alone, although Liz Norton sometimes shared her London flat with a globe-trotting brother who worked for an NGO and who came back to England only a few times a year. All four were devoted to their careers, although Pelletier, Espinoza, and Morini had doctorates and Pelletier and Espinoza also chaired their respective departments, whereas Norton was just preparing her dissertation and had no expectation of becoming the head of her university's German department.

That night, before he fell asleep, Pelletier didn't think back on the squabbles at the conference. Instead he thought about walking along the streets near the river and about Liz Norton walking beside him as Espinoza pushed Morini's wheelchair and the four of them laughed at the little animals of Bremen, which watched them or watched their shadows on the pavement while mounted harmoniously, innocently, on each other's backs.

•

From that day on or that night on, not a week went by without the four of them calling back and forth regularly, sometimes at the oddest hours, without a thought for the phone bill.

Sometimes it was Liz Norton who would call Espinoza and ask about Morini, whom she'd talked to the day before and whom she'd thought seemed a little depressed. That same day Espinoza would call Pelletier and inform him that according to Norton, Morini's health had taken a turn for the worse, to which Pelletier would respond by immediately calling Morini, asking him bluntly how he was, laughing with him (because Morini did his best never to talk seriously about his condition), exchanging a few unimportant remarks about work, and later telephoning Norton, maybe at midnight, after putting off the pleasure of the call with a frugal and exquisite dinner, and assuring her that as far as could be hoped, Morini was fine, normal, stable, and what Norton had taken for depression was just the Italian's natural state, sensitive as he was to changes in the weather (maybe the weather had been bad in Turin, maybe Morini had dreamed who knows what kind of horrible dream the night before), thus ending a cycle that would begin again a day later, or two days later, with Morini calling Espinoza for no reason, just to say hello, that was all, to talk for a while, the call invariably taken up with unimportant things, remarks about the weather (as if Morini and even Espinoza were adopting British conversational habits), film recommendations, dispassionate commentary on recent books, in short, a generally soporific or at best listless phone conversation, but one that Espinoza followed with odd enthusiasm, or feigned enthusiasm, or fondness, or at least civilized interest, and that Morini attended to as if his life depended on it, and which was succeeded two days or a few hours later by Espinoza calling Norton and having a conversation along essentially the same lines, and Norton calling Pelletier, and Pelletier calling Morini, with the whole process starting over again days later, the call transmuted into hyperspecialized code, signifier and signified in Archimboldi, text, subtext, and paratext, reconquest of the verbal and physical territoriality in the final pages of *Bitzius*, which under the circumstances was the same as talking about film or problems in the German department or the clouds that passed incessantly over their respective cities, morning to night.

•

They met again at the postwar European literature colloquium held in Avignon at the end of 1994. Norton and Morini went as spectators, although their trips were funded by their universities, and Pelletier and Espinoza presented papers on the import of Archimboldi's work. Pelletier's paper focused on insularity, on the rupture that seemed to separate the whole of Archimboldi's oeuvre from the German tradition, though not from a larger European tradition. Espinoza's paper, one of the most engaging he ever wrote, revolved around the mystery veiling the figure of Archimboldi, about whom virtually no one, not even his publisher, knew anything: his books appeared with no author photograph on the flaps or back cover; his biographical data was minimal (German writer born in Prussia in 1920); his place of residence was a mystery, although at some point his publisher let slip in front of a *Spiegel* reporter that one of his manuscripts had arrived from Sicily; none of his surviving fellow writers had ever seen him; no biography of him existed in German even though sales of his books were rising in Germany as well as in the rest of Europe and even in the United States, which likes vanished writers (vanished writers or millionaire writers) or the legend of vanished writers, and where his work was beginning to circulate widely, no longer just in German departments but on campus and off campus, in the vast cities with a love for the oral and the visual arts.

•

At night Pelletier, Morini, Espinoza, and Norton would have dinner together, sometimes accompanied by one or two German professors whom they'd known for a long time, and who would usually retire early to their hotels or stay until the end of the evening but remain discreetly in the background, as if they understood that the four-cornered figure formed by the Archimboldians was inviolable and also liable to react violently to any outside interference at that hour of the night. By the end it was always just the four of them walking the streets of Avignon, as blithely and happily as they'd walked the grimy, bureaucratic streets of Bremen and as they would walk the many streets awaiting them in the future, Norton pushing Morini with Pelletier to her left and Espinoza to her right, or

Pelletier pushing Morini with Espinoza to his left and Norton walking backward ahead of them and laughing with all the might of her twenty-six years, a magnificent laugh that they were quick to imitate although they would surely have preferred not to laugh but just to look at her, or the four of them abreast and halted beside the low wall of a storied river, in other words a river tamed, talking about their German obsession without interrupting one another, testing and savoring one another's intelligence, with long intervals of silence that not even the rain could disturb.

•

When Pelletier returned from Avignon at the end of 1994, when he opened the door to his apartment in Paris and set his bag on the floor and closed the door, when he poured himself a glass of whiskey and opened the drapes and saw the usual view, a slice of the Place de Breteuil with the UNESCO building in the background, when he took off his jacket and left the whiskey in the kitchen and listened to the messages on the answering machine, when he felt drowsiness, heaviness in his eyelids, but instead of getting into bed and going to sleep he undressed and took a shower, when wrapped in a white bathrobe that reached almost to his ankles he turned on the computer, only then did he realize that he missed Liz Norton and that he would have given anything to be with her at that moment, not just talking to her but in bed with her, telling her that he loved her and hearing from her lips that she loved him too.

Espinoza experienced something similar, though slightly different in two respects. First, the need to be near Liz Norton struck some time before he got back to his apartment in Madrid. By the time he was on the plane he'd realized that she was the perfect woman, the one he'd always hoped to find, and he began to suffer. Second, among the ideal images of Norton that passed at supersonic speed through his head as the plane flew toward Spain at four hundred miles an hour, there were more sex scenes than Pelletier had imagined. Not many more, but more.

Meanwhile, Morini, who traveled by train from Avignon to Turin, spent the trip reading the cultural supplement of *Il Manifesto*, and then he slept until a couple of ticket collectors (who would help him onto the platform in his wheelchair) let him know that they'd arrived.

As for what passed through Liz Norton's head, it's better not to say.

Still, the friendship of the four Archimboldians continued in the same fashion as ever, unshakable, shaped by a greater force that the four didn't resist, even though it meant relegating their personal desires to the background.

In 1995 they met at a panel discussion on contemporary German literature held in Amsterdam, a discussion within the framework of a larger discussion that was taking place in the same building (although in separate lecture halls), encompassing French, English, and Italian literature.

It goes without saying that most of the attendees of these curious discussions gravitated toward the hall where contemporary English literature was being discussed, next door to the German literature hall and separated from it by a wall that was clearly not made of stone, as walls used to be, but of fragile bricks covered with a thin layer of plaster, so that the shouts, howls, and especially the applause sparked by English literature could be heard in the German literature room as if the two talks or dialogues were one, or as if the Germans were being mocked, when not drowned out, by the English, not to mention by the massive audience attending the English (or Anglo-Indian) discussion, notably larger than the sparse and earnest audience attending the German discussion. Which in the final analysis was a good thing, because it's common knowledge that a conversation involving only a few people, with everyone listening to everyone else and taking time to think and not shouting, tends to be more productive or at least more relaxed than a mass conversation, which runs the permanent risk of becoming a rally, or, because of the necessary brevity of the speeches, a series of slogans that fade as soon as they're put into words.

But before coming to the crux of the matter, or of the discussion, a rather petty detail that nonetheless affected the course of events must be noted. On a last-minute whim, the organizers—the same people who'd left out contemporary Spanish and Polish and Swedish literature for lack of time or money—earmarked most of the funds to provide luxurious accommodations for the stars of English literature, and with the money left over they brought in three French novelists, an Italian poet, an Italian short story writer, and three German writers, the first two of them novelists from West and East Berlin, now reunified, both vaguely renowned (and both of whom arrived in Amsterdam by train and made no complaint when they were put up at a three-star hotel), and the third a rather shadowy figure about whom no one knew anything, not even Morini, who, presenter or not, knew quite a bit about contemporary German literature.

And when the shadowy writer, who was Swabian, began to reminisce during his talk (or discussion) about his stint as a journalist, as an editor of arts pages, as an interviewer of all kinds of writers and artists wary of interviews, and then began to recall the era in which he had served as cultural promoter in towns that were far-flung or simply forgotten but interested in culture, suddenly, out of the blue, Archimboldi's name cropped up (maybe prompted by the previous talk led by Espinoza and Pelletier), since the Swabian, as it happened, had met Archimboldi while he was cultural promoter for a Frisian town, north of Wilhelmshaven, facing the Black Sea coast and the East Frisian islands, a place where it was cold, very cold, and even wetter than it was cold, with a salty wetness that got into the bones, and there were only two ways of making it through the winter, one, drinking until you got cirrhosis, and two, listening to music (usually amateur string quartets) in the town hall auditorium or talking to writers who came from elsewhere and who were given very little, a room at the only boardinghouse in town and a few marks to cover the return trip by train, those trains so unlike German trains today, but on which the people were perhaps more talkative, more polite, more interested in their neighbors, but anyway, writers who, after being paid and subtracting transportation costs, left these places and went home (which was sometimes just a room in Frankfurt or Cologne) with a little money and possibly a few books sold, in the case of those writers or poets (especially poets) who, after reading a few pages and answering the townspeople's questions, would set up a table and make a few extra marks, a fairly profitable activity back then, because if the audience liked what the writer had read, or if the reading moved them or entertained them or made them think, then they would buy one of his books, sometimes to keep as a souvenir of a pleasant evening, as the wind whistled along the narrow streets of the Frisian town, cutting into the flesh it was so cold, sometimes to read or reread a poem or story, back at home now, weeks after the event, maybe by the light of an oil lamp because there wasn't always electricity, of course, since the war had just ended and there were still gaping wounds, social and economic, anyway, more or less the same as a literary reading today, with the exception that the books displayed on the table were self-published and now it's the publishing houses that set up the table, and one of these writers who came to the town where the Swabian was cultural promoter was Benno von Archimboldi, a writer of the stature of Gustav Heller or Rainer Kuhl or Wilhelm Frayn (writers whom Morini would later look up in his encyclopedia of German authors, without success), and he didn't bring books, and he read two chapters from a novel in progress, his second novel, the first, remembered the Swabian, had been published in Hamburg that year, although he didn't read anything from it, but that first novel did exist, said the Swabian, and Archimboldi, as if anticipating doubts, had brought a copy with him, a little novel about one hundred pages long, maybe longer, one hundred and twenty, one hundred and twenty-five pages, and he carried the novel in his jacket pocket, and, strangely, the Swabian remembered Archimboldi's jacket more clearly than the novel crammed into its pocket, a little novel with a dirty, creased cover that had once been deep ivory or a pale wheat color or gold shading into invisibility, but now was colorless and dull, just the title of the novel and the author's name and the colophon of the publishing house, whereas the jacket was unforgettable, a black leather jacket with a high collar, providing excellent protection against the snow and rain and cold, loose fitting, so it could be worn over heavy sweaters or two sweaters without anyone noticing, with horizontal pockets on each side, and a row of four buttons, neither very large nor very small, sewn on with something like fishing line, a jacket that brought to mind, why I don't know, the jackets worn by some Gestapo officers, although back then black leather jackets were in fashion and anyone who had the money to buy one or had inherited one wore it without stopping to think about what it suggested, and the writer who had come to that Frisian town was Benno von Archimboldi, the young Benno von Archimboldi, twenty-nine or thirty years old, and it had been he, the Swabian, who had gone to wait for him at the train station and who had accompanied him to the boardinghouse, talking about the weather, which was bad, and then had brought him to city hall, where Archimboldi hadn't set up any table and had read two chapters from a novel that wasn't finished yet, and then the Swabian had gone to dinner with him at the local tavern, along with the teacher and a widow who preferred music or painting to literature, but who, once resigned to not having music or painting, was in no way averse to a literary evening, and it was she who somehow or other kept up the conversation during dinner (sausages and potatoes and beer: neither the times, recalled the Swabian, nor the town's budget allowed for anything more extravagant), although it might be truer to say that she steered it with a firm hand on the rudder, and the men who were around the table, the mayor's secretary, a man in the salted fish business, an old schoolteacher who kept falling asleep even with his fork in his hand, and a town employee, a very nice boy named Fritz who was a good friend of the Swabian's, nodded or were careful not to contradict the redoubtable widow whose knowledge of the arts was much greater than anyone else's, even the Swabian's, and who had traveled in Italy and France and had even, on one of her voyages, an unforgettable ocean crossing, gone as far as Buenos Aires, in 1927 or 1928, when the city was a meat emporium and the refrigerator ships left port laden with meat, a sight to see, hundreds of ships arriving empty and leaving laden with tons of meat headed all over the world, and when she, the lady, went out on deck, say at night, half asleep or seasick or ailing, all she had to do was lean on the rail and let her eyes grow accustomed to the dark and then the view of the port was startling and it instantly cleared away any vestiges of sleep or seasickness or other ailments, the nervous system having no choice but to surrender unconditionally to such a picture, the parade of immigrants like ants loading the flesh of thousands of dead cattle into the ships' holds, the movements of pallets piled with the meat of thousands of sacrificed calves, and the gauzy tint that shaded every corner of the port from dawn until dusk and even during the night shifts, the red of barely cooked steak, of T-bones, of filet, of ribs grilled rare, terrible, thank goodness the lady, who wasn't a widow at the time, had to see it only the first night, then they disembarked and took rooms at one of the most expensive hotels in Buenos Aires, and they went to the opera and then to a ranch where her husband, an expert horseman, agreed to race with the rancher's son, who lost, and then with a ranch hand, the son's right-hand man, a gaucho, who also lost, and then with the gaucho's son, a little sixteen-year-old gaucho, thin as a reed and with bright eyes, so bright that when the lady looked at him he lowered his head and then lifted it a little and gave her such a wicked look that she was offended, what an insolent urchin, while her husband laughed and said in German: you've made quite an impression on the boy, a joke the lady didn't find the least bit funny, and then the little gaucho mounted his horse and they set off, the boy could really gallop, he clung to the horse so tightly it was as if he were glued to its neck, and he sweated and thrashed it with his whip, but in the end her husband won the race, he hadn't been captain of a cavalry regiment for nothing, and the rancher and the rancher's son got up from their seats and clapped, good losers, and the rest of the guests clapped too, excellent rider, this German, extraordinary rider, although when the little gaucho reached the finish line, or in other words the porch, he didn't look like a good loser, a dark, angry expression on his face, his head down, and while the men, speaking French, scattered along the porch in search of glasses of ice-cold champagne, the lady went up to the little gaucho, who was left standing alone, holding his horse's reins in his left hand (at the other end of the long yard the little gaucho's father headed off toward the stables with the horse the German had ridden), and told him, in an incomprehensible language, not to be sad, that he had ridden an excellent race but her husband was good too and more experienced, words that to the little gaucho sounded like the moon, like the passage of clouds across the moon, like a slow storm, and then the little gaucho looked up at the lady with the eyes of a bird of prey, ready to plunge a knife into her at the navel and slice up to the breasts, cutting her wide open, his eyes shining with a strange intensity, like the eyes of a clumsy young butcher, as the lady recalled, which didn't stop her from following him without protest when he took her by the hand and led her to the other side of the house, to a place where a wrought-iron pergola stood, bordered by flowers and trees that the lady had never seen in her life or which at that moment she thought she had never seen in her life, and she even saw a fountain in the park, a stone fountain, in the center of which, balanced on one little foot, a creole cherub with smiling features danced, part European and part cannibal, perpetually bathed by three jets of water that spouted at its feet, a fountain sculpted from a single piece of black marble, a fountain that the lady and the little gaucho admired at length, until a distant cousin of the rancher appeared (or a mistress whom the rancher had lost in the deep folds of memory), telling her in brusque and serviceable English that her husband had been looking for her for some time, and then the lady walked out of the enchanted park on the distant cousin's arm, and the little gaucho called to her, or so she thought, and when she turned he spoke a few hissing words, and the lady stroked his head and asked the cousin what the little gaucho had said, her fingers lost in the thick curls of his hair, and the cousin seemed to hesitate for a moment, but the lady, who wouldn't tolerate lies or half-truths, demanded an immediate, direct translation, and the cousin said: he says . . . he says the boss . . . arranged it so your husband would win the last two races, and then the cousin was quiet and the little gaucho went off toward the other end of the park, dragging on his horse's reins, and the lady rejoined the party but she couldn't stop thinking about what the little gaucho had confessed at the last moment, the sainted lamb, and no matter how much she thought, his words were still a riddle, a riddle that lasted the rest of the party, and tormented her as she tossed and turned in bed, unable to sleep, and made her listless the next day during a long horseback ride and barbecue, and followed her back to Buenos Aires and all through the days she was at the hotel or went out to receptions at the German embassy or the English embassy or the Ecuadorean embassy, and was solved only days after her ship set sail for Europe, one night, at four in the morning, when the lady went out to stroll the deck, not knowing or caring what parallel or longitude they were at, surrounded or partially surrounded by forty-one million square miles of salt water, just then, as the lady lit a cigarette on the first-class passengers' first deck, with her eyes fixed on the expanse of ocean that she couldn't see but could hear, the riddle was miraculously solved, and it was then, at that point in the story, said the Swabian, that the lady, the once rich and powerful and intelligent (in her fashion, at least) Frisian lady, fell silent, and a religious, or worse, superstitious hush fell over that sad postwar German tavern, where everyone began to feel more and more uncomfortable and hurried to mop up what was left of their sausage and potatoes and swallow the last drops of beer from their mugs, as if they were afraid that at any moment the lady would begin to howl like a Fury and they judged it wise to prepare themselves to face the cold journey home with full stomachs.

And then the lady spoke. She said:

"Can anyone solve the riddle?"

That's what she said, but she didn't look at any of the townspeople or address them directly.

"Does anyone know the answer to the riddle? Does anyone understand it? Is there by chance a man in this town who can tell me the solution, even if he has to whisper it in my ear?"

She said all of this with her eyes on her plate, where her sausage and her serving of potatoes remained almost untouched.

And then Archimboldi, who had kept his head down, eating, as the lady talked, said, without raising his voice, that it had been an act of hospitality, that the rancher and his son were sure the lady's husband would lose the first race, and they had rigged the second and third races so the former cavalry captain would win. Then the lady looked him in the eye and laughed and asked why her husband had won the first race.

"Why? why?" asked the lady.

"Because the rancher's son," said Archimboldi, "who surely rode better and had a better mount than your husband, was overcome at the last minute by selflessness. In other words, he chose extravagance, carried away by the impromptu festivities that he and his father had arranged. Everything had to be squandered, including his victory, and somehow everyone understood it had to be that way, including the woman who came looking for you in the park. Everyone except the little gaucho."

"Was that all?" asked the lady.

"Not for the little gaucho. If you'd spent any longer with him, I think he would have killed you, which would have been an extravagant gesture in its own right, though certainly not the kind the rancher and his son had in mind."

Then the lady got up, thanked everyone for a pleasant evening, and left.

"A few minutes later," said the Swabian, "I walked Archimboldi back to the boardinghouse. The next morning, when I went to get him to take him to the station, he was gone."

•

Astounding Swabian, said Espinoza. I want him all to myself, said Pelletier. Try not to overwhelm him, try not to seem too interested, said Morini. We have to treat the man with kid gloves, said Norton. Which means we have to be very nice to him.

•

But the Swabian had already said everything he had to say, and even though they coddled him and took him out to the best restaurant in Amsterdam and complimented him and talked to him about hospitality and extravagance and the fate of cultural promoters trapped in small provincial towns, it was impossible to get anything interesting out of him, although the four were careful to record every word he spoke, as if they'd met their Moses, a detail that didn't go unnoticed by the Swabian and in fact heightened his shyness (which, according to Espinoza and Pelletier, was such an unusual trait in a former cultural promoter that they thought the Swabian must be some kind of impostor), his reserve, his discretion, which verged on the improbable *omertà* of an old Nazi who smells danger.

•

Fifteen days later, Espinoza and Pelletier took a few days' leave and went to Hamburg to visit Archimboldi's publisher. They were received by the editor in chief, a thin, upright man in his sixties by the name of Schnell, which means quick, although Schnell was on the slow side. He had sleek dark brown hair, sprinkled with gray at the temples, which only accentuated his youthful appearance. When he got up to shake hands, it occurred to both Espinoza and Pelletier that he must be gay.

"That faggot is the closest thing to an eel I've ever seen," Espinoza said afterward, as they strolled through Hamburg.

Pelletier chided him for his comment, with its markedly homophobic overtones, although deep down he agreed, there was something eellike about Schnell, something of the fish that swims in dark, muddy waters.

Of course, there was little Schnell could tell them that they didn't already know. He had never seen Archimboldi, and the money, of which there was more and more, was deposited in a Swiss bank account. Once every two years, instructions were received from the writer, the letters usually postmarked Italy, although there were also letters in the publisher's files with Greek and Spanish and Moroccan stamps, letters, incidentally, that were addressed to Mrs. Bubis, the owner of the publishing house, and that he, naturally, hadn't read.

"There are only two people left here, besides Mrs. Bubis, of course, who've met Benno von Archimboldi in person," Schnell told them. "The publicity director and the copy chief. By the time I came to work here, Archimboldi had long since vanished."

Pelletier and Espinoza asked to speak to both women. The publicity director's office was full of plants and photographs, not necessarily of the house authors, and the only thing she could tell them about the vanished writer was that he was a good person.

"A tall man, very tall," she said. "When he walked beside the late Mr. Bubis they looked like a *ti*. Or a *li*."

Espinoza and Pelletier didn't understand what she meant and the publicity director wrote the letter *l* and then the letter *i* on a scrap of paper. Or maybe more like a *le*. Like this.

And again she wrote something on the scrap of paper.

Le

"The *l* is Archimboldi, the *e* is the late Mr. Bubis."

Then the publicity director laughed and watched them for a while, reclining in her swivel chair in silence. Later they talked to the copy chief. She was about the same age as the publicity director but not as cheery.

She said yes, she had met Archimboldi many years ago, but she didn't remember his face anymore, or what he was like, or any story about him that would be worth telling. She couldn't remember the last time he was at the publishing house. She advised them to speak to Mrs. Bubis, and then, without a word, she busied herself editing a galley, answering the other copy editors' questions, talking on the phone to people who might—Espinoza and Pelletier thought with pity—be translators. Before they left, refusing to be discouraged, they returned to Schnell's office and talked to him about Archimboldian conferences and colloquiums planned for the future. Schnell, attentive and cordial, told them they could count on him for whatever they might need.

•

Since they didn't have anything to do except wait for their flights back to Paris and Madrid, Pelletier and Espinoza went walking around Hamburg. The walk inevitably took them to the district of streetwalkers and peep shows, and then they both lapsed into gloom and began telling each other stories of love and disillusionment. Of course, they didn't give names or dates, they spoke in what might be called abstract terms, but despite the seemingly detached presentation of their misfortunes, the conversation and the walk only sank them deeper into a state of melancholy, to such a degree that after two hours they both felt as if they were suffocating.

They took a taxi back to the hotel in silence.

A surprise awaited them there. At the desk there was a note from Schnell addressed to both of them, in which he explained that after their conversation that morning, he'd decided to talk to Mrs. Bubis and she had agreed to see them. The next morning, Espinoza and Pelletier called at the publisher's apartment, on the third floor of an old building in Hamburg's upper town. As they waited they looked at the framed photographs on one wall. On the other two walls there were canvases by Soutine and Kandinsky, and several drawings by Grosz, Kokoschka, and Ensor. But Espinoza and Pelletier were much more interested in the photographs, which were almost all of writers they disdained or admired, and in any case had read: Thomas Mann with Bubis, Heinrich Mann with Bubis, Klaus Mann with Bubis, Alfred Döblin with Bubis, Hermann Hesse with Bubis, Walter Benjamin with Bubis, Anna Seghers with Bubis, Stefan Zweig with Bubis, Bertolt Brecht with Bubis, Feuchtwanger with Bubis, Johannes Becher with Bubis, Oskar Maria Graf with Bubis, bodies and faces and vague scenery, beautifully framed. With the innocence of the dead, who no longer mind being observed, the people in the photographs gazed out on the professors' barely contained enthusiasm. When Mrs. Bubis appeared, the two of them had their heads together trying to decide whether a man next to Bubis was Fallada or not.

Indeed, it is Fallada, said Mrs. Bubis. When they turned, Pelletier and Espinoza saw an older woman in a white blouse and black skirt, a woman with a figure like Marlene Dietrich, as Pelletier would say much later, a woman who despite her years was still as strong willed as ever, a woman who didn't cling to the edge of the abyss but plunged into it with curiosity and elegance. A woman who plunged into the abyss *sitting down.*

"My husband knew all the German writers and the German writers loved and respected my husband, even if a few of them said horrible things about him later that weren't always even accurate," said Mrs. Bubis, with a smile.

They talked about Archimboldi and Mrs. Bubis had tea and cakes brought in, although she drank vodka, which surprised Espinoza and Pelletier, not that she would start to drink so early, but that she wouldn't offer them a drink too, a drink they would in any case have refused.

"The only person at the press who knew Archimboldi's work to perfection," said Mrs. Bubis, "was Mr. Bubis, who published all his books."

But she asked herself (and by extension, the two of them) how well anyone could really know another person's work.

"For example, I love Grosz's work," she said, gesturing toward the Grosz drawings on the wall, "but do I really know it? His stories make me laugh, often I think Grosz drew what he did to make me laugh, sometimes I laugh to the point of hilarity, and hilarity becomes helpless mirth, but once I met an art critic who of course liked Grosz, and who nevertheless got very depressed when he attended a retrospective of his work or had to study some canvas or drawing in a professional capacity. And these bouts of depression or sadness would last for weeks. This art critic was a friend, but we'd never discussed Grosz. Once, however, I mentioned the effect Grosz had on me. At first he refused to believe me. Then he started to shake his head. Then he looked me up and down as if he'd never laid eyes on me before. I thought he'd gone mad. That was the end of our friendship. A while ago I was told that he still says I know nothing about Grosz and I have the aesthetic sense of a cow. Well, as far as I'm concerned he can say whatever he likes. Grosz makes me laugh, Grosz depresses him, but who can say they really know Grosz?

"Let's suppose," said Mrs. Bubis, "that at this very moment there's a knock on the door and my old friend the art critic comes in. He sits here on the sofa beside me, and one of you brings out an unsigned drawing and tells us it's by Grosz and you want to sell it. I look at the drawing and smile and I take out my checkbook and buy it. The art critic looks at the drawing and *isn't* depressed and tries to make me reconsider. He thinks it isn't a Grosz. I think it is. Which of us is right?

"Or let's tell the story a different way. You," said Mrs. Bubis, pointing to Espinoza, "present an unsigned drawing and say it's by Grosz and try to sell it. I don't laugh, I look at it coldly, I appreciate the line, the control, the satire, but nothing about it tickles me. The art critic examines it carefully and gets depressed, in his normal way, and then and there he makes an offer, an offer that exceeds his savings, and that if accepted will condemn him to endless afternoons of melancholy. I try to change his mind. I tell him the drawing strikes me as suspicious because it doesn't make me laugh. The critic says finally I'm looking at Grosz like an adult and gives me his congratulations. Which of the two of us is right?"

•

Then they went back to talking about Archimboldi and Mrs. Bubis showed them a very odd review that had appeared in a Berlin newspaper after the publication of *Lüdicke*, Archimboldi's first novel. The review, by someone named Schleiermacher, tried to sum up the novelist's personality in a few words.

Intelligence: average.

Character: epileptic.

Scholarship: sloppy.

Storytelling ability: chaotic.

Prosody: chaotic.

German usage: chaotic.

Average intelligence and sloppy scholarship are easy to understand. What did he mean by epileptic character, though? that Archimboldi had epilepsy? that he wasn't right in the head? that he suffered attacks of a mysterious nature? that he was a compulsive reader of Dostoevsky? There was no physical description of the writer in the piece.

"We never knew who this man Schleiermacher was," said Mrs. Bubis, "and sometimes my late husband would joke that Archimboldi himself had written the review. But he knew as well as I did that it wasn't true."

Near midday, when it was time to leave, Pelletier and Espinoza dared to ask the only question they thought really mattered: could she help them get in touch with Archimboldi? Mrs. Bubis's eyes lit up. As if she were at the scene of a fire, Pelletier told Liz Norton later. Not a raging blaze, but a fire that was about to go out, after burning for months. Her no came as a slight shake of the head that made Pelletier and Espinoza abruptly aware of the futility of their plea.

Still, they stayed a while longer. From somewhere in the house came the muted strains of an Italian popular song. Espinoza asked whether she knew Archimboldi, whether she had ever seen him in person while her husband was alive. Mrs. Bubis said she had and then, under her breath, she sang the song's final chorus. Her Italian, according to the two friends, was very good.

"What is Archimboldi like?" asked Espinoza.

"Very tall," said Mrs. Bubis, "very tall, a man of truly great height. If he'd been born in this day and age he likely would have played basketball."

Although by the way she said it, Archimboldi might as well have been a dwarf. In the taxi back to the hotel the two friends thought about Grosz and about Mrs. Bubis's cruel, crystalline laugh and about the impression left by that house full of photographs, where nevertheless the photograph of the only writer they cared about was missing. And although neither wanted to admit it, both believed (or sensed) that the flash of insight granted to them in the red-light district was more important than any revelation they might have scented as the guests of Mrs. Bubis.

•

In a word, and bluntly: as they walked around Sankt Pauli, it came to Pelletier and Espinoza that the search for Archimboldi could never fill their lives. They could read him, they could study him, they could pick him apart, but they couldn't laugh or be sad with him, partly because Archimboldi was always far away, partly because the deeper they went into his work, the more it devoured its explorers. In a word: in Sankt Pauli and later at Mrs. Bubis's house, hung with photographs of the late Mr. Bubis and his writers, Pelletier and Espinoza understood that what they wanted to make was love, not war.

•

That afternoon, and without indulging in any confidences beyond the strictly necessary—confidences in general, or maybe abstract, terms— they shared another taxi to the airport, and as they waited for their planes they talked about love, about the need for love. Pelletier was the first to go. When Espinoza was left alone (his flight was an hour later), his thoughts turned to Liz Norton and his real chances of wooing her. He imagined her and then he imagined himself, side by side, sharing an apartment in Madrid, going to the supermarket, both of them working in the German department. He imagined his office and her office, separated by a wall, and nights in Madrid next to her, eating with friends at good restaurants, and, back at home, an enormous bathtub, an enormous bed.

•

But Pelletier got there first. Three days after the meeting with Archimboldi's publisher, he showed up in London unannounced, and after telling Liz Norton the latest news, he invited her to dinner at a restaurant in Hammersmith that a colleague in the Russian department had recommended, where they ate goulash and chickpea puree with beets and fish macerated in lemon with yogurt, a dinner with candles and violins and real Russian waiters and Irish waiters disguised as Russians, all of it excessive from any point of view, and somewhat rustic and dubious from a gastronomic point of view, and they had vodka with their dinner and a bottle of Bordeaux, and the whole meal cost Pelletier an arm and a leg, but it was worth it because then Norton invited him home, officially to discuss Archimboldi and the few things that Mrs. Bubis had revealed, including, of course, the critic Schleiermacher's contemptuous appraisal of Archimboldi's first book, and then both of them started to laugh and Pelletier kissed Norton on the lips, with great tact, and she kissed him back much more ardently, thanks possibly to the dinner and the vodka and the Bordeaux, but Pelletier thought it showed promise, and then they went to bed and screwed for an hour until Norton fell asleep.

•

That night, while Liz Norton was sleeping, Pelletier remembered a long-ago afternoon when he and Espinoza had watched a horror film in a room at a German hotel.

The film was Japanese, and in one of the early scenes there were two teenage girls. One was telling a story. The story was about a boy spending his holidays in Kobe who wanted to go out to play with friends at the same time that his favorite TV show was on. So the boy found a videocassette and set the machine to record the show and went outside. The problem was that the boy was from Tokyo and in Tokyo his show was on Channel 34, whereas in Kobe, Channel 34 is blank, a channel on which all you see is snow.

And after he came back in, when he sat down in front of the TV and started the player, instead of his favorite show he saw a white-faced woman telling him he was going to die.

And that was all.

And then the phone rang and the boy answered and he heard the same woman's voice asking him did he think it was a joke. A day later they found him in the yard, dead.

And the first girl told the second girl this story, and the whole time she was talking it looked like she was about to crack up. The second girl was obviously scared. But the first girl, the one who was telling the story, looked like she was about to roll on the floor laughing.

And then, remembered Pelletier, Espinoza said the first girl was a two-bit psychopath and the second girl was a silly bitch, and the film could have been good if the second girl, instead of staring openmouthed and looking horrified, had told the first one to shut up. And not gently, not politely, instead she should have told the girl: "Shut up, you cunt, what's so funny? does it turn you on telling the story of a dead boy? does it make you come telling the story of a dead boy, you imaginary-dick-sucking bitch?"

And so on, in the same vein. And Pelletier remembered that Espinoza spoke so vehemently, he even did the voice the second girl should have used and the way she should have stood, that he thought it best to turn off the TV and take him to the bar for a drink before they went back to their rooms. And he also remembered that he felt tenderness toward Espinoza at that moment, a tenderness that brought back adolescence, adventures fiercely shared, and small-town afternoons.

•

That week, Liz Norton's home phone rang three or four times every afternoon and her cell phone rang two or three times every morning. The calls were from Pelletier and Espinoza, and although both produced elaborate Archimboldian pretexts, the pretexts were exhausted in a minute and the two professors proceeded to say what was really on their minds.

Pelletier talked about his colleagues in the German department, about a young Swiss poet and professor who was badgering him for a scholarship, about the sky in Paris (shades of Baudelaire, Verlaine, Banville), about the cars at dusk, their lights already on, heading home. Espinoza talked about his library, where he arranged his books in the strictest solitude, about the distant drums that he sometimes heard coming from a neighboring apartment that seemed to be home to a group of African musicians, about the neighborhoods of Madrid, Lavapiés, Malasaña, and about the area around the Gran Vía, where you could go for a walk at any time of night.

•

During this period, both Espinoza and Pelletier completely forgot about Morini. Only Norton called him now and then, carrying on the same conversations as ever.

In his way, Morini had vanished from sight.

•

Soon Pelletier got used to traveling to London whenever he wanted, though it must be emphasized that in terms of proximity and ready modes of transportation, he had it easiest.

These visits lasted only a single night. Pelletier would arrive just after nine, meeting Norton at ten at a restaurant where he had made reservations from Paris, and by one they were in bed.

Liz Norton was a passionate lover, although her passion was of limited duration. Not having much imagination of her own, she abandoned herself to any game her lover suggested, without ever taking the initiative, or thinking she ought to. These sessions rarely lasted more than three hours, a fact that occasionally saddened Pelletier, who would gladly have screwed till daybreak.

After the sexual act, and this was what frustrated Pelletier most, Norton preferred to talk about academic matters rather than to look frankly at what was developing between them. To Pelletier, Norton's coldness seemed a particularly feminine mode of self-protection. Hoping to get through to her, one night he decided to tell her the story of his own sentimental adventures. He drew up a long list of women he had known and exposed them to her frosty or indifferent gaze. She seemed unimpressed and showed no desire to repay his confession with one of her own.

In the mornings, after he called a cab, Pelletier slipped soundlessly into his clothes so as not to wake her and headed for the airport. Before he left he would spend a few seconds watching her, sprawled on the sheets, and sometimes he felt so full of love he could have burst into tears.

•

An hour later Liz Norton's alarm would sound and she'd jump out of bed. She'd take a shower, put water on to boil, drink tea with milk, dry her hair, and launch a thorough inspection of her apartment as if she were afraid that her nocturnal visitor had purloined some object of value. The living room and bedroom were almost always a wreck, and that bothered her. Impatiently, she would gather up the dirty glasses, empty the ashtrays, change the sheets, put back the books that Pelletier had taken down from the shelves and left on the floor, return the bottles to the rack in the kitchen, and then get dressed and go to the university. If she had a meeting with her department colleagues, she would go to the meeting, and if she didn't have a meeting she would shut herself up in the library to work or read until it was time for class.

•

One Saturday Espinoza told her that she must come to Madrid, she would be his guest, Madrid at this time of year was the most beautiful city in the world, and there was a Bacon retrospective on, too, which wasn't to be missed.

"I'll be there tomorrow," said Norton, which caught Espinoza off guard, since what his invitation had expressed was more a wish than any real hope that she might accept.

The certain knowledge that she would appear at his apartment the next day naturally sent Espinoza into a state of growing excitement and rampant insecurity. And yet they had a wonderful Sunday (Espinoza did everything in his power to assure they would), and that night they went to bed together, listening for the sound of the drums next door but hearing nothing, as if that day the African band had packed up for a tour of other Spanish cities. Espinoza had so many questions to ask that when the time came he didn't ask a single one. He didn't need to. Norton told him that she and Pelletier were lovers, although she put it another way, using some more ambiguous word, friends maybe, or maybe she said they'd been seeing each other, or words to that effect.

Espinoza would have liked to ask how long they'd been lovers, but all that came out was a sigh. Norton said she had many friends, without specifying whether she meant friend-friends or lover-friends, and always had ever since she was sixteen, when she made love for the first time with a thirty-four-year-old, a failed Pottery Lane musician, and this was how she saw things. Espinoza, who had never talked to a woman about love (or sex) in German, the two of them naked in bed, wanted to know how exactly she *did* see things, because he wasn't quite clear on that, but all he did was nod.

Then came the great surprise. Norton looked him in the eye and asked whether he thought he knew her. Espinoza said he wasn't sure, maybe in some ways he thought he did and in other ways he didn't, but he felt great respect for her and admired her work as a scholar and critic of the Archimboldian oeuvre. That was when Norton told him she'd been married and was now divorced.

"I had no idea," said Espinoza.

"Well, it's true," said Norton. "I'm a divorcée."

When Liz Norton flew back to London, Espinoza was left even more nervous than he'd been during her two days in Madrid. On the one hand, the encounter had been as successful as he could have hoped, of that there was no doubt. In bed, especially, the two of them seemed to understand each other, to be in sync, well matched, as if they'd known each other for a long time, but when the sex was over and Norton was in the mood to talk, everything changed. She entered a hypnotic state, as if she didn't have any woman friend to turn to, thought Espinoza, who in his heart believed that such confessions weren't intended for men's ears but should be heard by other women: Norton talked about menstrual cycles, for example, and the moon and black-and-white movies that turned without warning into horror films, which thoroughly depressed Espinoza, to the extent that when she stopped talking it took a superhuman effort for him to dress and go out for dinner or meet friends, arm in arm with Norton, not to mention the business with Pelletier, which when you really thought about it was chilling, and now who'll tell Pelletier that I'm sleeping with Liz?, all of which unsettled Espinoza and, when he was alone, gave him knots in his stomach and made him want to run to the bathroom, just as Norton had explained happened to her (how could I have let her tell me these things!) when she saw her ex-husband, six foot three and not very stable, a danger to himself and others, somebody who might have been a small-time thug or hooligan, the extent of his cultural education the old songs he sang in the pub with his mates from childhood, a bastard who believed in television and had the shrunken and shriveled soul of a religious fundamentalist. To put it plainly, the worst husband a woman could inflict on herself, no matter how you looked at it.

•

And even though Espinoza calmed himself with the promise that he wouldn't take things any further, four days later, once he was recovered, he called Norton and said he wanted to see her. Norton asked whether he'd rather meet in London or Madrid. Espinoza said it was up to her. Norton chose Madrid. Espinoza felt like the happiest man in the world.

Norton arrived Saturday evening and left Sunday night. Espinoza drove her to El Escorial and then they went to a flamenco show. He thought she seemed happy, and he was glad. Saturday night they made love for three hours, after which Norton, instead of starting to talk as she had before, said that she was exhausted and went to sleep. The next day, after they showered, they made love again and left for El Escorial. On the way back Espinoza asked her whether she'd seen Pelletier. Norton said she had, that Jean-Claude had been in London.

"How is he?" asked Espinoza.

"Fine," said Norton. "I told him about us."

Espinoza got nervous and concentrated on the road.

"So what did he think?" he asked.

"That it's my business," said Norton, "but sooner or later I'll have to choose."

Though he made no comment, Espinoza admired Pelletier's attitude. There's a man who knows how to play fair, he thought. Then Norton asked him how he felt about it.

"More or less the same," lied Espinoza, without taking his eyes off the road.

For a while they were silent and then Norton started to talk about her husband. This time the horror stories she told didn't affect Espinoza in the slightest.

•

Pelletier called Espinoza that Sunday night, just after Espinoza had dropped Norton off at the airport. He got straight to the point. He said he knew Espinoza knew what was going on. Espinoza said he appreciated the call, and whether Pelletier believed it or not, he'd been planning to call him that very night and the only reason he hadn't was because Pelletier had beaten him to it. Pelletier said he believed him.

"So what do we do now?" asked Espinoza.

"Leave it all in the hands of fate," answered Pelletier.

Then they started to talk—and laughed quite a bit—about a strange conference that had just been held in Salonika, to which only Morini had been invited.

•

In Salonika, Morini had a mild attack. One morning he woke up in his hotel room and couldn't see anything. He had gone blind. He panicked at first, but after a while he managed to regain control. He lay in bed without moving, trying to go back to sleep. He thought of pleasant things, trying out childhood scenes, a few films, still shots of faces, but nothing worked. He sat up in bed and felt around for his wheelchair. He unfolded it and swung into it with less effort than he had expected. Then, very slowly, he tried to turn himself toward the room's only window, a French door that opened onto a balcony with a view of bare, yellowish-brown hills and an office building topped with a neon sign for a real estate company advertising chalets in an area presumably near Salonika.

The development (which had yet to be built) boasted the name Apollo Residences, and the night before, Morini had been watching the sign from his balcony, a glass of whiskey in his hand, as it blinked on and off. When he reached the window at last and managed to open it, he felt dizzy, as if he were about to faint. First he thought about trying to find the door to the hallway and maybe calling for help or letting himself fall in the middle of the corridor. Then he decided that it would be best to go back to bed. An hour later he was woken by the light coming in the open window and by his own perspiration. He called the reception desk and asked whether there were any messages for him. He was told there were none. He undressed in bed and got back in the wheelchair sitting ready beside him. It took him half an hour to shower and dress himself in clean clothes. Then he closed the window, without looking out, and left the room for the conference.

•

The four of them met again at the contemporary German literature symposium held in Salzburg in 1996. Espinoza and Pelletier seemed very happy. Norton, on the other hand, was like an ice queen, indifferent to the city's cultural offerings and beauty. Morini showed up loaded with books and papers to grade, as if the Salzburg meeting had caught him at one of his busiest moments.

All four were put up at the same hotel. Morini and Norton were on the third floor, in rooms 305 and 311, respectively. Espinoza was on the fifth floor, in room 509. And Pelletier was on the sixth floor, in room 602. The hotel was literally overrun by a German orchestra and a Russian choir, and there was a constant musical hubbub in the hallways and on the stairs, sometimes louder and sometimes softer, as if the musicians never stopped humming overtures or as if a mental (and musical) static had settled over the hotel. Espinoza and Pelletier weren't bothered in the least by it, and Morini seemed not to notice, but this was just the sort of thing, Norton exclaimed, one of many others she wouldn't mention, that made Salzburg such a shithole.

Naturally, neither Pelletier nor Espinoza visited Norton in her room a single time. Instead, the room that Espinoza visited (once) was Pelletier's, and the room that Pelletier visited (twice) was Espinoza's, the two of them as excited as children at the news spreading like wildfire, like a nuclear conflagration, along the hallways and through the symposium gatherings in *petit comité*, to wit, that Archimboldi was a candidate for the Nobel that year, not only cause for great joy among Archimboldians everywhere but also a triumph and a vindication, so much so that in Salzburg, at the Red Bull beer hall, on a night of many toasts, peace was declared between the two main factions of Archimboldi scholars, that is, between Pelletier and Espinoza and Borchmeyer, Pohl, and Schwarz, who from then on decided, with respect for each other's differences and methods of interpretation, to pool their efforts and forswear sabotage, which in practical terms meant that Pelletier would no longer veto the publication of Schwarz's essays in the journals where he held sway, and Schwarz would no longer veto the publication of Pelletier's studies in the journals where he, Schwarz, was held in godlike esteem.

•

Morini, less excited than Pelletier and Espinoza, was the first to point out that until now, at least as far as he knew, Archimboldi had never received an important prize in Germany, no booksellers' award, or critics' award, or readers' award, or publishers' award, assuming there was such a thing, which meant that one might reasonably expect that, knowing Archimboldi was up for the biggest prize in world literature, his fellow Germans, even if only to play it safe, would offer him a national award or a symbolic award or an honorary award or at least an hour-long television interview, none of which happened, incensing the Archimboldians (united this time), who, rather than being disheartened by the poor treatment that Archimboldi continued to receive, redoubled their efforts, galvanized in their frustration and spurred on by the injustice with which a civilized state was treating not only—in their opinion—the best living writer in Germany, but the best living writer in Europe, and this triggered an avalanche of literary and even biographical studies of Archimboldi (about whom so little was known that it might as well be nothing at all), which in turn drew more readers, most captivated not by the German's work but by the life or nonlife of such a singular figure, which in turn translated into a word-of-mouth movement that increased sales considerably in Germany (a phenomenon not unrelated to the presence of Dieter Hellfeld, the latest acquisition of the Schwarz, Borchmeyer, and Pohl group), which in turn gave new impetus to the translations and the reissues of the old translations, none of which made Archimboldi a bestseller but did boost him, for two weeks, to ninth place on the bestseller list in Italy, and to twelfth place in France, also for two weeks, and although it never made the lists in Spain, a publishing house there bought the rights to the few novels that still belonged to other Spanish publishers and the rights to all of the writer's books that had yet to be translated into Spanish, and in this way a kind of Archimboldi Library was begun, which wasn't a bad business.

•

In the British Isles, it must be said, Archimboldi remained a decidedly marginal writer.

•

In these heady days, Pelletier happened on a piece written by the Swabian whom they'd had the pleasure of meeting in Amsterdam. In the piece the Swabian basically repeated what he'd already told them about Archimboldi's visit to the Frisian town and the dinner afterward with the lady who had traveled to Buenos Aires. The piece was published in the *Reutlingen Morning News* and differed from the Swabian's original account in that it reproduced an exchange between the lady and Archimboldi, pitched in a key of sardonic humor. The conversation began with her asking him where he was from. Archimboldi replied that he was Prussian. The lady asked whether his was a noble name, of the Prussian landed gentry. Archimboldi replied that it probably was. Then the lady murmured the name Benno von Archimboldi, as if biting a gold coin to test it. Immediately she said it didn't sound familiar and she mentioned a few other names, to see whether Archimboldi recognized them. He said he didn't, all he'd known of Prussia were its forests.

"And yet your name is of Italian origin," said the lady.

"French," replied Archimboldi. "It's Huguenot."

At this, the lady laughed. She had once been very beautiful, said the Swabian. Even then, in the dim light of the tavern, she looked beautiful, although when she laughed her false teeth slipped and she had to adjust them with her hand. Still, the operation was not ungraceful, as performed by her. The lady was so easy and natural with the fishermen and peasants that she inspired only respect and affection. She had been a widow for a long time. Sometimes she would go out riding on the dunes.

Other times she would wander down side roads buffeted by the wind off the North Sea.

•

When Pelletier discussed the Swabian's article with his three friends one morning as they were having breakfast at the hotel before going out into Salzburg, opinions and interpretations varied considerably.

According to Espinoza and Pelletier, the Swabian had probably been the lady's lover at the time when Archimboldi came to give his reading. According to Norton, the Swabian had a different version of events depending on his mood and his audience, and it was possible that he himself didn't even remember anymore what was really said and what had really happened on that momentous occasion. According to Morini, the Swabian was a grotesque double of Archimboldi, his twin, the negative image of a developed photograph that keeps looming larger, becoming more powerful, more oppressive, without ever losing its link to the negative (which undergoes the reverse process, gradually altered by time and fate), the two images somehow still the same: both young men in the years of terror and barbarism under Hitler, both World War II veterans, both writers, both citizens of a bankrupt nation, both poor bastards adrift at the moment when they meet and (in their grotesque fashion) recognize each other, Archimboldi as a struggling writer, the Swabian as "cultural promoter" in a town where culture was hardly a serious concern.

Was it even conceivable that the miserable and (why not?) contemptible Swabian was really Archimboldi? It wasn't Morini who asked this question, but Norton. And the answer was no, since the Swabian, to begin with, was short and of delicate constitution, which didn't match Archimboldi's physical description at all. Pelletier's and Espinoza's explanation was much more plausible: the Swabian as the noble lady's lover, even though she could have been his grandmother. The Swabian trudging each afternoon to the house of the lady who had traveled to Buenos Aires, to fill his belly with charcuterie and biscuits and cups of tea. The Swabian massaging the back of the former cavalry captain's widow, as the rain lashed the windows, a sad Frisian rain that made one want to weep, and although it didn't make the Swabian weep, it made him pale, and he approached the nearest window, where he stood looking out at what was beyond the curtains of frenzied rain, until the lady called him, peremptorily, and the Swabian turned his back on the window, not knowing why he had gone to it, not knowing what he hoped to see, and just at that moment, when there was no one at the window anymore and only a little lamp of colored glass at the back of the room flickering, it appeared.

•

So the days in Salzburg were generally pleasant, and although Archimboldi didn't receive the Nobel Prize that year, life for our four friends proceeded smoothly, flowing along on the placid river of European university German departments, not without racking up one upset or another that in the end simply added a dash of pepper, a dash of mustard, a drizzle of vinegar to orderly lives, or lives that looked orderly from without, although each of the four had his or her own cross to bear, like anyone, a strange cross in Norton's case, ghostly and phosphorescent, for Norton made frequent and rather tasteless references to her ex-husband as a lurking threat, ascribed to him the vices and defects of a monster, a horribly violent monster but one who never materialized, a monster all evocation and no action, although with her words Norton managed to give substance to a being whom neither Espinoza nor Pelletier had ever seen, as if her ex existed only in their dreams, until Pelletier, sharper than Espinoza, understood that Norton's unthinking diatribe, that endless list of grievances, was more than anything a punishment inflicted on herself, perhaps for the shame of having fallen in love with such a cretin and married him. Pelletier, of course, was wrong.

•

Around this time, Pelletier and Espinoza, worried about the current state of their mutual lover, had two long conversations on the phone.

Pelletier made the first call, which lasted an hour and fifteen minutes. The second was made three days later by Espinoza and lasted two hours and fifteen minutes. After they'd been talking for an hour and a half, Pelletier told Espinoza to hang up, the call would be expensive and he'd call right back, but Espinoza firmly refused.

The first conversation began awkwardly, although Espinoza had been expecting Pelletier's call, as if both men found it difficult to say what sooner or later they would have to say. The first twenty minutes were tragic in tone, with the word *fate* used ten times and the word *friendship* twenty-four times. Liz Norton's name was spoken fifty times, nine of them in vain. The word *Paris* was said seven times, *Madrid*, eight. The word *love* was spoken twice, once by each man. The word *horror* was spoken six times and the word *happiness* once (by Espinoza). The word *solution* was said twelve times. The word *solipsism* seven times. The word *euphemism* ten times. The word *category*, in the singular and the plural, nine times. The word *structuralism* once (Pelletier). The term *American literature* three times. The words *dinner* or *eating* or *breakfast* or *sandwich* nineteen times. The words *eyes* or *hands* or *hair* fourteen times. Then the conversation proceeded more smoothly. Pelletier told Espinoza a joke in German and Espinoza laughed. In fact, they both laughed, wrapped up in the waves or whatever it was that linked their voices and ears across the dark fields and the wind and the snow of the Pyrenees and the rivers and the lonely roads and the separate and interminable suburbs surrounding Paris and Madrid.

•

The second conversation, radically longer than the first, was a conversation between friends doing their best to clear up any murky points they might have overlooked, a conversation that refused to become technical or logistical and instead touched on subjects connected only tenuously to Norton, subjects that had nothing to do with surges of emotion, subjects easy to broach and then drop when they wished to return to the main subject, Liz Norton, whom, by the time the second call was nearing its close, both had recognized not as the Fury who destroyed their friendship, black clad with bloodstained wings, nor as Hecate, who began as an au pair, caring for children, and ended up learning witchcraft and turning herself into an animal, but as the angel who had fortified their friendship, forcibly shown them what they'd known all along, what they'd assumed all along, which was that they were civilized beings, beings capable of noble sentiments, not two dumb beasts debased by routine and regular sedentary work, no, that night Pelletier and Espinoza discovered that they were generous, so generous that if they'd been together they'd have felt the need to go out and celebrate, dazzled by the shine of their own virtue, a shine that might not last (since virtue, once recognized in a flash, has no shine and makes its home in a dark cave amid cave dwellers, some dangerous indeed), and for lack of celebration or revelry they hailed this virtue with an unspoken promise of eternal friendship, and sealed the vow, after they hung up their respective phones in their respective apartments crammed with books, by sipping whiskey with supreme slowness and watching the night outside their windows, maybe seeking unconsciously what the Swabian had sought outside the widow's window in vain.

•

Morini was the last to know, as one would expect, although in Morini's case the sentimental mathematics didn't always work out.

Even before Norton first went to bed with Pelletier, Morini had felt it coming. Not because of the way Pelletier behaved around Norton but because of her own detachment, a generalized detachment, Baudelaire would have called it spleen, Nerval melancholy, which left Norton liable to embark on an intimate relationship with anyone who came along.

Espinoza, of course, he hadn't predicted. When Norton called and told him she was involved with the two of them, Morini was surprised (although he wouldn't have been surprised if Norton had said she was involved with Pelletier and a colleague at the University of London or even a student), but he hid it well. Then he tried to think of other things, but he couldn't.

He asked Norton whether she was happy. Norton said she was. He told her he had received an e-mail from Borchmeyer with fresh news. Norton didn't seem very interested. He asked her whether she'd heard from her husband.

"Ex-husband," said Norton.

No, she hadn't heard from him, although an old friend had called to tell her that her ex was living with another old friend. Morini asked whether the woman had been a very close friend. Norton didn't understand the question.

"What close friend?"

"The one who's living with your ex now," said Morini.

"She doesn't live with him, she's supporting him, it's completely different."

"Ah," said Morini, and he tried to change the subject, but he drew a blank.

Maybe I should talk to her about my illness, he thought bitterly. But that he would never do.

•

Around this time, Morini was the first of the four to read an article about the killings in Sonora, which appeared in *Il Manifesto* and was written by an Italian reporter who had gone to Mexico to cover the Zapatista guerrillas. The news was horrible, he thought. In Italy there were serial killers, too, but they hardly ever killed more than ten people, whereas in Sonora the dead numbered well over one hundred.

Then he thought about the reporter from *Il Manifesto* and it struck him as odd that she had gone to Chiapas, which is at the southern tip of the country, and that she had ended up writing about events in Sonora, which, if he wasn't mistaken, was in the north, the northwest, on the border with the United States. He imagined her traveling by bus, a long way from Mexico City to the desert lands of the north. He imagined her talking to Subcomandante Marcos. He imagined her in the Mexican capital. Someone there must have told her what was happening in Sonora. And instead of getting on the next plane to Italy, she had decided to buy a bus ticket and set off on a long trip to Sonora. For an instant, Morini felt a wild desire to travel with the reporter.

I'd love her until the end of time, he thought. An hour later he'd already forgotten the matter completely.

•

A little later he got an e-mail from Norton. He thought it was strange that Norton would write and not call. Once he had read the letter, though, he understood that she needed to express her thoughts as precisely as possible and that was why she'd decided to write. In the letter she asked his forgiveness for what she called her egotism, an egotism that expressed itself in the contemplation of her own misfortunes, real or imaginary. She went on to say that she'd finally resolved her lingering quarrel with her ex-husband. The dark clouds had vanished from her life. Now she wanted to be happy and sing [*sic*]. Until probably the week before, she added, she'd loved him still, and now she could attest that the part of her past that included him was behind her for good. I'm suddenly keen on my work, she said, and on all those little everyday things that make human beings happy. And she also said: I wanted you, my patient Piero, to be the first to know.

Morini read the letter three times. With a heavy heart, he thought how wrong Norton was when she said her love and her ex-husband and everything they'd been through were behind her. Nothing is ever behind us.

•

Pelletier and Espinoza, meanwhile, received no such confidences. But Pelletier noticed something that Espinoza didn't. The London–Paris trips had become more frequent than the Paris–London trips. And as often as not, Norton would show up with a gift—a collection of essays, an art book, catalogs of exhibitions that Pelletier would never see, even a shirt or a handkerchief—which had never happened before.

Otherwise, everything was the same. They screwed, went out to dinner, discussed the latest news about Archimboldi. They never talked about their future as a couple. Each time Espinoza came up in conversation (which was rare), both adopted a strictly impartial, cautious, and above all friendly tone. Some nights they even fell asleep in each other's arms without making love, something Pelletier was sure didn't happen with Espinoza. But he was wrong, because relations between Norton and Espinoza were often a faithful simulacrum of Norton's relations with Pelletier.

The meals were different, better in Paris; the setting and the scenery were different, more modern in Paris; and the language was different, because with Espinoza Norton spoke mostly German and with Pelletier mostly English, but overall the similarities outweighed the differences. Naturally, with Espinoza there had also been nights without sex.

•

If Norton's closest friend (she had none) had asked which of the two friends she had a better time with in bed, Norton wouldn't have known what to say.

Sometimes she thought Pelletier was the more skillful lover. Other times, Espinoza. Viewed from outside, say from a rigorously academic standpoint, one could maintain that Pelletier had a longer bibliography than Espinoza, who relied more on instinct than intellect in such matters, and who had the disadvantage of being Spanish, that is, of belonging to a culture that tended to confuse eroticism with scatology and pornography with coprophagy, a confusion evident (because unaddressed) in Espinoza's mental library, for he had only just read the Marquis de Sade in order to check (and refute) an article by Pohl in which the latter drew connections from *Justine* and *Philosophy in the Boudoir* to one of Archimboldi's novels of the 1950s.

Pelletier, on the other hand, had read the divine Marquis when he was sixteen and at eighteen had participated in a ménage à trois with two female fellow students, and his adolescent predilection for erotic comics had flowered into a reasonable, restrained adult collection of licentious literature of the seventeenth and eighteenth centuries. In figurative terms: Pelletier was more intimately acquainted than Espinoza with Mnemosyne, mountain goddess and mother of the nine muses. In plain speech: Pelletier could screw for six hours (without coming) thanks to his bibliography, whereas Espinoza could go for the same amount of time (coming twice, sometimes three times, and finishing half dead) sheerly on the basis of strength and force of will.

•

And speaking of the Greeks, it would be fair to say that Espinoza and Pelletier believed themselves to be (and in their perverse way, were) incarnations of Ulysses, and that both thought of Morini as Eurylochus, the loyal friend about whom two very different stories are told in the *Odyssey*. The first, in which he escapes being turned into a pig, suggests shrewdness or a solitary and individualistic nature, careful skepticism, the craftiness of an old seaman. The second, however, involves an impious and sacrilegous adventure: the cattle of Zeus or another powerful god are grazing peacefully on the island of the Sun when they wake the powerful appetite of Eurylochus, so that with clever words he cajoles his friends to kill the cattle and prepare a feast, which angers Zeus or whichever god it is no end, who curses Eurylochus for putting on airs and presuming to be enlightened or atheistic or Promethean, since the god in question is more incensed by Eurylochus's attitude, by the dialectic of his hunger, than by the act itself of eating the cattle, and because of this act, or because of the feast, the ship that bears Eurylochus capsizes and all the sailors die, which was what Pelletier and Espinoza believed would happen to Morini, not in a conscious way, of course, but in a kind of disjointed or instinctual way, a dark thought in the form of a microscopic sign throbbing in a dark and microscopic part of the two friends' souls.

•

Near the end of 1996, Morini had a nightmare. He dreamed that Norton was diving into a pool as he, Pelletier, and Espinoza played cards around a stone table. Espinoza and Pelletier had their backs to the pool, which seemed at first glance to be an ordinary hotel pool. As they played, Morini watched the other tables, the parasols, the deck chairs lined up along both sides of the pool. In the distance there was a park with deep green hedges, shining as if with fresh rain. Little by little people began to leave, vanishing through the different doors connecting the outdoor space, the bar, and the building's rooms or little suites, suites that Morini imagined consisted of a double room with kitchenette and bathroom. Soon there was no one left outside, not even the bored waiters he'd seen earlier bustling around. Pelletier and Espinoza were still absorbed in the game. Next to Pelletier he saw a pile of poker chips, as well as coins from various countries, so he guessed Pelletier was winning. And yet Espinoza didn't look ready to give up. Just then, Morini glanced at his cards and saw he had nothing to play. He discarded and asked for four cards, which he left facedown on the stone table, without looking at them, and with some difficulty he set his wheelchair in motion. Pelletier and Espinoza didn't even ask where he was going. He rolled the wheelchair to the edge of the pool. Only then did he realize how enormous it was. It must have been at least a thousand feet wide and more than two miles long, calculated Morini. The water was dark and in some places there were oily patches, the kind you see in harbors. There was no trace of Norton. Morini shouted.

"Liz."

He thought he saw a shadow at the other end of the pool, and he moved his wheelchair in that direction. It was a long way. The one time he looked back, Pelletier and Espinoza had vanished from sight. A fog had settled over that part of the terrace. He went on. The water in the pool seemed to scale the edges, as if somewhere a squall were brewing or worse, although where Morini was heading everything was calm and silent, and there was no sign of a storm. Soon the fog settled over Morini. At first he tried to keep going, but then he realized that he was in danger of tipping his wheelchair into the pool, and he decided not to risk it. When his eyes had adjusted, he saw a rock jutting from the pool, like a dark and iridescent reef. This didn't seem strange to him. He went over to the edge and shouted Liz's name once more, afraid now that he would never see her again. A half turn of the wheels was all it would take to topple him in. Then he saw that the pool had emptied and was enormously deep, as if a gulf of moldy black tiles were opening at his feet. At the bottom he seemed to make out the figure of a woman (though it was impossible to be sure) heading toward the slope of rock. Morini was about to shout again and wave when he sensed someone at his back. Two things were instantly certain: the thing was evil and it wanted Morini to turn around and see its face. Carefully, he backed away and continued around the pool, trying not to look at whoever was following him, searching for the ladder that might take him down to the bottom. But of course the ladder, which should logically be in a corner, never appeared, and after he had rolled a few feet Morini stopped and turned and looked into the stranger's face, controlling his fear, a fear all the worse for his dawning certainty that he knew the person following him, who gave off a stench of evil that Morini could hardly bear. In the fog, Liz Norton's face appeared. A younger Norton—twenty, if that—staring so seriously and intently that Morini had to look away. Who was the person at the bottom of the pool? Morini could still see him or her, a tiny speck trying to climb the rock that had now become a mountain, and the sight of this person, so far away, filled his eyes with tears and made him deeply and inconsolably sad, as if he were seeing his first love wandering in a labyrinth. Or himself, with legs that still worked, lost on a hopeless climb. Also, and he couldn't help it, and it was good that he didn't, he thought it looked like a painting by Gustave Moreau or Odilon Redon. Then he swung around to face Norton and she said:

"There's no turning back."

He heard the sentence not with his ears but in his head. Norton has acquired telepathic powers, Morini thought. She isn't bad, she's good. It isn't evil that I sensed, it's telepathy, he told himself to alter the course of a dream that in his heart of hearts he knew was fixed and inevitable. Then Norton repeated, in German, there's no turning back. And, paradoxically, she turned and walked off away from the pool and was lost in a forest that could barely be seen through the fog, a forest that gave off a red glow, and it was into this red glow that Norton disappeared.

•

A week later, having interpreted the dream in at least four different ways, Morini traveled to London. The decision to make the trip was a complete break from his usual routine, since normally he traveled only to conferences and meetings, his plane ticket and hotel room paid for by the organization in question. This time there was no professional excuse and he paid the hotel and transportation costs out of his own pocket. Nor can it be said that he was answering a call of help from Liz Norton. He had talked to her just four days before and told her he was planning to come to London, a city he hadn't visited in a long time.

Norton was delighted and invited him to stay with her, but Morini lied, saying he'd already made a reservation at a hotel. When he landed at Gatwick, Norton was waiting for him. That day they had breakfast together, in a restaurant near Morini's hotel, and that night they had dinner in Norton's apartment. During dinner, bland but praised politely by Morini, they talked about Archimboldi, about his growing renown and the innumerable gaps in his story that remained to be filled, but later, over dessert, the conversation took a more personal turn, tending more toward reminiscence, and until three in the morning, when they called a cab and Norton helped Morini into her building's old elevator, then down a flight of six steps, everything was, as the Italian reviewed it in his mind, much more pleasant than he'd expected.

Between breakfast and dinner, Morini was alone, hardly daring at first to leave his room, although later, driven by boredom, he decided to go out and went as far as Hyde Park, where he wandered aimlessly, lost in thought, without noticing or seeing anyone. Some people gazed after him in curiosity, because they had never seen a man in a wheelchair moving with such determination and at such a steady pace. When he finally came to a stop he found himself outside the Italian Gardens, or so they were called, although nothing about them struck him as Italian, but who knows, he mused, sometimes people are staggeringly ignorant of what's under their very noses.

He pulled a book out of his jacket pocket and began to read as he regained his strength. Soon he heard a voice saying hello, then the noise a heavy body makes when it drops to a wooden bench. He returned the greeting. The stranger had straw-colored hair, graying and dirty, and must have weighed at least two hundred and fifty pounds. They sat a moment looking at each other and the stranger asked whether he was a foreigner. Morini said he was Italian. The stranger wanted to know whether he lived in London, and then what the book he was reading was called. Morini answered that he didn't live in London and that the book he was reading was called *Il libro di cucina di Juana Inés de la Cruz*, by Angelo Morino, and that it was written in Italian, of course, although it was about a Mexican nun. About the nun's life and some of her recipes.

"So this Mexican nun liked to cook?" asked the stranger.

"In a way she did, although she also wrote poems," Morini replied.

"I don't trust nuns," said the stranger.

"Well, this nun was a great poet," said Morini.

"I don't trust people who cook from recipes," said the stranger, as if he hadn't heard him.

"So whom do you trust?" asked Morini.

"People who eat when they're hungry, I guess," said the stranger.

Then he went on to explain that a long time ago he had worked for a company that made mugs, just mugs, the plain kind and the kind decorated with phrases or mottoes or jokes: *Sorry, I'm On My Coffee Break!* or *Daddy Loves Mummy* or *Last Round Today, Last Round Forever*, that sort of thing, mugs with anodyne captions, and one day, surely due to demand, the inscriptions on the mugs changed drastically and they started using pictures, black-and-white at first, but then the venture did so well they switched to pictures in color, some humorous but some dirty, too.

"They even gave me a raise," the stranger said. "Do mugs like that exist in Italy?" he asked then.

"Yes," said Morini, "some with phrases in English and others with phrases in Italian."

"Well, it was everything we could have asked for," said the stranger. "We all worked more happily. The managers worked more happily, too, and the boss looked happy. But after a few months of making those mugs I realized that my happiness was artificial. I felt happy because I saw the others were happy and because I knew I should feel happy, but I wasn't really happy. In fact, I felt worse than before they'd given me a raise. I thought I was going through a bad patch and I tried not to think about it, but after three months I couldn't keep pretending nothing was wrong. I was in a terrible mood, I was much more violent than I'd been before, any little thing would make me angry, I started to drink. So I faced up to the problem, and finally I realized that I didn't like to make that particular kind of mug. At night, I swear, I suffered like a dog. I thought I was going crazy, that I didn't know what I was doing or thinking. Some of the thoughts I had back then still scare me. One day I confronted one of the managers. I told him I was sick of making those idiotic mugs. This manager was a good man, his name was Andy, and he always tried to make conversation with the workers. He asked me whether I'd preferred making the mugs we'd made before. That's right, I said. Are you serious, Dick? he asked me. Completely serious, I answered. Are the new mugs more work? Not at all, I said, the work is the same, but the fucking mugs didn't do damage to me this way before. What do you mean? said Andy. That the bloody mugs didn't bother me before and now they're destroying me inside. So what the hell makes them different, aside from being more modern? asked Andy. That's it exactly, I answered, the mugs weren't so modern before, and even if they tried to hurt me, they couldn't, I didn't feel their sting, but now the fucking mugs are like samurais armed with those fucking samurai swords and they're driving me insane. Anyway, it was a long conversation," said the stranger. "The manager listened to me, but he didn't understand a single word I was saying. The next day I asked for the pay I was due and I left the company. I haven't worked since. What do you think of that?"

Morini hesitated before answering.

"I don't know," he said finally.

"That's what everyone says: they don't know," said the stranger.

"What do you do now?" asked Morini.

"Nothing, I don't work anymore, I'm a London bum," the stranger said.

It's as if he's pointing out a tourist attraction, thought Morini, but he was careful not to say this out loud.

"So what do you think of that book?" asked the stranger.

"What book?" asked Morini.

The stranger pointed one of his thick fingers at the book, published by Sellerio, in Palermo, that Morini was holding delicately in one hand.

"Oh, I think it's very good," he said.

"Read me some recipes," said the stranger, in a tone of voice that struck Morini as threatening.

"I don't know whether I have time," he said, "I have to meet a friend."

"What's your friend's name?" asked the stranger in the same tone of voice.

"Liz Norton," said Morini.

"Liz, pretty name," said the stranger. "And what's your name, if you don't mind me asking?"

"Piero Morini," said Morini.

"Odd," said the stranger, "your name is almost the same as the name of the author of the book."

"No," said Morini, "my name is Piero Morini, and his name is Angelo Morino."

"If you wouldn't mind," said the stranger, "at least read me the names of some recipes. I'll close my eyes and imagine them."

"All right," said Morini.

The stranger closed his eyes and Morini began to read some of the names of the recipes attributed to Sor Juana Inés de la Cruz, slowly and with an actor's intonation.

Sgonfiotti al formaggio
Sgonfiotti alla ricotta
Sgonfiotti di vento
Crespelle
Dolce di tuorli di uovo
Uova regali
Dolce alla panna
Dolce alle noci
Dolce di testoline di moro
Dolce alle barbabietole
Dolce di burro e zucchero
Dolce alla crema
Dolce di mamey

By the time he got to *dolce di mamey*, the stranger seemed to have fallen asleep and Morini left the Italian Gardens.

•

The next day was much like the first. This time Norton came to meet him at the hotel, and as Morini was paying the bill she put his only suitcase in the boot of her car. When they left, she drove the same way he'd taken to Hyde Park the day before.

Morini realized it and watched the streets in silence, and then the appearance of the park, which looked to him like a film of the jungle, the colors wrong, terribly sad, exalted, until the car turned and disappeared down other streets.

They ate together in a neighborhood that Norton had discovered, a neighborhood near the river, where there had once been a few factories and dry docks and where boutiques and food shops and fashionable restaurants had now opened in the renovated buildings. A small boutique occupied the same number of square feet as four workers' houses, calculated Morini. The restaurant, twelve or sixteen. Liz Norton's voice praised the neighborhood and the efforts of the people who were setting it back afloat.

Morini thought that *afloat* was wrong, despite its maritime ring. In fact, as they ate dessert he felt like weeping, or better yet, fainting, sliding gently out of his chair with his eyes fixed on Norton's face, and never waking up. But now Norton was telling a story about a painter, the first to settle in the neighborhood.

He was a young man, thirty-three or so, known on the scene but not what you'd call famous. The real reason he came was because it was cheaper to rent a studio here than anywhere else. The neighborhood was less lively in those days. There were still old workmen living here on their pensions, but no young people or children. Women were notably absent: they had either died or spent all day inside, never going out. There was just one pub, as tumbledown as the rest of the neighborhood. In short, a lonely, decrepit place. But it seemed this sparked the painter's imagination and inspired him to work. He was a solitary kind of person, too. Or else just comfortable being alone.

So the neighborhood didn't frighten him. He fell in love with it, actually. He liked to come home at night and walk for blocks and blocks without seeing anyone. He liked the color of the streetlamps and the light that spilled over the fronts of the houses. The shadows that moved as he moved. The ashen, sooty dawns. The men of few words who gathered in the pub, where he became a regular. The pain, or the memory of pain, that here was literally sucked away by something nameless until only a void was left. The knowledge that this question was possible: pain that turns finally into emptiness. The knowledge that the same equation applied to everything, more or less.

The point is, he set to work more eagerly than ever. A year later he had a show at the Emma Waterson gallery, an alternative space in Wapping, and it was an enormous success. He ushered in something that would later be known as the *new decadence* or *English animalism*. The paintings in the inaugural show of this school were big, ten feet by seven, and they portrayed the remains of the shipwreck of his neighborhood, awash in a mingling of grays. It was as if painter and neighborhood had achieved total symbiosis. As if, in other words, the painter were painting the neighborhood or the neighborhood were painting the painter, in savage, gloomy strokes. The paintings weren't bad. Still, the show wouldn't have been so successful or had such an impact if not for the central painting, much smaller than the rest, the masterpiece that years later led so many British artists down the path of new decadence. This painting, viewed properly (although one could never be sure of viewing it properly), was an ellipsis of self-portraits, sometimes a spiral of self-portraits (depending on the angle from which it was seen), seven feet by three and a half feet, in the center of which hung the painter's mummified right hand.

It happened like this. One morning, after two days of feverish work on the self-portraits, the painter cut off his painting hand. He immediately applied a tourniquet to his arm and took the hand to a taxidermist he knew, who'd already been informed of the nature of the assignment. Then he went to the hospital, where they stanched the bleeding and proceeded to suture his arm. At some point someone asked how the accident had happened. He answered that he had cut off his hand with a machete blow while he was working, by mistake. The doctors asked where the amputated hand was, because there was always the possibility that it might be reattached. He said he'd thrown it in the river on his way to the hospital, out of sheer rage and pain.

Although the prices were astronomical, the show sold out. The masterpiece, it was said, went to an Arab who worked in the City, as did four of the big paintings. Shortly thereafter, the painter went mad and his wife (he was married by then) had no choice but to send him to a convalescent home on the outskirts of Lausanne or Montreux.

He lives there to this day.

Other painters, meanwhile, began to move into the neighborhood. Mostly because it was cheap, but also because they were attracted by the legend of the man who had painted the most radical self-portrait of our time. Then came the architects, then some families who bought houses that had been renovated and remodeled. Then came the boutiques, the black-box theaters, the cutting-edge restaurants, until it was one of the trendiest neighborhoods in London, nowhere near as cheap as it was reputed to be.

"What do you think of that story?"

"I don't know what to think," said Morini.

The urge to weep—or else, faint—persisted, but he restrained it.

•

They had tea at Norton's apartment. Only then did she begin to talk about Espinoza and Pelletier, but casually, as if the matter was too familiar to be worthy of interest or discussion with Morini (whom she had noticed was upset, although she was careful not to pry, knowing there was rarely anything soothing about being pestered with questions), and not even something she cared to discuss herself.

It was a very pleasant afternoon. From his armchair, Morini admired Norton's sitting room—her books and her framed prints hanging on white walls, her mysterious photographs and souvenirs, her preferences expressed in things as simple as the choice of furniture, which was tasteful, comfortable, and modest, and even in the sliver of tree-lined street that she surely saw each morning before she left the apartment—and he began to feel good, as if he were swaddled in these various manifestations of his friend, as if they were also an expression of affirmation, the words of which he might not understand but that brought him comfort nevertheless.

Shortly before he left, he asked the name of the painter whose story he'd just heard and whether there'd been a catalog for that terrible show. His name is Edwin Johns, said Norton. Then she got up and searched one of the bookcases. She found a large catalog and handed it to Morini. Before he opened it he asked himself whether it was a good idea to insist on this, precisely now that he was so relaxed. But if I don't do it I'll die, he told himself, and he opened the catalog, which more than a catalog was an art book that covered or tried to cover the trajectory of Johns's career. There was a photograph of Johns on the first page, from before his self-mutilation, which showed a young man of about twenty-five looking straight at the camera and smiling a half smile that might be shy or mocking. His hair was dark and straight.

"It's a gift," he heard Norton say.

"Thank you," he heard himself answer.

An hour later they left together for the airport, and an hour after that Morini was on his way back to Italy.

•

Around this time, a previously insignificant Serbian critic, a German professor at the University of Belgrade, published a strange article in the journal overseen by Pelletier, an article reminiscent in a certain sense of the minuscule findings on the Marquis de Sade published many years ago by a French critic, which comprised the facsimile reproduction of loose papers testifying vaguely to the Marquis's visit to a laundry, an aide-mémoire of his relations with a certain theater impresario, a doctor's bill complete with medicines prescribed, an order for a doublet specifying buttonwork and color, etc., all of it accompanied by lengthy notes from which only a single conclusion could be drawn: Sade had existed, Sade had washed his clothes and bought new clothes and maintained a correspondence with beings now definitively wiped from the slate of time.

The Serb's text was very similar. In this case, the person traced was Archimboldi, not Sade, and the article consisted of a painstaking and often frustrating investigation that began in Germany, continued through France, Switzerland, Italy, Greece, returned to Italy, and ended at a travel agency in Palermo, where it seemed Archimboldi had bought a plane ticket to Morocco. An old man, a German, said the Serbian. The words *old man* and *German* he waved like magic wands to uncover a secret, and at the same time they supplied the stamp of ultraconcrete critical literature, a nonspeculative literature free of ideas, assertions, denials, doubts, free of any intent to serve as guide, neither pro nor con, just an eye seeking out the tangible elements, not judging them but simply displaying them coldly, archaeology of the facsimile, and, by the same token, of the photocopier.

•

To Pelletier it seemed an odd text. Before he published it, he sent copies to Espinoza, Morini, and Norton. Espinoza said it could lead somewhere, and even though researching and writing that way might seem like drudge work, like the lowest of menial tasks, he thought, and said, that it was good to have a place in the Archimboldian project for these single-minded fanatics. Norton said she'd always had the feeling (feminine intuition) that sooner or later Archimboldi would show up somewhere in the Maghreb, and that the only part of the Serb's paper that was worth anything was the ticket in the name of Benno von Archimboldi, bought a week before the Italian plane was scheduled to depart for Rabat. From now on we can imagine him lost in a cave in the Atlas Mountains, she said. Morini held his tongue.

•

Here we should clarify in the interest of properly (or improperly) understanding the Serb's text. A reservation was indeed made in the name of Benno von Archimboldi. And yet, that reservation was never confirmed and at the departure time no Benno von Archimboldi appeared at the airport. By the Serb's lights, the matter couldn't be clearer. Archimboldi had doubtless made the reservation himself. We can imagine him at his hotel, likely upset about something or other, maybe drunk, perhaps even half asleep, at that abysslike hour (with its ineffably nauseating scent) when momentous decisions are made, speaking to the girl at Alitalia and mistakenly giving her his pen name instead of booking the seat under the name on his passport, an error that later, the next day, he would rectify by going in person to the airline office and buying a ticket in his own name. This explained the absence of an Archimboldi on the flight to Morocco. Of course, there were other possibilities: at the last minute, after having second (or fourth) thoughts, Archimboldi may have decided not to take the trip, or to travel somewhere else instead, say the United States, or maybe it was all simply a joke or misunderstanding.

The Serb's text contained a physical description of Archimboldi. This description was plainly based on the Swabian's account. Of course, in the Swabian's account Archimboldi was a young postwar writer. All the Serbian had done was age him, turning that same young man, who had traveled with his single published book to Friesland in 1949, into an old man, seventy-five or eighty, who now had a substantial oeuvre behind him but the same attributes more or less, as if Archimboldi, unlike most people, hadn't changed and were still the same person. To judge by his work, our writer is unquestionably a stubborn man, said the Serb, he's stubborn as a mule, as a pachyderm, and if during the saddest stretch of a Sicilian afternoon he hatched a plan to travel to Morocco, no matter that he made the reservation under the name Archimboldi by mistake, instead of his legal name, there's no reason to think he might not have changed his mind the very next day and gone personally to the travel agency to buy the ticket, this time under his legal name and with his legal passport, and that he didn't set off, like any of the thousands of old men, German bachelors, who each day cross the skies alone heading for any of the countries of North Africa.

•

Old and alone, thought Pelletier. Just one of thousands of old men on their own. Like the *machine célibataire*. Like the bachelor who suddenly grows old, or like the bachelor who, when he returns from a trip at light speed, finds the other bachelors grown old or turned into pillars of salt.

Thousands, hundreds of thousands of *machines célibataires* crossing an amniotic sea each day, on Alitalia, eating *spaghetti al pomodoro* and drinking Chianti or grappa, their eyes half closed, positive that the paradise of retirees isn't in Italy (or, therefore, anywhere in Europe), bachelors flying to the hectic airports of Africa or America, burial ground of elephants. The great cemeteries at light speed. I don't know why I'm thinking this, thought Pelletier. Spots on the wall and spots on the skin, thought Pelletier, looking at his hands. Fuck the Serb.

•

In the end, after the article came out, Espinoza and Pelletier were forced to recognize flaws in the Serb's approach. There had to be research, literary criticism, interpretive essays, even informational pamphlets if required, but not this hybrid between science fiction and half-finished *roman noir*, said Espinoza, and Pelletier was in complete agreement.

•

Around this time, at the beginning of 1997, Norton felt a desire for change. To get away. To visit Ireland or New York. To distance herself abruptly from Espinoza and Pelletier. She summoned them both to London. Pelletier had a feeling that nothing serious would happen, nothing irrevocable at least, and he arrived calm, ready to listen and say little. By contrast, Espinoza feared the worst (that Norton had summoned them to tell them she preferred Pelletier, but also to assure him that they'd still be friends, maybe even to ask if he'd give her away at her approaching wedding).

Pelletier was the first to show up at Norton's apartment. He asked whether anything serious was wrong. Norton said she'd rather discuss it when Espinoza got there, to keep from making the same speech twice. As they had nothing else important to say, they began to talk about the weather. Pelletier soon rebelled and changed the subject. Then Norton started to talk about Archimboldi. This new subject of conversation almost did Pelletier in. He thought again about the Serb, he thought again about that poor writer, old and alone and possibly misanthropic (Archimboldi), he thought again about the lost years of his own life before Norton had appeared.

Espinoza was late. Life is shit, thought Pelletier in astonishment, all of it. And then: if we hadn't teamed up, she would be mine now. And then: if there hadn't been mutual understanding and friendship and affinity and alliance, she would be mine now. And a little later: if there hadn't been anything, I wouldn't even have met her. And: I might have met her, since each of us has an independent interest in Archimboldi that doesn't spring from our mutual friendship. And: it's possible, too, that she might have hated me, found me pedantic, cold, arrogant, narcissistic, an intellectual elitist. The term *intellectual elitist* amused him. Espinoza was late. Norton seemed very calm. Actually, Pelletier seemed very calm too, but that was far from how he felt.

Norton said there was nothing strange about Espinoza's lateness. Planes get delayed, she said. Pelletier imagined Espinoza's plane engulfed in flames, crashing onto a runway at the Madrid airport in a screech of twisted steel.

"Maybe we should turn on the television," he said.

Norton looked at him and smiled. I never turn on the television, she said, smiling, surprised that Pelletier didn't already know that. Of course, Pelletier did know it. But he hadn't had the spirit to say: let's watch the news, let's see whether some plane wreck appears on the screen.

"Can I turn it on?" he asked.

"Of course," said Norton, and as Pelletier bent over the knobs of the set, he saw her out of the corner of his eye, luminous, so natural, making a cup of tea or moving from one room to another, putting away a book that she had just shown him, answering the phone and talking to someone who wasn't Espinoza.

He turned on the television. He clicked through different channels. He saw a man with a beard dressed in cheap clothes. He saw a group of blacks walking along a dirt track. He saw two men in suits and ties talking slowly and deliberately, both with their legs crossed, both glancing every so often at a map that appeared and disappeared behind their backs. He saw a chubby woman saying: daughter . . . factory . . . meeting . . . doctors . . . inevitable, and then smiling a little and lowering her gaze. He saw the face of a Belgian minister. He saw the smoldering remains of a plane next to a runway, surrounded by ambulances and fire trucks. He shouted for Norton. She was still talking on the phone.

•

Espinoza's plane has crashed, said Pelletier, this time not raising his voice, and Norton, instead of looking at the television screen, looked at him. It took her only a few seconds to realize that the plane in flames wasn't a Spanish plane. In addition to the firemen and rescue teams, passengers could be seen walking away, some limping, others wrapped in blankets, their faces contorted in fear or shock, but apparently unharmed.

•

Twenty minutes later, Espinoza arrived, and during lunch Norton told him that Pelletier had thought he was in the plane that went down. Espinoza laughed but gave Pelletier a strange look, which Norton didn't notice, but Pelletier caught immediately. It was a sad meal, all things considered, although Norton's behavior was perfectly normal, as if she had run into the two of them by chance and hadn't expressly asked them to come to London. They guessed what she had to tell them before she said anything: Norton wanted to end her romantic involvement with both of them, at least for the time being. The reason she gave was that she needed to think and get her bearings. Then she said she didn't want to stop being friends with either of them. She needed to think, that was all.

Espinoza accepted Norton's explanation without asking a single question. Pelletier would have liked to ask whether her ex-husband had anything to do with her decision, but following Espinoza's example, he kept quiet. After they ate they went out for a drive around London in Norton's car. Pelletier insisted on sitting in back, until he saw a sarcastic flash in Norton's eyes, and then he said he would sit anywhere, which happened to be the backseat.

As she drove along Cromwell Road, Norton said that maybe that night it would make most sense for her to sleep with both of them. Espinoza laughed and said something meant to be funny, a continuation of the joke, but Pelletier wasn't sure Norton was joking and he was even less sure he was ready to participate in a ménage à trois. Then they went to watch the sun set near the Peter Pan statue in Kensington Gardens. They sat on a bench by a giant oak tree, Norton's favorite spot, a place she'd been drawn to ever since she was a child. At first there were people lying on the grass, but little by little the area began to empty. Couples or elegantly dressed single women passed briskly, toward the Serpentine Gallery or the Albert Memorial, and in the opposite direction men with crumpled newspapers or mothers pushing baby carriages headed toward Bayswater Road.

As dusk fell, they watched a young Spanish-speaking couple approach the Peter Pan statue. The woman had black hair and was very pretty, and she reached out as if to touch Peter Pan's leg. The man beside her was tall and had a beard and mustache and pulled a notepad out of his pocket and jotted something down. Then he said out loud:

"Kensington Gardens."

The woman wasn't looking at the statue anymore but at the lake, or rather at something moving in the grass and weeds that separated the little path from the lake.

"What's she looking at?" asked Norton in German.

"It seems to be a snake," said Espinoza.

"There aren't any snakes here!" said Norton.

Then the woman called to the man: Rodrigo, come see this, she said. The man seemed not to hear. He had put the little notepad away in a pocket of his leather jacket and he was gazing silently at the statue of Peter Pan. The woman bent down and something beneath the leaves slithered toward the lake.

"It does actually seem to be a snake," said Pelletier.

"That's what I thought," said Espinoza.

Norton didn't answer but she stood to get a better look.

•

That night Pelletier and Espinoza slept for a few hours in Norton's sitting room. Although they had the sofa bed and the rug at their disposal, they had difficulty dozing off. Pelletier tried to talk, explain the plane wreck thing to Espinoza, but Espinoza said there was no need for explanations, he understood everything.

At four in the morning, by common accord, they turned on the light and started to read. Pelletier opened a book on the work of Berthe Morisot, the first woman impressionist, but soon he felt like hurling it against the wall. Espinoza, meanwhile, pulled Archimboldi's latest novel, *The Head*, out of his bag and started to go over the notes he had written in the margins, notes that were the nucleus of an essay he planned to publish in the journal edited by Borchmeyer.

Espinoza's thesis, also espoused by Pelletier, was that with this novel Archimboldi was drawing his literary adventures to a close. After *The Head*, said Espinoza, there'll be no new books on the market, an opinion that another illustrious Archimboldian, Dieter Hellfeld, considered too risky, based as it was on no more than the writer's age, and the same thing had been said when Archimboldi came out with *Railroad Perfection*; a few Berlin professors had even said it when *Bitzius* was published. At five in the morning Pelletier took a shower, then made coffee. At six Espinoza was asleep again but at six-thirty he woke in a foul mood. At a quarter to seven they called a cab and straightened up the sitting room.

Espinoza wrote a goodbye note. Pelletier glanced at it and after thinking for a few seconds, decided to leave another note himself. Before they left he asked Espinoza whether he didn't want to shower. I'll shower in Madrid, Espinoza answered. The water is better there. True, said Pelletier, although his reply struck him as stupid and appeasing. Then the two of them left without making a sound and had breakfast at the airport, as they'd done so many times before.

·

On the plane back to Paris, Pelletier began to think, inexplicably, about the Berthe Morisot book he'd wanted to slam against the wall the night before. Why? Pelletier asked himself. Was it that he didn't like Berthe Morisot or something she stood for in some momentary way? Actually, he liked Berthe Morisot. All at once it struck him that Norton hadn't bought the book, that he'd been the one who traveled from Paris to London with the gift-wrapped volume, that the first Berthe Morisot reproductions Norton had ever seen were the ones in that book, with Pelletier next to her, massaging the back of her neck and walking her through each painting. Did he regret having given her the book now? No, of course not. Did the painter have anything to do with their separation? The idea was ridiculous. Then why had he wanted to slam the book against the wall? And more to the point: why was he thinking about Berthe Morisot and the book and Norton's neck and not about the real possibility of a ménage à trois that had hovered in Norton's apartment that night like a howling Indian witch doctor without ever materializing?

·

On the plane back to Madrid, Espinoza, unlike Pelletier, thought about the book he believed to be Archimboldi's last novel, and how—if he was right, which he thought he was—there would be no more novels by Archimboldi, and he thought about all that entailed, and about a plane in flames and Pelletier's hidden desires (the son of a bitch could be oh so modern, but only when it was to his advantage), and every once in a while he looked out the window and glanced at the engines and dearly wished he was back in Madrid.

•

For a while Pelletier and Espinoza didn't call each other. Pelletier called Norton occasionally, although their conversations were increasingly, how to put it, stilted, as if good manners were the only thing sustaining their relationship, and he called Morini just as frequently as ever, for with him nothing had changed.

It was the same for Espinoza, although it took him a little longer to realize that Norton meant what she said. Naturally, Morini noticed something wrong, but out of discretion or laziness, the awkward and sometimes painful laziness that gripped him now and then, he preferred to behave as if he hadn't noticed, for which Pelletier and Espinoza were grateful.

Even Borchmeyer, who in some ways feared the tandem of Espinoza and Pelletier, noticed something new in the correspondence he maintained with each, veiled insinuations, tiny retractions, the faintest of doubts (all extremely eloquent, naturally, coming from them) about the methodology they had previously shared.

•

Then came an assembly of Germanists in Berlin, a twentieth-century German literature congress in Stuttgart, a symposium on German literature in Hamburg, and a conference on the future of German literature in Mainz. Norton, Morini, Pelletier, and Espinoza attended the Berlin assembly, but for one reason or another all four of them were able to meet only once, at breakfast, where they were surrounded by other Germanists fighting doggedly over the butter and jam. Pelletier, Espinoza, and Norton attended the congress, and just as Pelletier managed to speak to Norton alone (while Espinoza was exchanging views with Schwarz), when it was Espinoza's turn to talk to Norton, Pelletier went off discreetly with Dieter Hellfeld.

This time Norton noticed that her friends were doing their best not to speak to each other, sometimes even avoiding each other's company, which couldn't help affecting her since she felt in some way responsible for the rift between them.

Only Espinoza and Morini attended the symposium, and since they were in Hamburg anyway and killing time they went to visit the Bubis publishing house and paid their compliments to Schnell, but they couldn't see Mrs. Bubis, for whom they'd brought a bouquet of roses, since she was on a trip to Moscow. That woman, Schnell said to them, I don't know where she gets her energy, and then he gave a pleased laugh that Espinoza and Morini thought was a bit much. Before they left the publishing house they gave the roses to Schnell.

Only Pelletier and Espinoza attended the conference, and this time they had no choice but to meet and lay their cards on the table. At first, as was natural, they tried to avoid each other, politely most of the time or brusquely on a few occasions, but in the end there was nothing to do but talk. This event took place at the hotel bar, late at night, when only one waiter was left, the youngest one, a tall, blond, sleepy boy.

Pelletier was sitting at one end of the bar and Espinoza at the other. Then the bar began gradually to empty, and when only the two of them were left Pelletier got up and sat down next to Espinoza. They tried to discuss the conference, but after a few minutes it came to seem ridiculous going on, or pretending to go on, in that vein. Once again it was Pelletier, better versed in the art of conciliation and confidences, who took the first step. He asked how Norton was. Espinoza confessed he didn't know. Then he said that he called her sometimes and it was like talking to a stranger. This last part Pelletier inferred, because Espinoza, who at times expressed himself in unintelligible ellipses, didn't call Norton a stranger but used the word *busy*, then the word *distracted*. For a while, the phone in Norton's apartment floated in their conversation. A white telephone in the grasp of a white hand, the white forearm of a stranger. But she wasn't a stranger. Not insofar as both had slept with her. Oh white hind, little hind, white hind, murmured Espinoza. Pelletier assumed he was quoting a classic, but without comment asked him whether they were really going to become enemies. The question seemed to surprise Espinoza, as if the possibility had never occurred to him.

"That's absurd, Jean-Claude," he said, although Pelletier noticed he thought for a long time before he answered.

By the end of the night, they were drunk and the young waiter had to help them both out of the bar. What Pelletier remembered best was the strength of the waiter who hauled them, one on each side, to the elevators in the lobby, as if he and Espinoza were adolescents, no older than fifteen, two weedy adolescents clamped in the powerful arms of this young German who had stayed until closing time, when all the veteran waiters had already gone home, a country boy, to judge by his face and build, or a laborer, and he also remembered something like a whisper that he later understood was a kind of laugh, Espinoza's laugh as he was lugged by the peasant waiter, a soft chuckle, a discreet laugh, as if the situation weren't merely ridiculous but also an escape valve for his unspoken sorrows.

•

One day, when more than three months had gone by since their visit to Norton, one of them called the other and suggested a weekend in London. It's unclear whether Pelletier or Espinoza made the call. In theory, it must have been the one with the strongest sense of loyalty, or of friendship, which amounts to the same thing, but in truth neither Pelletier nor Espinoza had a strong sense of any such virtue. Both of them paid it lip service, of course. But in practice, neither believed in friendship or loyalty. They believed in passion, they believed in a hybrid form of social or public happiness (both voted Socialist, albeit with the occasional abstention), they believed in the possibility of self-realization.

The salient point is that one called and the other said yes, and one Friday afternoon they met at the London airport and got a cab to a hotel, then another cab, now very close to dinnertime (they had made a reservation for three at Jane & Chloe), to Norton's apartment.

From the sidewalk, after they paid the driver, they looked up at the lighted windows. Then, as the cab drove off, they saw Liz's silhouette, the beloved silhouette, and then, as if a breath of foul air had wafted into a commercial for sanitary pads, the silhouette of a man that made them freeze, Espinoza with a bouquet of flowers in his hand, Pelletier with a Jacob Epstein book wrapped in the finest paper. But the pantomime above didn't end there. In one window, Norton's silhouette gestured, as if trying to explain something that her interlocutor refused to understand. In the other window, the man's silhouette, to the horror of its two gaping spectators, made a kind of hula-hooping motion, or what looked to Pelletier and Espinoza like a hula-hooping motion, first the hips, then the legs, the torso, even the neck! a motion that contained a hint of sarcasm and mockery, unless behind the curtains the man was undressing or melting, which seemed very unlikely; the motion, or the series of motions, expressed not only sarcasm but cruelty and assurance too, the assurance plain, since he was the strongest one in the apartment, the tallest, the most muscular, the hula-hooper.

And yet there was something strange about Liz's silhouette. To the extent that they knew her, and they thought they knew her well, Norton wasn't the sort to stand for slights, especially in her own apartment. So it was possible, they decided, that the man's silhouette wasn't actually hula-hooping or insulting Liz but laughing, and laughing with her, not at her. But Liz's silhouette didn't seem to be laughing. Then the man's silhouette disappeared: maybe he had gone to look at books, maybe to the bathroom or the kitchen. Maybe he had dropped onto the sofa, still laughing. And just then Norton's silhouette drew near the window, seeming to shrink, and then pushed back the curtains and opened the window. Norton's eyes were closed, as if she needed to breathe the night air of London, and then she opened her eyes and looked down, into the abyss, and saw them.

•

They called hello as if the taxi had just left them there. Espinoza waved his bouquet of flowers in the air and Pelletier his book, and then, without waiting to see Norton's confused face, they headed to the door of the building and waited for Liz to buzz them in.

They were sure all was lost. As they climbed the stairs, without talking, they heard a door being opened, and although they didn't see her, both sensed Norton's luminous presence on the landing. The apartment smelled of Dutch tobacco. Leaning in the doorway, Norton looked at them as if they were two friends who had died long ago, ghosts returning from the sea. The man waiting for them in the sitting room was younger, probably born in the seventies, not the sixties—even the midseventies. He was wearing a turtleneck sweater, although the neck seemed to sag, and faded jeans and sneakers. He looked like a student of Norton's or a substitute teacher.

Norton said his name was Alex Pritchard. A friend. Pelletier and Espinoza shook his hand and smiled, knowing their smiles would be pathetic. Pritchard didn't smile. Two minutes later they were all sitting drinking whiskey in silence. Pritchard, who was drinking orange juice, sat next to Norton and slung an arm over her shoulders, a gesture she didn't seem to mind at first (in fact, Pritchard's long arm was resting on the back of the sofa and only his fingers, long as a spider's or a pianist's, occasionally brushed Norton's blouse), but as the minutes went by Norton became more and more nervous and her trips to the kitchen or bedroom became more frequent.

Pelletier attempted a few subjects of conversation. He tried to talk about film, music, recent theater productions, without getting any help even from Espinoza, who seemed to vie with Pritchard in his muteness, although Pritchard's muteness was at least that of the observer, equal parts distracted and engaged, and Espinoza's muteness was that of the observed, sunk in misery and shame. Suddenly, without anyone being able to say for sure who had started it, they began to talk about Archimboldian studies. It was probably Norton, from the kitchen, who mentioned the work they all did. Pritchard waited for her to come back and then, his arm stretched once again along the back of the sofa and his spider fingers on Norton's shoulder, said he thought German literature was a scam.

Norton laughed, as if someone had told a joke. Pelletier asked him what he, Pritchard, knew about German literature.

"Not much, really," he said.

"Then you're a cretin," said Espinoza.

"Or an ignoramus, at least," said Pelletier.

"In any case, a *badulaque*," said Espinoza.

Espinoza had said *badulaque* in Spanish, and Pritchard didn't know what it meant. Norton didn't understand it either and wanted to know what it was.

"A *badulaque*," said Espinoza, "is someone of no consequence. It's a word that can also be applied to fools, but there are fools of consequence, and *badulaque* applies only to fools of no consequence."

"Are you insulting me?" Pritchard wanted to know.

"Do you feel insulted?" asked Espinoza, who had begun to sweat profusely.

Pritchard took a swallow of his orange juice and said that he did, he really did feel insulted.

"Then you have a problem, sir," said Espinoza.

"Typical reaction of a *badulaque*," added Pelletier.

Pritchard got up from the sofa. Espinoza got up from his armchair. Norton said that's enough, you're behaving like stupid children. Pelletier started to laugh. Pritchard went over to Espinoza and tapped him on the chest with his index finger, which was almost as long as his middle finger. He tapped his chest, one, two, three, four times, as he said:

"First: I don't like to be insulted. Second: I don't like to be taken for a fool. Third: I don't like it when some Spanish fucker takes the piss. Fourth: if you have anything else to say to me, let's go outside."

Espinoza looked at Pelletier and asked him, in German, of course, what he should do.

"Don't go outside," said Pelletier.

"Alex, leave now," said Norton.

And since Pritchard didn't really intend to hit anyone, he kissed Norton on the cheek and left without saying goodbye.

•

That night the three of them ate at Jane & Chloe. At first they were a little subdued, but the dinner and wine cheered them up and in the end they went home laughing. Still, they were reluctant to ask Norton who Pritchard was and she didn't say anything that might cast light on the lanky figure of that disagreeable youth. Instead, toward the end of dinner, they talked about themselves, about how close they'd come to destroying, possibly forever, the friendship they felt for one another.

Sex, they agreed, was too wonderful (although almost immediately they regretted the adjective) to get in the way of a friendship based as much on emotional as intellectual affinities. Pelletier and Espinoza took pains, however, to make it clear there in front of each other that the ideal thing for them, and they imagined for Norton too, was that she ultimately and in a nontraumatic way (try to make it a soft landing, said Pelletier) choose one of them, or neither of them, said Espinoza, either way the decision was in her hands, Norton's hands, and it was a decision she could make whenever she wanted, whenever was most convenient for her, or never make, put off, defer, postpone, draw out, delay, adjourn until her deathbed, they didn't care, because they were as in love with her now, while Liz was keeping them in limbo, as they had been before, when they were her active lovers or colovers, as in love with her as they would be when she chose one of them or the other, or when she (in a possible future that was only slightly more bitter, a future of shared bitterness, of somehow mitigated bitterness), if such was her wish, chose neither of them. To which Norton replied with a question, no doubt partly rhetorical, but a plausible question all the same: what would happen if, while she took her time considering the options, one of them, Pelletier for example, suddenly fell in love with a student who was younger and prettier than she, and richer, too, and more charming? Should she consider the pact broken and automatically give up on Espinoza? Or should she take the Spaniard, since he was the only one left? To which Pelletier and Espinoza responded that the real possibility of such a thing happening was extremely remote, and anyway she could do as she liked, even become a nun if she so desired.

"The only thing either of us wants is to marry you, live with you, have children with you, grow old with you, but at this point in our lives, what matters to us is preserving your friendship."

•

After that night, the plane trips to London began again. Sometimes it would be Espinoza who came to visit, other times Pelletier, and once in a while both. When this happened they would always stay at the same place, a small, uncomfortable hotel on Foley Street, near the Middlesex Hospital. When they left Norton's apartment, they would often take a walk near the hotel, usually in silence, frustrated, somehow exhausted by the goodwill and cheer they felt required to display during these joint visits. Many times they would just stand there under the streetlight on the corner, watching the ambulances going in and out. The English nurses spoke at the top of their lungs, although from where they stood the sound of the braying voices was muted.

One night, as they were watching the unusually quiet entrance to the hospital, they asked themselves why, when they came to London together, neither of them stayed at Liz's apartment. Out of politeness, probably, they said. But neither one of them believed in that kind of politeness anymore. And they also asked themselves, at first hesitantly and then vehemently, why the three of them didn't sleep together. That night a green, sickly light seeped from under the hospital doors, a transparent green swimming pool light, and an orderly smoked a cigarette, standing on the curb, and among the parked cars there was one with its light on, a yellow light as in a nest, though not just any nest but a post-nuclear nest, a nest with no room for any certainties but cold, despair, and apathy.

One night, while talking to Norton on the phone from Paris or Madrid, one of them brought the subject up. Surprisingly, Norton said she'd been asking herself the same question for a while.

"I don't think we'll ever suggest it," said the person on the phone.

"I know," said Norton. "You're afraid to. You're waiting for me to make the first move."

"I don't know," said the person on the phone, "maybe it isn't as simple as that."

They saw Pritchard again a few times. The lanky youth didn't seem as ill-humored as before, although in truth their encounters were fleeting, too brief for rudeness or violence. Espinoza was on his way into Norton's apartment as Pritchard was leaving; Pelletier crossed paths with him once on the stairs. Brief though it was, however, this latter encounter was significant. Pelletier said hello to Pritchard. Pritchard said hello to Pelletier, and after they had passed each other Pritchard turned around and called after Pelletier.

"Do you want some advice?" he asked. Pelletier gazed at him in alarm. "I know you don't, old man, but here it is. Be careful," said Pritchard.

"Careful of what?" Pelletier managed to ask.

"Of the Medusa," said Pritchard. "Beware of the Medusa."

And then, before he continued down the stairs, he added: "When you've got her in your hands she'll blow you to pieces."

For a while Pelletier stood there motionless, listening to Pritchard's footsteps on the stairs, then the noise of the street door opening and closing. Only when the silence became unbearable did he continue upstairs, thoughtful and in the dark.

•

He said nothing to Norton about the incident with Pritchard, but on his return to Paris he wasted no time calling Espinoza and telling him the story of the enigmatic encounter.

"Odd," said the Spaniard. "It sounds like a warning but also a threat."

"There's this, too," said Pelletier. "Medusa is one of the three daughters of Phorcys and Ceto, the so-called Gorgons, three sea monsters. According to Hesiod, the other two sisters, Stheno and Euryale, were immortal. But not Medusa."

"Have you been reading the Greek myths?" asked Espinoza.

"It's the first thing I did when I got home," said Pelletier. "Listen to this: when Perseus cut Medusa's head off, Chrysaor, father of the monster Geryon, emerged, and so did the horse Pegasus."

"Pegasus came out of Medusa's body? Fuck," said Espinoza.

"That's right. The winged horse Pegasus, which to me stands for love."

"You think Pegasus stands for love?"

"That's right."

"Strange," said Espinoza.

"It's a lycée thing," said Pelletier.

"And you think Pritchard knows this stuff?"

"Impossible," said Pelletier. "Although who's to say, but no, I doubt it."

"Then what do you think it all means?"

"I'd say Pritchard is alerting me, alerting us, to a danger we can't see. Or rather, he was trying to tell me that only after Norton's death would I, or we, find true love."

"After Norton's death?" said Espinoza.

"Of course, don't you understand? Pritchard sees himself as Perseus, Medusa's assassin."

•

For a while, Espinoza and Pelletier wandered around as if possessed. Archimboldi, who was again rumored to stand a clear chance for the Nobel, left them cold. They resented their work at the university, their periodic contributions to the journals of German departments around the world, their classes, and even the conferences they attended like sleepwalkers or drugged detectives. They were there but they weren't there. They talked, but their minds were on something else. Only Pritchard held their interest, the ominous presence of Pritchard, Norton's constant companion. A Pritchard who saw Norton as the Medusa, as a Gorgon, a Pritchard about whom, as reticent spectators, they knew almost nothing at all.

To fill in the gaps, they began to question the one person who could give them answers. At first Norton was reluctant to talk. He was a teacher, as they had suspected, though not at the university but at a secondary school. He wasn't from London but a town near Bournemouth. He had studied at Oxford for a year, and then, incomprehensibly to Espinoza and Pelletier, had moved to London and finished his studies there. He was on the Left, the *pragmatic* Left, and, according to Norton, on occasion he had mentioned plans (which never hardened into action) to become active in the Labour Party. The school where he taught was a council school with a good number of students from immigrant families.

He was headstrong and generous and lacked imagination, something Pelletier and Espinoza had already gathered. But that didn't make them feel any better.

"A bastard may have no imagination and then do one imaginative thing when you least expect it," said Espinoza.

"England is full of swine like him," was Pelletier's opinion.

Talking on the phone one night, they discovered without surprise (without even a shadow of surprise) that both of them hated Pritchard, and that they hated him more each day.

•

During the next conference they attended ("Reflecting the Twentieth Century: The Work of Benno von Archimboldi," a two-day event in Bologna packed with young Italian Archimboldians and a crop of Archimboldian neostructuralists from all over Europe), they decided to tell Morini everything that had happened to them in the last few months and all the fears they harbored concerning Norton and Pritchard.

Morini, whose health had deteriorated slightly since the last time (although neither Espinoza nor Pelletier knew), listened patiently at the hotel bar and at a trattoria near the conference headquarters and at an extremely expensive restaurant in the old part of the city and also as they strolled aimlessly along the streets of Bologna, Espinoza and Pelletier pushing Morini's wheelchair and talking nonstop. In the end, when they requested his opinion on the romantic imbroglio, real or imaginary, in which they found themselves, Morini only asked if either of them, or both, had asked Norton whether she loved Pritchard or was attracted to him. They had to confess that out of delicacy, tact, and good taste—out of consideration for Norton, essentially—they hadn't asked.

"Well, that's where you should have begun," said Morini, who, although he felt ill, and dizzy, too, after taking so many turns, breathed not a sigh of complaint.

•

(And at this point it must be said that there's truth to the saying *make your name, then sleep and reap fame*, because Espinoza's and Pelletier's participation in the conference "Reflecting the Twentieth Century: The Work of Benno von Archimboldi," not to mention their contribution to it, was at best null, at worst catatonic, as if they were suddenly spent or absent, prematurely aged or in a state of shock, a fact that didn't pass un-noticed by the attendees used to Espinoza's and Pelletier's displays of energy [sometimes brazen] at this sort of event, nor did it go unnoticed by the latest litter of Archimboldians, recent graduates, boys and girls, their doctorates tucked still warm under their arms, who planned, by any means necessary, to impose their particular readings of Archimboldi, like missionaries ready to instill faith in God, even if to do so meant signing a pact with the devil, for most were what you might call rationalists, not in the philosophical sense but in the pejorative literal sense, denoting people less interested in literature than in literary criticism, the one field, according to them—some of them, anyway—where revolution was still possible, and in some way they behaved not like youths but like *nou-veaux* youths, in the sense that there are the rich and the *nouveaux riches*, all of them generally rational thinkers, let us repeat, although of-ten incapable of telling their asses from their elbows, and although they noticed a there and a not-there, an absence-presence in the fleeting pas-sage of Pelletier and Espinoza through Bologna, they were incapable of seeing what was really important: Pelletier's and Espinoza's absolute boredom regarding everything said there about Archimboldi or their neg-ligent disregard for the gaze of others, as if the two were so much canni-bal fodder, a disregard lost on the young conferencegoers, those eager and insatiable cannibals, their thirtysomething faces bloated with suc-cess, their expressions shifting from boredom to madness, their coded stutterings speaking only two words: *love me*, or maybe two words and a phrase: *love me, let me love you*, though obviously no one understood.)

•

So Pelletier and Espinoza, who drifted through Bologna like two ghosts, asked Norton on their next visit to London, almost panting, as if they'd been running or jogging (without pause, in dreams or in reality), whether she, their beloved Liz who hadn't been able to go to Bologna, loved or lusted after Pritchard.

And Norton told them no. And then she said maybe she did, it was hard to give a conclusive answer in that regard. And Pelletier and Es-pinoza said they needed to know, that is, they needed definitive confir-mation. And Norton asked them why now, precisely, they were so interested in Pritchard.

And Pelletier and Espinoza said, almost on the verge of tears, if not now, when?

And Norton asked whether they were jealous. And they said that was simply too much, jealousy had nothing to do with it, it was almost an insult to accuse them of being jealous considering the nature of their friendship.

And Norton said it was only a question. And Pelletier and Espinoza said they weren't prepared to answer such a hurtful or captious or ill-intentioned question. And then they went out to dinner and the three of them drank too much, happy as children, talking about jealousy and its disastrous consequences. And they also talked about the inevitability of jealousy. And about the need for jealousy, as if jealousy were a middle-of-the-night urge. Not to mention the sweetness and the open, in some cases, to some people, delectable wounds. And on the way out they got in a cab and the discourse went on.

And for the first few minutes, the driver, a Pakistani, watched them in his rearview mirror, in silence, as if he couldn't believe what his ears were hearing, and then he said something in his language and the cab passed Harmsworth Park and the Imperial War Musuem, heading along Brook Drive and then Austral Street and then Geraldine Street, driving around the park, an unnecessary maneuver no matter how you looked at it. And when Norton told him he was lost and said which streets he should take to find his way, the driver fell silent again, with no more murmurings in his incomprehensible tongue, until he confessed that London was such a labyrinth, he really had lost his bearings.

Which led Espinoza to remark that he'd be damned if the cabbie hadn't just quoted Borges, who once said London was like a labyrinth—unintentionally, of course. To which Norton replied that Dickens and Stevenson had used the same trope long before Borges in their descriptions of London. This seemed to set the driver off, for he burst out that as a Pakistani he might not know this Borges, and he might not have read the famous Dickens and Stevenson either, and he might not even know London and its streets as well as he should, that's why he'd said they were like a labyrinth, but he knew very well what decency and dignity were, and by what he had heard, the woman here present, in other words Norton, was lacking in decency and dignity, and in his country there was a word for what she was, the same word they had for it in London as it happened, and the word was *bitch* or *slut* or *pig*, and the gentlemen here present, gentlemen who, to judge by their accents, weren't English, also had a name in his country and that name was *pimp* or *hustler* or *whoremonger*.

This speech, it may be said without exaggeration, took the Archimboldians by surprise, and they were slow to respond. If they were on Geraldine Street when the driver let them have it, they didn't manage to speak till they came to Saint George's Road. And then all they managed to say was: stop the cab right here, we're getting out. Or rather: stop this filthy car, we're not going any farther. Which the Pakistani promptly did, punching the meter as he pulled up to the curb and announcing to his passengers what they owed him, a fait accompli or final scene or parting token that seemed more or less normal to Norton and Pelletier, no doubt still reeling from the ugly surprise, but which was absolutely the last straw for Espinoza, who stepped down and opened the driver's door and jerked the driver out, the latter not expecting anything of the sort from such a well-dressed gentleman. Much less did he expect the hail of Iberian kicks that proceeded to rain down on him, kicks delivered at first by Espinoza alone, but then by Pelletier, too, when Espinoza flagged, despite Norton's shouts at them to stop, despite Norton's objecting that violence didn't solve anything, that in fact after this beating the Pakistani would hate the English even more, something that apparently mattered little to Pelletier, who wasn't English, and even less to Espinoza, both of whom nevertheless insulted the Pakistani in English as they kicked him, without caring in the least that he was down, curled into a ball on the ground, as they delivered kick after kick, shove Islam up your ass, which is where it belongs, this one is for Salman Rushdie (an author neither of them happened to think was much good but whose mention seemed pertinent), this one is for the feminists of Paris (will you fucking stop, Norton was shouting), this one is for the feminists of New York (you're going to kill him, shouted Norton), this one is for the ghost of Valerie Solanas, you son of a bitch, and on and on, until he was unconscious and bleeding from every orifice in the head, except the eyes.

•

When they stopped kicking him they were sunk for a few seconds in the strangest calm of their lives. It was as if they'd finally had the ménage à trois they'd so often dreamed of.

Pelletier felt as if he had come. Espinoza felt the same, to a slightly different degree. Norton, who was staring at them without seeing them in the dark, seemed to have experienced multiple orgasms. A few cars were passing by on St. George's Road, but the three of them were invisible to anyone traveling in a vehicle at that hour. There wasn't a single star in the sky. And yet the night was clear: they could see everything in great detail, even the outlines of the smallest things, as if an angel had suddenly clapped night-vision goggles on their eyes. Their skin felt smooth, extremely soft to the touch, although in fact the three of them were sweating. For a moment Espinoza and Pelletier thought they'd killed the Pakistani. A similar idea seemed to be passing through Norton's mind, because she bent over the cabbie and felt for his pulse. To move, to kneel down, hurt her as if the bones of her legs were dislocated.

A group of people came from Garden Row singing a song. They were laughing. Three men and two women. Without moving, Norton, Pelletier, and Espinoza turned their heads toward them and waited. The group began to walk in their direction.

"The cab," said Pelletier, "they want the cab."

Only at that moment did they realize the interior light of the cab was still on.

"Let's go," said Espinoza.

Pelletier took Norton by the shoulders and helped her up. Espinoza had gotten behind the wheel and was urging them to hurry. Pelletier pushed Norton into the backseat and then got in himself. The group from Garden Row headed straight toward the spot where the driver lay.

"He's alive, he's breathing," said Norton.

Espinoza started the car and they drove away. On the other side of the Thames, on a little street near Old Marylebone, they left the cab and walked for a while. They wanted to talk to Norton, explain what had happened, but she wouldn't even let them take her home.

•

The next day, as they ate a big breakfast at the hotel, they searched the papers for news about the Pakistani cabbie, but he wasn't mentioned anywhere. After breakfast they went out to get the tabloids. They didn't find anything there either.

They called Norton, who didn't seem as angry as she had the night before. They said they had to see her that afternoon. There was something important they needed to tell her. Norton said she had something important to tell them, too. To kill time they went out for a walk around the neighborhood. For a few minutes they entertained themselves by watching the ambulances coming in and out of Middlesex Hospital, imagining that each sick or hurt person who went in looked like the Pakistani they'd beaten so badly, until they got bored and went for a walk, their minds calmer, along Charing Cross toward the Strand. They confided in each other, as is natural. They shared their innermost feelings. What worried them most was that the police would come after them and catch them in the end.

"Before I got out of the cab," confessed Espinoza, "I wiped my fingerprints away with a handkerchief."

"I know," said Pelletier, "I saw you do it and I did the same. I wiped my fingerprints away, and Liz's, too."

More calmly each time, they went over and over the concatenation of events that had driven them, finally, to give the cabbie a beating. Pritchard, no question about it. And the Gorgon, that innocent and mortal Medusa, set apart from her immortal sisters. And the veiled or not so veiled threat. And nerves. And the rudeness of that ignorant wretch. They wished they had a radio so they could hear the latest news. They talked about what they'd felt as they rained blows on the fallen body. A combination of sleepiness and sexual desire. Desire to fuck the poor bastard? Not at all! More as if they were fucking themselves. As if they were digging into themselves. With long nails and empty hands. Though if your fingernails are long enough your hands are never really empty. But in this dreamlike state, they dug and dug, rending fabric and ripping veins and puncturing vital organs. What were they looking for? They didn't know. Nor, at that stage, did they care.

•

In the afternoon they saw Norton and they told her everything they knew or feared about Pritchard. The Gorgon, the death of the Gorgon. The exploding woman. She let them talk until they ran out of words. Then she soothed them. Pritchard couldn't hurt a fly, she said. They thought of Anthony Perkins, who claimed he wouldn't hurt a fly and look what happened, but they were content not to argue and they accepted her arguments, unconvinced. Then Norton sat down and said that the thing that couldn't be explained was what had happened the night before.

As if to divert blame, they asked her whether she'd heard anything about the Pakistani. Norton said she had. There'd been something on a local television station. A group of friends, probably the people they saw coming from Garden Row, had found the driver's body and called the police. He had four broken ribs, a concussion, a broken nose, and he'd lost all his top teeth. Now he was in the hospital.

"It was my fault," said Espinoza. "When he said what I did, I lost control."

"It would be best if we didn't see each other for a while," said Norton, "I have to think this over."

Pelletier agreed, but Espinoza kept blaming himself: it seemed fair that Norton should stop seeing him but not that she should stop seeing Pelletier.

"Stop talking nonsense," Pelletier said to him in a low voice, and only then did Espinoza realize that what he was saying was, in fact, stupid.

That night they both flew home.

•

When he got back to Madrid, Espinoza had a minor breakdown. In the cab home he started to cry, discreetly, covering his eyes with his hand, but the driver saw him crying and asked him if anything was wrong, whether he felt ill.

"I feel all right," said Espinoza, "I'm just a little on edge."

"Are you from here?" asked the driver.

"Yes," said Espinoza, "I was born in Madrid."

For a while neither of them said anything. Then the driver renewed his attack and asked whether he was interested in soccer. Espinoza said no, he'd never been interested in soccer or any other sport. And he added, as if not to put an abrupt end to the conversation, that the night before he had almost killed a man.

"Really," said the driver.

"That's right," said Espinoza, "I almost killed him."

"How's that?" asked the driver.

"It was in a rage," said Espinoza.

"Abroad?" asked the driver.

"Yes," said Espinoza, laughing for the first time, "far from here, and the man had a strange job, too."

Pelletier, meanwhile, neither had a breakdown nor talked to the driver who brought him back to his apartment. When he got home he took a shower and made himself some pasta with olive oil and cheese.

Then he checked his e-mail, answered a few messages, and went to bed with a novel by a young French author, nothing of great significance but amusing, and a journal of literary studies. A little while later he was asleep and he had the following extremely strange dream: he was married to Norton and they lived in a big house, near a cliff from which one could see a beach full of people in bathing suits lying in the sun or swimming, though never getting too far from shore.

The days were short. From his window he watched an almost unending succession of sunrises and sunsets. From time to time Norton would approach the room he was in and say something to him, but she never crossed the threshold. The people on the beach were always there. Sometimes he had the impression that at night they didn't go home, or that they all left together when it was dark, returning in a long procession before the sun came up. Other times, if he closed his eyes, he could soar over the beach like a seagull and see the bathers from up close. They came in every shape and size, although most were adults, in their thirties, forties, fifties, and all gave the impression of being focused on foolish activities, like rubbing oil on themselves, eating sandwiches, listening with more politeness than interest to the conversation of friends, relatives, or towel mates. Sometimes, however, the bathers would get up circumspectly and gaze at the horizon, even if for only a second or two. It was a calm horizon, cloudless, of a transparent blue.

When Pelletier opened his eyes he thought about the bathers' behavior. It was clear they were waiting for something, but you couldn't say there was anything desperate in their waiting. Every once in a while they'd simply look more alert, their eyes scanning the horizon for a second or two, and then they would once again become part of the flow of time on the beach, fluidly, without a moment of hesitation. Absorbed in watching the bathers, Pelletier forgot about Norton, trusting, perhaps, in her presence in the house, a presence evidenced by the noises that occasionally drifted from within, from the rooms that had no windows or windows that overlooked the fields or the mountains, not the sea or the crowded beach. He slept, or so he discovered deep into the dream, sitting in a chair, near his desk and the window. And he didn't seem to do much sleeping. Even when the sun set he tried to stay awake as long as possible, with his eyes fixed on the beach, now a black canvas or the bottom of a well, watching for any light, the trace of a flashlight, the flickering flame of a bonfire. He lost all notion of time. He vaguely remembered a confusing scene, at once embarrassing and exciting. The papers he had on the table were manuscripts by Archimboldi, or at least that was what he'd been told when he bought them, although when he looked through them he realized that they were written in French, not German. Next to him was a phone that never rang. The days grew hotter and hotter.

One morning, near midday, he saw the bathers halt their activities and turn to watch the horizon, all at once, in the usual way. Nothing happened. But then, for the first time, the bathers turned around and began to leave the beach. Some headed along a dirt road between two hills. Others struck off cross-country, clinging to bushes and stones. A few moved toward the cliff and Pelletier couldn't see them but he knew they were beginning a slow climb. All that was left on the beach was a mass, a dark form projecting from a yellow pit. For an instant Pelletier wondered whether he should go down to the beach and bury the mass at the bottom of the hole, taking all necessary precautions. But just imagining how far he would have to walk to get to the beach made him sweat, and he kept sweating more and more, as if once you turned the spigot you couldn't turn it off.

And then he spied a tremor in the sea, as if the water were sweating too, or as if it were about to boil. A barely perceptible simmer that spilled into ripples, building into waves that came to die on the beach. And then Pelletier felt dizzy and a hum of bees came from outside. And when the hum faded, a silence that was even worse fell over the house and everywhere around. And Pelletier shouted Norton's name and called to her, but no one answered his calls, as if the silence had swallowed up his cries for help. And then Pelletier began to weep and he watched as what was left of a statue emerged from the bottom of the metallic sea. A formless chunk of stone, gigantic, eroded by time and water, though a hand, a wrist, part of a forearm could still be made out with total clarity. And this statue came out of the sea and rose above the beach and it was horrific and at the same time very beautiful.

•

For a few days, Pelletier and Espinoza were, quite independently, filled with remorse by the business with the Pakistani driver, which circled in their guilty consciences like a ghost or an electric charge.

Espinoza wondered whether his behavior didn't reveal what he truly was, in other words a violent, xenophobic reactionary. Pelletier's guilt, on the other hand, was driven by having kicked the Pakistani when he was already on the ground, which was frankly unsportsmanlike. What need was there for that? he asked himself. The cabbie had already got what he deserved and there was no need to heap violence on violence.

One night the two of them talked on the phone for a long time. They expressed their respective fears. They comforted each other. But after a few minutes they were again lamenting what had happened, even though deep inside they were convinced that it was the Pakistani who was the real reactionary and misogynist, the violent one, the intolerant and offensive one, that the Pakistani had asked for it a thousand times over. The truth is that at moments like these, if the Pakistani had materialized before them, they probably would have killed him.

•

For a long time they forgot their weekly trips to London. They forgot Pritchard and the Gorgon. They forgot Archimboldi, whose renown continued to grow while their backs were turned. They forgot their papers, which they wrote in a perfunctory and uninspired way and which were really the work of their acolytes or of assistant professors from their respective departments recruited for the Archimboldian cause on the basis of vague promises of tenure-track positions or higher pay.

During a conference, as Pohl was giving a brilliant lecture on Archimboldi and shame in postwar German literature, the two visited a brothel in Berlin, where they slept with two tall and long-legged blondes. Upon leaving, near midnight, they were so happy they began to sing like children in the pouring rain. The experience, something new in their lives, was repeated several times in different European cities and finally ended up becoming part of their daily routine in Paris and Madrid. Others might have slept with students. They, afraid of falling in love, or of falling out of love with Norton, turned to whores.

In Paris, Pelletier went looking for them on the Internet, with excellent results. In Madrid, Espinoza found them by reading the sex ads in *El País*, which provided a much more reliable and practical service than the newspaper's arts pages, where Archimboldi was hardly ever mentioned and Portuguese heroes abounded, just as in the arts pages of *ABC*.

"You know," complained Espinoza in his conversations with Pelletier, perhaps seeking some consolation, "we Spaniards have always been provincials."

"True," replied Pelletier, after considering his answer for exactly two seconds.

Nor did they emerge unscathed from their adventures in prostitution.

•

Pelletier met a girl called Vanessa. She was married and had a son. Sometimes she would go weeks without seeing her husband and son. According to her, her husband was a saint. He had some flaws—for example he was an Arab, Moroccan to be precise, plus he was lazy—but overall, according to Vanessa, he was a good person, who almost never got angry about anything, and when he did, he wasn't violent or cruel like other men but instead melancholy, sad, filled with sorrow in the face of a world that suddenly struck him as overwhelming and incomprehensible. When Pelletier asked whether the Arab knew she worked as a prostitute, Vanessa said he did, that he knew but didn't care, because he believed in the freedom of individuals.

"Then he's your pimp," said Pelletier.

To this Vanessa replied that he might be, that if you thought about it he probably was, but he wasn't like other pimps, who were always demanding too much of their women. The Moroccan made no demands. There were periods, said Vanessa, when she, too, lapsed into a kind of habitual laziness, a persistent languor, and then money was tight. At times like these, the Moroccan contented himself with what there was and tried, without much luck, to find odd jobs so the three of them could scrape by. He was a Muslim, and sometimes he prayed toward Mecca, but clearly he was his own kind of Muslim. According to him, Allah permitted everything, or almost everything. To consciously hurt a child was not allowed. To abuse a child, kill a child, abandon a child to certain death, was forbidden. Everything else was relative and, in the end, permitted.

At some point, Vanessa told Pelletier, they had traveled to Spain. She, her son, and the Moroccan. In Barcelona they met up with the Moroccan's younger brother, who lived with another Frenchwoman, a tall, fat girl. They were musicians, the Moroccan told Vanessa, but really they were beggars. She had never seen the Moroccan so happy. He was constantly laughing and telling stories and he never got tired of walking around Barcelona, all the way to the suburbs or the mountains with views of the whole city and the gleam of the Mediterranean. Never, according to Vanessa, had she seen a man with such energy. Children, yes. A few, not many. But no adults.

When Pelletier asked Vanessa whether her son was the Moroccan's son too, she answered that he wasn't, and something about the way she said it made it plain that the question struck her as offensive or hurtful, an insult to her son. He was light-skinned, almost blond, she said, and he had turned six by the time she met the Moroccan, if she remembered correctly. A terrible time in my life, she said without going into details. The Moroccan's appearance could hardly be called providential. When she met him, it was a bad time for her, but he was literally starving.

Pelletier liked Vanessa and they saw each other several times. She was a tall girl, with a straight Greek nose and a steely, arrogant gaze. Her disdain for culture, especially book culture, was schoolgirlish somehow, a combination of innocence and elegance so thoroughly immaculate, or so Pelletier believed, that Vanessa could make the most idiotic remarks without provoking the slightest annoyance. One night, after they had made love, Pelletier got up naked and went looking among his books for a novel by Archimboldi. After hesitating for a moment he decided on *The Leather Mask*, thinking that with some luck Vanessa might read it as a horror novel, might be attracted by the sinister side of the book. She was surprised at first by the gift, then touched, since she was used to her clients giving her clothes or shoes or lingerie. Really, she was very happy with it, especially when Pelletier explained who Archimboldi was and the role the German writer played in his life.

"It's as if you were giving me a part of you," said Vanessa.

This remark left Pelletier a bit confused, since in a way it was perfectly true, Archimboldi was by now a part of him, the author belonged to him insofar as Pelletier had, along with a few others, instituted a new reading of the German, a reading that would endure, a reading as ambitious as Archimboldi's writing, and this reading would keep pace with Archimboldi's writing for a long time, until the reading was exhausted or until Archimboldi's writing—the capacity of the Archimboldian oeuvre to spark emotion and revelations—was exhausted (but he didn't believe that would happen), though in another way it wasn't true, because sometimes, especially since he and Espinoza had given up their trips to London and stopped seeing Norton, Archimboldi's work, his novels and stories, that is, seemed completely foreign, a shapeless and mysterious verbal mass, something that appeared and disappeared capriciously, literally a pretext, a false door, a murderer's alias, a hotel bathtub full of amniotic liquid in which he, Jean-Claude Pelletier, would end up committing suicide for no reason, gratuitously, in bewilderment, just because.

As he expected, Vanessa never told him what she thought of the book. One morning he went home with her. She lived in a working-class neighborhood full of immigrants. When they got there, her son was watching TV and Vanessa scolded him because he hadn't gone to school. The boy said he had a stomachache and Vanessa immediately made him some herbal tea. Pelletier watched her move around the kitchen. The energy Vanessa expended was boundless and ninety percent of it was lost in wasted movement. The house was a complete mess, which he attributed in part to the boy and the Moroccan, though it was essentially her fault.

Soon, drawn by the noise from the kitchen (spoons dropping on the floor, a broken glass, shouts demanding to know of no one in particular where the hell the tea was), the Moroccan appeared. Without anyone introducing them, they shook hands. The Moroccan was small and thin. Soon the boy would be taller and stronger than he was. He had a heavy mustache and he was balding. After greeting Pelletier he sat on the sofa, still half asleep, and began to watch cartoons with the boy. When Vanessa came out of the kitchen, Pelletier told her he had to leave.

"That's fine with me," she said.

He thought there was something belligerent about her reply, but then he remembered Vanessa was like that. The boy took a sip of the tea and said it needed sugar, then he left the steaming glass untouched. A few leaves floated in the liquid, leaves that struck Pelletier as strange and suspicious.

That morning, while he was at the university, he spent his idle moments thinking about Vanessa. When he saw her again they didn't make love, though he paid her as if they had, and they talked for hours. Before he fell asleep, Pelletier had come to some conclusions. Vanessa was perfectly suited to live in the Middle Ages, emotionally as well as physically. For her, the concept of "modern life" was meaningless. She had much more faith in what she could see than in the media. She was mistrustful and brave, although paradoxically her bravery made her trust people—

waiters, train conductors, friends in trouble, for example—who almost always let her down or betrayed her trust. These betrayals drove her wild and could lead her into unthinkably violent situations. She held grudges, too, and she boasted of saying things to people's faces without beating around the bush. She considered herself a free woman and had an answer for everything. Whatever she didn't understand didn't interest her. She never thought about the future, even her son's future, but only the present, a perpetual present. She was pretty but didn't consider herself pretty. More than half her friends were Moroccan immigrants, but she, who never got around to voting for Le Pen, saw immigration as a danger to France.

"Whores are there to be fucked," Espinoza said the night Pelletier talked to him about Vanessa, "not psychoanalyzed."

•

Espinoza, unlike his friend, didn't remember any of their names. On one side were the bodies and faces, and on the other side, flowing in a kind of ventilation tube, the Lorenas, the Lolas, the Martas, the Paulas, the Susanas, names without bodies, faces without names.

He never saw the same girl twice. He was with a Dominican, a Brazilian, three Andalusians, a Catalan woman. He learned from the start to be the silent type, the well-dressed man who pays and makes it known what he wants, sometimes with a gesture, and then gets dressed and leaves as if he'd never been there. He met a Chilean who advertised herself as a Chilean and a Colombian who advertised herself as a Colombian, as if the two nationalities held a special fascination. He did it with a Frenchwoman, two Poles, a Russian, a Ukrainian, a German. One night he slept with a Mexican and that was the best.

As always, they went to a hotel, and when he woke up in the morning the Mexican was gone. That day was strange. As if something inside of him had burst. He spent a long time sitting in bed, naked, with his feet resting on the floor, trying to remember something vague. When he got in the shower he realized that he had a mark on his inner thigh. It was as if someone had sucked there or set a leech on his left leg. The bruise was as big as a child's fist. The first thing he thought was that the whore had given him a love bite, and he tried to remember it, but he couldn't, the only images that came were of him on top of her, her legs around his shoulders, and some vague, indecipherable words, whether spoken by him or the Mexican he wasn't sure, probably obscene.

For a few days he thought he'd forgotten her, until one night he found himself searching for her along the streets of Madrid where the whores went or in the Casa de Campo. One night he thought he saw her and he followed her and touched her shoulder. The woman who turned around was Spanish and didn't look like the Mexican whore at all. Another night, in a dream, he thought he remembered what she'd said. He realized that he was dreaming, realized the dream was going to end badly, realized there was a good chance he would forget her words and maybe that was for the best, but he resolved to do everything he could to remember them before he woke up. In the middle of the dream, with the sky spinning in slow motion, he even tried to force himself awake, to turn on the light, to shout so that the sound of his own voice would return him to wakefulness, but the bulbs in the house seemed to have burned out and instead of a shout all he heard was a distant moan, as if of a boy or a girl or maybe an animal sheltering in a faraway room.

When he woke up, of course, he couldn't remember a thing, except that he had dreamed about the Mexican, that she was standing in the middle of a long, dimly lit hallway and he was watching her, unseen. The Mexican seemed to read something written in felt-tip pen on the wall, graffiti or obscene messages that she was spelling out slowly, as if she didn't know how to read. He kept looking for her for a few more days, but then he got tired of it and slept with a Hungarian, two Spanish women, a Gambian, a Senegalese, and an Argentinian. He never dreamed of her again, and finally he managed to forget her.

•

Time, which heals all wounds, finally erased the sense of guilt that had been instilled in them by the violent episode in London. One day they returned to their respective labors as fresh as daisies. They began writing and attending conferences again with uncommon energy, as if the time of the whores had been a Mediterranean rest cruise. They got back in touch with Morini, whom they'd somehow sidelined at first during their adventures and then forgotten altogether. They found the Italian in slightly worse health than usual, but just as warm, intelligent, and discreet, which meant that he didn't ask a single question, didn't demand a single confidence. One night, to their mutual surprise, Pelletier said to Espinoza that Morini was like a gift. A gift from the gods to the two of them. It was a silly thing to say and to argue it would have been to wade directly into a swamp of sentimentalism, but Espinoza, who felt the same way, even if he'd have put it differently, instantly agreed. Life smiled on them once again. They traveled to conferences here and there. They partook of the pleasures of gastronomy. They read and were lighthearted. Everything around them that had stopped and grown creaky and rusted sprang into motion again. The lives of other people grew visible, to a point. Their remorse vanished like laughter on a spring night. Once more they began to call Norton.

·

Deeply affected by their reunion, Pelletier, Espinoza, and Norton met at a bar, or rather at the tiny cafeteria (truly Lilliputian: two tables and a counter at which no more than four people fit shoulder to shoulder) of an unorthodox gallery only a little bigger than the bar, which exhibited paintings but also sold used books and clothes and shoes, located on Hyde Park Gate, very near the Dutch embassy. The three expressed their admiration for the Netherlands, a thoroughly democratic country.

At this bar, according to Norton, they made the best margaritas in London, a distinction of little interest to Pelletier and Espinoza, although they feigned enthusiasm. They were the only ones there, of course, and despite the time of day, the single employee or owner looked as if he were asleep or had just woken up, in contrast to Pelletier and Espinoza, who, though each had woken at seven and taken a plane, then separately endured the delays of their respective flights, were fresh and full of energy, ready to make the most of their London weekend.

Conversation, it's true, was difficult at first. In the silence, Pelletier and Espinoza watched Norton: she was as pretty and seductive as ever. Sometimes they were distracted by the little ant steps of the gallery owner, who was taking dresses off a rack and carrying them into a back room, returning with identical or very similar dresses, which he left where the others had been hanging.

Though the silence didn't bother Pelletier or Espinoza, Norton found it stifling and felt obliged to tell them, quickly and rather ferociously, about her teaching activities during the time they hadn't seen each other. It was a boring subject, and soon exhausted, so Norton went on to describe everything she had done the day before and the day before that, but once again she was left with nothing to say. For a while, smiling like squirrels, the three of them turned to their margaritas, but the quiet became more and more unbearable, as if within it, in the interregnum of silence, cutting words and cutting ideas were slowly being formed, never a performance or dance to be observed with indifference. So Espinoza decided it would be a good idea to describe a trip to Switzerland, a trip that hadn't involved Norton and that might amuse her.

•

In his telling, Espinoza didn't leave out the tidy cities or the rivers that invited contemplation or the springtime mountainsides clothed in green. And then he spoke of a trip by train, once the work that had brought the three friends together was finished, into the countryside, toward one of the towns halfway between Montreux and the foothills of the Bernese Alps, where they hired a car that took them along a winding but scrupulously paved road toward a rest clinic that bore the name of a late nineteenth-century Swiss politician or financier, the Auguste Demarre Clinic, an unobjectionable name behind which lay concealed a civilized and discreet lunatic asylum.

It hadn't been Pelletier's or Espinoza's idea to visit such a place. It was Morini's idea, because Morini had somehow learned that a man he considered to be one of the most disturbing painters of the twentieth century was living there. Or not. Maybe Morini hadn't said that. Either way, the name of this painter was Edwin Johns and he had cut off his right hand, the hand he painted with, then had it embalmed, and attached it to a kind of multiple self-portrait.

"How is it you never told me this story?" interrupted Norton.

Espinoza shrugged his shoulders.

"I thought you'd heard it from me," said Pelletier.

Although after a few seconds he realized that in fact she hadn't.

Norton, to everyone's surprise, burst into inappropriate laughter and ordered another margarita. For a while, as they were waiting for their drinks to be brought by the owner, who was still taking down and hanging up dresses, the three of them sat in silence. Then, at Norton's pleading, Espinoza had to resume his tale. But he didn't want to.

"You tell it," he said to Pelletier, "you were there, too."

Pelletier's story then began with the three Archimboldians contemplating the iron gate that rose in welcome to the Auguste Demarre lunatic asylum, while also blocking the way out (and preventing the entrance of any importunate guests). Or rather, the story begins seconds before, with Espinoza and Morini in his wheelchair surveying the iron gate and the iron railings that vanished to right and left, shaded by a venerable and well-tended grove of trees, as Pelletier, half in and half out of the car, paid the driver and arranged a reasonable time for him to drive up from the town to retrieve them. Then the three turned to face the bulk of the asylum, which could just be seen at the end of the road, like a fifteenth-century fortress, not in its architecture but in the effect of its inertness.

And what was this effect? An odd conviction. The certainty that the American continent, for example, had never been discovered, or in other words had never *existed*, and that this had in no way impeded the sustained economic growth or normal demographic growth or democratic advancement of the Helvetian republic. Just one of those strange and pointless ideas, said Pelletier, that people exchange on trips, especially if the trip is manifestly pointless, as this one was shaping up to be.

Next they made their way through all the formalities and red tape of a Swiss lunatic asylum. At last, without having seen a single one of the mental patients taking the cure, they were led by a middle-aged nurse with an inscrutable face to a small cottage in the rear grounds of the clinic, huge grounds that enjoyed a splendid view but sloped downward, which Pelletier, who was pushing Morini's wheelchair, thought must not be very calming for the disturbed or the severely disturbed.

To their surprise, the cottage turned out to be a cozy place, surrounded by pine trees, with rosebushes along a low wall, and armchairs within that mimicked the comfort of the English countryside, a fireplace, an oak table, a half-empty bookcase (the titles were almost all in German and French, besides a few in English), a special table with a computer and modem, a Turkish divan that clashed with the rest of the furnishings, a bathroom containing a toilet, a sink, and even a shower with a sliding plastic door.

"They don't have it too bad," said Espinoza.

Pelletier went over to a window and looked out at the view. At the foot of the mountains, he thought he saw a city. Maybe it's Montreux, he said to himself. Or maybe it was the town where they'd hired the car. After all, you couldn't see the lake. When Espinoza came over to the window he thought the houses were the town, certainly not Montreux. Morini sat still in his wheelchair, his gaze fixed on the door.

•

When the door opened, Morini was the first to see him. Edwin Johns had straight hair, starting to thin on top, and pale skin. He wasn't especially tall, but he was still thin. He wore a gray turtleneck sweater and a leather blazer. The first thing he noticed was Morini's wheelchair, which evinced pleasant surprise, as if clearly he hadn't been expecting anything quite so concrete. Morini, meanwhile, couldn't help glancing at Johns's right arm, where the hand was missing, and to his own great surprise, not at all pleasant, he discovered that where there should only have been emptiness, a hand emerged from Johns's jacket cuff, plastic of course, but so well made that only a careful and informed observer could tell it was artificial.

Behind Johns a nurse came in, not the one who had attended them but another one, a little younger and much blonder, who sat in a chair by one of the windows and took out a fat paperback, which she began to read, oblivious to Johns and the visitors. Morini introduced himself as a professor of literature from the University of Turin and an admirer of Johns's work, and then proceeded to introduce his friends. Johns, who had remained standing all this time, offered his hand to Espinoza and Pelletier, who shook it carefully, then sat in a chair at the table and watched Morini, as if they were the only two people in the cottage.

At first Johns made a slight, almost imperceptible effort to start a conversation. He asked whether Morini had bought any of his art. Morini replied in the negative. He said no, then he added that he couldn't afford Johns's work. Espinoza noticed then that the book the nurse was reading so intently was an anthology of twentieth-century German literature. He elbowed Pelletier, and the latter asked the nurse, more to break the ice than because he was curious, whether Benno von Archimboldi was included in the anthology. At that moment they all heard the caw or squawk of a crow. The nurse said yes. Johns began to blink and then he closed his eyes and ran his prosthetic hand over his face.

"It's my book," he said, "I loaned it to her."

"Unbelievable," said Morini, "what a coincidence."

"But of course I haven't read it, I don't speak German."

Espinoza asked why he'd bought it, then.

"For the cover," said Johns. "The drawing is by Hans Wette, a fine painter. And as far as coincidence is concerned, it's never a question of believing in it or not. The whole world is a coincidence. I had a friend who told me I was wrong to think that way. My friend said the world isn't a coincidence for someone traveling by rail, even if the train should cross foreign lands, places the traveler will never see again in his life. And it isn't a coincidence for the person who gets up at six in the morning, exhausted, to go to work; for the person who has no choice but to get up and pile more suffering on the suffering he's already accumulated. Suffering is accumulated, said my friend, that's a fact, and the greater the suffering, the smaller the coincidence."

"As if coincidence were a luxury?" asked Morini.

At that moment, Espinoza, who had been following Johns's monologue, noticed Pelletier next to the nurse, one elbow propped on the window ledge as with the other hand, in a polite gesture, he helped her find the page where the story by Archimboldi began. The blond nurse, sitting in the chair with the book on her lap, and Pelletier, standing by her side, in a pose not lacking in gallantry. And the window ledge and the roses outside and beyond them the grass and the trees and the evening advancing across ridges and ravines and lonely crags. The shadows that crept imperceptibly across the inside of the cottage, creating angles where none had existed before, vague sketches that suddenly appeared on the walls, circles that faded like mute explosions.

"Coincidence isn't a luxury, it's the flip side of fate, and something else besides," said Johns.

"What else?" asked Morini.

"Something my friend couldn't grasp, for a reason that's simple and easy to understand. My friend (if I may still call him that) believed in humanity, and so he also believed in order, in the order of painting and the order of words, since words are what we paint with. He believed in redemption. Deep down he may even have believed in progress. Coincidence, on the other hand, is total freedom, our natural destiny. Coincidence obeys no laws and if it does we don't know what they are. Coincidence, if you'll permit me the simile, is like the manifestation of God at every moment on our planet. A senseless God making senseless gestures at his senseless creatures. In that hurricane, in that osseous implosion, we find communion. The communion of coincidence and effect and the communion of effect with us."

Then, just then, Espinoza—and Pelletier, too—heard or sensed that Morini was formulating the question he had come to ask, his voice low, his torso so far inclined they feared he would tumble out of his wheelchair.

"Why did you mutilate yourself?"

Morini's face seemed to be pierced by the last lights rolling across the grounds of the asylum. Johns listened impassively. His attitude suggested a presentiment that the man in the wheelchair had come on this visit in search of an answer, like so many others before him. Then Johns smiled and posed a question of his own.

"Are you going to publish this conversation?"

"Certainly not," said Morini.

"Then why ask me a question like that?"

"I want to hear you say it yourself," whispered Morini.

In a movement that to Pelletier seemed slow and rehearsed, Johns lifted his right hand and held it an inch or so from Morini's expectant face.

"Do you think you're like me?" asked Johns.

"No, I'm not an artist," answered Morini.

"I'm not an artist either," said Johns. "Do you think you're like me?"

Morini shook his head back and forth, and his wheelchair moved too. For a few seconds Johns looked at him with a faint smile on his thin, bloodless lips.

"Why do you think I did it?" he asked.

"Honestly, I don't know," said Morini, looking him in the eye.

Dusk had settled around Morini and Johns now. The nurse made a move as if to get up and turn on the light, but Pelletier lifted a finger to his lips and stopped her. The nurse sat down again. The nurse's shoes were white. Pelletier's and Espinoza's shoes were black. Morini's shoes were brown. Johns's shoes were white and made for running long distance, on the paved streets of a city or cross-country. That was the last thing Pelletier saw, the color of the shoes and their shape and stillness, before night plunged them into the cold nothingness of the Alps.

"I'll tell you why I did it," said Johns, and for the first time his body relaxed, abandoning its stiff, martial stance, and he bent toward Morini, saying something into his ear.

Then he straightened up and went over to Espinoza and shook his hand very politely and then he shook Pelletier's hand too, and then he left the cottage and the nurse went out after him.

As he turned on the light, Espinoza pointed out, in case they hadn't noticed, that Johns hadn't shaken Morini's hand at the beginning or end of the interview. Pelletier answered that he had noticed. Morini said nothing. After a time the first nurse came and led them to the exit. As they crossed the grounds she told them a car was waiting for them at the gate.

The car took them back to Montreux, where they spent the night at the Hotel Helvetia. All three were tired and they decided not to go out to dinner. A few hours later, however, Espinoza called Pelletier's room and said he was hungry and was going to see whether he could find anything open. Pelletier told him to wait, he'd come too. When they met in the lobby, Pelletier asked whether he'd called Morini.

"I did," said Espinoza, "but no one answered."

They decided the Italian must already be asleep. That night they got back to the hotel late and slightly tipsy. The next morning they went to Morini's room to get him and he wasn't there. The clerk told them that according to the computer Mr. Piero Morini had settled his bill and left the hotel at midnight (as Pelletier and Espinoza were having dinner at an Italian restaurant). Around that time he had come down to the reception desk and asked for a car.

"He left at midnight? Where was he going?"

The clerk, of course, didn't know.

That morning, after they made sure Morini wasn't at any of the hospitals in or around Montreux, Pelletier and Espinoza took the train to Geneva. From the Geneva airport they called Morini's apartment in Turin. All they got was the answering machine, which they lavished with abuse. Then each caught a flight back to his city.

As soon as he got to Madrid Espinoza called Pelletier. The latter, who had been home for an hour, said he had nothing new to report. All day long, both Espinoza and Pelletier left short and increasingly hopeless messages on Morini's answering machine. By the second day they were in a state of anguish and even considered catching the next flights to Turin and notifying the authorities if they couldn't find Morini. But they didn't want to be rash or look foolish, and they didn't do anything.

The third day was the same as the second: they called Morini, they called each other, they weighed several courses of action, they considered Morini's mental health, his undeniable maturity and common sense, and did nothing. On the fourth day, Pelletier called the University of Turin directly. He spoke to a young Austrian who was working temporarily in the German department. The Austrian had no idea where Morini might be. Pelletier asked him to put the department secretary on the phone. The Austrian informed him that the secretary had gone out for breakfast and wasn't back yet. Pelletier immediately called Espinoza and gave him a detailed account of the phone call. Espinoza said he would try his luck.

This time it wasn't the Austrian who answered the phone but a German literature student. The student's German wasn't the best, so Espinoza switched to Italian. He asked whether the department secretary had come back yet. The student replied that he was alone, that everyone had gone out, presumably for breakfast, and there was no one in the department. Espinoza wanted to know what time people had breakfast at the University of Turin and how long breakfast usually lasted. The student didn't understand Espinoza's poor Italian and Espinoza had to repeat the question twice, the second time in slightly offensive terms.

The student said that he, for example, almost never had breakfast, but that didn't mean anything, everyone did things their own way. Did he understand or not?

"I understand," said Espinoza, gritting his teeth, "but I need to talk to someone in a position of authority."

"Talk to me," said the student.

Espinoza asked whether Dr. Morini had missed any of his classes.

"Let's see, let me think," said the student.

And then Espinoza heard someone, the student himself, whispering Morini . . . Morini . . . Morini, in a voice that didn't sound like his but rather like the voice of a sorcerer, or more specifically, a sorceress, a soothsayer from the times of the Roman Empire, a voice that reached Espinoza like the dripping of a basalt fountain but that soon swelled and overflowed with a deafening roar, with the sound of thousands of voices, the thunder of a great river in flood comprising the shared fate of every voice.

"Yesterday he had a class and he wasn't here," said the student after some thought.

Espinoza thanked him and hung up. That afternoon he tried Morini again at home and then he called Pelletier. There was no one at either place and he had to content himself with leaving messages. Then he began to reflect. But his thoughts only returned to what had just happened, the strict past, the past that seems deceptively like the present. He remembered the voice on Morini's answering machine, which is to say Morini's own recorded voice, saying briefly but politely that this was

Piero Morini's number and to please leave a message, and Pelletier's voice, which, instead of saying this is Pelletier, repeated the number to eliminate any uncertainty, then urged whoever was calling to leave his name and phone number, promising vaguely to call back.

That night Pelletier called Espinoza and they agreed, after each had dispelled the other's forebodings, to let a few days go by, not to fall into vulgar hysteria, and to bear in mind that whatever Morini might do, he was free to do it and there was nothing they could (or should) do to prevent it. That night, for the first time since they'd returned from Switzerland, they had a good night's sleep.

The next morning both men left for work rested in body and easy in mind, although by eleven, a little before he went out for lunch with colleagues, Espinoza broke down and called the German department at the University of Turin, with the same futile results as before. Later Pelletier called from Paris and they discussed the advisability of letting Norton know what was going on.

They weighed the pros and cons and decided to shield Morini's privacy behind a veil of silence, at least until they had more concrete information. Two days later, almost reflexively, Pelletier called Morini's apartment and this time someone picked up the phone. Pelletier's first words expressed the astonishment he felt upon hearing his friend's voice at the other end of the line.

"It can't be," shouted Pelletier, "how can it be, it's impossible."

Morini's voice sounded the same as always. Then came the delight, the relief, the waking from a bad dream, a baffling dream. In the middle of the conversation, Pelletier said he had to let Espinoza know right away.

"You won't go anywhere, will you?" he asked before he hung up.

"Where would I go?" asked Morini.

But Pelletier didn't call Espinoza. Instead he poured himself some whiskey and went into the kitchen and then the bathroom and then his office, turning on all the lights in the apartment. Only then did he call Espinoza and tell him he'd found Morini safe and sound and that he'd just talked to him on the phone, but he couldn't talk any longer. After he hung up he drank more whiskey. Half an hour later Espinoza called from Madrid. It was true, Morini was fine. He wouldn't say where he'd been over the last few days. He said he'd needed to rest. To collect his thoughts. According to Espinoza, who'd been reluctant to bombard him with questions, Morini seemed to be trying to hide something. Why? Espinoza hadn't the remotest idea.

"We really know very little about him," said Pelletier, who was beginning to tire of Morini, Espinoza, the phone.

"Did you ask him how he felt?" Pelletier asked.

Espinoza said yes and that Morini had assured him he was fine.

"There's nothing we can do now," concluded Pelletier in a tone of sadness that wasn't lost on Espinoza.

A little later they hung up and Espinoza picked up a book and tried to read, but he couldn't.

•

Then, as the gallery employee or owner kept taking down dresses and hanging them up, Norton told them that during the time he disappeared, Morini had been in London.

"He spent the first two days alone, without calling me once."

When she saw him he said he'd spent his time going to museums and wandering through unfamiliar neighborhoods, neighborhoods that were vaguely reminiscent of Chesterton stories but no longer had anything to do with Chesterton, although the spirit of Father Brown still hovered over them, not in a religious way, said Morini, as if he were trying not to overdramatize his solitary ramblings, but really Norton imagined him shut in his hotel room, with the drapes open, staring at the drab backs of buildings and reading for hour after hour. Then he called her and invited her out to lunch.

Naturally, Norton was happy to hear from him and to learn he was in the city and at the agreed-upon time she appeared in the hotel lobby, where Morini, sitting in his wheelchair with a package on his lap, was patiently and impassively deflecting the flow of guests and visitors that convulsed the lobby in an ever-changing display of luggage, tired faces, perfumes trailing after meteroidian bodies, bellhops with their stern jitters, the philosophical circles under the eyes of the manager or associate manager, each with his brace of assistants radiating freshness, the same freshness of eager sacrifice emitted by young women (in the form of ghostly laughter), which Morini tactfully chose to ignore. When Norton got there they left for a restaurant in Notting Hill, a Brazilian vegetarian restaurant she had recently discovered.

When Norton learned that Morini had spent two days in London already, she demanded to know what on earth he'd been doing and why he hadn't called. That was when Morini brought up Chesterton, said he'd spent the time wandering, praised the way the city accommodated the handicapped, unlike Turin, which was full of obstacles for wheelchairs, said he'd been to some secondhand bookshops where he'd bought a few books he didn't name, mentioned two visits to Sherlock Holmes's house, Baker Street being one of his favorite streets, a street that for him, a middle-aged Italian, cultured and crippled and a reader of detective novels, was timeless or outside time, lovingly (although the word wasn't lovingly but immaculately) preserved in Dr. Watson's tales. Then they went to Norton's house and there Morini gave her the gift he'd bought her, a book on Brunelleschi, with excellent photographs by photographers from four different countries of the same buildings by the great Renaissance architect.

"They're interpretations," said Morini. "The French photographer is the best," he said. "The one I like least is the American. Too showy. He's too eager to discover Brunelleschi. To *be* Brunelleschi. The German isn't bad, but the French one is best, I'd say. You'll have to tell me what you think."

Although she'd never seen the book, exquisite in paper and binding alone, something about it struck Norton as familiar. The next day they met in front of a theater. Morini had two tickets that he'd bought at the hotel, and they saw a bad, vulgar comedy that made them laugh, Norton more than Morini, who couldn't follow some of the cockney slang. That night they went to dinner and when Norton asked how Morini had spent his day he said he'd visited Kensington Gardens and the Italian Gardens in Hyde Park and roamed around, although Norton, for some reason, imagined him sitting still in the park, sometimes craning to see something he couldn't quite make out, most of the time with his eyes closed, pretending to sleep. Over dinner, Norton explained the parts of the play he hadn't understood. Only then did Morini realize it had been worse than he'd thought. The acting, however, rose greatly in his esteem, and back at the hotel, as he partially undressed without getting out of the wheelchair, in front of the silent television where he and the room were mirrored like ghostly figures in a performance that prudence and fear would keep anyone from staging, he concluded that the play hadn't been so bad after all, it had been good, he had laughed, the actors were good, the seats comfortable, the price of the tickets not too high.

The next day he told Norton he had to leave. Norton drove him to the airport. As they were waiting, Morini, adopting a casual tone of voice, said he thought he knew why Johns had cut off his right hand.

"Johns who?" asked Norton.

"Edwin Johns, the painter you told me about," said Morini.

"Oh, Edwin Johns," said Norton. "Why?"

"For money," said Morini.

"Money?"

"Because he believed in investments, the flow of capital, one has to play the game to win, that kind of thing."

Norton looked doubtful and then said: maybe.

"He did it for money," said Morini.

Then Norton asked him (for the first time) how Pelletier and Espinoza were.

"I'd prefer it if they didn't know I was here," said Morini.

Norton looked at him quizzically and told him not to worry, his secret was safe. Then she asked him to call when he got to Turin.

"Of course," said Morini.

A flight hostess asked to speak with them and a few minutes later she went away smiling. The line of passengers began to move. Norton gave Morini a kiss on the cheek and departed.

•

Before they left the gallery, thoughtful but hardly downcast, the owner and only attendant told them that the establishment would soon be closing its doors. With a lamé dress over one arm, he said that the house, of which the gallery was part, had belonged to his grandmother, a very respectable lady, ahead of her times. When she died the house was passed down to her three grandchildren, in theory equally. But back then, he, who was one of the grandchildren, lived in the Caribbean, where in addition to learning to make margaritas he did intel and spy work. A hippie spy with some rather bad habits, was how he described himself. When he got back to England he discovered that his cousins had taken over the entire house. That's when the quarreling began. Lawyers cost money, though, and in the end he had to settle for three rooms, where he set up his gallery. But the business was a flop: he didn't sell paintings or used clothes and hardly anyone came to try his cocktails. This neighborhood is too chic for my customers, he said, now the galleries are in the old working-class neighborhoods, the bars are on the traditional bar circuit, and people in this part of town don't buy used clothes. When Norton, Pelletier, and Espinoza had gotten up and were heading down the little metal staircase that led to the street, the gallery owner told them that, on top of it all, he'd recently begun to see his grandmother's ghost. This confession piqued the interest of Norton and her companions.

Have you seen her? they asked. I have, said the gallery owner, though at first I just heard strange noises, like water and bubbles. Noises he'd never heard in this house, although since it had been divided up to be sold as flats and new bathrooms had been installed, there might be some logical explanation for the sounds. But next came the moans, expressions not exactly of pain but more of puzzlement and frustration, as if the ghost of his grandmother were moving around her old house and not recognizing it, converted as it was into several smaller homes, with walls she didn't remember and modern furniture that must have struck her as common and mirrors where there never used to be mirrors.

Sometimes the owner got so depressed he slept in the store. What depressed him wasn't the sounds the ghost made, of course, but his business on the brink of ruin. On those nights he could clearly hear his grandmother's steps and her moans as she moved about upstairs as if she understood nothing about the world of the dead or the world of the living. One night, before he closed the gallery, he saw her reflected in the only mirror, an old full-length Victorian looking glass that stood in a corner for the use of customers trying on dresses. His grandmother peered at one of the paintings on the wall, then shifted her gaze to the clothing on hangers, then she looked at the gallery's two lone tables, as if they were the ultimate indignity.

She shuddered in horror, said the owner. That was the first and last time he'd seen her, though every now and then he heard her wandering on the upper floors, where surely she was moving through walls that hadn't used to exist. When Espinoza asked what his old job in the Caribbean had been like, the owner smiled sadly and promised them he wasn't mad, as anyone might think. He'd been a spy, he told them, in the same way that others work for the census bureau or in some statistics department. His words saddened them greatly, though they couldn't say why.

●

During a seminar in Toulouse they met Rodolfo Alatorre, a young Mexican whose scattershot reading included the work of Archimboldi. The Mexican, who was living on a creative writing scholarship and spent his days striving, apparently in vain, to write a modern novel, attended a few lectures then introduced himself to Norton and Espinoza, who lost no time giving him the brush-off, and then to Pelletier, who supremely ignored him, since nothing distinguished Alatorre from the hordes of generally irritating young European university students who swarmed around the Archimboldian apostles. To his greater discredit, Alatorre didn't speak German, which disqualified him from the outset. Meanwhile, the Toulouse seminar was a great success, and amid the fauna of critics and specialists who knew each other from previous conferences and who, at least on the surface, seemed happy to see each other again and eager to resume old discussions, the Mexican could either go home, which was something he was loath to do because home was a dreary scholarship student's room where only his books and papers awaited him, or stand in a corner and smile right and left pretending to be deep in thought, which is what in the end he did. As it happened, it was thanks to this position or pose that he noticed Morini, who, confined to his wheelchair and responding distractedly to everyone's greetings, displayed—or so it seemed to Alatorre—a forlornness resembling his own. A little while later, after Alatorre had introduced himself, the Mexican and the Italian went out for a walk along the streets of Toulouse.

First they discussed Alfonso Reyes, with whom Morini was reasonably well acquainted, then Sor Juana, Morini unable to forget the book by Morino—that Morino who might almost have been Morini himself—on the Mexican nun's recipes. Then they talked about Alatorre's novel, the novel he planned to write and the one novel he'd written so far, and they talked about the life of a young Mexican in Toulouse, about the winter days that dragged on, short but endless, Alatorre's few French friends (the librarian, another scholarship student from Ecuador he saw only every so often, the barman whose image of Mexico struck Alatorre as half bizarre, half offensive), about the friends he'd left behind in Mexico City and to whom he daily wrote long monothematic e-mails about his novel in progress, and about melancholy.

One of these Mexico City friends, said Alatorre, and he said it innocently, with that slight hint of clumsy boasting typical of minor writers, had met Archimboldi *just the other day*.

At first Morini, who wasn't paying close attention and was letting himself be dragged to all the places Alatorre considered worthy of interest, places that in fact, while not being obligatory tourist stops, were in some way interesting, as if Alatorre's secret calling was to be a tour guide, not a novelist, decided that the Mexican, who had in any case read only two novels by Archimboldi, was bragging or mistaken or else didn't know that Archimboldi had vanished long ago.

The story Alatorre told was in short as follows: his friend, an essayist and novelist and poet by the name of Almendro, a man in his forties better known to his friends as El Cerdo, or the Pig, had received a phone call at midnight. El Cerdo, after a brief conversation in German, got dressed and set off in his car to a hotel near the Mexico City airport. Even though there wasn't much traffic at that time of night, it was past one when he reached the hotel. A clerk and a policeman were in the lobby. El Cerdo showed his credentials, identifying him as a top government official, and then he accompanied the policeman to a room on the third floor. There were two other policemen there and an old German who was sitting on the bed, his hair uncombed, dressed in a gray T-shirt and jeans, barefoot, as if the arrival of the police had caught him sleeping. Evidently the German, thought El Cerdo, slept in his clothes. One of the two policemen was watching TV. The other was smoking, leaning against the wall. The policeman who had arrived with El Cerdo turned off the TV and told them to follow him. The policeman leaning against the wall demanded an explanation, but the policeman who had come up with El Cerdo told him to keep his mouth shut. Before the policemen left the room, El Cerdo asked, in German, whether they had stolen anything from him. The old man said no. They wanted money, but they hadn't stolen anything.

"That's good," said El Cerdo in German. "That's progress."

Then he asked the policemen which station they were from and let them go. When the policemen had gone, El Cerdo sat down next to the TV and said he was sorry. The old German got up from the bed without saying anything and went into the bathroom. He was huge, El Cerdo wrote to Alatorre. Nearly seven feet tall. Six foot six at least. In any case: enormous and imposing. When the old man came out of the bathroom, El Cerdo realized that now he had his shoes on and he asked him whether he felt like taking a drive around Mexico City or going out for a drink.

"If you're tired," he added, "just tell me and I'll leave this instant."

"My flight is at seven in the morning," the old man said.

El Cerdo looked at his watch. It was after two. He didn't know what to say. He, like Alatorre, hardly knew the old man's work. Any of his books that were translated into Spanish were published in Spain and were late coming to Mexico. Three years ago, when he was the head of a publishing house, before he became one of the top cultural officials in the new government, he had tried to publish *The Berlin Underworld*, but the rights already belonged to a house in Barcelona. He wondered how the old man had gotten his phone number, who had given it to him. Simply posing the question, a question to which he didn't expect an answer, made him happy, filled him with a happiness that somehow vindicated him as a person and a writer.

"We can go out," he said. "I'm game."

The old man put on a leather jacket over his gray T-shirt and followed him. El Cerdo took him to Plaza Garibaldi. There weren't many people there when they arrived, most of the tourists had gone back to their hotels, leaving only drunks and night owls, people on their way to supper, and mariachi bands rehashing the latest soccer match. Shadowy figures slunk around the streets leading into the plaza, occasionally halting to scrutinize them. El Cerdo fingered the pistol he had begun to carry since he began to work for the government. They went into a bar and El Cerdo ordered pork tacos. The old man was drinking tequila and he had a beer. As the old man ate, El Cerdo thought about the changes life brings. Not even ten years ago, if he'd walked into this same bar and started speaking in German to a gangling old man, someone would inevitably have insulted him or taken offense on the slenderest of pretexts. Then the looming fight would have been staved off by El Cerdo begging someone's pardon or making explanations or buying a round of tequila. Now no one bothered him, as if the act of wearing a gun under his shirt or working high up in the government gave him an aura of sainthood that even the killers and drunks could sense from a distance. Pussies, thought El Cerdo. They smell me, they smell me and they're shitting in their pants. Then he started to think about Voltaire (why Voltaire, for fuck's sake?) and then he started to think about an old idea he'd been mulling over for a while, requesting an ambassadorship in Europe, or at least a post as cultural attaché, although with his connections the least they could make him was ambassador. The problem was that at an embassy he would make only a salary, an ambassador's salary. As the German ate, El Cerdo weighed the pros and cons of leaving Mexico. One of the pros, absolutely, would be the chance to write again. He was attracted by the idea of living in Italy or near Italy and spending long periods in Tuscany and Rome writing an essay on Piranesi and his imaginary prisons, which he saw extrapolated not exactly in Mexican prisons but in the imaginary and iconographic versions of some Mexican prisons. One of the cons, no question about it, was the physical separation from power. Distancing oneself from power is never good, he'd discovered that early on, before he'd been granted real power, when he was head of the house that tried to publish Archimboldi.

"Listen," he said suddenly, "weren't you supposed to have disappeared?"

The old man looked at him and smiled politely.

•

That same night, after Alatorre had repeated his story for Pelletier, Espinoza, and Norton, they called Almendro, alias El Cerdo, who had no trouble relating to Espinoza what, along general lines, Alatorre had already told him. In a certain sense, the relationship between Alatorre and El Cerdo was teacher-student or big brother–little brother. In fact, it had been El Cerdo who had gotten Alatorre the scholarship in Toulouse, which in a sense testified to the degree of El Cerdo's regard for his little brother, since it was in his power to grant flashier scholarships in more prestigious locales, to say nothing of appointing a cultural attaché in Athens or Caracas, which might not have been much but would've been something, and Alatorre would have thanked him for the appointment with all his heart, although God knows he didn't turn up his nose at the little scholarship in Toulouse. The next time around, he was sure, El Cerdo would be more munificent. Almendro, meanwhile, wasn't yet fifty, and outside the limits of Mexico City his work was widely unknown. But in Mexico City, and, to be fair, at some American universities, his name was familiar, even overfamiliar. How, then, did Archimboldi, supposing that the old German really was Archimboldi and not a prankster, get his number? El Cerdo believed it had come from Archimboldi's German editor, Mrs. Bubis. Espinoza asked, not without some perplexity, whether he knew the great lady.

"Of course," said El Cerdo. "I was at a party in Berlin, a cultural *charreada* with some German editors, and we were introduced there."

What the hell is a cultural *charreada*? wrote Espinoza on a piece of paper, the question seen by all but deciphered by Alatorre alone, for whom it was intended.

"I must have given her my card," said El Cerdo from Mexico City.

"And your home phone number was on your card."

"That's right," said El Cerdo. "I must have given her my A card. The B card only has my office number. And it's just my secretary's number on the C card."

"I understand," said Espinoza, mustering patience.

"There's nothing on the D card, it's blank, just my name, that's all," said El Cerdo, laughing.

"I see, I see," said Espinoza, "just your name."

"Exactly," said El Cerdo. "My name, period. No phone number or title or street where I live or anything, you know what I'm saying?"

"I do," said Espinoza.

"So obviously I gave the A card to Mrs. Bubis."

"And she must have given it to Archimboldi," said Espinoza.

"Correct," said El Cerdo.

•

El Cerdo was with the German until five in the morning. After they ate (the old man was hungry and ordered more tacos and more tequila, while El Cerdo buried his head like an ostrich in reflections on melancholy and power), they went for a walk around the Zócalo, visiting the plaza and the Aztec ruins springing like lilacs from wasteland, as El Cerdo put it, stone flowers among other stone flowers, a chaos that would surely lead nowhere, only to further chaos, said El Cerdo, as he and the German walked the streets around the Zócalo, toward the Plaza Santo Domingo, where, during the day, under the arches, scribes with their typewriters set up shop to type letters or legal claims. Then they went to see the Angel on Reforma, but that night the Angel was dark and as they drove around the traffic circle, El Cerdo could only describe it to the German, who looked up from his open window.

At five in the morning they returned to the hotel. El Cerdo waited in the lobby, smoking a cigarette. When the old man emerged from the elevator he was carrying a single suitcase and was dressed in the same gray T-shirt and jeans. The streets leading to the airport were empty and El Cerdo ran several red lights. He hunted around for a topic of conversation, but couldn't come up with one. He had already asked the old man, as they were eating, whether he had been to Mexico before, and the old man had answered no, which was odd, because almost every European writer had been there at some time or other. But the old man said this was his first time. Near the airport there were more cars and the traffic no longer moved smoothly. When they drove into the parking lot, the old man tried to say goodbye, but El Cerdo insisted on accompanying him.

"Give me your suitcase," he said.

The suitcase had wheels and hardly weighed a thing. The old man was flying from Mexico City to Hermosillo.

"Hermosillo?" said Espinoza. "Where's that?"

"The state of Sonora," said El Cerdo. "It's the capital of Sonora, in northwestern Mexico, on the border with the United States."

"What are you going to do in Sonora?" asked El Cerdo.

The old man hesitated a moment before answering, as if he'd forgotten how to talk.

"I'm going to see what it's like," he said.

Although El Cerdo wasn't sure. Maybe what he actually said was that he was going to learn something.

"Hermosillo?" said El Cerdo.

"No, Santa Teresa," said the old man. "Do you know it?"

"No," said El Cerdo. "I've been to Hermosillo a few times, giving talks on literature, a while ago, but never to Santa Teresa."

"I think it's a big city," said the old man.

"It's big, yes," said El Cerdo. "There are factories there, and problems too. I don't think it's a nice place."

El Cerdo pulled out his ID and was able to accompany the old man to the departure gate. Before they parted he gave him a card. An A card.

"In case you run into any trouble," he said.

"Many thanks," said the old man.

Then they shook hands and El Cerdo never saw him again.

•

They decided not to tell anyone else what they knew. By keeping quiet, they reasoned, they weren't betraying anyone, merely behaving with prudence and discretion, as the case merited. They soon convinced themselves that it was best not to raise false hopes. According to Borchmeyer, Archimboldi had come up again as a possible Nobel candidate this year. His name had been in the prize pool the year before, too. False hopes.

According to Dieter Hellfeld, a member of the Swedish Academy or the secretary of a member of the academy had been in touch with Archimboldi's publisher to get an idea how the writer would respond if he were awarded the prize. What could a man past eighty have to say? What could the Nobel mean to such a man, with no family, no heirs, no public face? Mrs. Bubis said he would be delighted. Probably on her own recognizance, thinking of sales. But did the baroness concern herself with sales, with the books piling up in the warehouses of the Bubis publishing house in Hamburg? No, surely not, said Dieter Hellfeld. The baroness was nearing ninety, and warehouses were of no interest to her. She traveled a lot, Milan, Paris, Frankfurt. Sometimes she could be seen talking to Signora Sellerio at the Bubis stand in Frankfurt. Or at the German embassy in Moscow, in a Chanel suit, with two Russian poets in her retinue, declaiming on Bulgakov and the (incomparable) beauty of Russian rivers in the fall, before the winter frosts. Sometimes, said Pelletier, it's as if Mrs. Bubis has forgotten that Archimboldi even exists. That's the way it always is in Mexico, said young Alatorre. In any case, according to Schwarz, Archimboldi was on the short list, so the Nobel was within the realm of possibility. And maybe the Swedish academicians wanted a change. A veteran, a World War II deserter still on the run, a reminder of the past for Europe in troubled times. A writer on the Left whom even the situationists respected. A person who didn't pretend to reconcile the irreconcilable, as was the fashion these days. Imagine, said Pelletier, Archimboldi wins the Nobel and at that very moment we appear, leading him by the hand.

·

They couldn't explain to themselves what Archimboldi was doing in Mexico. Why would someone in his eighties travel to a country he had never visited before? Sudden interest? Research for the setting of a novel in progress? It was improbable, they thought, not least because the four believed there would be no more books by Archimboldi.

Tacitly, they inclined toward the simplest but also the most outlandish answer: Archimboldi had gone to Mexico as a tourist, like so many retired Germans and other Europeans. The explanation didn't hold water. They imagined a misanthropic old Prussian waking up one morning, out of his head. They weighed the possibilities of senile dementia. They discarded their hypotheses and cleaved strictly to what El Cerdo had said. What if Archimboldi were fleeing? What if Archimboldi had suddenly found a new reason to flee?

At first Norton was least eager to go tracking him down. The image of them returning to Europe with Archimboldi by the hand seemed to her the image of a gang of kidnappers. Of course, no one planned to kidnap Archimboldi. Or even barrage him with questions. Espinoza would be satisfied just to see him. Pelletier would be satisfied if he could ask him whose skin the leather mask was made of in his homonymous novel. Morini would be satisfied if he could see the pictures they took of him in Sonora.

Alatorre, whose opinion no one had requested, would be satisfied to strike up an epistolary friendship with Pelletier, Espinoza, Morini, and Norton, and maybe, if it wasn't too much bother, visit them every so often in their respective cities. Only Norton had reservations. But in the end she decided to make the trip. I think Archimboldi lives in Greece, said Dieter Hellfeld, and the author we know by the name of Archimboldi is really Mrs. Bubis.

"Yes, of course," said our four friends, "Mrs. Bubis."

•

At the last minute, Morini decided not to travel. His ill health, he said, made it impossible. Marcel Schwob, whose health was equally fragile, had set off in 1901 on a more difficult trip to visit Stevenson's grave on an island in the Pacific. Schwob's trip lasted many days, first on the *Ville de la Ciotat*, then on the *Polynésienne*, and then on the *Manapouri*. In January 1902 he fell ill with pneumonia and nearly died. Schwob was traveling with his Chinese manservant, Ting, who got seasick at the drop of a hat. Or maybe he got seasick only if the sea was rough. In any case the trip was plagued by rough seas and seasickness. At one point, Schwob, in bed in his stateroom and convinced he was on the verge of death, felt someone lie down beside him. When he turned to see who the intruder was he discovered his Oriental servant, his skin as green as grass. Only then did he realize what kind of venture he had embarked on. When he got to Samoa, after many hardships, he didn't visit Stevenson's grave. Partly because he was too sick, and partly because what's the point of visiting the grave of someone who hasn't died? Stevenson—and Schwob owed this simple revelation to his trip—lived inside him.

Morini, who admired Schwob (or, more precisely, felt a great fondness for him), thought at first that his trip to Sonora could be a kind of lesser homage to the French writer and also to the English writer whose grave the French writer had gone to visit, but when he got back to Turin he saw that travel was beyond him. So he called his friends and lied, saying the doctor had strictly forbidden anything of the kind. Pelletier and Espinoza accepted his explanation and promised they would call regularly to keep him posted on the search they were undertaking, the definitive search this time.

With Norton it was different. Morini repeated that he wasn't going. That the doctor had forbidden it. That he planned to write them every day. He even laughed and indulged in a silly joke that Norton didn't understand. A joke on Italians. An Italian, a Frenchman, and an Englishman are in a plane with only two parachutes. Norton thought it was a political joke. Actually, it was a children's joke, although because of the way Morini told it, the Italian in the plane (which first lost one engine then the other and then went into a tailspin) resembled Berlusconi. Norton hardly opened her mouth. She said mm-hmm, mm-hmm, mm-hmm. And then she said good night, Piero, in English and very sweetly, or at least in a way that seemed to Morini unbearably sweet, and then she hung up.

Norton felt somehow insulted by Morini's decision not to go with them. They didn't call each other again. Morini might have called Norton, but before his friends set off on their search for Archimboldi, he, in his own way, like Schwob in Samoa, had already begun a voyage, a voyage that would end not at the grave of a brave man but in a kind of resignation, what might be called a new experience, since this wasn't resignation in any ordinary sense of the word, or even patience or conformity, but rather a state of meekness, a refined and incomprehensible humility that made him cry for no reason and in which his own image, what Morini saw as Morini, gradually and helplessly dissolved, like a river that stops being a river or a tree that burns on the horizon, not knowing that it's burning.

•

Pelletier, Espinoza, and Norton traveled from Paris to Mexico City, where El Cerdo was waiting. They spent the night in a hotel, and the next morning they flew to Hermosillo. El Cerdo, who didn't understand much of what was going on, was thrilled to play host to such distinguished European academics even though, to his disappointment, they refused to give a lecture at Bellas Artes or UNAM or the Colegio de México.

The night they spent in Mexico City, Espinoza and Pelletier went with El Cerdo to the hotel where Archimboldi had stayed. The clerk had no problem letting them see the computer. With the mouse, El Cerdo scrolled over the names that appeared on the glowing screen under the date he'd met Archimboldi. Pelletier noticed that his fingernails were dirty and understood why he'd been given his nickname.

"Here he is," said El Cerdo, "this is it."

Pelletier and Espinoza searched for the name the Mexican was pointing to. Hans Reiter. One night. Paid in cash. He hadn't used a credit card or taken anything from the minibar. Then they went back to their own hotel, although El Cerdo asked them whether they'd like to see any tourist sites. No, said Espinoza and Pelletier, we're not interested.

Norton, meanwhile, was at the hotel, and although she wasn't tired she had turned off the lights and left just the television on with the volume turned down low. Through the open windows of her room came a distant buzzing, as if many miles away, in a neighborhood on the outskirts of the city, people were being evacuated. She thought it was the television and turned it off, but the noise persisted. She sat on the windowsill and looked out at the city. A sea of flickering lights stretched toward the south. If she leaned half her body out the window, the humming stopped. The air was cold and felt good.

At the entrance to the hotel a couple of doormen were arguing with a guest and a taxi driver. The guest was drunk. One of the doormen was propping him up with one arm and the other doorman was listening to the taxi driver, who, to judge by his gestures, was getting more and more upset. Soon afterward a car stopped in front of the hotel and Norton watched as Espinoza and Pelletier climbed out, followed by the Mexican. From up above she wasn't entirely sure they were her friends. In any case, if they were, they seemed different, they were walking differently, in a more virile way, if such a thing were possible, although the word *virile*, especially applied to a form of walking, sounded grotesque to Norton, completely absurd. The Mexican handed the car keys to one of the doormen and then the three men went into the hotel. The doorman who had El Cerdo's keys got in the car, then the taxi driver directed his arm waving at the doorman propping up the drunk. Norton had the impression that the taxi driver was demanding more money and the drunk hotel guest didn't want to pay. From where she was, Norton thought the drunk might be American. He was wearing an untucked white shirt over his khaki trousers, the color of cappuccino or milky iced coffee. She couldn't tell his age. When the other doorman came back, the taxi driver retreated two steps and said something.

His attitude, thought Norton, was menacing. Then one of the doormen, the one who was supporting the drunk guest, leaped forward and grabbed him by the neck. The taxi driver wasn't expecting this reaction and barely managed to step back, but he couldn't shake off the doorman. In the sky, presumably full of black clouds heavy with pollution, the lights of a plane appeared. Norton lifted her gaze, surprised, because then all the air began to buzz, as if millions of bees were surrounding the hotel. For an instant the idea of a suicide bomber or a plane accident passed through her mind. At the entrance to the hotel, the two doormen were beating the taxi driver, who was on the ground. It wasn't a sustained attack. They might kick him four or six times, then stop and give him the chance to talk or go, but the taxi driver, doubled over, would open his mouth and swear at them, then another round of blows would follow.

The plane descended a little farther in the dark and Norton thought she could see the expectant faces of the passengers through the windows. Then it turned and climbed again, and a few seconds later it disappeared into the belly of the clouds. The taillights, red and blue sparks, were the last thing she saw before it disappeared. When she looked down, one of the hotel clerks had come out and was helping the drunk guest, who could hardly walk, as if he were wounded, while the two doormen dragged the taxi driver not toward the taxi but toward the underground parking garage.

•

Her first impulse was to go down to the bar, where she would find Pelletier and Espinoza talking to the Mexican, but in the end she decided to close the window and go to bed. The hum continued and Norton thought it must be the air-conditioning.

•

"There's a kind of war between taxi drivers and doormen," said El Cerdo. "An undeclared war, with its ups and downs, moments of tension and moments of truce."

"So what will happen now?" asked Espinoza.

They were sitting at the hotel bar, next to one of the big windows that overlooked the street. Outside the air had a liquid texture. Black water, jet-black, that made one want to reach out and stroke its back.

"The doormen will teach the taxi driver a lesson and it'll be a long time before he comes back to the hotel," said El Cerdo. "It's about tips."

Then El Cerdo pulled out his electronic organizer and they copied the phone number of the rector at the University of Santa Teresa into their address books.

"I talked to him today," said El Cerdo, "and I asked him to give you all the help he could."

"Who'll get the taxi driver out of here?" asked Pelletier.

"He'll walk out on his own two feet," said El Cerdo. "They'll beat the shit out of him in the garage and then they'll wake him up with buckets of cold water so that he gets in his car and hightails it out of here."

"But if the doormen and the taxi drivers are at war, what do the guests do when they need a taxi?" asked Espinoza.

"Oh, then the hotel calls a radio taxi. The radio taxis are at peace with everyone," said El Cerdo.

When they went out to say goodbye to him at the entrance to the hotel they saw the taxi driver emerge limping from the garage. His face was unmarked and his clothes didn't seem to be wet.

"He probably cut a deal," said El Cerdo.

"A deal?"

"A deal with the doormen. Money," said El Cerdo, "he must have given them money."

For a second, Pelletier and Espinoza imagined that El Cerdo would leave in the taxi, which was parked a few feet away, across the street, with an abandoned look about it, but El Cerdo nodded to one of the doormen, who went to get his car.

•

The next morning they flew to Hermosillo and from the airport they called the rector of the University of Santa Teresa, then they rented a car and set off toward the border. As they left the airport, the three of them noticed how bright it was in Sonora. It was as if the light were buried in the Pacific Ocean, producing an enormous curvature of space. It made a person hungry to travel in that light, although also, and maybe more insistently, thought Norton, it made you want to bear your hunger until the end.

•

They drove into Santa Teresa from the south and the city looked to them like an enormous camp of gypsies or refugees ready to pick up and move at the slightest prompting. They took three rooms on the fourth floor of the Hotel México. The three rooms were the same, but they were full of small distinguishing characteristics. In Espinoza's room there was a giant painting of the desert, with a group of men on horseback to the left, dressed in beige shirts, as if they were in the army or a riding club. In Norton's room there were two mirrors instead of one. The first mirror was by the door, as it was in the other rooms. The second was on the opposite wall, next to the window overlooking the street, hung in such a way that if one stood in a certain spot, the two mirrors reflected each other. In Pelletier's bathroom the toilet bowl was missing a chunk. It wasn't visible at first glance, but when the toilet seat was lifted, the missing piece suddenly leaped into sight, almost like a bark. How the hell did no one notice this? wondered Pelletier. Norton had never seen a toilet in such bad shape. Some eight inches were missing. Under the white porcelain was a red substance, like brick wafers spread with plaster. The missing piece was in the shape of a half-moon. It looked as if someone had ripped it off with a hammer. Or as if someone had picked up another person who was already on the floor and smashed that person's head against the toilet, thought Norton.

•

The rector of the University of Santa Teresa had a pleasant, timid appearance. He was very tall, with lightly tanned skin, as if every day he took long meditative walks in the country. He offered them coffee and listened to their story with patience and feigned interest. Then he gave them a tour of the university, pointing out the buildings and telling them which departments were housed in each. When Pelletier, to change the subject, talked about the light in Sonora, the rector waxed poetic about sunsets in the desert and mentioned a few painters, with names they didn't recognize, who had come to live in Sonora or nearby Arizona.

When they got back to his office he offered them more coffee and asked where they were staying. When they told him he wrote down the name of the hotel on a slip of paper that he tucked into the breast pocket of his jacket, then he invited them to dinner at his house. They left soon afterward. As they made their way from the rector's office to the parking lot they saw a group of students of both sexes walking across a lawn just as the sprinklers came on. The students screamed and scattered.

•

Before they went back to the hotel they took a drive around the city. It made them laugh it seemed so chaotic. Until then they hadn't been in good spirits. They had looked at things and listened to the people who could help them, but only as part of a grander scheme. On the ride back to the hotel, they lost the sense of being in a hostile environment, although *hostile* wasn't the word, an environment whose language they refused to recognize, an environment that existed on some parallel plane where they couldn't make their presence felt, imprint themselves, unless they raised their voices, unless they argued, something they had no intention of doing.

At the hotel they found a note from Augusto Guerra, the dean of the Faculty of Arts and Letters. The note was addressed to his "colleagues" Espinoza, Pelletier, and Norton. Dear Colleagues, he had written without a hint of irony. This made them laugh even more, although then they were immediately sad, since the ridiculousness of "colleague" somehow erected bridges of reinforced concrete between Europe and this drifters' retreat. It's like hearing a child cry, said Norton. In his note, after wishing them a pleasant and enjoyable stay in his city, Augusto Guerra talked about a certain Professor Amalfitano, "an expert on Benno von Archimboldi," who would diligently present himself at the hotel that very afternoon to help them as best he could. In a poetic turn of phrase, the flowery closing compared the desert to a petrified garden.

They decided not to leave the hotel as they waited for the Archimboldi expert. According to what they could see out the windows of the bar, this was a decision shared by a group of American tourists who were getting deliberately drunk on the terrace, which was decorated with some surprising varieties of cactus, some almost ten feet tall. Every once in a while one of the tourists would get up from the table and go over to the railing draped in half-dead plants and glance out into the street.

Then, stumbling, he would return to his friends and after a while they would all laugh, as if the one who had gotten up was telling them a dirty and very funny joke. None of them was young, though none was old either. They were a group of tourists in their forties and fifties who would probably return to the United States that same day. Little by little the hotel terrace filled up, until there wasn't a single empty table. As night began to creep in from the east, the first notes of a Willie Nelson song sounded on the terrace speakers.

When one of the drunks recognized the song, he gave a shout and rose to his feet. Espinoza, Pelletier, and Norton thought he was about to start dancing, but instead he went over to the terrace railing and looked up and down the street, craning his neck, then went calmly back to sit with his wife and friends. These people are crazy, said Espinoza and Pelletier. But Norton thought something strange was going on, on the street, on the terrace, in the hotel rooms, even in Mexico City with those unreal taxi drivers and doormen, unreal or at least logically ungraspable, and even in Europe something strange had been happening, something she didn't understand, at the Paris airport where the three of them had met, and maybe before, with Morini and his refusal to accompany them, with that slightly repulsive young man they had met in Toulouse, with Dieter Hellfeld and his sudden news about Archimboldi. And something strange was going on even with Archimboldi and everything Archimboldi had written about, and with Norton, unrecognizable to herself, if only intermittently, who read and made notes on and interpreted Archimboldi's books.

•

"Have you said the toilet in your room needs to be fixed?" asked Espinoza.

"I did tell them to do something about it," said Pelletier. "But at the desk they suggested I change rooms. They wanted to put me on the third floor. So I told them I was fine, I planned to stay in *my* room and they could fix the toilet when I left. I'd rather we stick together," said Pelletier with a smile.

"You did the right thing," said Espinoza.

"The clerk told me they were planning to replace the toilet but they couldn't find the right model. He didn't want me to leave with a negative impression of the hotel. A nice person, after all," said Pelletier.

The first impression the critics had of Amalfitano was mostly negative, perfectly in keeping with the mediocrity of the place, except that the place, the sprawling city in the desert, could be seen as something authentic, something full of local color, more evidence of the often terrible richness of the human landscape, whereas Amalfitano could only be considered a castaway, a carelessly dressed man, a nonexistent professor at a nonexistent university, the unknown soldier in a doomed battle against barbarism, or, less melodramatically, as what he ultimately was, a melancholy literature professor put out to pasture in his own field, on the back of a capricious and childish beast that would have swallowed Heidegger in a single gulp if Heidegger had had the bad luck to be born on the Mexican-U.S. border. Espinoza and Pelletier saw him as a failed man, failed above all because he had lived and taught in Europe, who tried to protect himself with a veneer of toughness but whose innate gentleness gave him away in the act. But Norton's impression was of a sad man whose life was ebbing swiftly away and who would rather do anything than serve them as guide to Santa Teresa.

·

That night the three critics went to bed on the early side. Pelletier dreamed of his toilet. A muffled noise woke him and he got up naked and saw from under the door that someone had turned on the bathroom light. At first he thought it was Norton, even Espinoza, but as he came closer he knew it couldn't be either of them. When he opened the door the bathroom was empty. On the floor he saw big smears of blood. The bathtub and the shower curtain were crusted with a substance that wasn't entirely dry yet and that Pelletier at first thought was mud or vomit, but which he soon discovered was shit. He was much more revolted by the shit than frightened by the blood. As he began to retch he woke up.

Espinoza dreamed about the painting of the desert. In the dream Espinoza sat up in bed, and from there, as if watching TV on a screen more than five feet square, he could see the still, bright desert, such a solar yellow it hurt his eyes, and the figures on horseback, whose movements—the movements of horses and riders—were barely perceptible, as if they were living in a world different from ours, where speed was different, a kind of speed that looked to Espinoza like slowness, although he knew it was only the slowness that kept whoever watched the painting from losing his mind. And then there were the voices. Espinoza listened to them. Barely audible voices, at first only syllables, brief moans shooting like meteorites over the desert and the framed space of the hotel room and the dream. He recognized a few stray words. *Quickness, urgency, speed, agility.* The words tunneled through the rarefied air of the room like virulent roots through dead flesh. Our culture, said a voice. Our freedom. The word *freedom* sounded to Espinoza like the crack of a whip in an empty classroom. He woke up in a sweat.

In Norton's dream she saw herself reflected in both mirrors. From the front in one and from the back in the other. Her body was slightly aslant. It was impossible to say for sure whether she was about to move forward or backward. The light in the room was dim and uncertain, like the light of an English dusk. No lamp was lit. Her image in the mirrors was dressed to go out, in a tailored gray suit and, oddly, since Norton hardly ever wore such things, a little gray hat that brought to mind the fashion pages of the fifties. She was probably wearing black pumps, although they weren't visible. The stillness of her body, something reminiscent of inertia and also of defenselessness, made her wonder, nevertheless, what she was waiting for to leave, what signal she was waiting for before she stepped out of the field between the watching mirrors and opened the door and disappeared. Had she heard a noise in the hall? Had someone passing by tried to open her door? A confused hotel guest? A worker, someone sent up by reception, a chambermaid? And yet the silence was total, and there was a certain calm about it, the calm of long early-evening silences. All at once Norton realized that the woman reflected in the mirror wasn't her. She felt afraid and curious, and she didn't move, watching the figure in the mirror even more carefully, if possible. Objectively, she said to herself, she looks just like me and there's no reason why I should think otherwise. She's me. But then she looked at the woman's neck: a vein, swollen as if to bursting, ran down from her ear and vanished at the shoulder blade. A vein that didn't seem real, that seemed drawn on. Then Norton thought: I have to get out of here. And she scanned the room, trying to pinpoint the exact spot where the woman was, but it was impossible to see her. In order for her to be reflected in both mirrors, she said to herself, she must be just between the little entryway and the room. But she couldn't see her. When she watched her in the mirrors she noticed a change. The woman's head was turning almost imperceptibly. I'm being reflected in the mirrors too, Norton said to herself. And if she keeps moving, in the end we'll see each other. Each of us will see the other's face. Norton clenched her fists and waited. The woman in the mirror clenched her fists too, as if she were making a superhuman effort. The light coming into the room was ashen. Norton had the impression that outside, in the streets, a fire was raging. She began to sweat. She lowered her head and closed her eyes. When she looked in the mirrors again, the woman's swollen vein had grown and her profile was beginning to appear. I have to escape, she thought. She also thought: where are Jean-Claude and Manuel? She thought about Morini. All she saw was an empty wheelchair and behind it an enormous, impenetrable forest, so dark green it was almost black, which it took her a while to recognize as Hyde Park. When she opened her eyes, the gaze of the woman in the mirror and her own gaze intersected at some indeterminate point in the room. The woman's eyes were just like her eyes. The cheekbones, the lips, the forehead, the nose. Norton started to cry in sorrow or fear, or thought she was crying. She's just like me, she said to herself, but she's dead. The woman smiled tentatively and then, almost without transition, a grimace of fear twisted her face. Startled, Norton looked behind her, but there was no one there, just the wall. The woman smiled at her again. This time the smile grew not out of a grimace but out of a look of despair. And then the woman smiled at her again and her face became anxious, then blank, then nervous, then resigned, and then all the expressions of madness passed over it and after each she always smiled. Meanwhile, Norton, regaining her composure, had taken out a small notebook and was rapidly taking notes about everything as it happened, as if her fate or her share of happiness on earth depended on it, and this went on until she woke up.

•

When Amalfitano told them he had translated *The Endless Rose* for an Argentinian publishing house in 1974, the critics' opinion of him changed. They wanted to know where he had learned German, how he had discovered Archimboldi, which books of his he had read, what he thought of him. Amalfitano said he had learned German in Chile, at the German School, which he had attended from the time he was small, although when he turned fifteen he had moved, for reasons that were neither here nor there, to a public high school. He had come into contact with Archimboldi's work, as far as he could recall, at the age of twenty, when he read *The Endless Rose, The Leather Mask,* and *Rivers of Europe* in German, books he borrowed from a library in Santiago. The library had only those three and *Bifurcaria Bifurcata,* but this last he had begun and couldn't finish. It was a public library, augmented by the collection of a German man who had accumulated many books in German and who had donated them before he died to the municipality of Ñuñoa, in Santiago.

Of course, Amalfitano admired Archimboldi, although he felt nothing like the adoration the critics felt for him. Amalfitano, for example, thought that Günter Grass or Arno Schmidt was just as good. When the critics wanted to know whether the translation of *The Endless Rose* had been his idea or an assignment, Amalfitano said that as far as he remembered, it had been the Argentinian publisher's idea. In those days, he said, I translated everything I could and I worked as a proofreader, too. As far as he knew, it had been a pirate edition, although the possibility didn't occur to him till much later and he couldn't say for sure.

When the critics, much more kindly disposed toward him now, asked what he was doing in Argentina in 1974, Amalfitano looked at them and then at his margarita and said, as if he had repeated it many times, that in 1974 he was in Argentina because of the coup in Chile, which had obliged him to choose the path of exile. And then he apologized for expressing himself so grandiloquently. Everything becomes a habit, he said, but none of the critics paid much attention to this last remark.

"Exile must be a terrible thing," said Norton sympathetically.

"Actually," said Amalfitano, "now I see it as a natural movement, something that, in its way, helps to abolish fate, or what is generally thought of as fate."

"But exile," said Pelletier, "is full of inconveniences, of skips and breaks that essentially keep recurring and interfere with anything you try to do that's important."

"That's just what I mean by abolishing fate," said Amalfitano. "But again, I beg your pardon."

•

The next morning Amalfitano was waiting for them in the hotel lobby. If the Chilean professor hadn't been there they would surely have told one another the nightmares they'd had the night before and who knows what might have come to light. But there was Amalfitano, and the four set off together to have breakfast and plan the day's activities. They went over the possibilities. In the first place, it was clear that Archimboldi hadn't stopped by the university. At least not the Faculty of Arts and Letters. There was no German consulate in Santa Teresa, so any steps in that direction could be ruled out from the start. They asked Amalfitano how many hotels there were in town. He said he didn't know, but he could find out right away, as soon as they were done with breakfast.

"How?" Espinoza wanted to know.

"By asking at the reception desk," said Amalfitano. "They must have a list of all the hotels and motels in the area."

"Of course," said Pelletier and Norton.

As they finished breakfast they speculated again about the motives that might have compelled Archimboldi to travel to Santa Teresa. That was when Amalfitano learned that no one had ever seen Archimboldi in person. The story struck him as amusing, though he couldn't say exactly why, and he asked why they wanted to find him when it was clear Archimboldi didn't want to be seen. Because we're studying his work, said the critics. Because he's dying and it isn't right that the greatest German writer of the twentieth century should die without being offered the chance to speak to the readers who know his novels best. Because, they said, we want to convince him to come back to Europe.

"I thought," said Amalfitano, "that Kafka was the greatest German writer of the twentieth century."

Well, then the greatest postwar German writer or the greatest German writer of the second half of the twentieth century, said the critics.

"Have you read Peter Handke?" Amalfitano asked them. "And what about Thomas Bernhard?"

Ugh, said the critics, and until breakfast was over Amalfitano was attacked until he resembled the bird in Azuela's *Mangy Parrot*, gutted and plucked to the last feather.

•

At the reception desk they were given the list of every hotel in the city. Amalfitano suggested that they call from the university, since it appeared that Guerra and the critics were on such excellent terms, or that Guerra felt a respect for them bordering on reverence and even fear, a fear, in turn, not without its element of vanity or coquetry, although cunning, to be fair, crouched behind the coquetry and fear, since even if Guerra's cooperation came down to the wishes of Rector Negrete, it was no secret to Amalfitano that Guerra planned to get something out of the visit of the distinguished European professors, for as we all know the future is a mystery and we never know when we may come to a bend in the road or what unexpected places our steps may lead us. But the critics didn't want to use the university phone and they made calls on their room accounts. To save time, Espinoza and Norton called from Espinoza's room, and Amalfitano and Pelletier called from Pelletier's room. After an hour the results couldn't have been more disheartening. No Hans Reiter was registered at any hotel. After two hours they decided to give up calling and go down to the bar for a drink. All they had left were a few hotels and some motels on the outskirts of the city. Looking over the list more carefully, Amalfitano said most of the motels on the list rented rooms by the hour or were really brothels, places where it was hard to imagine a German tourist.

"We aren't looking for a German tourist, we're looking for Archimboldi," Espinoza replied.

"True," said Amalfitano, and the truth was he could imagine Archimboldi at one of the motels.

•

The question is, what did Archimboldi come to this city to do, said Norton. After some argument, the three critics concluded, and Amalfitano agreed, that he could have come to Santa Teresa only to see a friend or to collect information for a novel in progress or for both reasons at once. Pelletier inclined toward the possibility of the friend.

"An old friend," he conjectured. "In other words, a German like himself."

"A German he hasn't seen for years, maybe since the end of the war," said Espinoza.

"An army friend, someone who meant a lot to Archimboldi and disappeared as soon as the war ended, maybe even before it ended," said Norton.

"But it must be someone who knows Archimboldi is Hans Reiter," said Espinoza.

"Not necessarily. Maybe Archimboldi's friend has no idea that Hans

Reiter and Archimboldi are the same person. He only knows Reiter and how to get in touch with Reiter and that's it," said Norton.

"Which isn't likely," said Pelletier.

"No, it isn't, since it assumes that Reiter has been at the same address since the last time he saw his friend, say in 1945," said Amalfitano.

"Statistically speaking, there isn't a single German born in 1920 who hasn't changed addresses at least once in his life," said Pelletier.

"So maybe it isn't this friend who got in touch with Archimboldi but Archimboldi himself who got in touch with him," said Espinoza.

"Him or her," said Norton.

"I'm more inclined to think it's a man than a woman," said Pelletier.

"Unless it's neither a man nor a woman and we're all groping in the dark," said Espinoza.

"But then why would Archimboldi come here?" asked Norton.

"It must be a friend, a dear friend, dear enough that Archimboldi felt he had to make the trip," said Pelletier.

"What if we're wrong? What if Almendro lied to us or was confused or someone lied to him?" said Norton.

"Almendro who? Héctor Enrique Almendro?" said Amalfitano.

"That's the one. You know him?" asked Espinoza.

"Not personally, but I wouldn't bet much on a tip from Almendro," said Amalfitano.

"Why?" asked Norton.

"Well, because he's a typical Mexican intellectual, his main concern is getting by," said Amalfitano.

"Isn't that the main concern of all Latin American intellectuals?" asked Pelletier.

"I wouldn't say that. Some of them are more interested in writing, for example," said Amalfitano.

"Tell us what you mean," said Espinoza.

"I don't really know how to explain it," said Amalfitano. "It's an old story, the relationship of Mexican intellectuals with power. I'm not saying they're all the same. There are some notable exceptions. Nor am I saying that those who surrender do so in bad faith. Or even that they surrender completely. You could say it's just a job. But they're working for the state. In Europe, intellectuals work for publishing houses or for the papers or their wives support them or their parents are well-off and give them a monthly allowance or they're laborers or criminals and they make an honest living from their jobs. In Mexico, and this might be true across Latin America, except in Argentina, intellectuals work for the state. It was like that under the PRI and it'll be the same under the PAN. The intellectual himself may be a passionate defender of the state or a critic of the state. The state doesn't care. The state feeds him and watches over him in silence. And it puts this giant cohort of essentially useless writers to use. How? It exorcises demons, it alters the national climate or at least tries to sway it. It adds layers of lime to a pit that may or may not exist, no one knows for sure. Not that it's always this way, of course. An intellectual can work at the university, or, better, go to work for an American university, where the literature departments are just as bad as in Mexico, but that doesn't mean they won't get a late-night call from someone speaking in the name of the state, someone who offers them a better job, better pay, something the intellectual thinks he deserves, and intellectuals *always* think they deserve better. This mechanism somehow crops the ears off Mexican writers. It drives them insane. Some, for example, will set out to translate Japanese poetry without knowing Japanese and others just spend their time drinking. Take Almendro—as far as I know he does both. Literature in Mexico is like a nursery school, a kindergarten, a playground, a kiddie club, if you follow me. The weather is good, it's sunny, you can go out and sit in the park and open a book by Valéry, possibly the writer most read by Mexican writers, and then you go over to a friend's house and talk. And yet your shadow isn't following you anymore. At some point your shadow has quietly slipped away. You pretend you don't notice, but you have, you're missing your fucking shadow, though there are plenty of ways to explain it, the angle of the sun, the degree of oblivion induced by the sun beating down on hatless heads, the quantity of alcohol ingested, the movement of something like subterranean tanks of pain, the fear of more contingent things, a disease that begins to become apparent, wounded vanity, the desire just for once in your life to be on time. But the point is, your shadow is lost and you, momentarily, forget it. And so you arrive on a kind of stage, without your shadow, and you start to translate reality or reinterpret it or sing it. The stage is really a proscenium and upstage there's an enormous tube, something like a mine shaft or the gigantic opening of a mine. Let's call it a cave. But a mine works, too. From the opening of the mine come unintelligible noises. Onomatopoeic noises, syllables of rage or of seduction or of seductive rage or maybe just murmurs and whispers and moans. The point is, no one sees, really sees, the mouth of the mine. Stage machinery, the play of light and shadows, a trick of time, hides the real shape of the opening from the gaze of the audience. In fact, only the spectators who are closest to the stage, right up against the orchestra pit, can see the shape of something behind the dense veil of camouflage, not the real shape, but at any rate it's the shape of something. The other spectators can't see anything beyond the proscenium, and it's fair to say they'd rather not. Meanwhile, the shadowless intellectuals are always facing the audience, so unless they have eyes in the backs of their heads, they can't see anything. They only hear the sounds that come from deep in the mine. And they translate or reinterpret or re-create them. Their work, it goes without saying, is of a very low standard. They employ rhetoric where they sense a hurricane, they try to be eloquent where they sense fury unleashed, they strive to maintain the discipline of meter where there's only a deafening and hopeless silence. They say cheep cheep, bowwow, meow meow, because they're incapable of imagining an animal of colossal proportions, or the absence of such an animal. Meanwhile, the stage on which they work is very pretty, very well designed, very charming, but it grows smaller and smaller with the passage of time. This shrinking of the stage doesn't spoil it in any way. It simply gets smaller and smaller and the hall gets smaller too, and naturally there are fewer and fewer people watching. Next to this stage there are others, of course. New stages that have sprung up over time. There's the painting stage, which is enormous, and the audience is tiny, though all elegant, for lack of a better word. There's the film stage and the television stage. Here the capacity is huge, the hall is always full, and year after year the proscenium grows by leaps and bounds. Sometimes the performers from the stage where the intellectuals give their talks are invited to perform on the television stage. On this stage the opening of the mine is the same, the perspective slightly altered, although maybe the camouflage is denser and, paradoxically, bespeaks a mysterious sense of humor, but it still stinks. This humorous camouflage, naturally, lends itself to many interpretations, which are finally reduced to two for the public's convenience or for the convenience of the public's collective eye. Sometimes intellectuals take up permanent residence on the television proscenium. The roars keep coming from the opening of the mine and the intellectuals keep misinterpreting them. In fact, they, in theory the masters of language, can't even enrich it themselves. Their best words are borrowings

that they hear spoken by the spectators in the front row. These spectators are called *flagellants*. They're sick, and from time to time they invent
hideous words and there's a spike in their mortality rate. When the work-
day ends the theaters are closed and they cover the openings of the
mines with big sheets of steel. The intellectuals retire for the night. The
moon is fat and the night air is so pure it seems edible. Songs can be
heard in some bars, the notes reaching the street. Sometimes an intellectual wanders off course and goes into one of these places and drinks
mezcal. Then he thinks what would happen if one day he. But no. He
doesn't think anything. He just drinks and sings. Sometimes he thinks
he sees a legendary German writer. But all he's really seen is a shadow,
sometimes all he's seen is his *own* shadow, which comes home every
night so that the intellectual won't burst or hang himself from the lintel.
But he swears he's seen a German writer and his own happiness, his
sense of order, his bustle, his spirit of revelry rest on that conviction. The
next morning it's nice out. The sun shoots sparks but doesn't burn. A
person can go out reasonably relaxed, with his shadow on his heels, and
stop in a park and read a few pages of Valéry. And so on until the end."

"I don't understand a word you've said," said Norton.

"Really I've just been talking nonsense," said Amalfitano.

•

Later they called the remaining hotels and motels and Archimboldi
wasn't at any of them. For a few hours they thought Amalfitano was
right, that Almendro's tip was probably the product of an overheated
imagination, that Archimboldi's trip to Mexico existed only in the re-
cesses of El Cerdo's brain. The rest of the day they spent reading and
drinking, and none of the three could muster the energy to leave the
hotel.

•

That night, while Norton was checking her e-mail on the hotel computer, she found a message from Morini. In his message Morini talked
about the weather, as if he had nothing better to say, about the slanting
rain that had begun to fall on Turin at eight and hadn't stopped until one
in the morning, and he sincerely wished Norton better weather in the
north of Mexico, where he believed it never rained and it was cold only
at night, and then only in the desert. That night, too, after replying to

some messages (not Morini's), Norton went up to her room, combed her hair, brushed her teeth, put moisturizing cream on her face, sat on the edge of the bed for a while, thinking, and then went out into the hallway and knocked at Pelletier's door and next at Espinoza's door and without a word she led them to her room, where she made love to both of them until five in the morning, at which time the critics, at Norton's request, returned to their rooms, where they soon fell into a deep sleep, a sleep that eluded Norton, who straightened the sheets of her bed a little and turned out the lights but remained wide awake.

•

She thought about Morini, or rather she saw Morini sitting in his wheelchair at a window in his apartment in Turin, an apartment she had never been to, looking out at the street and the façades of the surrounding buildings and watching the rain falling incessantly. The buildings across the street were gray. The street was dark and wide, a boulevard, although not a single car went by, with a spindly tree planted every sixty feet, like a bad joke on the part of the mayor or city planner. The sky was a blanket on top of a blanket, with another blanket on top of that, even thicker and wetter. The window Morini looked out was big, almost like a French door, narrower than it was wide but very tall, and so clean that the glass, with the raindrops sliding over it, was like pure crystal. The window frame was wooden, painted white. The lights were on in the room. The parquet shone, the bookshelves looked meticulously organized, and just a few paintings, in impeccable taste, hung on the walls. There were no rugs, and the furniture—a black leather sofa and two white leather armchairs—in no way impeded the passage of the wheelchair. Through double doors, half open, stretched a dark hallway.

And what to say about Morini? His position in the wheelchair expressed a certain degree of surrender, as if watching the night rain and the sleeping neighborhood fulfilled all his expectations. Sometimes he would rest his two arms on the chair, other times he would rest his head in one hand and prop his elbow on the chair's armrest. His useless legs, like the legs of an adolescent near death, were clothed in jeans possibly too big for him. He was wearing a white shirt with the top buttons undone, and on his left wrist his watch strap was too loose, though not so loose that the watch would fall off. He wasn't wearing shoes but rather very old slippers, of a cloth as black and shiny as the night. Everything he had on was comfortable, intended for wearing around the house, and by Morini's attitude it seemed clear that he had no intention of going in to work the next day, or that he planned to go in late.

The rain out the window, as he'd said in his e-mail, was falling obliquely, and there was something of the peasant fatalist in Morini's lassitude, his stillness and surrender, his uncomplaining and total abandonment to insomnia.

•

The next day they went to see the crafts market, which had been meant as a trading post for everyone living near Santa Teresa, where craftspeople and peasants from all over the region would bring their goods by cart or burro, even cattlemen came from Nogales and Vicente Guerrero and horse dealers from Agua Prieta and Cananea, but now the market was kept up solely for American tourists from Phoenix, who arrived by bus or in caravans of three or four cars and left the city before nightfall. Still, the critics liked the market, and even though they weren't planning to buy anything, in the end Pelletier picked up a clay figurine of a man sitting on a stone reading the newspaper, for next to nothing. The man was blond and two little devil horns sprouted from his forehead. Espinoza bought an Indian rug from a girl who had a rug and serape stall. He didn't actually like the rug very much, but the girl was nice and he spent a long time talking to her. He asked her where she was from, because he had the sense that she'd traveled from somewhere far away with her rugs, but the girl said she was from right here, Santa Teresa, from a neighborhood west of the market. She also said she was in high school and that if things went well, she planned to study to become a nurse. She wasn't just pretty but intelligent, too, thought Espinoza, though possibly too thin and delicate for his taste.

Amalfitano was waiting for them at the hotel. They took him out to lunch and then the four of them went to visit the offices of all the newspapers in Santa Teresa. At each place they looked through the papers dating from a month before Almendro saw Archimboldi in Mexico City to the previous day. They couldn't find a single sign to indicate that Archimboldi had passed through the city. First they looked in the death notices. Then they plowed through Society and Politics and they even read the items in Agriculture and Livestock. One of the papers didn't have an arts section. Another devoted one page a week to book reviews and listings of arts events in Santa Teresa, although it would have been better off allotting the page to sports. At six that evening they left the Chilean professor outside one of the newspaper offices and went back to the hotel. They showered and then each checked his or her e-mail. Pelletier and Espinoza wrote to Morini informing him of their meager findings. In both messages they announced that if nothing changed soon, they would return to Europe within the next few days. Norton didn't write to him. She hadn't answered his previous message and she didn't feel like facing up to that motionless Morini watching the rain, as if he had something to tell her and at the last moment had decided not to. Instead, and without saying anything to her two friends, she called Almendro's number in Mexico City and, after some fruitless efforts (El Cerdo's secretary and then his maid couldn't speak English, although both tried) she managed to reach him.

With enviable patience, and in English polished at Stanford, El Cerdo once again told her everything that had happened, beginning with the call from the hotel where Archimboldi was being interrogated by three policemen. Without contradicting himself, he again described his first meeting with Archimboldi, the time they spent in Plaza Garibaldi, the return to the hotel where Archimboldi collected his suitcase, the mostly silent trip to the airport, and then Archimboldi's departure for Hermosillo, after which he never saw him again. Following this, Norton's questions were all about Archimboldi's physical appearance. Nearly six and a half feet tall; his hair gray and thick, though he had a bald spot in back; thin; obviously strong.

"An old, old man," said Norton.

"No, I wouldn't say that," said El Cerdo. "When he opened his suitcase I saw lots of medicine. His skin was covered in age spots. Sometimes he seemed to get very tired but then he would recover easily or pretend to."

"What were his eyes like?" asked Norton.

"Blue," said El Cerdo.

"No, I already know they're blue, I've read all his books many times and they couldn't not be blue, I mean what were they like, what was your impression of them."

At the other end of the line there was a long silence, as if the question were completely unexpected or as if it were something El Cerdo had asked himself many times, and still couldn't answer.

"That's a hard question," said El Cerdo.

"You're the only person who can answer it. No one has seen him in a long time, and your situation is privileged, if I may say so," said Norton.

"Christ," said El Cerdo.

"What?" said Norton.

"Nothing, nothing, I'm thinking," said El Cerdo.

And after a while he said:

"He had the eyes of a blind man, I don't mean he couldn't see, but his eyes were just like the eyes of the blind, though I could be wrong about that."

•

That night they went to the party that Rector Negrete had planned in their honor, although it was only later that they discovered it was in their honor. Norton strolled through the gardens and admired the plants as the rector's wife named them one by one, although afterward she forgot all the names. Pelletier chatted for a long time with Guerra, the dean, and with another professor from the university who had written his thesis in Paris about a Mexican who wrote in French (a Mexican who wrote in French?), yes indeed, a most extraordinary, peculiar, excellent writer whose name the university professor mentioned several times (Fernández? García?), a man who came to a rather bad end because he had been a collaborator, yes indeed, a close friend of Céline and Drieu La Rochelle and a disciple of Maurras, shot by the Resistance, the Mexican writer, that is, not Maurras, a man who stood firm until the end, yes indeed, a real man, not like so many of his French counterparts who fled to Germany with their tails between their legs, this Fernández or García (or López or Pérez?) didn't leave home, he waited like a Mexican for them to come after him and his knees didn't buckle when they brought him (dragged him?) down the stairs and flung him against a wall, where they shot him.

Espinoza, meanwhile, was sitting the whole time next to Rector Negrete and various distinguished gentlemen of the same age as the host, men who spoke only Spanish and a very little bit of English, and he had to endure a conversation in praise of the latest signs of Santa Teresa's unstoppable progress.

None of the three critics failed to notice Amalfitano's constant companion that night. He was a handsome and athletic young man with very fair skin, who clung to the Chilean professor like a limpet and every so often gestured theatrically and grimaced like a madman, and other times just listened to what Amalfitano was saying, constantly shaking his head, small movements of almost spasmodic denial, as if he were abiding only grudgingly by the universal rules of conversation or as if Amalfitano's words (reprimands, to judge by his face) never hit their mark.

●

They left dinner having received a number of proposals, and with a suspicion. The proposals were: to give a class at the university on contemporary Spanish literature (Espinoza), to give a class on contemporary French literature (Pelletier), to give a class on contemporary English literature (Norton), to give a master class on Benno von Archimboldi and postwar German literature (Espinoza, Pelletier, and Norton), to take part in a panel discussion on economic and cultural relations between Europe and Mexico (Espinoza, Pelletier, and Norton, plus Dean Guerra and two economics professors from the university), to visit the foothills of the Sierra Madre, and, finally, to attend a lamb barbecue at a ranch near Santa Teresa, a barbecue that was predicted to be massive, with many professors in attendance, in a landscape, according to Guerra, of extraordinary beauty, although Rector Negrete declared that it was really quite severe and that some found it unsettling.

The suspicion was: that Amalfitano might be gay, and the vehement young man his lover, a dreadful suspicion since by the end of the night they had learned that the young man in question was the only son of Dean Guerra, Amalfitano's direct boss and the rector's right-hand man, and unless they were greatly mistaken, Guerra had no idea what kind of business his son was mixed up in.

"This could end in a hail of bullets," said Espinoza.

Then they talked about other things and afterward they went to sleep, exhausted.

●

The next day they went for a drive around the city, letting themselves be carried by chance, in no hurry, as if they were really hoping to find a tall old German man walking the streets. The western part of the city was very poor, with most streets unpaved and a sea of houses assembled out of scrap. The city center was old, with three- or four-story buildings and arcaded plazas in a state of neglect and young office workers in shirt-sleeves and Indian women with bundles on their backs hurrying down cobblestoned streets, and they saw streetwalkers and young thugs loitering on the corners, Mexican types straight out of a black-and-white movie. Toward the east were the middle- and upper-class neighborhoods. There they saw streets with carefully pruned trees and public playgrounds and shopping centers. The university was there, too. To the north were abandoned factories and sheds, and a street of bars and souvenir shops and small hotels, where it was said no one ever slept, and farther out there were more poor neighborhoods, though they were less crowded, and vacant lots out of which every so often there rose a school. To the south they discovered rail lines and slum soccer fields surrounded by shacks, and they even watched a match, without getting out of the car, between a team of the terminally ill and a team of the starving to death, and there were two highways that led out of the city, and a gully that had become a garbage dump, and neighborhoods that had grown up lame or mutilated or blind, and, sometimes, in the distance, the silhouettes of industrial warehouses, the horizon of the maquiladoras.

The city, like all cities, was endless. If you continued east, say, there came a moment when the middle-class neighborhoods ended and the slums began, like a reflection of what happened in the west but jumbled up, with a rougher orography: hills, valleys, the remains of old ranches, dry riverbeds, all of which went some way toward preventing overcrowding. To the north they saw a fence that separated the United States from Mexico and they gazed past it at the Arizona desert, this time getting out of the car. In the west they circled a couple of industrial parks that were in their turn being surrounded by slums.

They were convinced the city was growing by the second. On the far edge of Santa Teresa, they saw flocks of black vultures, watchful, walking through barren fields, birds that here were called turkey vultures, and also turkey buzzards. Where there were vultures, they noted, there were no other birds. They drank tequila and beer and ate tacos at a motel on the Santa Teresa–Caborca highway, at outdoor tables with a view. The sky, at sunset, looked like a carnivorous flower.

•

They returned to find Amalfitano waiting for them with Guerra's son, who invited them to dinner at a restaurant specializing in the food of northern Mexico. The place had a certain ambience, but the food didn't agree with them at all. They discovered, or believed they discovered, that the bond between the Chilean professor and the dean's son was more socratic than homosexual, and this in some way put their minds at ease, since the three of them had grown inexplicably fond of Amalfitano.

•

For three days they lived as if submerged in an undersea world. They watched television, seeking out the strangest and most random news, they reread novels by Archimboldi that suddenly they didn't understand, they took long naps, they were the last to leave the terrace at night, they talked about their childhoods as they had never done before. For the first time, the three of them felt like siblings or like the veterans of some shock troop who've lost their interest in most things of this world. They got drunk and they got up late and only every so often did they deign to go out with Amalfitano on walks around the city, to visit any attractions that might possibly be of interest to a hypothetical German tourist getting on in years.

•

And yes, in fact, they went to the lamb barbecue, and their movements were measured and cautious, as if they were three astronauts recently arrived on a planet about which nothing was known for sure. On the patio where the barbecue was being held they gazed at several smoke pits. The professors of the University of Santa Teresa displayed a rare talent for feats of country living. Two of them raced on horseback. Another sang a *corrido* from 1915. In a practice ring for bullfights some of them tried their luck with the lasso, with mixed results. Upon the appearance of Rector Negrete, who had been shut up in the main house with a man who seemed to be the ranch foreman, they dug up the barbecue, and a smell of meat and hot earth spread over the patio in a thin curtain of smoke that enveloped them all like the fog that drifts before a murder, and vanished mysteriously as the women carried the plates to the table, leaving clothing and skin impregnated with its aroma.

•

That night, maybe because of the barbecue and all they'd had to drink, the three had nightmares, which they couldn't remember when they woke, no matter how hard they tried. Pelletier dreamed of a page, a page that he tried to read forward and backward, every which way, turning it and sometimes turning his head, faster and faster, unable to decipher it at all. Norton dreamed of a tree, an English oak that she picked up and moved from place to place in the countryside, no spot entirely satisfying her. Sometimes the oak had no roots, other times it trailed long roots like snakes or the locks of a Gorgon. Espinoza dreamed about a girl who sold rugs. He wanted to buy a rug, any rug, and the girl showed him lots of rugs, one after the other, without stopping. Her thin, dark arms were never still and that prevented him from speaking, prevented him from telling her something important, from seizing her by the arm and getting her out of there.

•

The next morning Norton didn't come down for breakfast. They called her, thinking she was sick, but Norton assured them she just felt like sleeping in, and they should do without her. Gloomily, they waited for Amalfitano and then drove out to the northeast of the city, where a circus was setting up. According to Amalfitano, there was a German magician with the circus who went by the name of Doktor Koenig. He'd heard about the circus the night before, on his way back from the barbecue, when he saw leaflets that someone had gone to the trouble of leaving in all the yards in the neighborhood. The next day, on the corner where he waited for the bus to the university, he saw a color poster pasted on a sky-blue wall that announced the stars of the circus. Among them was the German magician, and Amalfitano thought this Doktor Koenig might be Archimboldi in disguise. Examined coolly, it was a stupid idea, he realized, but the critics were in such low spirits that he thought it wouldn't hurt to suggest a visit to the circus. When he told them, they looked at him the way students look at the class idiot.

"What would Archimboldi be doing in a circus?" said Pelletier when they were in the car.

"I don't know," said Amalfitano, "you're the experts, all I know is this is the first German who's come our way."

•

The circus was called Circo Internacional and some men who were raising the big top with a complicated system of cords and pulleys (or so it seemed to the critics) directed them to the trailer where the owner lived. The owner was a Chicano in his fifties who had worked a long time in European circuses that crossed the continent from Copenhagen to Málaga, performing in small towns and with middling success, until he decided to go back to Earlimart, California, where he was from, and start a circus of his own. He called it Circo Internacional because one of his original ideas was to have performers from all over the world, although in the end they were mostly Mexican and American, except that every so often some Central American came looking for work and once he had a Canadian lion tamer in his seventies whom no other circus in the United States would employ. His circus wasn't fancy, he said, but it was the first circus owned by a Chicano.

When they weren't traveling they could be found in Bakersfield, not far from Earlimart, where he had his winter quarters, although sometimes he set up camp in Sinaloa, Mexico, not for long, just so he could travel to Mexico City and sign deals for sites in the south, all the way to the Guatemalan border, and from there they'd head back up to Bakersfield. When the foreigners asked him about Doktor Koenig, the impresario wanted to know whether they had some dispute or money problem with his magician, to which Amalfitano was quick to reply that they didn't, certainly not, these gentlemen were highly respected university professors from Spain and France respectively, and he himself, not to put too fine a point on it and with all due respect, was a professor at the University of Santa Teresa.

"Oh, well then," said the Chicano, "if that's the way it is I'll take you to see Doktor Koenig. I think he used to be a professor too."

The critics' hearts leaped at his words. Then they followed the impresario past the circus trailers and cages on wheels until they came to what was, for all intents and purposes, the edge of the camp. Farther out there was only yellow earth and a black hut or two and the fence along the Mexican-American border.

"He likes the quiet," said the impresario, though they hadn't asked.

He rapped with his knuckles on the door of the magician's little trailer. Someone opened the door and a voice from the darkness asked what he wanted. The impresario said it was him and he had some European friends with him who wanted to say hello. Come in, then, said the voice, and they went up the single step and into the trailer, where the curtains were drawn over the only two windows, which were just a little bigger than portholes.

"I don't know how we're all going to fit in here," said the impresario, and immediately he pulled back the curtains.

Lying on the only bed they saw an olive-skinned bald man wearing only a pair of enormous black shorts, who looked at them, blinking with difficulty. He couldn't have been more than sixty, if that, which ruled him out immediately, but they decided to stay for a while and at least thank him for seeing them. Amalfitano, who was in a better mood than the other two, explained that they were looking for a German friend, a writer, and they couldn't find him.

"So you thought you'd find him in my circus?" said the impresario.

"Not him, but someone who might know him," said Amalfitano.

"I've never hired a writer," said the impresario.

"I'm not German," said Doktor Koenig. "I'm American. My name is Andy López."

With these words he pulled his wallet out of a bag hanging on a hook and held out his driver's license.

"What's your magic act?" Pelletier asked him in English.

"I start by making fleas disappear," said Doktor Koenig, and the five of them laughed.

"It's the truth," said the impresario.

"Then I make pigeons disappear, then I make a cat disappear, then a dog, and I end the act by disappearing a kid."

•

After they left the Circo Internacional, Amalfitano invited them to his house for lunch.

Espinoza went out into the backyard and saw a book hanging from a clothesline. He didn't want to go over and see what book it was, but when he went back into the house he asked Amalfitano about it.

"It's Rafael Dieste's *Testamento geométrico*," said Amalfitano.

"Rafael Dieste, the Galician poet," said Espinoza.

"That's right," said Amalfitano, "but this is a book of geometry, not poetry, ideas that came to Dieste while he was a high school teacher."

Espinoza translated what Amalfitano had said for Pelletier.

"And it's hanging outside?" said Pelletier with a smile.

"Yes," said Espinoza as Amalfitano looked in the refrigerator for something to eat, "like a shirt left out to dry."

"Do you like beans?" asked Amalfitano.

"Anything is fine. We're used to everything now," said Espinoza.

Pelletier went over to the window and looked at the book, its pages stirring almost imperceptibly in the slight afternoon breeze. Then he went outside and spent a while examining it.

"Don't take it down," he heard Espinoza say behind him.

"This book wasn't left out to dry, it's been here a long time," said Pelletier.

"That's what I thought," said Espinoza, "but we'd better leave it alone and go home."

Amalfitano watched them from the window, biting his lip, although the look on his face (just then at least) wasn't of desperation or impotence but of deep, boundless sadness.

When the critics showed the first sign of turning around, Amalfitano retreated, returning rapidly to the kitchen, where he pretended to be intent on making lunch.

•

When they got back to the hotel, Norton told them she was leaving the next day and they received the news without surprise, as if they'd been expecting it for a while. The flight Norton had found was out of Tucson, and despite her protests—she'd been planning to take a taxi—they decided to drive her to the airport. That night they talked until late. They told Norton about their visit to the circus and promised that if nothing changed, they would spend three more days there at most. Then Norton got up to go to bed and Espinoza suggested they spend their last night in Santa Teresa together. Norton misunderstood and said that she was the only one who was leaving, they still had more nights in the city.

"I mean the three of us together," said Espinoza.

"In bed?" asked Norton.

"Yes, in bed," said Espinoza.

"I don't think that's a good idea," said Norton, "I'd rather sleep alone."

So they walked her to the elevator and then they went to the bar and ordered two Bloody Marys and sat waiting for them in silence.

"I really put my foot in it this time," said Espinoza when the bartender brought them their drinks.

"It seems that way," said Pelletier.

"Have you realized," said Espinoza, after another silence, "that during this whole trip we've only been to bed with her once?"

"Of course I've realized," said Pelletier.

"And whose fault is that," asked Espinoza, "hers or ours?"

"I don't know," said Pelletier, "the truth is I haven't been much in the mood for making love these days. What about you?"

"I haven't either," said Espinoza.

They were quiet again for a while.

"She probably feels more or less the same," said Pelletier.

•

They left Santa Teresa very early. First they called Amalfitano and told him they were going to the United States and probably wouldn't be back all day. At the border the American customs officer wanted to see the car's papers and then he let them pass. Following the instructions of the hotel clerk, they took a dirt road and for a while they drove through a patch of woods and streams, as if they'd stumbled into a dome with its own ecosystem. For a while they thought they'd never get to the airport, or anywhere else. But the dirt road ended in Sonoita and from there they took Route 83 to Interstate 10, which brought them straight to Tucson. At the airport there was still time for them to have coffee and talk about what they'd do when they saw each other again in Europe. Then Norton had to go to the boarding gate and half an hour later her plane took off for New York, where she would catch a connecting flight to London.

To get back they took Interstate 19 to Nogales, although they turned off a little after Rio Rico and followed the border on the Arizona side, to Lochiel, where they entered Mexico again. They were hungry and thirsty but they didn't stop in any town. At five in the afternoon they got back to the hotel and after they showered they went down to have a sandwich and call Amalfitano. He told them not to leave the hotel, he'd take a taxi and be there in ten minutes. We're in no hurry, they said.

•

After that moment, reality for Pelletier and Espinoza seemed to tear like paper scenery, and when it was stripped away it revealed what was behind it: a smoking landscape, as if someone, an angel, maybe, was tending hundreds of barbecue pits for a crowd of invisible beings. They stopped getting up early, they stopped eating at the hotel, among the American tourists, and they moved to the center of the city, choosing dark bars for breakfast (beer and fiery *chilaquiles*) and bars with big windows for lunch, where the waiters wrote the specials in white ink on the glass. Dinner they had wherever they happened to be.

They accepted the rector's offer and gave lectures on contemporary French and Spanish literature, lectures that were more like massacres and that at least had the virtue of striking fear into their listeners, mostly young men, readers of Michon and Rolin or Marías and Vila-Matas. Then, and this time together, they gave a master class on Benno von Archimboldi, feeling less like butchers than like gutters or disembowelers, but something in them urged restraint, something undetectable at first, though silently they sensed a fated encounter: in the audience, not counting Amalfitano, there were three young readers of Archimboldi who almost brought them to tears. One of them, who could speak French, even had one of the books translated by Pelletier. So miracles were possible, after all. The Internet bookstores worked. Culture, despite the disappearances and guilt, was still alive, in a permanent state of transformation, as they soon discovered when, after the lecture and at the express request of Pelletier and Espinoza, the young readers of Archimboldi accompanied them to the university's reception hall, where there was a love fest, or rather a cocktail hour, or maybe a cocktail half hour, or possibly just a polite nod to the distinguished lecturers, and where, for lack of a better subject, people talked about what good writers the Germans were, all of them, and about the historic significance of universities like the Sorbonne or the University of Salamanca, where, to the astonishment of the critics, two of the professors (one who taught Roman law and another who taught twentieth-century penal law) had studied. Later, Dean Guerra and one of the administration secretaries took them aside and gave them their checks and a little later, under cover of a fainting fit suffered by one of the professors' wives, they slipped out.

•

They were accompanied by Amalfitano, who hated these parties though he had no choice but to endure them from time to time, and the three readers of Archimboldi. First they had dinner in the center and then they drove up and down the street that never slept. The rental car was big, but they still had to sit almost on top of each other and the people on the sidewalks gave them curious looks, the kind of looks they gave everyone on the street, until they saw Amalfitano and the three students crammed in the backseat and then they quickly averted their eyes.

They went into a bar that one of the boys knew. The bar was big and in the back was a yard with trees and a little fenced-in space for cockfights. The boy said his father had brought him there once. They talked politics, and Espinoza translated what the boys said for Pelletier. None of them was older than twenty and they had a fresh, healthy look. They seemed eager to learn. Amalfitano, in contrast, seemed more tired and defeated than ever that night. In a low voice, Pelletier asked him whether something was the matter. Amalfitano shook his head and said no, although back at the hotel, the critics remarked that the way their friend had chain-smoked and hardly spoken a word all night, he was either extremely depressed or a nervous wreck.

The next day, when he got up, Espinoza found Pelletier sitting on the hotel terrace, dressed in Bermuda shorts and leather sandals, reading that day's Santa Teresa papers, armed with a Spanish-French dictionary he'd probably bought that very morning.

"Are we going to the center for breakfast?" asked Espinoza.

"No," said Pelletier, "enough alcohol and rotgut meals. I want to find out what's going on in this city."

Then Espinoza remembered that the night before, one of the boys had told them the story of the women who were being killed. All he remembered was that the boy had said there were more than two hundred of them and he'd had to repeat it two or three times because neither Espinoza nor Pelletier could believe his ears. Not believing your ears, though, thought Espinoza, is a form of exaggeration. You see something beautiful and you can't believe your eyes. Someone tells you something about . . . the natural beauty of Iceland . . . people bathing in thermal springs, among geysers . . . in fact you've seen it in pictures, but still you say you can't believe it . . . Although obviously you believe it . . . Exaggeration is a form of polite admiration . . . You set it up so the person you're talking to can say: it's true . . . And then you say: incredible. First you can't believe it and then you think it's incredible.

That was probably what he and Pelletier had said the night before when the boy, healthy and strong and pure, told them that more than two hundred women had died. But not over a short period of time, thought Espinoza. From 1993 or 1994 to the present day . . . And many more women might have been killed. Maybe two hundred and fifty or three hundred. No one will ever know, the boy had said in French. The boy had read a book by Archimboldi translated by Pelletier and obtained thanks to the good offices of an Internet bookstore. He didn't speak much French, thought Espinoza. But a person can speak a language badly or not at all and still be able to read it. In any case, there were lots of dead women.

"So who's guilty?" asked Pelletier.

"There are people who've been in prison a long time, but women keep dying," said one of the boys.

Amalfitano, Espinoza remembered, was quiet, with an absent look on his face, probably plastered. At a nearby table there were three men who kept looking at them as if they were very interested in what they were talking about. What else do I remember? Espinoza thought. Someone, one of the boys, talked about a murder epidemic. Someone said something about the copycat effect. Someone spoke the name Albert Kessler. At a certain moment Espinoza got up and went to the bathroom to vomit. As he was doing it he heard someone outside, someone who was probably washing his hands or his face or primping in front of the mirror, say to him:

"That's all right, buddy, go ahead and puke."

The voice soothed me, thought Espinoza, but that implies I was upset, and why should I have been upset? When he left the stall there was no one there, just the music from the bar drifting in faintly and the sound of the plumbing, deeper and spasmodic. Who brought us back to the hotel? he wondered.

"Who drove us back?" he asked Pelletier.

"You did," said Pelletier.

•

That day Espinoza left Pelletier reading newspapers at the hotel and went out on his own. Although it was late for breakfast he went into a bar on Calle Arizpe that was always empty and asked for something restorative.

"This is the best thing for a hangover, sir," said the bartender, and he put a glass of cold beer in front of him.

From inside came the sound of frying. He asked for something to eat.

"Quesadillas, sir?"

"Just one," said Espinoza.

The bartender shrugged his shoulders. The bar was empty and it wasn't quite as dark as the bars where he usually went in the morning. The door to the bathroom opened and a very tall man came out. Espinoza's eyes hurt and he was starting to feel sick again, but the appearance of the tall man startled him. In the darkness he couldn't see his face or tell how old he was. But the tall man sat down next to the window, and yellow and green light illuminated his features.

Espinoza realized it couldn't be Archimboldi. He looked like a farmer or a rancher on a visit to the city. The bartender put a quesadilla in front of him. When he picked it up in his hands he burned himself and he asked for a napkin. Then he asked the bartender to bring him three more quesadillas. When he left the bar he headed for the crafts market. Some of the vendors were gathering up their wares and stowing their folding tables. It was lunchtime and there weren't many people. At first he had a hard time finding the stall of the girl who sold rugs. The streets of the market were dirty, as if food or fruit and vegetables were sold there instead of crafts. When he saw the girl she was busy rolling up rugs and tying the ends. The smallest ones, the handwoven ones, she put in a long cardboard box. She had a vacant expression, as if she was far away. Espinoza approached and stroked one of the rugs. He asked whether she remembered him. The girl showed no sign of surprise. She raised her eyes, looked at him, and said yes with a naturalness that made him smile.

"Who am I?" asked Espinoza.

"The Spanish man who bought a rug from me," said the girl, "we talked for a while."

•

After deciphering the newspapers, Pelletier felt like showering and washing off all the filth that clung to his skin. He saw Amalfitano approaching from a long way off. He watched him come into the hotel and speak to the desk clerk. Before he came out onto the terrace, Amalfitano raised one hand weakly in a sign of recognition. Pelletier got up and told him to order whatever he liked, he was going to take a shower. As he left he noticed that Amalfitano's eyes were red and there were circles under them, as if he hadn't slept. Crossing the lobby he changed his mind and turned on one of the two computers that the hotel provided for its guests in a little room next to the bar. When he checked his e-mail he found a long message from Norton in which she gave him what she believed to be her real reasons for leaving so abruptly. He read it as if he were still drunk. He thought about the young Archimboldi readers from the night before, and he wanted, vaguely, to be like them, to exchange his life for one of theirs. This wish was, he told himself, a form of lassitude. Then he pressed the button for the elevator and rode up with an American woman in her seventies who was reading a Mexican paper, one of the same ones he'd read that morning. As he was undressing he thought about how he would tell Espinoza. There was probably a message waiting for him from Norton. What can I do? he wondered.

The bite out of the toilet bowl was still there and for a few seconds he stared at it and let the warm water run over his body. What's the reasonable thing to do? he thought. The most reasonable thing would be to go back and postpone any conclusion as long as possible. Only when soap got in his eyes was he able to look away from the toilet. He turned his face into the stream of water and closed his eyes. I'm not as sad as I'd have thought, he told himself. This is all unreal, he said to himself. Then he turned off the shower, dressed, and went down to join Amalfitano.

•

He went with Espinoza to check his e-mail. He stood behind him until he'd made sure there was a message from Norton, and when he saw that there was, certain it would say the same thing his had, he sat in an armchair a few feet away from the computers and leafed through a tourist magazine. Every so often he would lift his eyes and look at Espinoza, who didn't seem about to get up. He would've liked to pat him on the back, but he chose not to move. When Espinoza turned around to look at him, he said he'd gotten one just like it.

"I can't believe it," said Espinoza in a thread of a voice.

Pelletier left the magazine on the glass table and went over to the computer, where he glanced through Norton's letter. Then, without sitting down, and typing with one finger, he found his own e-mail and showed Espinoza the message he'd gotten. He asked him, very gently, to read it. Espinoza turned toward the screen again and read Pelletier's letter several times.

"It's almost exactly the same," he said.

"What does it matter?" said the Frenchman.

"She could have shown a bit more decency in that regard, at least," said Espinoza.

"In these cases, decency is informing the person at all," said Pelletier.

When they went out onto the terrace there was almost no one there.

A waiter, dressed in a white jacket and black pants, was gathering up glasses and bottles from the empty tables. At one end, near the railing, a couple in their twenties looked out at the silent, deep green street, holding hands. Espinoza asked Pelletier what he was thinking about.

"About her," said Pelletier, "of course."

He also said it was strange, or at least curious, that they were here, in this hotel, in this city, when Norton finally came to a decision. Espinoza gave him a long look and then said in disgust that he felt like throwing up.

•

The next day Espinoza went back to the crafts market and asked the girl what her name was. She said it was Rebeca, and Espinoza smiled, because the name, he thought, suited her perfectly. He stood there for three hours, talking to Rebeca, as tourists and browsers wandered around looking halfheartedly at the merchandise, as if under duress. Only twice did customers come up to Rebeca's stall, but both times they left without buying anything, which made Espinoza feel guilty because in some sense he blamed the girl's bad luck on himself, on his stubborn presence at the stall. He decided to make up for it by buying what he imagined the others would have bought. He chose a big rug, two small rugs, a serape that was mostly green, another that was mostly red, and a kind of knapsack made of the same cloth and with the same pattern as the serapes. Rebeca asked whether he was going back to his country soon and Espinoza smiled and said he didn't know. Then the girl called a boy, who loaded all of Espinoza's purchases onto his back and went with him to where he had parked the car.

Rebeca's voice when she called the boy (who had appeared out of nowhere or out of the crowd, which was essentially the same thing), her tone, the calm authority she projected, made Espinoza shudder. As he was walking behind the boy he noticed that most of the vendors were beginning to pack up. When he got to the car they put the rugs in the trunk and Espinoza asked the boy how long he'd been working with Rebeca. She's my sister, he said. They don't look alike at all, thought Espinoza. Then he glanced at the boy, who was short but also seemed strong, and gave him a ten-dollar bill.

•

When he got to the hotel, Pelletier was on the terrace reading Archimboldi. Espinoza asked him what book it was and Pelletier smiled and answered that it was *Saint Thomas*.

"How many times have you read it?" asked Espinoza.

"I've lost count, although this is one of the ones I've read least."

Just like me, thought Espinoza, just like me.

●

Rather than two letters, it was really a single one albeit with variations, brusque personalized twists that opened onto the same abyss. Santa Teresa, that horrible city, said Norton, had made her think. Think in the strict sense, for the first time in years. In other words: she had begun to think about practical, real, tangible things, and she had also begun to remember. She had thought about her family, her friends, and her job, and nearly simultaneously she had remembered family scenes or work scenes, scenes in which her friends raised their glasses and made toasts, maybe to her, maybe to someone she'd forgotten. Mexico is unbelievable (here she digressed, but only in Espinoza's letter, as if Pelletier wouldn't understand or as if she knew beforehand that they would compare letters), a place where one of the big fish in the cultural establishment, someone presumably refined, a writer who has reached the highest levels of government, is called El Cerdo, and no one even questions it, she said, and she saw a connection between this, the nickname or the cruelty of the nickname or the resignation to the nickname, and the criminal acts that had been occurring for some time in Santa Teresa.

When I was little there was a boy I liked. I don't know why I liked him, but I did. I was eight and so was he. He was called James Crawford. I think he was a very shy boy. He would speak only to other boys and kept his distance from the girls. He had dark hair and brown eyes. He always wore short pants, even when the other boys began to wear trousers. The first time I talked to him—this I remembered just a little while ago—I called him Jimmy instead of James. No one called him that. Only me. The two of us were eight years old. His face was very serious. What was my excuse for talking to him? I think he left something on the desk, maybe an eraser or a pencil, I can't remember now, and I said: Jimmy, you forgot your eraser. I do remember smiling. I do remember why I called him Jimmy and not James or Jim. Out of fondness. Because it made me happy. Because I liked Jimmy and I thought he was very handsome.

The next day Espinoza went to the crafts market first thing in the morning. The vendors and craftspeople were just beginning to set up their stalls and the cobblestoned street was still clean. His heart was beating faster than normal. Rebeca was arranging her rugs on a folding table and she smiled when she saw him. Some vendors were standing around drinking coffee or soda and chatting from stall to stall. Behind the stalls, on the sidewalk, under the old arches and the awnings of some of the more traditional stores, men were milling around arguing over wholesale batches of pottery that were guaranteed to sell in Tucson or Phoenix. Espinoza said hello to Rebeca and helped her set out the last rugs. Then he asked whether she'd like to have breakfast with him and the girl said she couldn't and anyway she'd already had breakfast at home. Refusing to give up, Espinoza asked where her brother was.

"At school," said Rebeca.

"So who helps you bring everything here?"

"My mother," said Rebeca.

For a while, Espinoza was silent, his eyes on the ground, not knowing whether to buy another rug from her or leave without a word.

"Have lunch with me," he said finally.

"All right," said the girl.

•

When Espinoza got back to the hotel he found Pelletier reading Archimboldi. Seen from the distance, Pelletier's face, and in fact not just his face but his whole body, radiated an enviable calm. When he got a little closer he saw that the book wasn't *Saint Thomas* but rather *The Blind Woman*, and he asked Pelletier whether he'd had the patience to reread the other book from start to finish. Pelletier looked up at him and didn't answer. He said instead that it was surprising, or that it would never cease to surprise him, the way Archimboldi depicted pain and shame.

"Delicately," said Espinoza.

"That's right," said Pelletier. "Delicately."

•

In Santa Teresa, in that horrible city, said Norton's letter, I thought about Jimmy, but mostly I thought about me, about what I was like at eight, and at first the ideas leaped, the images leaped, it was as if there were an earthquake in my head, I couldn't focus clearly or precisely on any single memory, but when I finally could it was worse, I saw myself saying Jimmy, I saw my smile, Jimmy Crawford's serious face, the flock of children, their backs, the sudden swell of them in the calm waters of the schoolyard, I saw my lips announcing to the boy that he'd forgotten something, I saw the eraser, or maybe it was a pencil, I saw the way my eyes looked then, saw them with the eyes I have now, and I heard my cry once more, the timbre of my voice, the extreme politeness of a girl of eight who shouts after a boy of eight to remind him not to forget his eraser and yet can't call him by his name, James, or Crawford, the way we do in school, and opts, consciously or unconsciously, for the diminutive Jimmy, which indicates fondness, a verbal fondness, a personal fondness, since only she, in that world-encompassing instant, calls him that, a name that somehow casts in a new light the fondness or solicitude implicit in the gesture of warning him he's forgotten something, don't forget your eraser, or your pencil, though in the end it's simply an expression, verbally poor or verbally rich, of happiness.

•

They ate at a cheap restaurant near the market, while Rebeca's little brother watched the cart that was used each morning to transport the rugs and folding table. Espinoza asked Rebeca whether it wasn't possible to leave the cart unguarded so the boy could eat with them, but Rebeca told him not to worry. If the cart was left unguarded then someone would probably take it. From the window of the restaurant Espinoza could see the boy on top of the heap of rugs like a bird, scanning the horizon.

"I'll take him something," he said, "what does your brother like?"

"Ice cream," said Rebeca, "but they don't have ice cream here."

For a few seconds Espinoza considered going out to find ice cream somewhere else, but he gave up the idea for fear the girl would be gone by the time he got back. She asked him what Spain was like.

"Different," said Espinoza, thinking about the ice cream.

"Different from Mexico?" she asked.

"No," said Espinoza, "different in different places, diverse."

Suddenly it occurred to Espinoza to take the boy a sandwich.

"They're called *tortas* in Mexico," said Rebeca, "and my brother likes ham."

She was like a princess or an ambassadress, thought Espinoza. He asked the waitress to bring him a ham sandwich and a soda. The waitress asked him how he wanted the sandwich.

"Tell her you want it with everything," said Rebeca.

"With everything," said Espinoza.

Later he went outside with the sandwich and the soda and handed them to the boy, who was still perched atop the cart. At first the boy shook his head and said he wasn't hungry. Espinoza saw that there were three slightly bigger boys on the corner watching them, holding back laughter.

"If you're not hungry, just drink the soda and keep the sandwich," he said, "or give it to the dogs."

When he sat back down with Rebeca he felt good. In fact, he felt replete.

"This won't work," he said, "it isn't right. Next time, the three of us will eat together."

Rebeca looked him in the eye, her fork halted in the air, and then a half smile appeared on her face and she conveyed the food to her mouth.

•

At the hotel, stretched out on a deck chair beside the empty pool, Pelletier was reading, and Espinoza knew, even before he saw the title, that it wasn't *Saint Thomas* or *The Blind Woman*, but another book by Archimboldi. When he sat down next to Pelletier he could see it was *Lethaea*, not one of his favorites, although to judge by Pelletier's face, the rereading was fruitful and thoroughly enjoyable. When he sat down in the next deck chair he asked Pelletier what he'd done all day.

"I read," answered Pelletier, who in turn asked him the same question.

"Not much," said Espinoza.

That night, as they ate together at the hotel restaurant, Espinoza told him he'd bought some souvenirs, including something for Pelletier. Pelletier was happy to hear it and asked what kind of souvenir Espinoza had bought for him.

"An Indian rug," said Espinoza.

•

When I reached London after an exhausting trip, said Norton in her letter, I started to think about Jimmy Crawford, or maybe I started to think about him as I was waiting for the New York–London flight, but either way Jimmy Crawford and my eight-year-old voice calling after him were already with me at the moment when I found the keys to my flat and turned on the light and left my bags on the floor in the hall. I went into the kitchen and made tea. Then I showered and went to bed. I had a feeling that I wouldn't be able to sleep, so I took a sleeping pill. I remember I started to leaf through a magazine, I remember I thought about the two of you, wandering that horrible city, I remember I thought about the hotel. In my room at the hotel there were two very odd mirrors that frightened me the last few days. When I felt myself dropping off, I barely had the strength to reach out and turn off the light.

I had no dreams at all. When I woke up I didn't know where I was, but the feeling lasted just a second or two, because straightaway I recognized the usual street noises. Everything's over, I thought. I feel rested, I'm home, I have lots to do. When I sat up in bed, though, all I did was start to cry like a fool, for no apparent reason. All day I was like that. At moments I wished I hadn't left Santa Teresa, that I'd stayed there with you until the end. More than once I felt the urge to rush to the airport and catch the first plane to Mexico. These urges were followed by other, more destructive ones: to set fire to my apartment, slit my wrists, never return to the university, and live on the streets forever after.

But in England at least, women who live on the streets are often subjected to terrible humiliations, I just read an article about it in some magazine or other. In England these street women are gang-raped, beaten, and it isn't unusual for them to be found dead outside hospitals. The people who do these things to them aren't, as I might have thought at eighteen, the police or gangs of neo-Nazi thugs, but other street people, which makes it seem somehow even worse. Feeling confused, I went out, hoping to cheer up and thinking I might call some friend to meet for dinner. How I don't know, but suddenly I found myself in front of a gallery hosting a retrospective of the work of Edwin Johns, the artist who cut off his right hand to display it in a self-portrait.

•

On his next visit, Espinoza managed to persuade the girl to let him take her home. They left the cart safe in the back room of the restaurant where they'd eaten before, among empty bottles and stacks of canned chiles and meat, after Espinoza paid a meager rent to a fat woman in an old factory worker's apron. Then they put the rugs and serapes in the backseat of the car and the three of them squeezed up in front. The boy was happy and Espinoza told him he could decide where they went to eat that day. They ended up at a McDonald's in the city center.

The girl's house was in one of the neighborhoods to the west, the area where most crimes were committed, according to what he'd read in the papers, but the neighborhood and the street where Rebeca lived just seemed like a poor neighborhood and a poor street, there was nothing ominous about them. He left the car parked in front of the house. There was a tiny garden in front, with three planter boxes made of cane and wire, full of pots of flowers and plants. Rebeca told her brother to stay outside and watch the car. The house was built of wood and when anyone walked on the floorboards they made a hollow sound, as if a drain ran underneath, or as if there was a secret room below.

Contrary to Espinoza's expectations, Rebeca's mother greeted him in a friendly way and offered him a soda. Then she herself introduced the rest of her children. Rebeca had two brothers and three sisters, although the oldest didn't live at home anymore because she'd gotten married. One of the sisters was just like Rebeca but younger. Her name was Cristina and everyone said she was the smartest in the family. Once a reasonable amount of time had passed, Espinoza asked Rebeca to go for a walk with him around the neighborhood. As they left they saw the boy up on the roof of the car. He was reading a comic book and had something in his mouth, probably candy. When they got back from the walk the boy was still there, although he wasn't reading anymore and his candy was gone.

•

When he returned to the hotel Pelletier was reading *Saint Thomas* again. When he sat down beside him Pelletier looked up from the book and said there were still things he didn't understand and probably never would. Espinoza laughed and said nothing.

"Amalfitano was here today," said Pelletier.

In his opinion, the Chilean professor's nerves were shot. Pelletier had invited him to take a dip in the pool. Since he didn't have bathing trunks Pelletier had picked up a pair for him at the reception desk. Everything seemed to be going fine. But when Amalfitano got in the pool, he froze, as if he'd suddenly seen the devil. Then he sank. Before he went under, Pelletier remembered, he covered his mouth with both hands. In any case, he made no attempt to swim. Fortunately, Pelletier was there and it was easy to dive down and bring him back up to the surface. Then they each had a whiskey, and Amalfitano explained that it had been a long time since he swam.

"We talked about Archimboldi," said Pelletier.

Then Amalfitano got dressed, returned the swimming trunks, and left.

"And what did you do?" asked Espinoza.

"I showered, got dressed, came down to eat, and kept reading."

•

For an instant, said Norton in her letter, I felt like a derelict dazzled by the sudden lights of a theater. I wasn't in the best state of mind to go into a gallery, but the name Edwin Johns drew me like a magnet. I went up to the gallery door, which was glass, and inside I saw many people and I saw waiters dressed in white who could scarcely move, balancing trays laden with glasses of champagne or red wine. I decided to wait and went back across the street. Little by little the gallery emptied and the moment came when I thought I could go in and at least see part of the retrospective.

When I opened the glass door I felt something strange, as if everything I saw or felt from that moment on would determine the course of my life to come. I stopped in front of a kind of landscape, a Surrey landscape from Johns's early period, that looked to me at once sad and sweet, profound and not at all grandiloquent, an English landscape as only the English can paint them. All at once I decided that seeing this one painting was enough and I was about to leave when a waiter, maybe the last of the waiters from the catering company, came over to me with a single glass of wine on his tray, a glass especially for me. He didn't say anything. He just offered it to me and I smiled at him and took the glass. Then I saw the poster for the show, across the room from where I was standing, a poster that showed the painting with the severed hand, Johns's masterpiece, and in white numerals gave his dates of birth and death.

I hadn't known he was dead, said Norton in her letter, I thought he was still living in Switzerland, in a comfortable asylum, laughing at himself and most of all at us. I remember the glass of wine fell from my hands. I remember that a couple, both tall and thin, turned away from a painting and peered over as if I might be an ex-lover or a living (and unfinished) painting that had just got news of the painter's death. I know I walked out without looking back and that I walked for a long time until I realized I wasn't crying, but that it was raining and I was soaked. That night I didn't sleep at all.

•

In the mornings Espinoza would pick Rebeca up at her house. He'd park the car out front, have a coffee, and then, without saying anything, he'd put the rugs in the backseat and occupy himself polishing the trim. If he'd been at all mechanically inclined he would have lifted the hood and looked at the engine, but he wasn't, and in any case the car ran perfectly. Then the girl and her brother would come out of the house and Espinoza would open the passenger door for them, without a word, as if they'd had the same routine for years, and then he would get in the driver's side, put the dust rag away in the glove compartment, and head to the crafts market. Once they were there he helped set up the stall and once they finished he'd go to a nearby restaurant and buy two coffees and one Coca-Cola to go, which they drank standing up, looking at the other booths or the squat but proud horizon of colonial buildings surrounding them. Sometimes Espinoza scolded the girl's brother, telling him that drinking Coca-Cola in the morning was a bad habit, but the boy, whose name was Eulogio, laughed and ignored him because he knew Espinoza's anger was ninety percent put-on. The rest of the morning Espinoza would spend at an outdoor café in the neighborhood, the only neighborhood in Santa Teresa he liked, besides Rebeca's, reading the local papers and drinking coffee and smoking. When he went into the bathroom and looked at himself in the mirror, he thought his features were changing. I look like a gentleman, he said to himself sometimes. I look younger. I look like someone else.

•

At the hotel, when he got back, Pelletier was always on the terrace or at the pool or sprawled in an armchair in one of the lounges, rereading *Saint Thomas* or *The Blind Woman* or *Lethaea*, which were, it seemed, the only books by Archimboldi he'd brought with him to Mexico. Espinoza asked whether he was preparing some article or essay on those three books in particular and Pelletier's answer was vague. At first he had been. Not anymore. He was reading them just because they were the ones he had. Espinoza considered lending him one of his, and all at once he realized with alarm that he'd forgotten all about the books by Archimboldi hidden away in his suitcase.

•

That night I didn't sleep a wink, said Norton in her letter, and it occurred to me to call Morini. It was very late, it was rude to bother him at that hour, it was rash of me, it was a terrible imposition, but I called him. I remember I dialed his number and immediately I turned out the light in the room, as if so long as I was in the dark Morini couldn't see my face. To my surprise, he picked up the phone instantly.

"Piero, it's me, Liz," I said. "Did you know Edwin Johns is dead?"

"Yes," said Morini's voice from Turin. "He died a few months ago."

"But I only found out just now, tonight," I said.

"I thought you already knew," said Morini.

"How did he die?" I asked.

"It was an accident," said Morini, "he went out for a walk, he wanted to sketch a little waterfall near the sanatorium, he climbed up on a rock and slipped. They found his body at the bottom of a ravine, one hundred and fifty feet down."

"It can't be," I said.

"It can," said Morini.

"He went for a walk alone? With no one watching him?"

"He wasn't alone," said Morini, "a nurse was with him, and one of those strong young men from the sanatorium, the kind who can pin a raving lunatic in no time."

I laughed—for the first time—at the expression *raving lunatic*, and Morini, at the other end of the line, laughed with me, although only for an instant.

"The word for those men is orderlies," I said.

"Well, he had a nurse and an orderly with him," he said. "Johns climbed up on a rock and the man climbed up too. The nurse sat on a stump, as Johns asked her to do, and pretended to read a book. Then Johns started to draw with his left hand, with which he had become quite proficient. He drew the waterfall, the mountains, the outcroppings of rock, the forest, and the nurse reading her book, far away from it all. Then the accident happened. Johns stood up on the rock and slipped, and although the man tried to catch him, he fell into the abyss."

That was all.

We were quiet for a time, said Norton in her letter, until Morini broke the silence and asked how things had gone in Mexico.

"Badly," I said.

He didn't ask any more questions. I listened to his steady breathing, and he listened to my breathing, which was growing steadily calmer.

"I'll call you tomorrow," I said to him.

"All right," he said, but for a few seconds neither of us was able to hang up the phone.

That night I thought about Edwin Johns, I thought about his hand, now doubtless on display in his retrospective, the hand that the sanatorium orderly couldn't grasp to prevent his fall, although this was too obvious, a false representation, having nothing to do with what Johns actually been. Much more real was the Swiss landscape, the landscape that you two saw and I've never seen, with its mountains and forests, its iridescent stones and waterfalls, its deadly ravines and reading nurses.

•

One night Espinoza took Rebeca dancing. They went to a club in the center of Santa Teresa where the girl had never been but that her friends highly recommended. As they drank Cuba libres, Rebeca told him that two of the girls who later showed up dead had been kidnapped on their way out of the club. Their bodies were dumped in the desert.

Espinoza thought it was a bad omen that she'd told him the killer made a habit of frequenting the club. When he'd brought her home he kissed her. Rebeca smelled like alcohol and her skin was very cold. He asked if she wanted to make love and she nodded, several times, without saying anything. Then they moved from the front seat into the back and did it. It was a quick fuck. But then she rested her head on his chest, without saying a word, and for a long time he stroked her hair. The smell of chemicals came in waves on the night air. Espinoza wondered whether there was a paper factory nearby. He asked Rebeca and she said there were only houses built by the people who lived in them and empty fields.

•

No matter what time he got back to the hotel, Pelletier was always awake, reading a book and waiting for him. This was his way of reaffirming their friendship, Espinoza thought. It was also possible that Pelletier couldn't sleep and his insomnia drove him to read in the empty hotel lounges until dawn.

Sometimes Pelletier was by the pool, in a sweater or wrapped in a towel, sipping whiskey. Other times Espinoza found him in a room presided over by an enormous border landscape, painted, one could see instantly, by someone who had never been to the border: there was more wishfulness than realism in the industriousness and harmony of the landscape. The waiters, even those on the night shift, made sure Pelletier lacked for nothing, because he was a decent tipper. When Espinoza got in, the two men spent a few minutes exchanging brief, pleasant remarks.

Sometimes, before he went to look for Pelletier in the hotel's empty lounges, he would go check his e-mail, in the hope of finding letters from Europe, from Hellfeld or Borchmeyer, that might shed some light on Archimboldi's whereabouts. Then he would go in search of Pelletier and later both of them would head silently up to their rooms.

•

The next day, said Norton in her letter, I tidied my apartment and put my papers in order. This was done much sooner than I expected. In the afternoon I went to see a film, and on the way out, though I felt calm, I couldn't reconstruct the plot or think who the actors had been. That night I had dinner with a friend and went to bed early, though it was midnight before I fell asleep. As soon as I got up, early in the morning and with no ticket, I went to the airport and booked a seat on the next flight to Italy. I flew from London to Milan, then I took the train to Turin. When Morini opened the door I told him I'd come to stay, that it was up to him to decide whether I should go to a hotel or stay with him. He didn't answer my question. He just moved aside in the wheelchair and asked me in. I went to the bathroom to wash my face. When I returned Morini had made tea and put three little biscuits on a plate, which he urged me to try. I tasted one and it was delicious. It was like a Greek pastry, filled with pistachio and fig paste. I made short work of all three and had two cups of tea. Morini, meanwhile, made a phone call, and then he sat listening to me, stopping me every now and then to ask a question, which I was happy to answer.

We talked for hours. We talked about the Italian Right, about the resurgence of fascism in Europe, about immigrants, about Islamic terrorists, about British and American politics, and as we talked I felt better and better, which is odd because the subjects we were discussing were depressing, until I couldn't go on any longer and I asked him for another magic biscuit, just one, and then Morini looked at the clock and said it was only natural I should be hungry, and he'd do better than give me a pistachio biscuit, he'd made us a reservation at a restaurant in Turin and he was going to take me there for dinner.

The restaurant was in the middle of a garden where there were benches and stone statues. I remember that I pushed Morini's chair and he showed me the statues. Some were of mythological figures, but others were of simple peasants lost in the night. In the park there were other couples strolling and sometimes we crossed paths with them and other times we only glimpsed their shadows. As we ate Morini asked about the two of you. I told him the tip we'd gotten about Archimboldi being in the north of Mexico was false, and that he'd probably never set foot in the country. I told him about your Mexican friend, the great intellectual El Cerdo, and we laughed for a long time. I really was feeling better and better.

•

One night, after making love with Rebeca for the second time in the backseat of the car, Espinoza asked what her family thought of him. The girl said her sisters thought he was handsome and her mother had said he had a responsible look. The smell of chemicals seemed to lift the car from the ground. The next day Espinoza bought five rugs. She asked him why he wanted so many rugs and Espinoza answered that he planned to give them as gifts. When he got back to the hotel he left the rugs on the bed he didn't sleep in, then he sat on his bed and for a fraction of a second the shadows retreated and he had a fleeting glimpse of reality. He felt dizzy and he closed his eyes. Without knowing it he fell asleep.

When he woke up his stomach hurt and he wanted to die. In the afternoon he went shopping. He went into a lingerie shop and a women's clothing shop and a shoe shop. That night he brought Rebeca to the hotel and after they had showered together he dressed her in a thong and garters and black tights and a black teddy and black spike-heeled shoes and fucked her until she was no more than a tremor in his arms. Then he ordered dinner for two from room service and after they ate he gave her the other gifts he'd bought her and then they fucked again until the sun began to come up. Then they both got dressed, she packed her gifts in the bags, and he took her home first and then to the crafts market, where he helped her set up. Before he said goodbye she asked him whether she would see him again. Espinoza, without knowing why, maybe just because he was tired, shrugged his shoulders and said you never know.

"You do know," said Rebeca, in a sad voice he didn't recognize. "Are you leaving Mexico?" she asked him.

"Someday I have to go," he answered.

•

When he got back to the hotel, Pelletier wasn't on the terrace or at the pool or in any of the lounges where he usually hid away to read. He asked at the desk whether it had been long since his friend went out and they told him that Pelletier hadn't left the hotel at all. He went up to Pelletier's room and knocked on the door, but no one answered. He knocked again, banging several times, to no avail. He told the clerk he was afraid something had happened to his friend, that he might have had a heart attack, and the clerk, who knew them both, went up with Espinoza.

"I doubt anything bad has happened," he said to Espinoza in the elevator.

After opening the door with the passkey, the clerk didn't cross the threshold. The room was dark and Espinoza turned on the light. On one of the beds he saw Pelletier with the bedspread pulled up to his chin. He was on his back, his face turned slightly to one side, and he had his hands folded on his chest. There was a peaceful expression on his face that Espinoza had never seen before. Espinoza called out to him:

"Pelletier, Pelletier."

The clerk, his curiosity getting the better of him, advanced a few steps and advised him not to touch Pelletier.

"Pelletier," shouted Espinoza, and he sat down beside him and shook him by the shoulders.

Then Pelletier opened his eyes and asked what was going on.

"We thought you were dead," said Espinoza.

"No," said Pelletier, "I was dreaming I was on vacation in the Greek islands and I rented a boat and I met a boy who spent the whole day diving.

"It was a beautiful dream," he said.

"It sure does sound relaxing," said the clerk.

"The strangest part of the dream," said Pelletier, "was that the water was alive."

●

The first few hours of my first night in Turin, said Norton in her letter, I spent in Morini's guest room. I had no trouble falling asleep, but all of a sudden a thunderclap, real or in my dream, woke me, and I thought I saw Morini and his wheelchair silhouetted at the end of the hallway. At first I ignored him and tried to go back to sleep, until suddenly it struck me what I'd seen: to one side the outline of the wheelchair in the hallway and to the other side the figure of Morini, not in the hallway but in the sitting room, with his back to me. I started awake, grabbed an ashtray, and turned on the light. The hallway was deserted. I went to the sitting room and no one was there. Months before, I would've just drunk a glass of water and gone back to bed, but nothing would ever be the same again. So I went to Morini's room. When I opened the door the first thing I saw was the wheelchair to one side of the bed, and then the bulk of Morini, who was breathing steadily. I whispered his name. He didn't move. I raised my voice and Morini's voice asked me what was wrong.

"I saw you in the hallway," I said.

"When?" asked Morini.

"A minute ago, when I heard the thunder."

"Is it raining?" asked Morini.

"It must be," I said.

"I wasn't in the hallway, Liz," said Morini.

"I saw you there. You had gotten up. The wheelchair was in the hallway, facing me, but you were at the end of the hallway, in the sitting room, with your back to me," I said.

"It must have been a dream," said Morini.

"The wheelchair was facing me and you had your back to me," I said.

"Calm down, Liz," said Morini.

"Don't tell me to calm down, don't treat me like a fool. The wheel-chair was looking at me, and you were standing there cool as can be, not looking at me. Do you understand?"

Morini allowed himself a few minutes to think, propped on his elbows.

"I think so," he said. "My chair was watching you while I was ignor-ing you, yes? As if the chair and I were a single person or a single being. And the chair was bad precisely because it was watching you, and I was bad too, because I had lied to you and I wasn't looking at you."

Then I started to laugh and I said that really, as far as I was con-cerned, he could never be bad, and neither could the wheelchair, since it was of such great use to him.

The rest of the night we spent together. I told him to move over and make room for me and Morini obeyed without a word.

"How could it have taken me so long to realize you loved me?" I asked him afterward. "How could it have taken me so long to realize I loved you?"

"It's my fault," said Morini in the dark, "I'm hopeless at these things."

•

In the morning Espinoza gave the clerks and the guards and the waiters at the hotel some of the rugs and serapes he'd been accumulating. He also gave rugs to the two women who cleaned his room. The last serape—a very pretty one, with a red, green, and lavender geometric motif—he put in a bag and told the clerk to have it sent up to Pelletier.

"An anonymous gift," he said.

The clerk winked at him and said he would take care of it.

When Espinoza got to the crafts market she was sitting on a wooden bench reading a pop magazine full of color photos, with articles on Mex-ican singers, their weddings, divorces, tours, their gold and platinum al-bums, their stints in prison, their deaths in poverty. He sat down next to her, on the curb, and wondered whether to greet her with a kiss or not. Across the way was a new stall that sold little clay figurines. From where he was Espinoza could make out some tiny gallows and he smiled sadly. He asked the girl where her brother was, and she said he'd gone to school, like every morning.

A woman with very wrinkled skin, dressed in white as if she were about to get married, stopped to talk to Rebeca, so he picked up the magazine, which the girl had left under the table on a lunch box, and leafed through it until Rebeca's friend was gone. A few times he tried to say something, but he couldn't. Her silence wasn't unpleasant, nor did it imply resentment or sadness. It was transparent, not dense. It took up almost no space. A person could even get used to silence like this, thought Espinoza, and be happy. But he would never get used to it, he knew that too.

When he got tired of sitting he went to a bar and asked for a beer at the counter. Around him there were only men and no one was alone. Espinoza swept the bar with a terrible gaze and immediately he saw that the men were drinking but eating too. He muttered the word *fuck* and spat on the floor, less than an inch from his own shoes. Then he had another beer and went back to the stall with the half-empty bottle. Rebeca looked at him and smiled. Espinoza sat on the sidewalk next to her and told her he was going home. The girl didn't say anything.

"I'll be coming back to Santa Teresa," he said, "in less than a year, I swear."

"Don't swear," said the girl, smiling in a pleased way.

"I'll come back to you," said Espinoza, swallowing the last of his beer. "And maybe we'll get married and you'll come to Madrid with me."

It sounded as if the girl said: that would be nice, but Espinoza couldn't hear her.

"What? What?" he asked.

Rebeca was silent.

•

When he got back that night, Pelletier was reading and drinking whiskey by the pool. Espinoza sat in the deck chair next to him and asked what their plans were. Pelletier smiled and set his book on the table.

"I found your gift in my room," he said, "and it's perfect. Even charming."

"Ah, the serape," said Espinoza, and he let himself fall back on the deck chair.

There were many stars in the sky. The green-blue water of the pool danced on the tables and on the pots of flowers and cacti, in a chain of reflections stretching off to a cream-colored brick wall, behind which lay a tennis court and a sauna that Espinoza had successfully avoided. Every so often the *pock* of a racquet could be heard, and muted voices commenting on the game.

Pelletier stood up and said let's walk. He headed toward the tennis court, followed by Espinoza. The court lights were on and two men with big bellies were struggling through an inept game, making the two women watching them laugh. The women were sitting on a wooden bench, under an umbrella like those around the pool. Beyond them, behind a wire fence, was the sauna, a cement box with two tiny windows like the portholes of a sunken ship. Sitting on the brick wall, Pelletier said:

"We aren't going to find Archimboldi."

"I've known that for days," said Espinoza.

Then he leaped and leaped again until he was sitting on the wall, his legs dangling down toward the tennis court.

"And yet," said Pelletier, "I'm sure Archimboldi is here, in Santa Teresa."

Espinoza looked at his hands, as if he feared he had hurt himself. One of the women got up from her seat and ran onto the court. When she reached one of the men, she said something in his ear and then she ran back off the court. The man she'd spoken to lifted his arms, opened his mouth, and threw back his head, all without making the slightest sound. The other man, dressed just like the first in spotless white, waited until his opponent had finished his silent rejoicing and was calm, and then he tossed the ball. The match started up again and the women laughed some more.

"Believe me," said Pelletier in a very soft voice, like the breeze that was blowing just then, suffusing everything with the scent of flowers, "I know Archimboldi is here."

"Where?" asked Espinoza.

"Somewhere, either in Santa Teresa or else nearby."

"So why haven't we found him?" asked Espinoza.

One of the tennis players fell and Pelletier smiled.

"That doesn't matter. Because we've been clumsy or because Archimboldi is extraordinarily good at self-concealment. It means nothing. The important thing is something else entirely."

"What?" asked Espinoza.

"That he's here," said Pelletier, and he motioned toward the sauna, the hotel, the court, the fence, the dry brush that could be glimpsed in the distance, on the unlit hotel grounds. The hair rose on the back of Espinoza's neck. The cement box where the sauna was looked like a bunker holding a corpse.

"I believe you," he said, and he really did believe what his friend was saying.

"Archimboldi is here," said Pelletier, "and we're here, and this is the closest we'll ever be to him."

•

I don't know how long we'll last together, said Norton in her letter. It doesn't matter to me or to Morini either (I think). We love each other and we're happy. I know the two of you will understand.

2.
THE PART ABOUT AMALFITANO

I don't know what I'm doing in Santa Teresa, Amalfitano said to himself after he'd been living in the city for a week. Don't you? Don't you really? he asked himself. Really I don't, he said to himself, and that was as eloquent as he could be.

•

He had a little single-story house, three bedrooms, a full bathroom and a half bathroom, a combined kitchen–living room–dining room with windows that faced west, a small brick porch where there was a wooden bench worn by the wind that came down from the mountains and the sea, the wind from the north, the wind through the gaps, the wind that smelled like smoke and came from the south. He had books he'd kept for more than twenty-five years. Not many. All of them old. He had books he'd bought in the last ten years, books he didn't mind lending, books that could've been lost or stolen for all he cared. He had books that he sometimes received neatly packaged and with unfamiliar return addresses, books he didn't even open anymore. He had a yard perfect for growing grass and planting flowers, but he didn't know what flowers would do best there—flowers, as opposed to cacti or succulents. There would be time (so he thought) for gardening. He had a wooden gate that needed a coat of paint. He had a monthly salary.

•

He had a daughter named Rosa who had always lived with him. Hard to believe, but true.

•

Sometimes, at night, he remembered Rosa's mother and sometimes he laughed and other times he felt like crying. He thought of her while he was shut in his office with Rosa asleep in her room. The living room was empty and quiet, and the lights were off. Anyone listening carefully on the porch would have heard the whine of a few mosquitoes. But no one was listening. The houses next door were silent and dark.

•

Rosa was seventeen and she was Spanish. Amalfitano was fifty and Chilean. Rosa had had a passport since she was ten. On some of their trips, remembered Amalfitano, they had found themselves in strange situations, because Rosa went through customs by the gate for EU citizens and Amalfitano went by the gate for non-EU citizens. The first time, Rosa threw a tantrum and started to cry and refused to be separated from her father. Another time, since the lines were moving at different speeds, the EU citizens' line quickly and the noncitizens' line more slowly and laboriously, Rosa got lost and it took Amalfitano half an hour to find her. Sometimes the customs officers would see Rosa, so little, and ask whether she was traveling alone or whether someone was waiting for her outside. Rosa would answer that she was traveling with her father, who was South American, and she was supposed to wait for him right there. Once Rosa's suitcase was searched because they suspected her father of smuggling drugs or arms under cover of his daughter's innocence and nationality. But Amalfitano had never trafficked in drugs, or for that matter arms.

•

It was Lola, Rosa's mother, who always traveled with a weapon, never going anywhere without her stainless-steel spring-loaded switchblade, Amalfitano remembered as he smoked a Mexican cigarette, sitting in his office or standing on the dark porch. Once they were stopped in an airport, before Rosa was born, and Lola was asked what she was doing with the knife. It's for peeling fruit, she said. Oranges, apples, pears, kiwis, all kinds of fruit. The officer gave her a long look and let her go. A year and a few months after that, Rosa was born. Two years later, Lola left, still carrying the knife.

•

Lola's pretext was a plan to visit her favorite poet, who lived in the insane asylum in Mondragón, near San Sebastián. Amalfitano listened to her explanations for a whole night as she packed her bag and promised she'd come home soon to him and Rosa. Lola, especially toward the end, used to claim that she knew the poet, that she'd met him at a party in Barcelona before Amalfitano became a part of her life. At this party, which Lola described as a wild party, a long overdue party that suddenly sprang to life in the middle of the summer heat and a traffic jam of cars with red lights on, she had slept with him and they'd made love all night, although Amalfitano knew it wasn't true, not just because the poet was gay, but because Lola had first heard of the poet's existence from him, when he'd given her one of his books. Then Lola took it upon herself to buy everything else the poet had written and to choose friends who thought the poet was a genius, an alien, God's messenger, friends who had themselves just been released from the Sant Boi asylum or had flipped out after repeated stints in rehab. The truth was, Amalfitano knew that sooner or later she would make her way to San Sebastián, so he chose not to argue but offered her part of his savings, begged her to come back in a few months, and promised to take good care of Rosa. Lola seemed not to hear a thing. When she had finished, she went into the kitchen, made coffee, and sat in silence, waiting for dawn, although Amalfitano tried to come up with subjects of conversation that might interest her or at least help pass the time. At six-thirty the doorbell rang and Lola jumped. They've come for me, she said, and since she didn't move, Amalfitano had to get up and ask over the intercom who it was. He heard a weak voice saying it's me. Who is it? asked Amalfitano. Let me in, it's me, said the voice. Who? asked Amalfitano. The voice, while still barely audible, seemed indignant at the interrogation. Me me me me, it said. Amalfitano closed his eyes and buzzed the door open. He heard the sound of the elevator cables and he went back to the kitchen. Lola was still sitting there, sipping the last of her coffee. I think it's for you, said Amalfitano. Lola gave no sign of having heard him. Are you going to say goodbye to Rosa? asked Amalfitano. Lola looked up and said it was better not to wake her. There were dark circles under her blue eyes. Then the doorbell rang twice and Amalfitano went to open the door. A small woman, no more than five feet tall, gave him a brief glance and murmured an unintelligible greeting, then brushed past him and went straight to the kitchen, as if she knew Lola's habits better than Amalfitano did. When he returned to the kitchen he noticed the woman's knapsack, which she had left on the floor by the refrigerator, smaller than Lola's, almost a miniature. The woman's name was Inmaculada, but Lola called her Imma. Amalfitano had encountered her a few times in the apartment when he came home from work, and then the woman had told him her name and what she liked to be called. Imma was short for Immaculada, in Catalan, but Lola's friend wasn't Catalan and her name wasn't Immaculada with a double *m*, either, it was Inmaculada, and Amalfitano, for phonetic reasons, preferred to call her Inma, although each time he did his wife scolded him, until he decided not to call her anything. He watched them from the kitchen door. He felt much calmer than he had expected. Lola and her friend had their eyes fixed on the Formica table, although Amalfitano couldn't help noticing that both looked up now and then and stared at each other with an intensity unfamiliar to him. Lola asked whether anyone wanted more coffee. She means me, thought Amalfitano. Inmaculada shook her head and said there was no time, they should get moving, since before long there would be no way out of Barcelona. She talks as if Barcelona were a medieval city, thought Amalfitano. Lola and her friend stood up. Amalfitano stepped forward and opened the refrigerator door to get a beer, driven by a sudden thirst. To do so, he had to move Imma's backpack. It was so light it might've held just two shirts and another pair of black pants. It's like a fetus, was what Amalfitano thought, and he dropped it to one side. Then Lola kissed him on both cheeks and she and her friend were gone.

•

A week later Amalfitano got a letter from Lola, postmarked Pamplona. In the letter she told him that their trip so far had been full of pleasant and unpleasant experiences. Mostly pleasant. And although the unpleasant experiences could certainly be called unpleasant, *experiences* might not be the right word. Nothing unpleasant that happens to us can take us by surprise, said Lola, because Imma has lived through all of this already. For two days, said Lola, we were working at a roadside restaurant in Lérida, for a man who also owned an apple orchard. It was a big orchard and there were already green apples on the trees. In a little while the apple harvest would begin, and the owner had asked them to stay till then. Imma had gone to talk to him while Lola read a book by the Mondragón poet (she had all the books he'd published so far in her backpack), sitting by the Canadian tent where the two of them slept. The tent was pitched in the shade of a poplar, the only poplar she'd seen in the orchard, next to a garage that no one used anymore. A little while later, Imma came back, and she didn't want to explain the deal the restaurant owner had offered her. The next day they headed back out to the highway to hitchhike, without telling anyone goodbye. In Zaragoza they stayed with an old friend of Imma's from university. Lola was very tired and she went to bed early and in her dreams she heard laughter and loud voices and scolding, almost all Imma's but some her friend's, too. They talked about the old days, about the struggle against Franco, about the women's prison in Zaragoza. They talked about a pit, a very deep hole from which oil or coal could be extracted, about an underground jungle, about a commando team of female suicide bombers. Then Lola's letter took an abrupt turn. I'm not a lesbian, she said, I don't know why I'm telling you this, I don't know why I'm treating you like a child by saying it. Homosexuality is a lie, it's an act of violence committed against us in our adolescence, she said. Imma knows this. She knows it, she knows it, she's too clearsighted not to, but all she can do is help. Imma is a lesbian, every day hundreds of thousands of cows are sacrificed, every day a herd of herbivores or several herds cross the valley, from north to south, so slowly but so fast it makes me sick, right now, now, now, do you understand, Óscar? No, thought Amalfitano, I don't, as he held the letter in his two hands like a life raft of reeds and grasses, and with his foot he steadily rocked his daughter in her seat.

•

Then Lola described again the night when she'd made love with the poet, who lay in majestic and semisecret repose in the Mondragón asylum. He was still free back then, he hadn't yet been committed to any institution. He lived in Barcelona, with a gay philosopher, and they threw parties together once a week or once every two weeks. This was before I knew you. I don't know whether you'd come to Spain yet or whether you were in Italy or France or some filthy Latin American hole. The gay philosopher's parties were famous in Barcelona. People said the poet and the philosopher were lovers, but it never looked that way. One had an apartment and ideas and money, and the other had his legend and his poetry and the fervor of the true believer, a doglike fervor, the fervor of the whipped dog that's spent the night or all its youth in the rain, Spain's endless storm of dandruff, and has finally found a place to lay its head, no matter if it's a bucket of putrid water, a vaguely familiar bucket of water. One day fortune smiled on me and I attended one of these parties. To say I met the philosopher would be an exaggeration. I saw him. In a corner of the room, talking to another poet and another philosopher. He appeared to be giving a lecture. Then everything seemed slightly off. The guests were waiting for the poet to make his entrance. They were waiting for him to pick a fight. Or to defecate in the middle of the living room, on a Turkish carpet like the threadbare carpet from the *Thousand and One Nights*, a battered carpet that sometimes functioned as a mirror, reflecting all of us from below. I mean: it turned into a mirror at the command of our spasms. Neurochemical spasms. When the poet showed up, though, nothing happened. At first all eyes turned to him, to see what could be had. Then everybody went back to what they'd been doing and the poet said hello to certain writer friends and joined the group around the gay philosopher. I had been dancing with myself and I kept dancing with myself. At five in the morning I went into one of the bedrooms. The poet was leading me by the hand. Without getting undressed, I began to make love with him. I came three times, feeling the poet's breath on my neck. It took him quite a while longer. In the semidarkness I made out three shadowy figures in a corner of the room. One of them was smoking. Another one never stopped whispering. The third was the philosopher and I realized that the bed was his and the room was the room where, the gossip was, he and the poet made love. But now I was the one making love and the poet was gentle with me and the only thing I didn't understand was why the other three were watching, although I didn't much care, in those days, if you remember, nothing really mattered. When the poet finally came, crying out and turning his head to look at his three friends, I was sorry it wasn't the right time of month, because I would've loved to have his baby. Then he got up and went over to the shadowy figures. One of them put a hand on his shoulder. Another one gave him something. I got up and went to the bathroom without even looking at them. The last party guests were in the living room. In the bathroom, a girl was asleep in the tub. I washed my face and hands. I combed my hair. When I came out the philosopher was kicking everyone out who could still walk. He didn't look the least bit drunk or high. He looked fresh, as if he'd just got up and drunk a big glass of orange juice. I left with a couple of people I'd met at the party. At that hour only the Drugstore on Las Ramblas was open and we headed there without a word. At the Drugstore I ran into a girl I'd known a few years before who was a reporter for *Ajoblanco*, although it disgusted her to work there. She started to talk to me about moving to Madrid. She asked if I felt like I needed a change. I shrugged my shoulders. All cities are more or less the same, I said. What I was really thinking about was the poet and what he and I had just done. A gay man doesn't do that. Everyone said he was gay, but I knew it wasn't true. Then I thought about the confusion of the senses and I understood everything. I knew the poet had lost his way, he was a lost child and I could save him, give him back a small part of all he'd given me. For almost a month I kept watch outside the philosopher's building hoping one day I'd see the poet and he'd ask me to make love with him again. I didn't see him, but one night I saw the philosopher. I noticed that something was wrong with his face. When he got closer (he didn't recognize me) I could see he had a black eye and was covered in bruises. No sign of the poet. Sometimes I tried to guess, by the lights, what floor the apartment was on. Sometimes I saw shadows behind the curtains. Sometimes someone, an older woman, a man in a tie, a long-faced adolescent, would open a window and look out at the grid of Barcelona at dusk. One night I discovered I wasn't the only one there, spying on the poet or waiting for him to appear. A kid, maybe eighteen, maybe younger, was quietly keeping watch from the opposite sidewalk. He hadn't noticed me because clearly he was the heedless type, a dreamer. He would sit at a bar, at an outside table, and he always ordered a can of Coca-Cola, sipping it slowly as he wrote in a school notebook or read books that I recognized at a glance. One night, before he could get up from the table and dash away, I went over and sat down next to him. I told him I knew what he was doing. Who are you? he asked me, terrified. I smiled and said I was someone like him. He looked at me the way you look at a crazy person. Don't get the wrong idea, I said, I'm not crazy, I'm in full possession of my faculties. He laughed. You look crazy, he said, even if you aren't. Then he motioned for the check and he was about to get up when I confessed that I was looking for the poet, too. He sat down again abruptly, as if I'd clapped a gun to his head. I ordered a chamomile tea and told him my story. He told me that he wrote poetry, too, and he wanted the poet to read his poems. There was no need to ask to know that he was gay and very lonely. Let me see them, I said, and I pulled the notebook out of his hands. His poems weren't bad. His only problem was that he wrote just like the poet. These things can't have happened to you, I said, you're too young to have suffered this much. He made a gesture as if to say that he didn't care whether I believed him or not. What matters is that it's well written, he said. No, I told him, you know that isn't what matters. Wrong, wrong, wrong, I said, and finally he had to cede the point. His name was Jordi and today he may be teaching at the university or writing reviews for *La Vanguardia* or *El Periódico*.

·

Amalfitano received the next letter from San Sebastián. In it, Lola told him that she'd gone with Imma to the asylum at Mondragón to visit the poet, who lived there, raving and demented, and that the guards, priests disguised as security guards, wouldn't let them in. In San Sebastián they had plans to stay with a friend of Imma's, a Basque girl named Edurne, who had been an ETA commando and had given up the armed struggle when democracy came, and who didn't want them in her house for more than one night, saying she had lots to do and her husband didn't like unexpected guests. Her husband's name was Jon, and guests really did make him nervous, as Lola had opportunity to observe. He shook, he flushed as red as a glowing clay pot, he always seemed about to burst out shouting although he never spoke a word, he was sweaty and his hands shook, he was constantly moving, as if he couldn't sit still for two minutes at a time. Edurne herself was very relaxed. She had a little boy (though Lola and Imma never saw him, because Jon always found a reason to keep them out of his room) and she worked almost full-time as a street educator, with junkie families and the street people who huddled on the steps of the cathedral of San Sebastián and only wanted to be left alone, as Edurne explained, laughing, as if she'd just told a joke that only Imma understood, because neither Lola nor Jon laughed. That night they had dinner together and the next day they left. They found a cheap boardinghouse that Edurne had told them about and they hitchhiked back to Mondragón. They weren't allowed into the asylum this time either, but they settled for studying it from the outside, noting and committing to memory all the dirt and gravel roads they could see, the gray walls, the rises and curves of the land, the walks taken by the inmates and their caretakers, whom they watched from a distance, the curtains of trees following one after the other at unpredictable intervals or in a pattern they didn't understand, and the brush where they thought they saw flies, by which they deduced that some of the inmates and maybe even a worker or two urinated there in the dark or as night fell. Then they sat together by the side of the road and ate the cheese sandwiches they'd brought from San Sebastián, without talking, or musing as if to themselves on the fractured shadows that the asylum of Mondragón cast over its surroundings.

•

For their third try, they called to make an appointment. Imma passed herself off as a reporter from a Barcelona newspaper and Lola claimed to be a poet. This time they got to see him. Lola thought he looked older, his eyes sunken, his hair thinner than before. At first they were accompanied by a doctor or priest, who led them down the endless corridors, painted blue and white, until they came to a nondescript room where the poet was waiting. It was Lola's impression that the asylum people were proud to have him as a patient. All of them knew him, all of them greeted him as he headed to the garden or went to receive his daily dose of tranquilizers. When they were alone she told him that she'd missed him, that for a while she'd kept watch over the philosopher's apartment in the Ensanche, and that despite her perseverance she'd never seen him again. It's not my fault, she said, I did everything I could. The poet looked her in the eyes and asked for a cigarette. Imma was standing next to the bench where they were sitting and wordlessly she handed him a cigarette. The poet said thank you and then he said perseverance. I was, I was, I was, said Lola, who was turned toward him, her gaze fixed on him, although out of the corner of her eye she saw that Imma, after flicking her lighter, had taken a book out of her bag and begun to read, standing there like a tiny and infinitely patient Amazon, the lighter still visible in one of her hands as she held the book. Then Lola started to talk about the trip they had made together. She spoke of highways and back roads, problems with chauvinist truck drivers, cities and towns, nameless forests where they had pitched camp, rivers and gas station bathrooms where they had washed. The poet, meanwhile, blew smoke out of his mouth and nose, making perfect rings, bluish nimbuses, gray cumulonimbuses that dissolved in the park breeze or were carried off toward the edge of the grounds where a dark forest rose, the branches of the trees silver in the light falling from the hills. As if to gain time, Lola described the two previous visits, fruitless but eventful. And then she told him what she had really come to say: that she knew he wasn't gay, she knew he was a prisoner and wanted to escape, she knew that love, no matter how mistreated or mutilated, always left room for hope, and that hope was her plan (or the other way around), and that its materialization, its objectification, consisted of his fleeing the asylum with her and heading for France. What about her? asked the poet, who was taking sixteen pills a day and recording his visions, and he pointed at Imma, who read on undaunted, still standing, as if her skirts and underskirts were made of concrete and she couldn't sit down. She'll help us, said Lola. In fact, the plan was hers in the first place. We'll cross into France over the mountains, like pilgrims. We'll make our way to Saint-Jean-de-Luz and take the train to Paris, traveling through the countryside, which is the prettiest in the world at this time of year. We'll live in hostels. That's Imma's plan. She and I will work cleaning or taking care of children in the wealthy neighborhoods of Paris while you write poetry. At night you'll read us your poems and make love to me. That's Imma's plan, worked out to the last detail. After three or four months I'll be pregnant, and that will prove for once and for all that you aren't a nonbreeder, the last of your line. What more can our enemy families want! I'll keep working a few more months, but when the time comes, Imma will have to work twice as hard. We'll live like mendicants or child prophets while Paris trains a distant eye on fashion, movies, games of chance, French and American literature, gastronomy, the gross domestic product, arms exports, the manufacture of massive batches of anesthesia, all mere backdrop for our fetus's first few months. Then, when I'm six months pregnant, we'll go back to Spain, though this time we won't cross over at Irún but at La Jonquera or Port Bou, into Catalan country. The poet looked at her with interest (and also at Imma, who never took her eyes off his poems, poems he'd written perhaps five years ago, he thought), and he began to blow smoke rings again, in the most unlikely shapes, as if he'd spent his long stay in Mondragón perfecting that peculiar art. How do you do it? asked Lola. With the tongue, and by pursing the lips a certain way, he said. Sometimes by making a kind of fluted shape. Sometimes like someone who's burned himself. Sometimes like sucking a small to medium dick. Sometimes like shooting a Zen arrow with a Zen bow into a Zen pavilion. Ah, I understand, said Lola. You, read a poem, said the poet. Imma looked at him and raised the book a little higher, as if she was trying to hide behind it. Which poem? Whichever one you like best, said the poet. I like them all, said Imma. So read one, said the poet. When Imma had finished reading a poem about a labyrinth and Ariadne lost in the labyrinth and a young Spaniard who lived in a Paris garret, the poet asked if they had any chocolate. No, said Lola. We don't smoke these days, said Imma, we're focusing all our efforts on getting you out of here. The poet smiled. I didn't mean that kind of chocolate, he said, I meant the other kind, the kind made with cocoa and milk and sugar. Oh, I see, said Lola, and they both were forced to admit they hadn't brought anything like that either. They remembered that they had cheese sandwiches in their bags, wrapped in napkins and aluminum foil, and they offered them to him, but the poet seemed not to hear. Before it began to get dark, a flock of big blackbirds flew over the park, vanishing northward. A doctor approached along the gravel path, his white robe flapping in the evening breeze. When he reached them he asked the poet how he felt, calling him by his first name as if they'd been friends since adolescence. The poet gave him a blank look, and, calling him by his first name too, said he was a little tired. The doctor, whose name was Gorka and who couldn't have been more than thirty, sat down beside him and put a hand on his forehead, then took his pulse. You're doing fucking great, man, he said. And how are the ladies? he asked, with a smile full of health and cheer. Imma didn't answer. Lola had the sense that Imma was dying behind her book. Just fine, she said, it's been a while since we saw each other and we're having a wonderful time. So you knew each other already? asked the doctor. Not me, said Imma, and she turned the page. I knew him, said Lola, we were friends a few years ago, in Barcelona, when he lived in Barcelona. In fact, she said, looking up at the last blackbirds, the stragglers, taking flight just as someone turned on the park lights from a hidden switch in the asylum, we were more than friends. How interesting, said Gorka, his eyes on the birds, which at that time of day and in the artificial light had a burnished glow. What year was that? asked the doctor. It was 1979 or 1978, I can't remember now, said Lola in a faint voice. I hope you won't think I'm indiscreet, said the doctor, but I'm writing a biography of our friend and the more information I can gather on his life, the better, wouldn't you say? Someday he'll leave here, said Gorka, smoothing his eyebrows, someday the Spanish public will have to recognize him as one of the greats, I don't mean they'll give him a prize, hardly, no Príncipe de Asturias or Cervantes for him, let alone a seat in the Academy, literary careers in Spain are for social climbers, operators, and ass kissers, if you'll pardon the expression. But someday he'll leave here. There's no question about that. Someday I'll leave, too. And so will my patients and my colleagues' patients. Someday all of us will finally leave Mondragón, and this noble institution, ecclesiastical in origin, charitable in aim, will stand abandoned. Then my biography will be of interest and I'll be able to publish it, but in the meantime, as you can imagine, it's my duty to collect information, dates, names, confirm stories, some in questionable taste, even damaging, others more picturesque, stories that revolve around a chaotic center of gravity, which is our friend here, or what he's willing to reveal, the ordered self he presents, ordered verbally, I mean, according to a strategy I think I understand, although its purpose is a mystery to me, an order concealing a verbal disorder that would shake us to the core if ever we were to experience it, even as spectators of a staged performance. Doctor, you're a sweetheart, said Lola. Imma ground her teeth. Then Lola began to tell Gorka about her heterosexual experience with the poet, but her friend sidled over and kicked her in the ankle with the pointed toe of her shoe. Just then, the poet, who had begun to blow smoke rings again, remembered the apartment in Barcelona's Ensanche and remembered the philosopher, and although his eyes didn't light up, part of his bone structure did: the jaws, the chin, the hollow cheeks, as if he'd been lost in the Amazon and three Sevillian friars had rescued him, or a monstrous three-headed friar, which held no terror for him either. So, turning to Lola, he asked her about the philosopher, said the philosopher's name, talked about his stay in the philosopher's apartment, the months he'd spent in Barcelona with no job, playing stupid jokes, throwing books that he hadn't bought out the window (as the philosopher ran down the stairs to retrieve them, which wasn't always possible), playing loud music, practically never sleeping and laughing all the time, taking the occasional assignment as a translator or lead reviewer, a liquid star of boiling water. And then Lola was afraid and she covered her face with her hands. And Imma, who had at last put the book of poems away in her pocket, did the same, covering her face with her small, knotty hands. And Gorka looked from the two women to the poet and laughter bubbled up inside him. But before the laughter could fade in his placid heart, Lola said the philosopher had recently died of AIDS. Well, well,

well, said the poet. He who laughs last, laughs best, said the poet. The early bird doesn't always catch the worm, the poet said. I love you, said Lola. The poet got up and asked Imma for another cigarette. For tomorrow, he said. The doctor and the poet made their way down one path toward the asylum. Lola and Imma took a different path toward the gate, where they ran into the sister of another lunatic and the son of a laborer, also mad, and a woman with a sorrowful look whose cousin was interned in the asylum.

•

They returned the next day but were told that the patient was on bedrest. The same thing happened the following days. One day their money ran out, and Imma decided to take to the road again, this time heading south, to Madrid, where she had a brother who had done well for himself under the democracy and whom she planned to ask for a loan. Lola didn't have the strength to travel and the two women agreed that she should wait at the boardinghouse, as if nothing had happened, and Imma would be back in a week. Alone, Lola killed time writing long letters to Amalfitano in which she described her daily life in San Sebastián and the area around the asylum, which she visited every day. Clinging to the fence, she imagined that she was establishing telepathic contact with the poet. Most of the time she would find a clearing in the nearby woods and read or pick little flowers and bunches of grasses with which she made bouquets that she dropped through the railings or took back to the boardinghouse. Once one of the drivers who picked her up on the highway asked if she wanted to see the Mondragón cemetery and she said she did. He parked the car outside, under an acacia tree, and for a while they walked among the graves, most of them with Basque names, until they came to the niche where the driver's mother was buried. Then he told Lola that he'd like to fuck her right there. Lola laughed and warned him that they would be in plain view of any visitor coming along the cemetery's main path. The driver thought for a few seconds, then he said: Christ, you're right. They went looking for a more private spot and it was all over in less than fifteen minutes. The driver's last name was Larrazábal, and although he had a first name, he didn't want to tell her what it was. Just Larrazábal, like my friends call me, he said. Then he told Lola that this wasn't the first time he'd made love in the cemetery. He'd been there with a sort-of girlfriend before, with a girl

175

he'd met at a club, and with two prostitutes from San Sebastián. As they were leaving, he tried to give her money, but she wouldn't take it. They talked for a long time in the car. Larrazábal asked her whether she had a relative at the asylum, and Lola told him her story. Larrazábal said he'd never read a poem. He added that he didn't understand Lola's obsession with the poet. I don't understand your fascination with fucking in the cemetery either, said Lola, but I don't judge you for it. True, Larrazábal admitted, everyone's got obsessions. Before Lola got out of the car, at the entrance to the asylum, Larrazábal snuck a five-thousand-peseta note into her pocket. Lola noticed but didn't say anything and then she was left alone under the trees, in front of the iron gate to the madhouse, home to the poet who was supremely ignoring her.

●

After a week Imma still wasn't back. Lola imagined her tiny, impassively staring, with her face like an educated peasant's or a high school teacher's looking out over a vast prehistoric field, a woman near fifty, dressed in black, walking without looking to either side, without looking back, through a valley where it was still possible to distinguish the tracks of the great predators from the tracks of the scurrying herbivores. She imagined her stopped at a crossroads as the trucks with their many tons of cargo passed at full speed, raising dust clouds that didn't touch her, as if her hesitance and vulnerability constituted a state of grace, a dome that protected her from the inclemencies of fate, nature, and her fellow beings. On the ninth day the owner of the boardinghouse kicked her out. After that she slept at the railroad station, or in an abandoned warehouse where some tramps slept, each keeping to himself, or in the open country, near the border between the asylum and the outside world. One night she hitchhiked to the cemetery and slept in an empty niche. The next morning she felt happy and lucky and she decided to wait there for Imma to come back. She had water to drink and wash her face and brush her teeth, she was near the asylum, it was a peaceful spot. One afternoon, as she was laying a shirt that she had just washed out to dry on a white slab propped against the cemetery wall, she heard voices coming from a mausoleum, and she went to see what was happening. The mausoleum belonged to the Lagasca family, and judging by the state it was in, the last of the Lagascas had long since died or moved far away. Inside the crypt she saw the beam of a flashlight and she asked who was there.

Christ, it's you, she heard a voice say inside. She thought it might be thieves or workers restoring the mausoleum or grave robbers, then she heard a kind of meow and when she was about to turn away she saw Larrazábal's sallow face at the barred door of the crypt. Then a woman came out. Larrazábal ordered her to wait for him by his car, and for a while he and Lola talked and strolled arm in arm along the cemetery paths until the sun began to drop behind the worn edges of the niches.

•

Madness is contagious, thought Amalfitano, sitting on the floor of his front porch as the sky grew suddenly overcast and the moon and the stars disappeared, along with the ghostly lights that are famously visible without binoculars or telescope in northern Sonora and southern Arizona.

•

Madness really is contagious, and friends are a blessing, especially when you're on your own. It was in these words, years before, in a letter with no postmark, that Lola had told Amalfitano about her chance encounter with Larrazábal, which ended with him forcing her to accept a loan of ten thousand pesetas and promising to come back the next day, before he got in his car, motioning to the prostitute who was waiting impatiently for him to do the same. That night Lola slept in her niche, although she was tempted to try the open crypt, happy because things were looking up. The next morning, she scrubbed herself all over with a wet rag, brushed her teeth, combed her hair, put on clean clothes, then went out to the highway to hitchhike to Mondragón. In town she bought some goat cheese and bread and had breakfast in the square, hungrily, since she honestly couldn't remember the last time she'd eaten. Then she went into a bar full of construction workers and had coffee. She'd forgotten when Larrazábal had said he'd come to the cemetery, but that didn't matter, and in the same distant way, Larrazábal and the cemetery and the town and the tremulous early morning landscape didn't matter to her either. Before she left the bar she went into the bathroom and looked at herself in the mirror. She walked back to the highway and stood there waiting until a woman stopped and asked where she was going. To the asylum, said Lola. Her reply clearly took the woman aback, but she told her to get in nevertheless. That's where she was going. Are you visiting someone or are you an inmate? she asked Lola. I'm visiting, answered Lola. The woman's face was thin and long, her almost nonexistent lips giving her a cold, calculating look, although she had nice cheekbones and she dressed like a professional woman who is no longer single, who has a house, a husband, maybe even a child to care for. My father is there, she confessed. Lola didn't say anything. When they reached the entrance, Lola got out of the car and the woman went on alone. For a while Lola wandered along the edge of the asylum grounds. She heard the sound of horses and she guessed that somewhere, on the other side of the woods, there must be a riding club or school. At a certain point she spotted the red-tiled roof of a house that wasn't part of the asylum. She retraced her steps. She returned to the section of fence that gave the best view of the grounds. As the sun rose higher in the sky she saw a tight knot of patients emerge from a slate outbuilding, then they scattered to the benches in the park and lit cigarettes. She thought she saw the poet. He was with two inmates and he was wearing jeans and a very tight white T-shirt. She waved to him, shyly at first, as if her arms were stiff from the cold, then openly, tracing strange patterns in the still-cold air, trying to give her signals a laserlike urgency, trying to transmit telepathic messages in his direction. Five minutes later, she watched as the poet got up from his bench and one of the lunatics kicked him in the legs. With an effort she resisted the urge to scream. The poet turned around and kicked back. The lunatic, who was sitting down again, took it in the chest and dropped like a little bird. The inmate smoking next to him got up and chased the poet for thirty feet, aiming kicks at his ass and throwing punches at his back. Then he returned calmly to his seat, where the other inmate had revived and was rubbing his chest, neck, and head, which anyone would call excessive, since he had been kicked only in the chest. At that moment Lola stopped signaling. One of the lunatics on the bench began to masturbate. The other one, the one in exaggerated pain, felt in one of his pockets and pulled out a cigarette. The poet approached them. Lola thought she heard his laugh. An ironic laugh, as if he were saying: boys, you can't take a joke. But maybe the poet wasn't laughing. Maybe, Lola said in her letter to Amalfitano, it was my madness that was laughing. In any case, whether it was her madness or not, the poet went over to the other two and said something to them. Neither of the lunatics answered. Lola saw them: they were looking down, at the life throbbing at ground level, between the blades of grass and under the loose clumps of dirt. A blind life in which everything had the transparency of water. The poet, however, must have scanned the faces of his companions in misfortune, first one and then the other, looking for a sign that would tell him whether it was safe for him to sit down on the bench again. Which he finally did. He raised his hand in a gesture of truce or surrender and he sat between the other two. He raised his hand the way someone might raise a tattered flag. He moved his fingers, each finger, as if his fingers were a flag in flames, the flag of the unvanquished. And he sat between them and then he looked at the one who was masturbating and said something into his ear. This time Lola couldn't hear him but she saw clearly how the poet's left hand groped its way into the other inmate's robe. And then she watched the three of them smoke. And she watched the artful spirals issuing from the poet's mouth and nose.

•

The next and final letter Amalfitano received from his wife wasn't postmarked but the stamps were French. In it Lola recounted a conversation with Larrazábal. Christ, you're lucky, said Larrazábal, my whole life I've wanted to live in a cemetery, and look at you, the minute you get here, you move right in. A good person, Larrazábal. He invited her to stay at his apartment. He offered to drive her each morning to the Mondragón asylum, where Spain's greatest and most self-deluding poet was studying osteology. He offered her money without asking for anything in return. One night he took her to the movies. Another night he went with her to the boardinghouse to ask whether there was any word from Imma. Once, late one Saturday night, after they'd made love for hours, he proposed to her and he didn't feel offended or stupid when Lola reminded him that she was already married. A good person, Larrazábal. He bought her a skirt at a little street fair and he bought her some brand-name jeans at a store in downtown San Sebastián. He talked to her about his mother, whom he'd loved dearly, and about his siblings, to whom he wasn't close. None of this had much of an effect on Lola, or rather it did, but not in the way he had hoped. For her, those days were like a prolonged parachute landing after a long space flight. She went to Mondragón once every three days now, instead of once a day, and she looked through the fence with no hope at all of seeing the poet, seeking at most some sign, a sign that she knew beforehand she would never understand or that she would understand only many years later, when none of it mattered anymore. Sometimes, without calling first or leaving a note, she wouldn't sleep at Larrazábal's apartment and he would go looking for her at the cemetery, the asylum, the old boardinghouse where she'd stayed, the places where the tramps and transients of San Sebastián gathered. Once he found her in the waiting room of the train station. Another time he found her sitting on a seafront bench at La Concha, at an hour when the only people out walking were two opposite types: those running out of time and those with time to burn. In the morning it was Larrazábal who made breakfast. At night, when he came home from work, he was the one who made dinner. During the day Lola drank only water, lots of it, and ate a little piece of bread or a roll small enough to fit in her pocket, which she would buy at the corner bakery before she went roaming. One night, as they were showering, she told Larrazábal that she was planning to leave and asked him for money for the train. I'll give you everything I've got, he answered, but I can't give you money to go away so I never see you again. Lola didn't insist. Somehow, though she didn't tell Amalfitano how she did it, she scraped together just enough money for a ticket, and one day at noon she took the train to France. She was in Bayonne for a while. She left for Landes. She returned to Bayonne. She was in Pau and in Lourdes. One morning she saw a train full of sick people, paralyzed people, adolescents with cerebral palsy, farmers with skin cancer, terminally ill Castilian bureaucrats, polite old ladies dressed like Carmelite nuns, people with rashes, blind children, and without knowing how she began to help them, as if she were a nun in jeans stationed there by the church to aid and direct the desperate, who one by one got on buses parked outside the train station or waited in long lines as if each person were a scale on a giant and old and cruel but vigorous snake. Then trains came from Italy and from the north of France, and Lola went back and forth like a sleepwalker, her big blue eyes unblinking, moving slowly, since the weariness of her days was beginning to weigh on her, and she was permitted entry to every part of the station, some rooms converted into first aid posts, others into resuscitation posts, and just one, discreetly located, converted into an improvised morgue for the bodies of those whose strength hadn't been equal to the accelerated wear and tear of the train trip. At night she slept in the most modern building in Lourdes, a functionalist monster of steel and glass that buried its head, bristling with antennas, in the white clouds that floated down from the north, big and sorrowful, or marched from the west like a ragtag army whose only strength was its numbers, or dropped down from the Pyrenees like the ghosts of dead beasts. There she would sleep in the trash compartments, which she entered through a tiny door. Other times she would stay at the station, at the station bar, when the chaos of the trains subsided, and let the old men buy her coffee and talk to her about movies and crops. One afternoon she thought she saw Imma get off the train from Madrid escorted by a troop of cripples. She was the same height as Imma, she was wearing long black skirts like Imma, her doleful Castilian nun's face was just like Imma's face. Lola sat still until she had gone by and didn't call out to her, and five minutes later she elbowed her way out of the Lourdes station and the town of Lourdes and walked to the highway and only then did she try to thumb a ride.

•

For five years, Amalfitano had no news of Lola. One afternoon, when he was at the playground with his daughter, he saw a woman leaning against the wooden fence that separated the playground from the rest of the park. He thought she looked like Imma and he followed her gaze and was relieved to discover that it was another child who had attracted her madwoman's attention. The boy was wearing shorts and was a little older than Amalfitano's daughter, and he had dark, very silky hair that kept falling in his face. Between the fence and the benches that the city had put there so parents could sit and watch their children, a hedge struggled to grow, reaching all the way to an old oak tree outside the playground. Imma's hand, her hard, gnarled hand, roughened by the sun and icy rivers, stroked the freshly clipped top of the hedge as one might stroke a dog's back. Next to her was a big plastic bag. Amalfitano walked toward her, willing himself futilely to be calm. His daughter was in line for the slide. Suddenly, before he could speak to Imma, Amalfitano saw that the boy had at last noticed her watchful presence, and once he had brushed a lock of hair out of his eyes he raised his right arm and waved to her several times. Then Imma, as if this were the sign she'd been waiting for, silently raised her left arm, waved, and went walking out of the park through the north gate, which led onto a busy street.

•

Five years after she left, Amalfitano heard from Lola again. The letter was short and came from Paris. In it Lola told him that she had a job cleaning big office buildings. It was a night job that started at ten and ended at four or five or six in the morning. Paris was pretty then, like all big cities when everyone is asleep. She would take the metro home. The metro at that hour was the saddest thing in the world. She'd had another child, a son, named Benoît, with whom she lived. She'd also been in the hospital. She didn't say why, or whether she was still sick. She didn't mention any man. She didn't ask about Rosa. For her it's as if Rosa doesn't exist, thought Amalfitano, but then it struck him that this might not be the case at all. He cried for a while with the letter in his hands. It was only as he was drying his eyes that he noticed the letter was typed. He knew, without a doubt, that Lola had written it from one of the offices she said she cleaned. For a second he thought it was all a lie, that Lola was working as an administrative assistant or secretary in some big company. Then he saw it clearly. He saw the vacuum cleaner parked between two rows of desks, saw the floor waxer like a cross between a mastiff and a pig sitting next to a plant, he saw an enormous window through which the lights of Paris blinked, he saw Lola in the cleaning company's smock, a worn blue smock, sitting writing the letter and maybe taking slow drags on a cigarette, he saw Lola's fingers, Lola's wrists, Lola's blank eyes, he saw another Lola reflected in the quicksilver of the window, floating weightless in the skies of Paris, like a trick photograph that isn't a trick, floating, floating pensively in the skies of Paris, weary, sending messages from the coldest, iciest realm of passion.

•

Two years after she sent this last letter, seven years after she'd abandoned Amalfitano and her daughter, Lola came home and found them gone. She spent three weeks asking around at old addresses for her husband's whereabouts. Some people didn't let her in, because they couldn't figure out who she was or they had forgotten her long ago. Others kept her standing in the doorway, because they didn't trust her or because Lola had simply got the address wrong. A few asked her in and offered her a cup of coffee or tea that Lola never accepted, since she was apparently in a hurry to see her daughter and Amalfitano. At first the search was discouraging and unreal. She talked to people even she had forgotten. At night she slept in a boardinghouse near Las Ramblas, where foreign workers crammed into tiny rooms. She found the city changed but she couldn't say what exactly was different. In the afternoons, after walking all day, she would sit on the steps of a church to rest and listen to the conversations of the people going in and out, mostly tourists. She read books in French about Greece or witchcraft or healthy living. Sometimes she felt like Electra, daughter of Agamemnon and Clytemnestra, wandering in disguise through Mycenae, the killer mingling with the plebes, the masses, the killer whose mind no one understands, not even the FBI special agents or the charitable people who dropped coins in her hands. Other times she saw herself as the mother of Medon and Strophius, a happy mother who watches her children play from the window while behind them the blue sky struggles in the white arms of the Mediterranean. She whispered: Pylades, Orestes, and those two names stood in her mind for the faces of many men, except Amalfitano's, the face of the man she was looking for now. One night she met an ex-student of her husband's, who recognized her at once, as if in his university days he had been in love with her. The ex-student took her home, told her she could stay as long as she wanted, fixed up the guest room for her exclusive use. The second night, as they were having dinner together, the ex-student embraced her and she let him embrace her for a few seconds, as if she needed him too, and then she said something into his ear and the ex-student moved away and went to sit on the floor in a corner of the living room. They were like that for hours, she sitting in her chair and he sitting on the floor, which was a very odd parquet, dark yellow, so that it looked more like a tightly woven straw rug. The candles on the table went out and only then did she go and sit in the living room, in the opposite corner. In the dark she thought she heard faint sobs. She supposed the young man was crying and she fell asleep, lulled by his weeping. For the next few days she and the ex-student redoubled their efforts. When she saw Amalfitano at last she didn't recognize him. He was fatter than before and he'd lost some of his hair. She spotted him from a distance and didn't hesitate for a second as she approached him. Amalfitano was sitting under a larch and smoking with an absent look on his face. You've changed a lot, she said. Amalfitano recognized her instantly. You haven't, he said. Thank you, she said. Then Amalfitano stood up and they left.

•

In those days, Amalfitano was living in Sant Cugat and teaching philosophy classes at Barcelona's Universidad Autónoma, not far away. Rosa went to a public elementary school in town and left at eight-thirty in the morning and didn't come home until five. Lola saw Rosa and told her she was her mother. Rosa screamed and hugged her and then almost immediately ran away to hide in her bedroom. That night, after showering and making up her bed on the sofa, Lola told Amalfitano that she was very sick, she would probably die, and she had wanted to see Rosa one last time. Amalfitano offered to take her to the hospital the next day, but Lola refused, saying French doctors had always been better than Spanish doctors, and she took some papers out of her bag that stated in no uncertain terms and in French that she had AIDS. The next day, when he got back from the university, Amalfitano spotted Lola and Rosa walking near the station holding hands. He didn't want to disturb them and he followed them from a distance. When he got home they were sitting together watching TV. Later, when Rosa was asleep, he asked Lola about her son Benoît. For a while she was silent, recalling with near photographic memory each part of her son's body, each gesture, each expression of astonishment or surprise, then she said that Benoît was an intelligent and sensitive boy, and that he had been the first to know she was going to die. Amalfitano asked her who had told him, although he thought, with resignation, that he knew the answer. He realized it without anyone telling him, said Lola, just by looking. It's terrible for a child to know his mother is going to die, said Amalfitano. It's worse to lie to them, children should never be lied to, said Lola. On her fifth morning with them, when the medicine she had brought with her from France was about to run out, Lola told them she had to leave. Benoît is little and he needs me, she said. Actually, he doesn't need me, but that doesn't mean he isn't little, she said. I don't know who needs who, she said at last, but the fact is I have to go see how he is. Amalfitano left a note on the table and an envelope containing a good part of his savings. When he got back from work he thought Lola would be gone. He picked Rosa up at school and they walked home. When they got there Lola was sitting in front of the TV, which was on but with the sound off, reading her book on Greece. They had dinner together. Rosa went to bed near midnight. Amalfitano took her to her bedroom, undressed her, and tucked her in. Lola was waiting for him in the living room, with her suitcase packed. You should stay the night, said Amalfitano. It's too late to go. There aren't any more trains to Barcelona, he lied. I'm not taking the train, said Lola. I'm going to hitchhike. Amalfitano bowed his head and said she could go whenever she wanted. Lola gave him a kiss on the cheek and left. The next day Amalfitano got up at six and turned on the radio, to make sure no hitchhiker on any highway nearby had been murdered or raped. Nothing.

•

And yet this vision of Lola lingered in his mind for many years, like a memory rising up from glacial seas, although in fact he hadn't seen anything, which meant there was nothing to remember, only the shadow of his ex-wife projected on the neighboring buildings in the beam of the streetlights, and then the dream: Lola walking off down one of the highways out of Sant Cugat, walking along the side of the road, an almost deserted road since most cars took the new toll highway to save time, a woman bowed by the weight of her suitcase, fearless, walking fearlessly along the side of the road.

•

The University of Santa Teresa was like a cemetery that suddenly begins to think, in vain. It also was like an empty dance club.

•

One afternoon Amalfitano went into the yard in his shirtsleeves, like a feudal lord riding out on horseback to survey his lands. The moment before, he'd been sitting on the floor of his study opening boxes of books with a kitchen knife, and in one of the boxes he'd found a strange book, a book he didn't remember ever buying or receiving as a gift. The book was Rafael Dieste's *Testamento geométrico*, published by Ediciones del Castro in La Coruña, in 1975, a book evidently about geometry, a subject that meant next to nothing to Amalfitano, divided into three parts, the first an "Introduction to Euclid, Lobachevsky and Riemann," the second concerning "The Geometry of Motion," and the third titled "Three Proofs of the V Postulate." This last was the most enigmatic by far since Amalfitano had no idea what the V Postulate was or what it consisted of, nor did he mean to find out, although this was probably owing not to a lack of curiosity, of which he possessed an ample supply, but to the heat that swept Santa Teresa in the afternoons, the dry, dusty heat of a bitter sun, inescapable unless you lived in a new apartment with air-conditioning, which Amalfitano didn't. The publication of the book had been made possible thanks to the support of some friends of the author, friends who'd been immortalized, in a photograph that looked as if it was taken at the end of a party, on page 4, where the publisher's information usually appears. What it said there was: *The present edition is offered as a tribute to Rafael Dieste by: Ramón BALTAR DOMÍNGUEZ, Isaac DÍAZ PARDO, Felipe FERNÁNDEZ ARMESTO, Francisco FERNÁNDEZ DEL RIEGO, Álvaro GIL VARELA, Domingo GARCÍA-SABELL, Valentín PAZ-ANDRADE and Luis SEOANE LÓPEZ.* It struck Amalfitano as odd, to say the least, that the friends' last names had been printed in capitals while the name of the man being honored was in small letters. On the front flap, the reader was informed that the *Testamento geométrico* was really three books, "each independent, but functionally correlated by the sweep of the whole," and then it said "this work representing the final distillation of Dieste's reflections and research on Space, the notion of which is involved in any methodical discussion of the fundamentals of Geometry." At that moment, Amalfitano thought he remembered that Rafael Dieste was a poet. A Galician poet, of course, or long settled in Galicia. And his friends and patrons were also Galician, naturally, or long settled in Galicia, where Dieste probably gave classes at the University of La Coruña or Santiago de Compostela, or maybe he was a high school teacher, teaching geometry to kids of fifteen or sixteen and looking out the window at the permanently overcast winter sky of Galicia and the pouring rain. And on the back flap there was more about Dieste. It said: "Of the books that make up Dieste's varied but in no way uneven body of work, which always cleaves to the demands of a personal process in which poetic creation and speculative creation are focused on a single object, the closest forerunners of the present book are *Nuevo tratado del paralelismo* (Buenos Aires, 1958) and more recent works: *Variaciones sobre Zenón de Elea* and *¿Qué es un axioma?* this followed by *Movilidad y Semejanza* together in one volume." So, thought Amalfitano, his face running with sweat to which microscopic particles of dust adhered, Dieste's passion for geometry wasn't something new. And his patrons, in this new light, were no longer friends who got together every night at the club to drink and talk politics or football or mistresses. Instead, in a flash, they became distinguished university colleagues, some doubtless retired but others fully active, and all well-to-do or relatively well-to-do, which of course didn't mean that they didn't meet up every so often like provincial intellectuals, or in other words like deeply self-sufficient men, at the La Coruña club to drink good cognac or whiskey and talk about intrigues and mistresses while their wives, or in the case of the widowers, their housekeepers, were sitting in front of the TV or preparing supper. But the question for Amalfitano was how this book had ended up in one of his boxes. For half an hour he searched his memory, leafing distractedly through Dieste's book. Finally he concluded that for the moment it was a mystery beyond his powers to solve, but he didn't give up. He asked Rosa, who was in the bathroom putting on makeup, if the book was hers. Rosa looked at it and said no. Amalfitano begged her to look again and tell him for sure whether it was hers or not. Rosa asked him if he was feeling all right. I feel fine, said Amalfitano, but this book isn't mine and it showed up in one of the boxes of books I sent from Barcelona. Rosa told him, in Catalan, not to worry, and kept putting on her makeup. How can I not worry, said Amalfitano, also in Catalan, when it feels like I'm losing my memory. Rosa looked at the book again and said: it might be mine. Are you sure? asked Amalfitano. No, it isn't mine, said Rosa, I'm sure it isn't, in fact, I've never seen it before. Amalfitano left his daughter in front of the bathroom mirror and went back out into the desolate yard, where everything was a dusty brown, as if the desert had settled around his new house, with the book dangling from his hand. He thought back on the bookstores where he might have bought it. He looked at the first page and the last page and the back cover for some sign, and on the first page he found a stamp reading Librería Follas Novas, S.L., Montero Ríos 37, phone 981-59-44-06 and 981-59-44-18, Santiago. Clearly it wasn't Santiago de Chile, the only place in the world where Amalfitano could see himself in a state of total catatonia, walking into a bookstore, choosing some book without even looking at the cover, paying for it, and leaving. Obviously, it was Santiago de Compostela, in Galicia. For an instant Amalfitano envisioned a pilgrimage along the Camino de Santiago. He walked to the back of the yard, where his wooden fence met the cement wall surrounding the house behind his. He had never really looked at it. Glass shards, he thought, the owners' fear of unwanted guests. The edges of the shards were reflecting the afternoon sun when Amalfitano resumed his walk around the desolate yard. The wall of the house next door was also bristling with glass, here mostly green and brown glass from beer and liquor bottles. Never, even in dreams, had he been in Santiago de Compostela, Amalfitano had to acknowledge, halting in the shadow of the left-hand wall. But that hardly mattered. Some of the bookstores he frequented in Barcelona carried stock bought directly from other bookstores in Spain, from bookstores that were selling off their inventories or closing, or, in a few cases, that functioned as both bookstore and distributor. I probably picked it up at Laie, he thought, or maybe at La Central, the time I stopped in to buy some philosophy book and the clerk was excited because Pere Gimferrer, Rodrigo Rey Rosa, and Juan Villoro were all there, arguing about whether it was a good idea to fly, and plane accidents, and which was more dangerous, taking off or landing, and she mistakenly put this book in my bag. La Central, that makes sense. But if that was the way it happened I'd have discovered the book when I got home and opened the bag or the package or whatever it was, unless, of course, something terrible or upsetting happened to me on the walk home that eliminated any desire or curiosity I had to examine my new book or books. It's even possible that I might have opened the package like a zombie and left the new book on the night table and Dieste's book on the bookshelf, shaken by something I'd just seen on the street, maybe a car accident, maybe a mugging, maybe a suicide in the subway, although if I had seen something like that, thought Amalfitano, I would surely remember it now or at least retain a vague memory of it. I wouldn't remember the *Testamento geométrico*, but I would remember whatever had made me forget the *Testamento geométrico*. And as if this wasn't enough, the biggest problem wasn't really where the book had come from but how it had ended up in Santa Teresa in one of Amalfitano's boxes of books, books he had chosen in Barcelona before he left. At what point of utter obliviousness had he put it there? How could he have packed a book without noticing what he was doing? Had he planned to read it when he got to the north of Mexico? Had he planned to use it as the starting point for a desultory study of geometry? And if that was his plan, why had he forgotten the moment he arrived in this city rising up in the middle of nowhere? Had the book disappeared from his memory while he and his daughter were flying east to west? Or had it disappeared from his memory as he was waiting for his boxes of books to arrive, once he was in Santa Teresa? Had Dieste's book vanished as a side effect of jet lag?

•

Amalfitano had some rather idiosyncratic ideas about jet lag. They weren't consistent, so it might be an exaggeration to call them ideas. They were feelings. Make-believe ideas. As if he were looking out the window and forcing himself to see an extraterrestrial landscape. He believed (or liked to think he believed) that when a person was in Barcelona, the people living and present in Buenos Aires and Mexico City didn't exist. The time difference only masked their nonexistence. And so if you suddenly traveled to cities that, according to this theory, didn't exist or hadn't yet had time to put themselves together, the result was the phenomenon known as jet lag, which arose not from your exhaustion but from the exhaustion of the people who would still have been asleep if you hadn't traveled. This was something he'd probably read in some science fiction novel or story and that he'd forgotten having read.

•

Anyway, these ideas or feelings or ramblings had their satisfactions. They turned the pain of others into memories of one's own. They turned pain, which is natural, enduring, and eternally triumphant, into personal memory, which is human, brief, and eternally elusive. They turned a brutal story of injustice and abuse, an incoherent howl with no beginning or end, into a neatly structured story in which suicide was always held out as a possibility. They turned flight into freedom, even if freedom meant no more than the perpetuation of flight. They turned chaos into order, even if it was at the cost of what is commonly known as sanity.

•

And although Amalfitano later found more information on the life and works of Rafael Dieste at the University of Santa Teresa library—information that confirmed what he had already guessed or what Don Domingo García-Sabell had insinuated in his prologue, titled "Enlightened Intuition," which went so far as to quote Heidegger (*Es gibt Zeit: there is time*)—on the afternoon when he'd ranged over his humble and barren lands like a medieval squire, as his daughter, like a medieval princess, finished applying her makeup in front of the bathroom mirror, he could in no way remember why or where he'd bought the book or how it had ended up packed and sent with other more familiar and cherished volumes to this populous city that stood in defiance of the desert on the border of Sonora and Arizona. And it was then, just then, as if it were the pistol shot inaugurating a series of events that would build upon each other with sometimes happy and sometimes disastrous consequences, Rosa left the house and said she was going to the movies with a friend and asked if he had his keys and Amalfitano said yes and he heard the door bang shut and then he heard his daughter's footsteps along the path of uneven paving stones to the tiny wooden gate that didn't even come up to her waist and then he heard his daughter's footsteps on the sidewalk, heading off toward the bus stop, and then he heard the engine of a car starting. And then Amalfitano walked into his devastated front yard and looked up and down the street, craning his neck, and didn't see any car or Rosa and he gripped Dieste's book tightly, which he was still holding in his left hand. And then he looked up at the sky and saw the moon, too big and too wrinkled, although it wasn't night yet. And then he returned to his ravaged backyard and for a few seconds he stopped, looking left and right, ahead and behind, trying to see his shadow, but although it was still daytime and the sun was still shining in the west, toward Tijuana, he couldn't see it. And then his eyes fell on the four rows of cord, each tied at one end to a kind of miniature soccer goal, two posts perhaps six feet tall planted in the ground, and a third post bolted horizontally across the top, making them sturdier, the cords strung from this top bar to hooks fixed in the side of the house. It was the clothesline, although the only things he saw hanging on it were a shirt of Rosa's, white with ocher embroidery around the neck, and a pair of underpants and two towels, still dripping. In the corner, in a brick hut, was the washing machine. For a while he didn't move, breathing with his mouth open, leaning on the horizontal bar of the clothesline. Then he went into the hut as if he were short of oxygen, and from a plastic bag with the logo of the supermarket where he went with his daughter to do the weekly shopping, he took out three clothespins, which he persisted in calling *perritos*, as they were called in Chile, and with them he clamped the book and hung it from one of the cords and then he went back into the house, feeling much calmer.

•

The idea, of course, was Duchamp's.

•

All that exists, or remains, of Duchamp's stay in Buenos Aires is a readymade. Though of course his whole life was a readymade, which was his way of appeasing fate and at the same time sending out signals of distress. As Calvin Tomkins writes: *As a wedding present for his sister Suzanne and his close friend Jean Crotti, who were married in Paris on April 14, 1919, Duchamp instructed the couple by letter to hang a geometry book by strings on the balcony of their apartment so that the wind could "go through the book, choose its own problems, turn and tear out the pages."* Clearly, then, Duchamp wasn't just playing chess in Buenos Aires. Tompkins continues: *This* Unhappy Readymade, *as he called it, might strike some newlyweds as an oddly cheerless wedding gift, but Suzanne and Jean carried out Duchamp's instructions in good spirit; they took a photograph of the open book dangling in midair (the only existing record of the work, which did not survive its exposure to the elements), and Suzanne later painted a picture of it called* Le Readymade malheureux de Marcel. *As Duchamp later told Cabanne, "It amused me to bring the idea of happy and unhappy into readymades, and then the rain, the wind, the pages flying, it was an amusing idea."* I take it back: all Duchamp did while he was in Buenos Aires was play chess. Yvonne, who was with him, got sick of all his play-science and left for France. According to Tompkins: *Duchamp told one interviewer in later years that he had liked disparaging "the seriousness of a book full of principles," and suggested to another that, in its exposure to the weather, "the treatise seriously got the facts of life."*

•

That night, when Rosa got back from the movies, Amalfitano was watching television in the living room and he told her he'd hung Dieste's book on the clothesline. Rosa looked at him as if she had no idea what he was talking about. I mean, said Amalfitano, I didn't hang it out because it got sprayed with the hose or dropped in the water, I hung it there just because, to see how it survives the assault of nature, to see how it survives this desert climate. I hope you aren't going crazy, said Rosa. No, don't worry, said Amalfitano, in fact looking quite cheerful. I'm telling you so you don't take it down. Just pretend the book doesn't exist. Fine, Rosa said, and she shut herself in her room.

•

The next day, as his students wrote, or as he himself was talking, Amalfitano began to draw very simple geometric figures, a triangle, a rectangle, and at each vertex he wrote whatever name came to him, dictated by fate or lethargy or the immense boredom he felt thanks to his students and the classes and the oppressive heat that had settled over the city. Like this:

Drawing 1

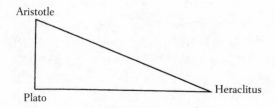

Or like this:

Drawing 2

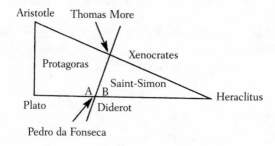

Or like this:

Drawing 3

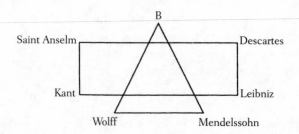

When he returned to his cubicle he discovered the paper and before he threw it in the trash he examined it for a few minutes. The only possible explanation for Drawing 1 was boredom. Drawing 2 seemed an extension of Drawing 1, but the names he had added struck him as insane. Xenocrates made sense, there was a fleeting logic there, and Protagoras, too, but why Thomas More and Saint-Simon? Why Diderot, what was he doing there, and God in heaven, why the Portuguese Jesuit Pedro da Fonseca, one of the thousands of commentators on Aristotle, who by no amount of forceps wiggling could be taken for anything but a very minor thinker? In contrast, there was a certain logic to Drawing 3, the logic of a teenage moron, or a teen bum in the desert, his clothes in tatters, but clothes even so. All the names, it could be said, were of philosophers who concerned themselves with ontological questions. The B that appeared at the apex of the triangle superimposed on the rectangle could be God or the existence of God as derived from his essence. Only then did Amalfitano notice that an A and a B also appeared in Drawing 2, and he no longer had any doubt that the heat, to which he was unaccustomed, was affecting his mind as he taught his classes.

•

That night, however, after he had finished his dinner and watched the TV news and talked on the phone to Professor Silvia Pérez, who was outraged at the way the Sonora police and the local Santa Teresa police were carrying out the investigation of the crimes, Amalfitano found three more diagrams on his desk. It was clear he had drawn them himself. In fact, he remembered doodling absentmindedly on a blank sheet of paper as he thought other things. Drawing 1 (or Drawing 4) was like this:

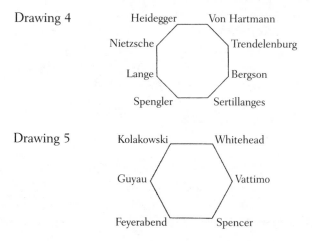

Drawing 4

Heidegger   Von Hartmann
Nietzsche   Trendelenburg
Lange   Bergson
Spengler   Sertillanges

Drawing 5

Kolakowski   Whitehead
Guyau   Vattimo
Feyerabend   Spencer

And Drawing 6

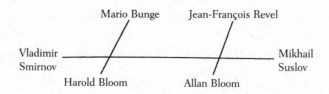

Mario Bunge   Jean-François Revel

Vladimir _____ /_____/_____ Mikhail
Smirnov   /   /   Suslov

Harold Bloom   Allan Bloom

Drawing 4 was odd. Trendelenburg—it had been years since he thought about Trendelenburg. Adolf Trendelenburg. Why now, precisely, and why in the company of Bergson and Heidegger and Nietzsche and Spengler? Drawing 5 was even odder. The appearance of Kolakowski and Vattimo. The presence of Whitehead, forgotten until now. But especially the unexpected materialization of poor Guyau, Jean-Marie Guyau, dead at thirty-four in 1888, called the French Nietzsche by some jokers, with no more than ten disciples in the whole world, although really there were only six, and Amalfitano knew this because in Barcelona he had met the only Spanish Guyautist, a professor from Gerona, shy and a zealot in his own way, whose great quest was to find a text (it might have been a poem or a philosophical piece or an article, he wasn't sure) that Guyau had written in English and published in a San Francisco newspaper sometime around 1886–1887. Finally, Drawing 6 was the oddest of all (and the least "philosophical"). What said it all was the appearance at opposite ends of the horizontal axis of Vladimir Smirnov, who disappeared in Stalin's concentration camps in 1938 (not to be confused with Ivan Nikitich Smirnov, executed by the Stalinists in 1936 after the first Moscow show trial), and Suslov, party ideologue, prepared to countenance any atrocity or crime. But the intersection of the horizontal by two slanted lines, reading Bunge and Revel above and Harold Bloom and Allan Bloom below, was something like a joke. And yet it was a joke Amalfitano didn't understand, especially the appearance of the two Blooms. There had to be something funny about it, but whatever it might be, he couldn't put his finger on it, no matter how he tried.

•

That night, as his daughter slept, and after he listened to the last news broadcast on Santa Teresa's most popular radio station, Voice of the Border, Amalfitano went out into the yard. He smoked a cigarette, staring into the deserted street, then he headed for the back, moving hesitantly, as if he feared stepping in a hole or was afraid of the reigning darkness. Dieste's book was still hanging with the clothes Rosa had washed that day, clothes that seemed to be made of cement or some very heavy material, because they didn't move at all, while the fitful breeze swung the book back and forth, as if it were grudgingly rocking it or trying to detach it from the clothespins holding it to the line. Amalfitano felt the breeze on his face. He was sweating and the irregular gusts of air dried the little drops of perspiration and occluded his soul. As if I were in Trendelenburg's study, he thought, as if I were following in Whitehead's footsteps along the edge of a canal, as if I were approaching Guyau's sickbed and asking him for advice. What would his response have been? Be happy. Live in the moment. Be good. Or rather: Who are you? What are you doing here? Go away.

•

Help.

•

The next day, searching in the university library, he found more information on Dieste. Born in Rianxo, La Coruña, in 1899. Begins writing in Galician, although later he switches to Castilian or writes in both. Man of the theater. Anti-Fascist during the Civil War. After his side's defeat he goes into exile, ending up in Buenos Aires, where he publishes *Viaje, duelo y perdición: tragedia, humorada y comedia*, in 1945, a book made up of three previously published works. Poet. Essayist. In 1958 (Amalfitano is seven), he publishes the aforementioned *Nuevo tratado del paralelismo*. As a short story writer, his most important work is *Historia e invenciones de Félix Muriel* (1943). Returns to Spain, returns to Galicia. Dies in Santiago de Compostela in 1981.

•

What's the experiment? asked Rosa. What experiment? asked Amalfitano. With the hanging book, said Rosa. It isn't an experiment in the literal sense of the word, said Amalfitano. Why is it there? asked Rosa. It occurred to me all of a sudden, said Amalfitano, it's a Duchamp idea, leaving a geometry book hanging exposed to the elements to see if it learns something about real life. You're going to destroy it, said Rosa. Not me, said Amalfitano, nature. You're getting crazier every day, you know, said Rosa. Amalfitano smiled. I've never seen you do a thing like that to a book, said Rosa. It isn't mine, said Amalfitano. It doesn't matter, Rosa said, it's yours now. It's funny, said Amalfitano, that's how I should feel, but I really don't have the sense it belongs to me, and anyway I'm almost sure I'm not doing it any harm. Well, pretend it's mine and take it down, said Rosa, the neighbors are going to think you're crazy. The neighbors who top their walls with broken glass? They don't even know we exist, said Amalfitano, and they're a thousand times crazier than me. No, not them, said Rosa, the other ones, the ones who can see exactly what's going on in our yard. Have any of them bothered you? asked Amalfitano. No, said Rosa. Then it's not a problem, said Amalfitano, it's silly to worry about it when much worse things are happening in this city than a book being hung from a cord. Two wrongs don't make a right, said Rosa, we're not animals. Leave the book alone, pretend it doesn't exist, forget about it, said Amalfitano, you've never been interested in geometry.

•

In the mornings, before he left for the university, Amalfitano would go out the back door to watch the book while he finished his coffee. No doubt about it: it had been printed on good paper and the binding was stoically withstanding nature's onslaught. Rafael Dieste's old friends had chosen good materials for their tribute, a tribute that amounted to an early farewell from a circle of learned old men (or old men with a patina of learning) to another learned old man. In any case, nature in northwestern Mexico, and particularly in his desolate yard, thought Amalfitano, was in short supply. One morning, as he was waiting for the bus to the university, he made firm plans to plant grass or a lawn, and also to buy a little tree in some store that sold that kind of thing, and plant flowers along the fence. Another morning he thought that any work he did to make the yard nicer would ultimately be pointless, since he didn't plan to stay long in Santa Teresa. I have to go back now, he said to himself, but where? And then he asked himself: what made me come here? Why did I bring my daughter to this cursed city? Because it was one of the few hellholes in the world I hadn't seen yet? Because I really just want to die? And then he looked at Dieste's book, the *Testamento geométrico*, hanging impassively from the line, held there by two clothespins, and he felt the urge to take it down and wipe off the ocher dust that had begun to cling to it here and there, but he didn't dare.

•

Sometimes, after he came home from the University of Santa Teresa or while he sat on the porch and read his students' essays, Amalfitano remembered his father, who followed boxing. Amalfitano's father used to say that all Chileans were faggots. Amalfitano, who was ten, said: but Dad, it's really the Italians who are faggots, just look at World War II. Amalfitano's father gave his son a very serious look when he heard him say that. His own father, Amalfitano's grandfather, was born in Naples. And he himself always felt more Italian than Chilean. But anyway, he liked to talk about boxing, or rather he liked to talk about fights that he'd only read about in the usual articles in boxing magazines or the sports page. So he would talk about the Loayza brothers, Mario and Rubén, nephews of El Tani, and about Godfrey Stevens, a stately faggot with no punch, and about Humberto Loayza, also a nephew of El Tani, who had a good punch but no stamina, about Arturo Godoy, a wily fighter and martyr, about Luis Vicentini, a powerfully built Italian from Chillán who was defeated by the sad fate of being born in Chile, and about Estanislao Loayza, El Tani, who was robbed of the world title in the United States in the most ridiculous way, when the referee stepped on his foot in the first round and El Tani fractured his ankle. Can you imagine? Amalfitano's father asked. I can't imagine, Amalfitano said. Let's give it a try, said Amalfitano's father, shadowbox around me and I'll step on your foot. I'd rather not, said Amalfitano. You can trust me, you'll be fine, said Amalfitano's father. Some other time, said Amalfitano. It has to be now, said his father. Then Amalfitano put up his fists and moved around his father with surprising agility, throwing a few jabs with his left and hooks with his right, and suddenly his father moved in and stepped on his foot and that was the end of it, Amalfitano stood still or tried to go in for a clinch or pulled away, but in no way fractured his ankle. I think the referee did it on purpose, said Amalfitano's father. You can't fuck up somebody's ankle by stomping on his foot. Then came the rant: Chilean boxers are all faggots, all the people in this shitty country are faggots, every one of them, happy to be cheated, happy to be bought, happy to pull down their pants the minute someone asks them to take off their watches. It was at this point that Amalfitano, who at ten read history magazines, especially military history magazines, not sports magazines, answered that the Italians had already claimed that role, all the way back to World War II. His father was silent then, looking at his son with frank admiration and pride, as if asking himself where the hell the kid had come from, and then he was silent for a while longer and afterward he said in a low voice, as if telling a secret, that Italians were brave individually. In large numbers, he admitted, they were hopeless. And this, he explained, was precisely what gave a person hope.

•

By which you might guess, thought Amalfitano, as he went out the front door and paused on the porch with his whiskey and then looked out into the street where a few cars were parked, cars that had been left there for hours and smelled, or so it seemed to him, of scrap metal and blood, before he turned and headed around the side of the house to the backyard where the *Testamento geométrico* was waiting for him in the stillness and the dark, by which you might guess that he himself, deep down, very deep down, was still a hopeful person, since he was Italian by blood, as well as an individualist and a civilized person. And it was even possible that he wasn't a coward. Although he didn't like boxing. But then Dieste's book fluttered and the black handkerchief of the breeze dried the sweat beading on his forehead and Amalfitano closed his eyes and tried to conjure up any image of his father, in vain. When he went back inside, not through the back door but through the front door, he peered over the gate and looked both ways down the street. Some nights he had the feeling he was being spied on.

•

In the mornings, when Amalfitano came into the kitchen and left his coffee cup in the sink after his obligatory visit to Dieste's book, Rosa was the first to leave. They didn't usually speak, although sometimes, if Amalfitano came in sooner than usual or put off going into the backyard, he would say goodbye, remind her to take care of herself, or give her a kiss. One morning he managed only to say goodbye, then he sat at the table looking out the window at the clothesline. The *Testamento geométrico* was moving imperceptibly. Suddenly, it stopped. The birds that had been singing in the neighboring yards were quiet. Everything was plunged into complete silence for an instant. Amalfitano thought he heard the sound of the gate and his daughter's footsteps receding. Then he heard a car start. That night, as Rosa watched a movie she'd rented, Amalfitano called Professor Pérez and confessed that he was turning into a nervous wreck. Professor Pérez soothed him, told him not to worry so much, all you had to do was be careful, there was no point giving in to paranoia. She reminded him that the victims were usually kidnapped in other parts of the city. Amalfitano listened to her talk and all of a sudden he laughed. He told her his nerves were in tatters. Professor Pérez didn't get the joke. Nobody gets anything here, thought Amalfitano angrily. Then Professor Pérez tried to convince him to come out that weekend, with Rosa and Professor Pérez's son. Where to, asked Amalfitano, almost inaudibly. We could go eat at a *merendero* ten miles out of the city, she said, a very nice place, with a pool for the kids and lots of outdoor tables in the shade with a view of the slopes of a quartz mountain, a silver mountain with black streaks. At the top of the mountain there was a chapel built of black adobe. The inside was dark, except for the light that came in through a kind of skylight, and the walls were covered in ex-votos written by travelers and Indians in the nineteenth century who had risked the pass between Chihuahua and Sonora.

•

Amalfitano's first few days in Santa Teresa and at the University of Santa Teresa were miserable, although Amalfitano was only half aware of the fact. He felt ill, but he thought it was jet lag and ignored it. A faculty colleague, a young professor from Hermosillo who had only recently finished his degree, asked what had made him choose the University of Santa Teresa over the University of Barcelona. I hope it wasn't the climate, he said. The climate here seems wonderful, answered Amalfitano. Oh, I agree, said the young professor, I just meant that the people who come here for the climate are usually ill and I sincerely hope that's not the case with you. No, said Amalfitano, it wasn't the climate, my contract had run out in Barcelona and Professor Pérez convinced me to take a job here. He had met Professor Silvia Pérez in Buenos Aires and then they had seen each other twice in Barcelona. It was she who had rented the house and bought some furniture for him. Amalfitano paid her back even before he collected his first paycheck to prevent any misunderstandings. The house was in Colonia Lindavista, an upper-middle-class neighborhood of one- and two-story houses with yards. The sidewalk, cracked by the roots of two enormous trees, was shady and pleasant, although behind the gates some of the houses were in advanced states of disrepair, as if the neighbors had left in a hurry, with no time even to sell, which would suggest that it hadn't been so hard to rent in the neighborhood, no matter what Professor Pérez claimed. He took a dislike to the dean of the Faculty of Literature, to whom Professor Pérez introduced him on his second day in Santa Teresa. The dean's name was Augusto Guerra and he had the pale, shiny skin of a fat man, but he was actually thin and wiry. He didn't seem very sure of himself, although he tried to disguise it with a combination of folk wisdom and a military air. He didn't really believe in philosophy either, or, by extension, in the teaching of philosophy, a discipline frankly on the decline in the face of the current and future marvels that science has to offer, he said. Amalfitano asked politely whether he felt the same way about literature. No, literature does have a future, believe it or not, and so does history, Augusto Guerra had said, take biographies, there used to be almost no supply or demand and today all anybody does is read them. Of course, I'm talking about biographies, not memoirs. People have a thirst to learn about other people's lives, the lives of their famous contemporaries, the ones who made it big or came close, and they also have a thirst to know what the old *chincuales* did, maybe even learn something, although they aren't prepared to jump through the same hoops themselves. Amalfitano asked politely what *chincuales* meant, since he had never heard the word. Really? asked Augusto Guerra. I swear, said Amalfitano. Then the dean asked Professor Pérez: Silvita, do you know what *chincuales* means? Professor Pérez took Amalfitano's arm, as if they were lovers, and confessed that really she didn't have the slightest idea, although the word rang a bell. What a pack of imbeciles, thought Amalfitano. The word *chincuales*, said Augusto Guerra, like all the words in the Mexican tongue, has a number of senses. First, it means flea or bedbug bites, those little red welts, you know? The bites itch, and the poor victims can't stop scratching, as you can readily imagine. Hence the second meaning, which is restless people who squirm and scratch and can't sit still, to the discomfort of anyone who's forced to watch them. Like European scabies, say, like all those people with scabies in Europe, who pick it up in public restrooms or in those horrendous French, Italian, and Spanish latrines. Related to this is the final sense, call it the Guerrist sense, which applies to a certain class of traveler, to adventurers of the mind, those who can't keep still *mentally*. Ah, said Amalfitano. Magnificent, said Professor Pérez. Also present at this impromptu gathering in the dean's office, which Amalfitano thought of as a welcome meeting, were three other professors from the literature department, and Guerra's secretary, who uncorked a bottle of Californian champagne and passed out paper cups and crackers. Then Guerra's son came in. He was maybe twenty-five years old, in sunglasses and a track suit, his skin very tanned. He spent all his time in a corner talking to his father's secretary and glancing every so often at Amalfitano with an amused look on his face.

•

The night before the excursion, Amalfitano heard the voice for the first time. Maybe he'd heard it before, in the street or while he was asleep, and thought it was part of someone else's conversation or that he was having a nightmare. But that night he heard it and he had no doubt whatsoever that it was addressing him. At first he thought he'd gone crazy. The voice said: hello, Óscar Amalfitano, please don't be afraid, there's nothing wrong. Amalfitano was afraid. He got up and rushed to his daughter's room. Rosa was sleeping peacefully. Amalfitano turned on the light and checked the window latch. Rosa woke up and asked what was wrong with him. Not what was wrong, what was wrong with him. I must look terrible, thought Amalfitano. He sat in a chair and told her he was ridiculously nervous, he'd thought he heard a noise, he was sorry he'd brought her to this disgusting city. Don't worry, it's no big deal, said Rosa. Amalfitano gave her a kiss on the cheek, stroked her hair, and went out but didn't turn off the light. After a while, as he was looking out the living room window at the yard and the street and the still branches of the trees, he heard Rosa turn off the light. He went out the back door, without making a sound. He wished he had a flashlight, but he went out anyway. No one was there. Hanging on the clothesline were the *Testamento geométrico* and some of his socks and a pair of his daughter's pants. He circled the yard. There was no one on the porch. He went over to the gate and inspected the street, without going out, and all he saw was a dog heading calmly toward Avenida Madero, to the bus stop. A dog on its way to the bus stop, Amalfitano said to himself. From where he was he thought he could tell that it was a mutt, not a purebreed. A *quiltro*, thought Amalfitano. He laughed to himself. Those Chilean words. Those cracks in the psyche. That hockey rink the size of Atacama where the players never saw a member of the opposing team and only every so often saw a member of their own. He went back into the house. He locked the door and windows, took a short, sturdy knife out of a drawer in the kitchen and set it down next to a history of German and French philosophy from 1900 to 1930, then sat back down at the table.

The voice said: don't think this is easy for me. If you think it's easy for me, you're one hundred percent wrong. In fact, it's hard. Ninety percent hard. Amalfitano closed his eyes and thought he was going crazy. He didn't have any tranquilizers in the house. He got up. He went into the kitchen and splashed water on his face with both hands. He dried himself with the kitchen towel and his sleeves. He tried to remember the psychiatric name for the auditory phenomenon he was experiencing. He went back into his office and after closing the door he sat down again, with his head bowed and his hands on the table. The voice said: I beg you to forgive me. I beg you to relax. I beg you not to consider this a violation of your freedom. Of my freedom? thought Amalfitano, surprised, as he sprang to the window and opened it and looked out at the side yard and the wall of the house next door, spiky with glass, and the reflection of the streetlights in the shards of broken bottles, very faint green and brown and orange gleams, as if at this time of night the wall stopped being a barricade and became or played at becoming ornamental, a tiny element in a choreography the basic features of which even the ostensible choreographer, the feudal lord next door, couldn't have identified, features that affected the stability, color, and offensive or defensive nature of his fortification. Or as if there was a vine growing on the wall, Amalfitano thought before he closed the window.

•

That night there were no further manifestations of the voice and Amalfitano slept very badly, his sleep plagued by jerks and starts, as if someone was scratching his arms and legs, his body drenched in sweat, although at five in the morning the torment ceased and Lola appeared in his sleep, waving to him from a park behind a tall fence (he was on the other side), along with the faces of two friends he hadn't seen for years (and would probably never see again), and a room full of philosophy books covered in dust but still magnificent. At that same moment the Santa Teresa police found the body of another teenage girl, half buried in a vacant lot in one of the neighborhoods on the edge of the city, and a strong wind from the west hurled itself against the slope of the mountains to the east, raising dust and a litter of newspaper and cardboard on its way through Santa Teresa, moving the clothes that Rosa had hung in the backyard, as if the wind, young and energetic in its brief life, were trying on Amalfitano's shirts and pants and slipping into his daughter's underpants and reading a few pages of the *Testamento geométrico* to see

whether there was anything in it that might be of use, anything that
might explain the strange landscape of streets and houses through which
it was galloping, or that would explain it to itself as wind.

●

At eight o'clock Amalfitano dragged himself into the kitchen. His daughter asked how he'd slept. A rhetorical question that Amalfitano answered with a shrug. When Rosa went out to buy provisions for their
day in the country, he made himself a cup of tea with milk and went
into the living room to drink it. Then he opened the curtains and asked
himself whether he was up to the trip planned by Professor Pérez. He
decided that he was, that what had happened to him the night before
might have been his body's response to the attack of a local virus or
the onset of the flu. Before he got in the shower he took his temperature. He didn't have a fever. For ten minutes he stood under the spray,
thinking about his behavior the night before, which embarrassed him
and even made him blush. Every so often he lifted his head so that the
water streamed directly onto his face. The water tasted different from
the water in Barcelona. The water in Santa Teresa seemed much denser,
as if it weren't filtered at all but came loaded with minerals, tasting of
earth. In the first few days he had acquired the habit, which he shared
with Rosa, of brushing his teeth twice as often as he had in Barcelona,
because it seemed to him that his teeth were turning brown, as if they
were being covered in a thin film of some substance from the underground rivers of Sonora. As time passed, though, he went back to brushing them three or four times a day. Rosa, more concerned about her
appearance, kept brushing six or seven times. In his class he noticed
some students with ocher-colored teeth. Professor Pérez had white
teeth. Once he asked her: was it true that the water in that part of
Sonora stained the teeth? Professor Pérez didn't know. It's the first I've
heard of it, she said, and she promised to find out. It's not important,
said Amalfitano, alarmed, it's not important, forget I asked. In the expression on Professor Pérez's face he had detected a hint of unease, as if
the question concealed some other question, this one highly offensive
and wounding. You have to watch what you say, sang Amalfitano in the
shower, feeling completely recovered, sure proof of his frequent irre-
sponsibility.

●

Rosa came back with two newspapers that she left on the table, then she started to make ham or tuna sandwiches with lettuce and slices of tomato and mayonnaise or *salsa rosa*. She wrapped the sandwiches in paper towels and aluminum foil and put them all in a plastic bag that she stowed in a small brown knapsack with the words *University of Phoenix* printed on it in an arc, and she also put in two bottles of water and a dozen paper cups. At nine-thirty they heard Professor Pérez's horn. Professor Pérez's son was sixteen and short, with a square face and broad shoulders, as if he played some sport. His face and part of his neck were covered in pimples. Professor Pérez was wearing jeans and a white shirt and a white bandanna. Sunglasses, possibly too big, hid her eyes. From a distance, thought Amalfitano, she looked like a Mexican actress from the seventies. When he got in the car the illusion vanished. Professor Pérez drove and he sat next to her. They headed east. For the first few miles the highway ran through a little valley dotted with rocks that seemed to have fallen from the sky. Chunks of granite with no origin or context. There were some fields, plots where invisible peasants grew crops that neither Professor Pérez nor Amalfitano could make out. Then they were in the desert and the mountains. There were the parents of the orphan rocks they'd just passed. Granitic formations, volcanic formations, peaks silhouetted against the sky in the shape and fashion of birds, but birds of sorrow, thought Amalfitano, as Professor Pérez talked to her son and Rosa about the place where they were going, painting it in colors that shaded from fun (a pool carved out of living rock) to mystery, exemplified for her by the voices to be heard from the lookout point, sounds clearly made by the wind. When Amalfitano turned his head to see the expression on Rosa's face and on the face of Professor Pérez's son, he saw four cars trailing them, waiting to pass. Inside each car he imagined a happy family, a mother, a picnic basket full of food, two children, and a father driving with the window rolled down. He smiled at his daughter and turned back to watch the road. Half an hour later they went up a hill, from the top of which he could see a wide expanse of desert behind them. They saw more cars. He supposed that the roadside bar or café or restaurant or by-the-hour motel was a fashionable destination for the inhabitants of Santa Teresa. He regretted having accepted the invitation. At some point he fell asleep. By the time he woke up, they were there. Professor Pérez's hand was on his face, a gesture that might have been a caress or not. Her hand was like a blind woman's hand. Rosa and Rafael were no longer in the car. He saw a parking lot, almost full, the sun glittering on the chrome-plated surfaces, an open terrace on a slightly higher level, a couple with their arms around each other's shoulders looking at something he couldn't see, the blinding sky full of small, low, white clouds, distant music and a voice that sang or muttered at great speed, so that it was impossible to understand the words. An inch away he saw Professor Pérez's face. He took her hand and kissed it. His shirt was damp with sweat, but what surprised him most was that the professor was sweating too.

•

Despite everything, they had a pleasant day. Rosa and Rafael swam in the pool and then joined Amalfitano and Professor Pérez, who were watching them from one of the tables. After that they all bought sodas and went out to walk around. In some places the mountain dropped straight down, and in the depths or on the cliff sides there were big gashes with different-colored rock showing through, or rock that looked different colors in the sun as it fled westward, lutites and andesites sandwiched between sandstone formations, vertical outcrops of tuff and great trays of basaltic rock. Here and there, a Sonora cactus dangled from the mountainside. And farther away there were more mountains and then tiny valleys and more mountains, finally giving way to an expanse veiled in haze, in mist, like a cloud cemetery, behind which were Chihuahua and New Mexico and Texas. Sitting on rocks and surveying this view, they ate in silence. Rosa and Rafael spoke only to exchange sandwiches. Professor Pérez seemed lost in her own thoughts. And Amalfitano felt tired and overwhelmed by the landscape, a landscape that seemed best suited to the young or the old, imbecilic or insensitive or evil and old who meant to impose impossible tasks on themselves and others until they breathed their last.

•

That night Amalfitano was up until very late. The first thing he did when he got home was go out into the backyard to see whether Dieste's book was still there. On the ride home Professor Pérez had tried to be nice and start a conversation in which all four of them could participate, but her son fell asleep as soon as they began the descent and soon afterward Rosa did, too, with her head against the window. It wasn't long before

Amalfitano followed his daughter's example. He dreamed of a woman's voice, not Professor Pérez's but a Frenchwoman's, talking to him about signs and numbers and something Amalfitano didn't understand, something the voice in the dream called "history broken down" or "history taken apart and put back together," although clearly the reassembled history became something else, a scribble in the margin, a clever footnote, a laugh slow to fade that leaped from an andesite rock to a rhyolite and then a tufa, and from that collection of prehistoric rocks there arose a kind of quicksilver, the American mirror, said the voice, the sad American mirror of wealth and poverty and constant useless metamorphosis, the mirror that sails and whose sails are pain. And then Amalfitano switched dreams and stopped hearing voices, which must have meant he was sleeping deeply, and he dreamed he was moving toward a woman, a woman who was only a pair of legs at the end of a dark hallway and then he heard someone laugh at his snoring, Professor Pérez's son, and he thought: good. As they were driving into Santa Teresa on the westbound highway, crowded at that time of day with dilapidated trucks and small pickups on their way back from the city market or from cities in Arizona, he woke up. Not only had he slept with his mouth open, but he had drooled on the collar of his shirt. Good, he thought, excellent. When he looked in satisfaction at Professor Pérez, he detected an air of sadness about her. Out of sight of their respective children, she lightly stroked Amalfitano's leg as he turned his head and looked at a taco stand where a couple of policemen with guns on their hips were drinking beer and talking and watching the red and black dusk, like a thick chili whose last simmer was fading in the west. When they got home it was dark but the shadow of Dieste's book hanging from the clothesline was clearer, steadier, more reasonable, thought Amalfitano, than anything they'd seen on the outskirts of Santa Teresa or in the city itself, images with no handhold, images freighted with all the orphanhood in the world, fragments, fragments.

•

That night he waited, dreading the voice. He tried to prepare for a class, but he soon realized it was a pointless task to prepare for something he knew backward and forward. He thought that if he drew on the blank piece of paper in front of him, the basic geometric figures would appear again. So he drew a face and erased it and then immersed himself in the memory of the obliterated face. He remembered (but fleetingly, as one remembers a lightning bolt) Ramon Llull and his fantastic machine. Fantastic in its uselessness. When he looked at the blank sheet again he had written the following names in three columns:

Pico della Mirandola	Hobbes	Boecio
Husserl	Locke	Alexander of Hales
Eugen Fink	Erich Becher	Marx
Merleau-Ponty	Wittgenstein	Lichtenberg
Bede	Llull	Sade
St. Bonaventure	Hegel	Condorcet
John Philoponus	Pascal	Fourier
Saint Augustine	Canetti	Lacan
Schopenhauer	Freud	Lessing

For a while, Amalfitano read and reread the names, horizontally and vertically, from the center outward, from bottom to top, skipping and at random, and then he laughed and thought that the whole thing was a truism, in other words a proposition too obvious to formulate. Then he drank a glass of tap water, water from the mountains of Sonora, and as he waited for the water to make its way down his throat he stopped shaking, an imperceptible shaking that only he could feel, and he began to think about the Sierra Madre aquifers running toward the city in the middle of the endless night, and he also thought about the aquifers rising from their hiding places closer to Santa Teresa, and about the water that coated teeth with a smooth ocher film. And when he'd drunk the whole glass of water he looked out the window and saw the long shadow, the coffinlike shadow, cast by Dieste's book hanging in the yard.

•

But the voice returned, and this time it asked him, begged him, to be a man, not a queer. Queer? asked Amalfitano. Yes, queer, faggot, cocksucker, said the voice. Ho-mo-sex-u-al, said the voice. In the next breath it asked him whether he happened to be one of those. One of what? asked Amalfitano, terrified. A ho-mo-sex-u-al, said the voice. And before Amalfitano could answer, it hastened to make clear that it was speaking figuratively, that it had nothing against faggots or queers, in fact it felt boundless admiration for certain poets who had professed such sexual leanings, not to mention certain painters and government clerks. Government clerks? asked Amalfitano. Yes, yes, yes, said the voice, young government clerks with short life spans. Clerks who stained official documents with senseless tears. Dead by their own hand. Then the voice was silent and Amalfitano remained sitting in his office. Much later, maybe a quarter of an hour later, maybe the next night, the voice said: let's say I'm your grandfather, your father's father, and let's say that as your grandfather I can ask you a personal question. You're free to answer or not, but I can ask the question. My grandfather? said Amalfitano. Yes, your grandfather, said the voice, you can call me *nono*. And my question for you is: are you a queer, are you going to go running out of this room, are you a ho-mo-sex-u-al, are you going to go wake up your daughter? No, said Amalfitano. I'm listening. Tell me what you have to say.

•

And the voice said: are you a queer? are you? and Amalfitano said no and shook his head, too. I'm not going to run away. You won't be seeing my back or the soles of my shoes. Assuming you see at all. And the voice said: see? as in *see*? to tell the truth, I can't. Not much, anyway. It's enough work just keeping one foot in. Where? asked Amalfitano. At your house, I suppose, said the voice. This is my house, said Amalfitano. Yes, I realize, said the voice, now why don't we relax. I'm relaxed, said Amalfitano, I'm here in my house. And he wondered: why is it telling me to relax? And the voice said: I think this is the first day of what I hope will be a long and mutually beneficial relationship. But if it's going to work out, it's absolutely crucial that we stay calm. Calm is the one thing that will never let us down. And Amalfitano said: everything else lets us down? And the voice: yes, that's right, it's hard to admit, I mean it's hard to have to admit it to you, but that's the honest-to-God truth. Ethics lets us down? The sense of duty lets us down? Honesty lets us down? Curiosity lets us down? Love lets us down? Bravery lets us down? Art lets us down? That's right, said the voice, everything lets us down, everything. Or lets you down, which isn't the same thing but for our purposes it might as well be, except calm, calm is the one thing that never lets us down, though that's no guarantee of anything, I have to tell you. You're wrong, said Amalfitano, bravery never lets us down. And neither does our love for our children. Oh no? said the voice. No, said Amalfitano, suddenly feeling calm.

•

And then, in a whisper, like everything he had said so far, he asked whether calm was therefore the opposite of madness. And the voice said: no, absolutely not, if you're worried that you've lost your mind, don't worry, you haven't, all you're doing is having a casual conversation. So I haven't lost my mind, said Amalfitano. No, absolutely not, said the voice. So you're my grandfather, said Amalfitano. Call me pops, said the voice. So everything lets us down, including curiosity and honesty and what we love best. Yes, said the voice, but cheer up, it's fun in the end.

•

There is no friendship, said the voice, there is no love, there is no epic, there is no lyric poetry that isn't the gurgle or chuckle of egoists, the murmur of cheats, the babble of traitors, the burble of social climbers, the warble of faggots. What is it you have against homosexuals? whispered Amalfitano. Nothing, said the voice. I'm speaking figuratively, said the voice. Are we in Santa Teresa? asked the voice. Is this city part of the state of Sonora? A pretty significant part of it, in fact? Yes, said Amalfitano. Well, there you go, said the voice. It's one thing to be a social climber, say, for example, said Amalfitano, tugging at his hair as if in slow motion, and something very different to be a faggot. I'm speaking figuratively, said the voice. I'm talking so you understand me. I'm talking like I'm in the studio of a ho-mo-sex-u-al painter, with you there behind me. I'm talking from a studio where the chaos is just a mask or the faint stink of anesthesia. I'm talking from a studio with the lights out, where the sinew of the will detaches itself from the rest of the body the way the snake tongue detaches itself from the body and slithers away, self-mutilated, amid the rubbish. I'm talking from the perspective of the simple things in life. You teach philosophy? said the voice. You teach Wittgenstein? said the voice. And have you asked yourself whether your hand is a hand? said the voice. I've asked myself, said Amalfitano. But now you have more important things to ask yourself, am I right? said the voice. No, said Amalfitano. For example, why not go to a nursery and buy seeds and plants and maybe even a little tree to plant in the middle of your backyard? said the voice. Yes, said Amalfitano. I've thought about my possible and conceivable yard and the plants and tools I need to buy. And you've also thought about your daughter, said the voice, and about the murders committed daily in this city, and about Baudelaire's faggoty

(I'm sorry) clouds, but you haven't thought seriously about whether your hand is really a hand. That isn't true, said Amalfitano, I have thought about it, I have. If you had thought about it, said the voice, you'd be dancing to the tune of a different piper. And Amalfitano was silent and he felt that the silence was a kind of eugenics. He looked at his watch. It was four in the morning. He heard someone starting a car. The engine took a while to turn over. He got up and went over to the window. The cars parked in front of the house were empty. He looked behind him and then put his hand on the doorknob. The voice said: be careful, but it said it as if it were very far away, at the bottom of a ravine revealing glimpses of volcanic rock, rhyolites, andesites, streaks of silver and gold, petrified puddles covered with tiny little eggs, while red-tailed hawks soared above in the sky, which was purple like the skin of an Indian woman beaten to death. Amalfitano went out onto the porch. To the left, some thirty feet from his house, the lights of a black car came on and its engine started. When it passed the yard the driver leaned out and looked at Amalfitano without stopping. He was a fat man with very black hair, dressed in a cheap suit with no tie. When he was gone, Amalfitano came back into the house. I didn't like the looks of him, said the voice the minute Amalfitano was through the door. And then: you'll have to be careful, my friend, things here seem to be coming to a head.

●

So who are you and how did you get here? asked Amalfitano. There's no point going into it, said the voice. No point? asked Amalfitano, laughing in a whisper, like a fly. There's no point, said the voice. Can I ask you a question? said Amalfitano. Go ahead, said the voice. Are you really the ghost of my grandfather? The things you come up with, said the voice. Of course not, I'm the spirit of your father. Your grandfather's spirit doesn't remember you anymore. But I'm your father and I'll never forget you. Do you understand? Yes, said Amalfitano. Do you understand that you have nothing to fear from me? Yes, said Amalfitano. Do something useful, then check that all the doors and windows are shut tight and go to sleep. Something useful like what? asked Amalfitano. For example, wash the dishes, said the voice. And Amalfitano lit a cigarette and began to do what the voice had suggested. You wash and I'll talk, said the voice. All is calm, said the voice. There's no bad blood between us. The headache, if you have a headache, will go away soon, and so will the buzzing in your ears, the racing pulse, the rapid heartbeat. You'll relax, you'll think some and relax, said the voice, while you do something useful for your daughter and yourself. Understood, whispered Amalfitano. Good, said the voice, this is like an endoscopy, but painless. Got it, whispered Amalfitano. And he scrubbed the plates and the pot with the remains of pasta and tomato sauce and the forks and the glasses and the stove and the table where they'd eaten, smoking one cigarette after another and also taking occasional gulps of water straight from the faucet. And at five in the morning he took the dirty clothes out of the bathroom hamper and went out into the backyard and put the clothes in the washing machine and pushed the button for a normal wash and looked at Dieste's book hanging motionless and then he went back into the living room and his eyes, like the eyes of an addict, sought out something else to clean or tidy or wash, but he couldn't find anything and he sat down, whispering yes or no or I don't remember or maybe. Everything is fine, said the voice. It's all a question of getting used to it. Without making a fuss. Without sweating and flailing around.

•

It was past six when Amalfitano fell into bed without undressing and slept like a baby. Rosa woke him at nine. It had been a long time since Amalfitano felt so good, although his classes that morning were entirely incomprehensible. At one o'clock he ate at the cafeteria and sat at one of the farthest, most out-of-the-way tables. He didn't want to see Professor Pérez, and he didn't want to run into any other colleagues either, least of all the dean, who made a habit of eating there every day, surrounded by professors and a few students who ceaselessly fawned over him. He ordered at the counter, almost stealthily, boiled chicken and salad, and he hurried to his table, dodging the students who crowded the cafeteria at that time of day. Then he sat down to eat and think some more about what had happened the previous night. He realized with astonishment that he was excited by what he had experienced. I feel like a nightingale, he thought happily. It was a simple and antiquated and ridiculous sentiment, but it was the only thing that fully expressed his current state of mind. He tried to relax. The students' laughter, their shouts to each other, the clatter of plates, made it a less than ideal spot for reflection. And yet after a few seconds he realized there could be no better place. Equally good, yes, but not better. So he took a long drink of bottled water (it didn't taste the same as the tap water, but it didn't taste very different either) and he began to think. First he thought about madness.

About the possibility—great—that he was losing his mind. It came as a surprise to him to realize that the thought (and the possibility) in no way diminished his excitement. Or his happiness. My excitement and my happiness are growing under the wing of a storm, he said to himself. I may be going crazy, but I feel good, he said to himself. He contemplated the possibility—great—that if he really was going crazy it would get worse, and then his excitement would turn into pain and helplessness and, especially, a source of pain and helplessness for his daughter. As if he had X-ray eyes he reviewed his savings and calculated that with what he had saved, Rosa could go back to Barcelona and still have money to start with. To start what? That was a question he preferred not to answer. He imagined himself locked up in an asylum in Santa Teresa or Hermosillo with Professor Pérez as his only occasional visitor, and every so often receiving letters from Rosa in Barcelona, where she would be working or finishing her studies, and where she would meet a Catalan boy, responsible and affectionate, who would fall in love with her and respect her and take care of her and be nice to her and with whom Rosa would end up living and going to the movies at night and traveling to Italy or Greece in July or August, and the scenario didn't seem so bad. Then he considered other possibilities. Of course, he said to himself, he didn't believe in ghosts or spirits, although during his childhood in the south of Chile people talked about the *mechona* who waited for riders on a tree branch, dropping onto horses' haunches, clinging to the back of the cowboy or smuggler without letting go, like a lover whose embrace maddened the horse as well as the rider, both of them dying of fright or ending up at the bottom of a ravine, or the *colocolo*, or the *chonchones*, or the *candelillas*, or so many other little creatures, lost souls, incubi and succubi, lesser demons that roamed between the Cordillera de la Costa and the Andes, but in which he didn't believe, not exactly because of his training in philosophy (Schopenhauer, after all, believed in ghosts, and it was surely a ghost that appeared to Nietzsche and drove him mad) but because of his materialist leanings. So he rejected the possibility of ghosts, at least until he had exhausted other lines of inquiry. The voice could be a ghost, he wouldn't rule it out, but he tried to come up with a different explanation. After much reflection, though, the only thing that made sense was the theory of the lost soul. He thought about the seer of Hermosillo, Madame Cristina, La Santa. He thought about his father. He decided that his father would never use the Mexican words the voice had used, no matter what kind of roving spirit he had become, whereas the slight tinge of homophobia suited him perfectly. With a happiness hard to disguise, he asked himself what kind of mess he had gotten himself into. That afternoon he taught another few classes and then he went walking home. As he passed the central plaza of Santa Teresa he saw a group of women protesting in front of the town hall. On one of the posters he read: No to impunity. On another: End the corruption. A group of policemen were watching the women from under the adobe arches of the colonial building. They weren't riot police but plain Santa Teresa uniformed policemen. As he walked past he heard someone call his name. When he turned he saw Professor Pérez and his daughter on the sidewalk across the street. He offered to buy them a soda. At the coffee shop they explained that the protest was to demand transparency in the investigation of the disappearances and killings of women. Professor Pérez said she had three feminists from Mexico City staying at her house, and that night she planned to have a dinner for them. I'd like you to come, she said. Rosa said yes. Amalfitano expressed no objection. Then his daughter and Professor Pérez returned to the protest and Amalfitano continued on his way.

•

But before he got home someone called his name again. Professor Amalfitano, he heard someone saying. He turned around and didn't see anyone. He wasn't in the center of the city anymore. He was walking along Avenida Madero, and the four-story buildings had given way to ranch houses, imitations of a kind of California house from the fifties, houses that had begun to suffer the ravages of time long ago, when their occupants moved to the neighborhood where Amalfitano now lived. Some houses had been converted into garages that also sold ice cream and others had become businesses dealing in bread or clothes, without any modifications whatsoever. Many of them displayed signs advertising doctors, lawyers specializing in divorce or criminal law. Others offered rooms by the day. Some had been divided without much skill into two or three separate shops, where newspapers and magazines or fruit and vegetables were sold, or passersby were promised a good deal on dentures. As Amalfitano was about to keep walking, someone called his name again. Then he saw who it was. The voice was coming from a car parked at the curb. At first he didn't recognize the young man who was calling him. He thought it was a student. Whoever it was had on sunglasses and a black shirt unbuttoned over his chest. He was very tan, like a singer or a Puerto Rican playboy. Get in, Professor, I'll give you a ride home. Amalfitano was about to tell him he'd rather walk when the young man identified himself. I'm Dean Guerra's son, he said as he got out of the car on the side of the street where the traffic thundered by, not looking either way, ignoring the danger in a way that struck Amalfitano as extremely bold. Walking around the car, he came up to Amalfitano and offered his hand. I'm Marco Antonio Guerra, he said, and he reminded him of their champagne toast at his father's office, Amalfitano's welcome to the department. You have nothing to fear from me, Professor, he said, and Amalfitano couldn't help but be surprised by the remark. The young Guerra stopped in front of him. He was smiling just as he had been the first time they met. A confident, mocking smile, like the smile of a cocksure sniper. He wore jeans and cowboy boots. Inside the car, on the backseat, lay a pearl-gray designer jacket and a folder full of papers. I was just driving by, said Marco Antonio Guerra. They headed toward Colonia Lindavista, but before they got there the dean's son suggested they get a drink. Amalfitano politely declined the invitation. Then let's go to your place and have a drink, said Marco Antonio Guerra. I don't have anything to offer, apologized Amalfitano. Then that's settled, said Marco Antonio Guerra, and he took the first turn. Soon there was a change in the urban scenery. West of Colonia Lindavista the houses were new, surrounded in some places by wide-open fields, and some streets weren't even paved. People say these neighborhoods are the city's future, said Marco Antonio Guerra, but in my opinion this shithole has no future. He drove straight onto a soccer field, across which were a pair of enormous sheds or warehouses surrounded by barbed wire. Beyond them ran a canal or creek carrying the neighborhood trash away to the north. Near another open field they saw the old railroad line that had once connected Santa Teresa to Ures and Hermosillo. A few dogs approached timidly. Marco Antonio rolled down the window and let them sniff his hand and lick it. To the left was the highway to Ures. They began to head out of Santa Teresa. Amalfitano asked where they were going. Guerra's son answered that they were on their way to one of the few places around where you could still drink real Mexican mezcal.

•

The place was called Los Zancudos and it was a rectangle three hundred feet long by one hundred feet wide, with a small stage at the end where *corrido* or *ranchera* groups performed on Fridays and Saturdays. The bar was at least one hundred and fifty feet long. The toilets were outside, and they could be entered directly from the outdoor patio or by way of a narrow passageway of galvanized tin connecting them to the restaurant. There weren't many people there. They were greeted by the waiters, whom Marco Antonio Guerra called by name, but no one came to wait on them. Only a few lights were on. I recommend the Los Suicidas, said Marco Antonio. Amalfitano smiled pleasantly and said yes, but just a small one. Marco Antonio raised his arm and snapped his fingers. The bastards must be deaf, he said. He got up and went to the bar. Some time passed before he came back with two glasses and a half-filled bottle of mezcal. Try it, he said. Amalfitano took a sip and thought it tasted good. There should be a worm at the bottom of the bottle, said Marco Antonio, but those scum probably ate it. It sounded like a joke and Amalfitano laughed. But I guarantee it's genuine Los Suicidas, drink up and enjoy, said Marco Antonio. At the second sip Amalfitano thought it really was an extraordinary drink. They don't make it anymore, said Marco Antonio, like so much in this fucking country. And after a while, fixing his gaze on Amalfitano, he said: we're going to hell, I suppose you've realized, Professor? Amalfitano answered that the situation certainly wasn't anything to applaud, without specifying what he meant or going into detail. It's all falling apart in our hands, said Marco Antonio Guerra. The politicians don't know how to govern. All the middle class wants is to move to the United States. And more and more people keep coming to work in the maquiladoras. You know what I would do? No, said Amalfitano. Burn a few of them down, you know? A few what? asked Amalfitano. A few maquiladoras. Interesting, said Amalfitano. I'd also send the army out into the streets, well, not the streets, the highways, to keep more scum from coming here. Highway checkpoints? asked Amalfitano. That's right. I can't see any other solution. There must be other solutions, said Amalfitano. People have lost all respect, said Marco Antonio Guerra. Respect for others and self-respect. Amalfitano glanced toward the bar. Three waiters were whispering, casting sidelong glances at their table. I think we should leave, said Amalfitano. Marco Antonio Guerra noticed the waiters and made an obscene gesture, then he laughed. Amalfitano took him by the arm and dragged him out into the parking lot. By now it was night and a huge glowing sign featuring a long-legged mosquito shone brightly on a metal scaffolding. I think these people have some problem with you, said Amalfitano. Don't worry, Professor, said Marco Antonio Guerra, I'm armed.

●

When he got home, Amalfitano immediately forgot about Marco Antonio Guerra and decided that maybe he wasn't as crazy as he'd thought he was, and that the voice he'd been hearing wasn't a bereaved soul. He thought about telepathy. He thought about the telepathic Mapuches or Araucanians. He remembered a very short book, scarcely one hundred pages long, by a certain Lonko Kilapán, published in Santiago de Chile in 1978, that an old friend, a wiseass of long standing, had sent him while he was living in Europe. This Kilapán presented himself with the following credentials: Historian of the Race, President of the Indigenous Confederation of Chile, and Secretary of the Academy of the Araucanian Language. The book was called *O'Higgins Is Araucanian*, and it was subtitled *17 Proofs, Taken from the Secret History of Araucanía*. Between the title and the subtitle was the following phrase: Text approved by the Araucanian History Council. Then came the prologue, which read like this: "*Prologue*. If proof were desired that any of the heroes of Chile's Independence shared kinship with the Araucanians, it would be difficult to find and harder to verify. Only Iberian blood flowed in the veins of the Carrera brothers, Mackenna, Freire, Manuel Rodríguez. But the dazzling light of Araucanian parentage shines bright in Bernardo O'Higgins, and to prove it we present these 17 proofs. Bernardo is not the illegitimate son described by historians, some with pity, others unable to hide their satisfaction. He is the dashing legitimate son of Irishman Ambrosio O'Higgins, Governor of Chile and Viceroy of Peru, and of an Araucanian woman who belonged to one of the principal tribes of Araucanía. The marriage was celebrated according to Admapu law, with the traditional Gapitun (abduction ceremony). The biography of the Liberator exposes the millenarian Araucanian secret on the very bicentenary of his birth; it springs from the Litrang* to paper, as faithfully as only an Epeutufe can render it." And that was the end of the prologue, by José R. Pichiñual, Cacique of Puerto Saavedra.

●

Odd, thought Amalfitano, with the book in his hands. Odd, extremely odd. For example, the single asterisk. *Litrang*: stone tablets on which the Araucanians engraved their writings. But why footnote *litrang* and not *admapu* or *epeutufe*? Did the Cacique of Puerto Saavedra assume that everyone would know what they meant? And then the sentence about whether or not O'Higgins was a bastard: *Bernardo is not the illegitimate son described by historians, some with* pity, *others unable to hide their* satisfaction. There you had the day-to-day history of Chile, the private history, the history behind closed doors. Pitying the father of the country because he was a bastard. Or being unable to conceal a certain satisfaction when discussing the subject. So telling, thought Amalfitano, and he thought about the first time he'd read Kilapán's book, laughing out loud, and the way he was reading it now, with something like laughter but also something like sorrow. Ambrosio O'Higgins as an Irishman was definitely a good joke. Ambrosio O'Higgins marrying an Araucanian woman, but under the aegis of *admapu* and even going so far as to cap it off with the traditional *gapitun* or abduction ceremony, struck him as a macabre joke that could point only to abuse, rape, a further mockery staged by fat Ambrosio to fuck the Indian woman in peace. I can't think of anything without the word *rape* popping up to stare with its helpless little mammal eyes, thought Amalfitano. Then he fell asleep in his chair, with the book in his hands. Maybe he dreamed something. Something short. Maybe he dreamed about his childhood. Maybe not.

•

Then he woke up and made himself and his daughter something to eat. Back in his office he felt extremely tired, unable to prepare a class or read anything serious, so he returned resignedly to Kilapán's book. Seventeen proofs. Proof number 1 was titled *He was born in the Araucanian state.* It went like this: "The Yekmonchi,[1] called Chile,[2] was geographically and politically identical to the Greek state, and, like it, forming a delta, between the respective latitudes of the 35th and 42nd parallels." Ignoring the construction of the sentence (where it read *forming* it should have read *formed*, and there were at least two commas too many), the most interesting thing about the first paragraph was what might be called its military slant. It began with a straight jab to the chin or a full artillery assault on the center of the enemy line. Note 1 clarified that *Yekmonchi* meant State. Note 2 stated that *Chile* was a Greek word whose translation was "distant tribe." Then came the geographic description of the Yekmonchi of Chile: "It stretched from the Maullis to the Chiligüe rivers, including the west of Argentina. The reigning Mother City, or that is Chile, properly speaking, was located between the Butaleufu and Toltén rivers; like the Greek state, it was surrounded by allied and interrelated peoples, those who were subject to the Küga Chiliches (that is to say the Chilean (or Chiliches: people of Chile) tribe (Küga). Che: people, as Kilapán meticulously took care to recall), who taught them the sciences, the arts, sports, and especially the science of war." Farther along Kilapán confessed: "In 1947," although Amalfitano suspected that this was an erratum and that the year was actually 1974, "I opened the tomb of Kurillanka, which was under the main Kuralwe, covered by a flat stone. All that remained was a katankura, a metawe, duck, an obsidian ornament, like an arrowhead to pay the 'toll' that the soul of Kurillanka had to pay to Zenpilkawe, the Greek Charon, to take him across the sea to his place of origin: a remote island in the sea. These pieces were distributed among the Araucanian museums of Temuco, the future Museo Abate Molina of Villa Alegre, and the Museo Araucano of Santiago, which will soon be open to the public." The mention of Villa Alegre prompted Kilapán to add the oddest note. It read: "In Villa Alegre, formerly Warakulen, lie the remains of Abate Juan Ignacio Molina, brought from Italy to his native city. He was a professor at the University of Bologna, where his statue presides over the entrance to the Pantheon of the Distinguished Sons of Italy, between the statues of Copernicus and Galileo. According to Molina, there is an unquestionable kinship between Greeks and Araucanians." This Molina was a Jesuit and a naturalist, and he lived from 1740 to 1829.

•

Shortly after the episode at Los Zancudos, Amalfitano saw Dean Guerra's son again. This time he was dressed like a cowboy, although he had shaved and he smelled of Calvin Klein cologne. Even so, all he lacked to look like a real cowboy was the hat. There was something mysterious about the way he accosted Amalfitano. It was late in the day, and as Amalfitano walked along a ridiculously long corridor at the university, deserted and dark at that hour, Marco Antonio Guerra burst out from a corner like someone playing a bad joke or about to attack him. Amalfitano jumped, then struck out automatically with his fist. It's me, Marco

Antonio, said the dean's son, after he was hit again. Then they recognized each other and relaxed and set off together toward the rectangle of light at the end of the hallway, which reminded Marco Antonio of the stories of people who'd been in comas or declared clinically dead and who claimed to have seen a dark tunnel with a white or dazzling brightness at the end, and sometimes these people even testified to the presence of loved ones who had passed away, who took their hands or soothed them or urged them to turn back because the hour or microfraction of a second in which the change took effect hadn't yet arrived. What do you think, Professor? Do people on the verge of death make this shit up, or is it real? Is it all just a dream, or is it within the realm of possibility? I don't know, said Amalfitano curtly, since he still hadn't gotten over his fright, and he wasn't in the mood for a repeat of their last meeting. Well, said Marco Antonio Guerra, if you want to know what I think, I don't believe it. People see what they want to see and what people want to see never has anything to do with the truth. People are cowards to the last breath. I'm telling you between you and me: the human being, broadly speaking, is the closest thing there is to a rat.

•

Despite what he had hoped (to get rid of Marco Antonio Guerra as soon as they emerged from the hallway with its aura of life after death), Amalfitano had to follow him without complaint because the dean's son was the bearer of an invitation to dinner that very evening at the house of the rector of the University of Santa Teresa, the august Dr. Pablo Negrete. So he climbed in Marco Antonio's car, and Marco Antonio drove him home, then chose, in an unwonted display of shyness, to wait for him outside, watching the car, as if there were thieves in Colonia Lindavista, while Amalfitano cleaned up and changed clothes, and his daughter, who of course was invited too, did the same, or not, since his daughter could go dressed as she liked, but he, Amalfitano, had better show up at Dr. Negrete's house in a jacket and tie at the very least. The dinner, as it happened, was nothing to worry about. Dr. Negrete simply wanted to meet him and had assumed, or been advised, that a first meeting in his office at the administration building would be much chillier than a first meeting in the comfort of his own home, a grand old two-story house surrounded by a lush garden with plants from all over Mexico and plenty of shady nooks where guests could gather in *petit comité*. Dr. Negrete was a man of silence and reserve who was happier listening to others than leading the conversation himself. He asked about Barcelona, recollected that in his youth he had attended a conference in Prague, mentioned a former professor at the University of Santa Teresa, an Argentinian who now taught at one of the branches of the University of California, and the rest of the time he was quiet. His wife, who carried herself with a distinction that the rector lacked, though to judge by her features she had never been a beauty, was much nicer to Amalfitano and especially to Rosa, who reminded her of her youngest daughter, whose name was Clara, like her mother's, and who had been living in Phoenix for years. At some point during the dinner Amalfitano thought he noticed a rather murky exchange of glances between the rector and his wife. In her eyes he glimpsed something that might have been hatred. At the same time, a sudden fear flitted as swiftly as a butterfly across the rector's face. But Amalfitano noticed it and for a moment (the second flutter of wings) the rector's fear nearly brushed his own skin. When he recovered and looked at the other dinner guests he realized that no one had noticed the slight shadow, like a hastily dug pit that gives off an alarming stench.

·

But he was wrong. Young Marco Antonio Guerra had noticed. And he had also noticed that Amalfitano had noticed. Life is worthless, he said into Amalfitano's ear when they went out into the garden. Rosa sat with the rector's wife and Professor Pérez. The rector sat in the gazebo's only rocking chair. Dean Guerra and two philosophy professors took seats near the rector's wife. A third professor, a bachelor, remained standing, next to Amalfitano and Marco Antonio Guerra. A servant, an almost elderly woman, came in after a while carrying an enormous tray of glasses that she set on a marble table. Amalfitano considered helping her, but then he thought it might be seen as disrespectful if he did. When the old woman reappeared, carrying more than seven bottles in precarious equilibrium, Amalfitano couldn't stop himself and went to help her. When she saw him, the old woman's eyes widened and the tray began to slip from her hands. Amalfitano heard a shriek, the ridiculous little shriek of one of the professors' wives, and at that same moment, as the tray was falling, he glimpsed the shadow of young Guerra setting everything right again. Don't worry, Chachita, he heard the rector's wife say.

Then he heard young Guerra, after he had set the bottles on the table, ask Doña Clara whether she kept any Los Suicidas mezcal in her liquor cabinet. And he heard Dean Guerra saying: pay no attention to my son and his foolish notions. And he heard Rosa say: Los Suicidas mezcal, what a pretty name. And he heard a professor's wife say: it certainly is unusual. And he heard Professor Pérez: what a fright, I thought she was going to drop them. And he heard a philosophy professor talking about *norteño* music, to change the subject. And he heard Dean Guerra say that the difference between *norteño* groups and groups from anywhere else in the country was that *norteño* groups were always made up of an accordion and a guitar, with the accompaniment of a *bajo sexto*, the twelve-string guitar, and some kind of *brinco*. And he heard the same philosophy professor asking what a *brinco* was. And he heard the dean answer that a *brinco* could be drums, for example, like a rock group's drum kit, or kettledrums, and in *norteño* music a proper *brinco* might be the *redova*, a hollow wooden block, or more commonly a pair of sticks. And he heard Rector Negrete saying: that's right. And then he accepted a glass of whiskey and sought the face of the person who had put it in his hand and found the face of young Guerra, pale in the moonlight.

•

Proof number 2, by far the most interesting to Amalfitano, was called *He was born to an Araucanian woman* and it began like this: "Upon the arrival of the Spaniards, the Araucanians established two channels for communication from Santiago: telepathy and Adkintuwe.[55] Lautaro,[56] because of his notable telepathic skills, was taken north with his mother when he was still a child to enter the service of the Spaniards. It was in this way that Lautaro contributed to the defeat of the Spaniards. Since telepaths could be eliminated and communications cut, Adkintuwe was created. Only after 1700 did the Spaniards become aware of this method of sending messages by the movement of branches. They were puzzled by the fact that the Araucanians knew everything that happened in the city of Concepción. Although they managed to discover Adkintuwe, they were never able to decipher it. They never suspected that the Araucanians were telepathic, believing instead that they had 'traffic with the devil,' who informed them of events in Santiago. There were three lines of Adkintuwe from the capital: one along the buttresses of the Andes, another along the coast, and a third along the central valley. Primitive man was ignorant of language; he communicated by brainwaves, as animals and plants do. When he resorted to sounds and gestures and hand signals to communicate, he began to lose the gift of telepathy, and this loss was accelerated when he went to live in cities, distancing himself from nature. Although the Araucanians had two kinds of writing—the rope knotting known as Prom,[57] and the triangle writing known as Adentunemul[58]—they never gave up telecommunication; on the contrary, some Kügas whose families were scattered all over America, the Pacific Islands, and the deepest south specialized in it so that no enemy would ever take them by surprise. By means of telepathy they kept in permanent contact with the Chilean migrants who first settled in the north of India, where they were called Aryans, then headed to the fields of ancient Germania and later descended to the Peloponnese, traveling from there to Chile along the traditional route to India and across the Pacific Ocean." Immediately following this and apropos of nothing, Kilapán wrote: "Killenkusi was a Machi[59] priestess. Her daughter Kinturay had to choose between succeeding her or becoming a spy; she chose the latter and her love for the Irishman; this opportunity afforded her the hope of having a child who, like Lautaro and mixed-race Alejo, would be raised among the Spaniards, and like them might one day lead the hosts of those who wished to push the conquistadors back beyond the Maule River, because Admapu law prohibited the Araucanians from fighting outside of Yekmonchi. Her hope was realized and in the spring[60] of the year 1777, in the place called Palpal, an Araucanian woman endured the pain of childbirth in a standing position because tradition decreed that a strong child could not be born of a weak mother. The son arrived and became the Liberator of Chile."

•

The footnotes made it very clear in what kind of drunken ship Kilapán had set sail, if it wasn't clear already. Note 55, *Adkintuwe*, read: "After many years the Spaniards became aware of its existence, but they were never able to decipher it." Note 56: "*Lautaro*, swift noise (*taros* in Greek means swift)." Note 57: "*Prom*, word handed down from the Greek by way of Prometheus, the Titan who stole writing from the gods to give to man." Note 58: "*Adentunemul*, secret writing consisting of triangles." Note 59: "*Machi*, seer. From the Greek verb *mantis*, which means to divine." Note 60: "*Spring*, Admapu law ordered that children should be conceived in summer, when all fruits were ripe; thus they would be born in spring when the land awakens in the fullness of its strength; when all the animals and birds are born."

•

From this one could conclude that: (1) all Araucanians or most of them were telepathic, (2) the Araucanian language was closely linked to the language of Homer, (3) Araucanians had traveled all over the globe, especially to India, ancient Germania, and the Peloponnese, (4) Araucanians were amazing sailors, (5) Araucanians had two kinds of writing, one based on knots and the other on triangles, the latter secret, (6) the exact nature of the mode of communication that Kilapán called Adkintuwe (and that had been discovered by the Spaniards, although they were unable to decipher it) wasn't very clear. Maybe it was the sending of messages by the movement of tree branches located in strategic places, like at the tops of hills? Something like the smoke signals of the Plains Indians of America? (7) in contrast, telepathic communication was never discovered and if at some point it stopped working this was because the Spaniards killed the telepaths, (8) telepathy also permitted the Araucanians of Chile to remain in permanent contact with Chilean migrants scattered in places as far-flung as populous India or green Germany, (9) should one deduce from this that Bernardo O'Higgins was also a telepath? Should one deduce that the author himself, Lonko Kilapán, was a telepath? Yes, in fact, one should.

•

One could also deduce (and, with a little effort, see) other things, thought Amalfitano as he diligently gauged his mood, watching Dieste's book hanging in the dark in the backyard. One could see, for example, the date that Kilapán's book was published, 1978, in other words during the military dictatorship, and deduce the atmosphere of triumph, loneliness, and fear in which it was published. One could see, for example, a gentleman of Indian appearance, half out of his head but hiding it well, dealing with the printers of the prestigious Editorial Universitaria, located on Calle San Francisco, number 454, in Santiago. One could see the sum that the publication of the little book would cost the Historian of the Race, the President of the Indigenous Confederation of Chile, and the Secretary of the Academy of the Araucanian Language, a sum that Mr. Kilapán tries to bargain down more wishfully than effectively, although the manager of the print shop knows that they aren't exactly overrun with work and that he could very well give this Mr. Kilapán a little discount, especially since the man swears he has two more books already finished and edited (*Araucanian Legends and Greek Legends* and *Origins of the American Man and Kinship Between Araucanians, Aryans, Early Germans, and Greeks*) and he swears up and down that he'll bring them here, because, gentlemen, a book published by the Editorial Universitaria is a book distinguished at first glance, a book of distinction, and it's this final argument that convinces the printer, the manager, the office drudge who handles these matters, to let him have his little discount. The word *distinguished*. The word *distinction*. Ah, ah, ah, ah, pants Amalfitano, struggling for breath as if he's having a sudden asthma attack. Ah, Chile.

•

Although it was possible to imagine other scenarios, of course, or it was possible to see the same sad picture from different angles. And just as the book began with a jab to the jaw ("the Yekmonchi, called Chile, was geographically and politically identical to the Greek state"), the active reader—the reader as envisioned by Cortázar—could begin his reading with a kick to the author's testicles, viewing him from the start as a straw man, a factotum in the service of some colonel in the intelligence services, or maybe of some general who fancied himself an intellectual, which wouldn't be so strange either, this being Chile, in fact the reverse would be stranger, in Chile military men behaved like writers, and writers, so as not to be outdone, behaved like military men, and politicians (of every stripe) behaved like writers and like military men, and diplomats behaved like cretinous cherubim, and doctors and lawyers behaved like thieves, and so on ad nauseam, impervious to discouragement. But picking up the thread where he had left off, it seemed possible that Kilapán hadn't been the one who wrote the book. And if Kilapán hadn't written the book, it might be that Kilapán didn't exist, in other words that there was no President of the Indigenous Confederation of Chile, among other reasons because perhaps the Indigenous Confederation didn't exist, nor was there any Secretary of the Academy of the Araucanian Language, among other reasons because perhaps said Academy of the Araucanian Language never existed. All fake. All nonexistent. Kilapán, from that perspective, thought Amalfitano, moving his head in time to the (very slight) swaying of Dieste's book outside the window, might easily be a nom de plume for Pinochet, representing Pinochet's long sleepless nights or his productive mornings, when he got up at six or five-thirty and after he showered and performed a few calisthenics he shut himself in his library to review international slights, to meditate on Chile's negative reputation abroad. But there was no reason to get too excited. Kilapán's prose could be Pinochet's, certainly. But it could also be Aylwin's or Lagos's. Kilapán's prose could be Frei's (which was saying something) or the prose of any right-wing neo-Fascist. Not only did Lonko Kilapán's prose encapsulate all of Chile's styles, it also represented all of its political factions, from the conservatives to the Communists, from the new liberals to the old survivors of the MIR. Kilapán was the high-grade Spanish spoken and written in Chile, its cadences revealing not only the leathery nose of Abate Molina, but also the butchery of Patricio Lynch, the endless shipwrecks of the *Esmeralda*, the Atacama desert and cattle grazing, the Guggenheim Fellowships, the Socialist politicians praising the economic policy of the junta, the corners where pumpkin fritters were sold, the *mote con huesillos*, the ghost of the Berlin Wall rippling on motionless red flags, the domestic abuse, the good-hearted whores, the cheap housing, what in Chile they called grudge holding and Amalfitano called madness.

•

But what he was really looking for was a name. The name of O'Higgins's telepathic mother. According to Kilapán: Kinturay Treulen, daughter of Killenkusi and Waramanke Treulen. According to the official story: Doña Isabel Riquelme. Having reached this point, Amalfitano decided to stop watching Dieste's book swaying (ever so slightly) in the darkness and sit down and think about his own mother's name: Doña Eugenia Riquelme (actually Doña Filia Maria Eugenia Riquelme Graña). He was briefly startled. For five seconds, his hair stood on end. He tried to laugh but he couldn't.

•

I understand you, Marco Antonio Guerra said to him. I mean, if I'm right, I think I understand you. You're like me and I'm like you. We aren't happy. The atmosphere around us is stifling. We pretend there's nothing wrong, but there is. What's wrong? We're being fucking stifled. You let off steam your own way. I beat the shit out of people or let them beat the shit out of me. But the fights I get into aren't just any fights, they're fucking apocalyptic mayhem. I'm going to tell you a secret. Sometimes I go out at night, to bars you can't even imagine. And I pretend to be a faggot. But not just any kind of faggot: smooth, stuck-up, sarcastic, a daisy in the filthiest pigsty in Sonora. Of course, I don't have a gay bone in me, I can swear that on the grave of my dead mother. But I pretend that's what I am. An arrogant little faggot with money who looks down on everyone. And then the inevitable happens. Two or three vultures ask me to step outside. And then the shit kicking begins. I know it and I don't care. Sometimes they're the ones who get the worst of it, especially when I have my gun. Other times it's me. I don't give a fuck. I need the fucking release. Sometimes my friends, the few friends I have, guys my age who are lawyers now, tell me I should be careful, I'm a time bomb, I'm a masochist. One of them, someone I was really close to, told me that only somebody like me could get away with what I did because I had my father to bail me out. Pure coincidence, that's all. I've never asked my father for a thing. The truth is, I don't have friends. I don't want any. At least, I'd rather not have friends who're Mexicans. Mexicans are rotten inside, did you know? Every last one of them. No one escapes. From the president of the republic to that clown Subcomandante Marcos. If I were Subcomandante Marcos, you know what I'd do? I'd launch an attack with my whole army on any city in Chiapas, so long as it had a strong military garrison. And there I'd sacrifice my poor Indians. And then I'd probably go live in Miami. What kind of music do you like? asked Amalfitano. Classical music, Professor, Vivaldi, Cimarosa, Bach. And what books do you read? I used to read everything, Professor, I read all the time. Now all I read is poetry. Poetry is the one thing that isn't contaminated, the one thing that isn't part of the game. I don't know if you follow me, Professor. Only poetry—and let me be clear, only some of it—is good for you, only poetry isn't shit.

•

Young Guerra's voice, breaking into flat, harmless shards, issued from a climbing vine, and he said: Georg Trakl is one of my favorites.

•

The mention of Trakl made Amalfitano think, as he went through the motions of teaching a class, about a drugstore near where he lived in Barcelona, a place he used to go when he needed medicine for Rosa. One of the employees was a young pharmacist, barely out of his teens, extremely thin and with big glasses, who would sit up at night reading a book when the pharmacy was open twenty-four hours. One night, while the kid was scanning the shelves, Amalfitano asked him what books he liked and what book he was reading, just to make conversation. Without turning, the pharmacist answered that he liked books like *The Metamorphosis*, *Bartleby*, *A Simple Heart*, *A Christmas Carol*. And then he said that he was reading Capote's *Breakfast at Tiffany's*. Leaving aside the fact that *A Simple Heart* and *A Christmas Carol* were stories, not books, there was something revelatory about the taste of this bookish young pharmacist, who in another life might have been Trakl or who in this life might still be writing poems as desperate as those of his distant Austrian counterpart, and who clearly and inarguably preferred minor works to major ones. He chose *The Metamorphosis* over *The Trial*, he chose *Bartleby* over *Moby-Dick*, he chose *A Simple Heart* over *Bouvard and Pécuchet*, and *A Christmas Carol* over *A Tale of Two Cities* or *The Pickwick Papers*. What a sad paradox, thought Amalfitano. Now even bookish pharmacists are afraid to take on the great, imperfect, torrential works, books that blaze paths into the unknown. They choose the perfect exercises of the great masters. Or what amounts to the same thing: they want to watch the great masters spar, but they have no interest in real combat, when the great masters struggle against that something, that something that terrifies us all, that something that cows us and spurs us on, amid blood and mortal wounds and stench.

•

That night, as young Guerra's grandiloquent words were still echoing in the depths of his brain, Amalfitano dreamed that he saw the last Communist philosopher of the twentieth century appear in a pink marble courtyard. He was speaking Russian. Or rather: he was singing a song in Russian as his big body went weaving toward a patch of red-streaked majolica that stood out on the flat plane of the courtyard like a kind of crater or latrine. The last Communist philosopher was dressed in a dark suit and sky-blue tie and had gray hair. Although he seemed about to collapse at any moment, he remained miraculously upright. The song wasn't always the same, since sometimes he mixed in words in English or French, words to other songs, pop ballads or tangos, tunes that celebrated drunkenness or love. And yet these interruptions were brief and sporadic and he soon returned to the original song, in Russian, the words of which Amalfitano didn't understand (although in dreams, as in the Gospels, one usually possesses the gift of tongues). Still, he sensed that the words were sad, the story or lament of a Volga boatman who sails all night and commiserates with the moon about the sad fate of men condemned to be born and to die. When the last Communist philosopher finally reached the crater or latrine, Amalfitano discovered in astonishment that it was none other than Boris Yeltsin. This is the last Communist philosopher? What kind of lunatic am I if this is the kind of nonsense I dream? And yet the dream was at peace with Amalfitano's soul. It wasn't a nightmare. And it also granted him a kind of featherlight sense of well-being. Then Boris Yeltsin looked at Amalfitano with curiosity, as if it were Amalfitano who had invaded his dream, not the other way around. And he said: listen carefully to what I have to say, comrade. I'm going to explain what the third leg of the human table is. I'm going to tell you. And then leave me alone. Life is demand and supply, or supply and demand, that's what it all boils down to, but that's no way to live. A third leg is needed to keep the table from collapsing into the garbage pit of history, which in turn is permanently collapsing into the garbage pit of the void. So take note. This is the equation: supply + demand + magic. And what is magic? Magic is epic and it's also sex and Dionysian mists and play. And then Yeltsin sat on the crater or the latrine and showed Amalfitano the fingers he was missing and talked about his childhood and about the Urals and Siberia and about a white tiger that roamed the infinite snowy spaces. And then he took a flask of vodka out of his suit pocket and said:

"I think it's time for a little drink."

And after he had drunk and given the poor Chilean professor the sly squint of a hunter, he began to sing again, if possible with even more brio. And then he disappeared, swallowed up by the crater streaked with red or by the latrine streaked with red, and Amalfitano was left alone and he didn't dare look down the hole, which meant he had no choice but to wake.

3

THE PART ABOUT FATE

When did it all begin? he thought. When did I go under? A dark, vaguely familiar Aztec lake. The nightmare. How do I get away? How do I take control? And the questions kept coming: Was getting away what he really wanted? Did he really want to leave it all behind? And he also thought: the pain doesn't matter anymore. And also: maybe it all began with my mother's death. And also: the pain doesn't matter, as long as it doesn't get any worse, as long as it isn't unbearable. And also: fuck, it hurts, fuck, it hurts. Pay it no mind, pay it no mind. And all around him, ghosts.

•

Quincy Williams was thirty when his mother died. A neighbor called him at work.

"Honey," she said, "Edna's dead."

He asked when she'd died. He heard the woman sobbing at the other end of the line, and other voices, probably other women. He asked how. No one said anything and he hung up. He dialed his mother's number.

"Who is this?" he heard a woman say angrily.

He thought: my mother is in hell. He hung up again. He called again. It was a young woman.

"This is Quincy, Edna Miller's son," he said.

There was an exclamation he couldn't make out, and a moment later another woman came to the phone. He asked to speak to the neighbor. She's in bed, the woman said, she just had a heart attack, Quincy, we're waiting for an ambulance to come and take her to the hospital. He didn't dare ask about his mother. He heard a man's voice cursing. The man must be in the hallway and his mother's door must be open. He put his hand to his forehead and waited, without hanging up, for someone to explain what was going on. Two women's voices scolded the man who had sworn. They spoke a man's name, but he couldn't hear it clearly.

The woman who was typing at the next desk asked whether something was wrong. He raised his hand as if he was listening to something important and shook his head. The woman went back to typing. Quincy waited awhile and hung up, put on the jacket that was hanging on the back of his chair, and said he had to leave.

•

When he got to his mother's apartment, the only person there was a fifteen-year-old girl who was sitting on the couch watching TV. She got up when she saw him come in. She must have been six feet tall and she was very thin. She was wearing jeans and over them a black dress with yellow flowers, very loose, like a robe.

"Where is she?" he asked.

"In the bedroom," said the girl.

His mother was on the bed with her eyes closed, dressed as if to go out. They'd even put lipstick on her. All she was missing was her shoes. Quincy stood for a time in the doorway, looking at her feet: there were corns on her two big toes and calluses on the soles of her feet, big calluses that must have hurt her. But he remembered that his mother went to a podiatrist on Lewis Street, a Dr. Johnson, always the same person, so they must not have bothered her too much after all. Then he looked at her face: it seemed to have been carved out of wax.

"I'm leaving," said the girl from the living room.

Quincy came out of the bedroom and tried to give her a twenty, but the girl said she didn't want money. He insisted. Finally the girl took the bill and put it in the pocket of her jeans. To do that she had to hitch her dress up to her hip. She looks like a nun, thought Quincy, or like she belongs to a dangerous cult. The girl gave him a piece of paper where someone had written the phone number of a neighborhood funeral home.

"They'll take care of everything," she said gravely.

"All right," he said.

He asked about the neighbor woman.

"She's in the hospital," said the girl. "I think they're putting in a pace-maker."

"A pacemaker?"

"Yes," said the girl, "in her heart."

When the girl left, Quincy thought that the people in the building and the neighborhood had loved his mother, but they had loved his mother's neighbor, whose face he couldn't remember clearly, even more.

•

He called the funeral home and talked to someone by the name of Tremayne. He said he was Edna Miller's son. Tremayne consulted his notes and expressed his condolences several times, until he found the paper he was looking for. Then he put him on hold and transferred him to someone called Lawrence. Lawrence asked him what kind of cere-mony he wanted.

"Something simple and intimate," said Quincy. "Very simple, very intimate."

In the end they agreed that his mother would be cremated, and the ceremony, barring unforeseen circumstances, would take place the next evening, at the funeral home, at seven. By seven forty-five it would all be over. He asked whether it was possible to do it sooner. It wasn't. Then Mr. Lawrence delicately approached the matter of payment. There was no problem. Quincy wanted to know whether he should call the police or the hospital. No, said Mr. Lawrence, Miss Holly already took care of that. Quincy asked himself who Miss Holly was and drew a blank.

"Miss Holly is your late mother's neighbor," said Mr. Lawrence.

"That's right," said Quincy.

For a moment they were both silent, as if they were trying to remem-ber or piece together the faces of Edna Miller and her neighbor. Mr. Lawrence cleared his throat. He asked whether Quincy knew what church his mother belonged to. He asked whether he himself had any religious preferences. Quincy said his mother belonged to the Chris-tian Church of Fallen Angels. Or no, maybe it had another name. He couldn't remember. You're right, said Mr. Lawrence, it does have a differ-ent name, it's the Christian Church of Angels Redeemed. That's the one, said Quincy. And he also said he had no religious leanings. So long as it was a Christian ceremony, that would be enough.

That night he slept on the couch in his mother's house. He went into her room just once and had a glance at the body. The next day, first thing in the morning, the people from the funeral home came and took her away. He got up to let them in, gave them a check, and watched how they carried the pine coffin down the stairs. Then he went back to sleep on the couch.

When he woke up he thought he'd dreamed about a movie he'd seen the other day. But everything was different. The characters were black, so the movie in the dream was like a negative of the real movie. And different things happened, too. The plot was the same, what happened was the same, but the ending was different or at some moment things took an unexpected turn and became something completely different. Most terrible of all, though, was that as he was dreaming he knew it didn't necessarily have to be that way, he noticed the resemblance to the movie, he thought he understood that both were based on the same premise, and that if the movie he'd seen was the real movie, then the other one, the one he had dreamed, might be a reasoned response, a reasoned critique, and not necessarily a nightmare. All criticism is ultimately a nightmare, he thought as he washed his face in the apartment where his mother's body no longer was.

He also thought about what she would have said to him. Be a man and bear your cross.

•

At work everybody called him Oscar Fate. When he came back no one said anything to him. There was no reason for anyone to say anything. He spent some time looking over his notes on Barry Seaman. The girl at the next desk wasn't there. Then he locked his notes in a drawer and went out to eat. In the elevator he ran into the editor of the magazine, who was with a fat young woman who wrote about teen killers. They nodded to each other and went their separate ways.

He had French onion soup and an omelet at a good, cheap restaurant two blocks away. He hadn't eaten anything since the day before and the food made him feel better. When he'd paid and was about to leave, a man who worked for the sports section called him over and offered to buy him a beer. As they were sitting waiting at the bar, the man told him that the chief boxing correspondent had died that morning outside Chicago. *Chief* was really an honorary term, since the dead man was the only boxing correspondent they had.

"How did he die?" asked Fate.

"Some black guys from Chicago stabbed him to death," said the other man.

The waiter set a hamburger on the bar. Fate finished his beer, clapped the man on the shoulder, and said he had to go. When he got to the glass door he turned around and contemplated the crowded restaurant and the back of the man from the sports section and the people in pairs, gazing into each other's eyes as they ate or talked, and the three waiters who were never still. Then he opened the door and went out. He looked back into the restaurant, but with the glass in between everything was different. He walked away.

•

"When are you heading out, Oscar?" asked his editor.

"Tomorrow."

"You got everything you need, are you set?"

"All set," said Fate. "Everything's ready to go."

"That's what I like to hear, son," said the boss. "Did you hear that Jimmy Lowell got whacked?"

"I heard something."

"It was in Paradise City, near Chicago," said the boss. "They say Jimmy had a girl there. Some bitch twenty years younger and married."

"How old was Jimmy?" asked Fate without the least interest.

"He must've been fifty-five or sixty," said the boss. "The police arrested the girl's husband, but our man in Chicago says she was probably mixed up in it too."

"Was Jimmy a big guy? Weighed about two hundred and fifty pounds?" asked Fate.

"No, Jimmy wasn't big, and he didn't weigh two hundred and fifty neither. He was five ten, maybe, maybe one seventy-five," said the boss.

"I must be mixing him up with someone else," said Fate, "a big guy who had lunch with Remy Burton sometimes. I used to see him in the elevator."

"No," said the boss, "Jimmy almost never came into the office. He stayed on the road. He showed up here once a year tops. I think he lived in Tampa, he may not even have had a place, spent his life in hotels and airports."

•

He showered and didn't shave. He listened to the messages on the answering machine. He left the Barry Seaman file that he'd brought from the office on the table. He put on clean clothes and went out. Since he still had time, he went to his mother's apartment first. He noticed that something there smelled bad. He went into the kitchen and when he didn't find anything rotten he tied up the garbage bag and opened the window. Then he sat on the couch and turned on the TV. On a shelf near the TV there were some videotapes. For a few seconds he thought about checking them out, but he gave up the idea almost as soon as it came to him. They had probably just been used to record shows that his mother watched later, at night. He tried to think about something pleasant. He tried to mentally run through all the things he had to do. He couldn't. After sitting absolutely still for a while, he turned off the TV, picked up the keys and the garbage bag, and left the apartment. Before he went down the stairs he knocked at the neighbor's door. No one answered. Outside he tossed the garbage bag into an overflowing Dumpster.

The ceremony was simple and businesslike. He signed a few papers. He wrote another check. He accepted the condolences first of Mr. Tremayne, then of Mr. Lawrence, who appeared at the end as Quincy was leaving with the urn that held his mother's ashes. Was the service satisfactory? asked Mr. Lawrence. During the ceremony, sitting at one end of the room, he saw the tall girl again. She was dressed just as she had been before, in jeans and the black dress with yellow flowers. He looked at her and tried to give her a friendly wave, but she wasn't looking his way. The rest of the people there were strangers, although they were mostly women, so he supposed they must be friends of his mother's. At the end, two of them came up to him and spoke words he didn't understand, words of consolation or rebuke. He went walking back to his mother's apartment. He set the urn next to the videotapes and turned the TV back on. The apartment had stopped smelling bad. The whole building was silent, as if no one was there, as if everyone had gone out on urgent business. From the window he saw teenagers playing and talking (or plotting) but doing the one thing on its own. In other words, they would play for a minute, stop, gather, talk for a minute, and go back to playing, and after that they'd stop and do the same thing over and over again.

He asked himself what kind of game it was and whether the pauses to talk were part of the game or a clear sign that they didn't know the rules. He made up his mind to take a walk. After a while he felt hungry and went into a little Middle Eastern restaurant (Egyptian or Jordanian, he didn't know which), where they served him a sandwich of ground lamb. When he came out he felt sick. In a dark alley he threw up the lamb and was left with a taste of bile and spices in his mouth. He saw a man pushing a hot dog cart. He caught up to him and asked for a beer. The man looked at him as if Fate was high and told him he wasn't allowed to sell alcoholic beverages.

"Give me whatever you have," Fate said.

The man handed him a Coke. He paid and drank the whole thing as the man with the cart went off down the dimly lit street. After a while he saw a movie theater marquee. He remembered that as a teenager he used to spend many evenings there. He decided to go in, even though the movie had already started some time ago, as the ticket seller informed him.

•

He sat through only one scene. A white man is arrested by three black cops. Instead of taking him to the police station, the cops take him to an airfield. There, the man who's been arrested sees the chief of police, who's also black. The man is no fool and he figures out they're working for the DEA. Through unspoken assurances and eloquent silences, they reach a kind of deal. As they talk, the man looks out a window. He sees the landing strip and a Cessna taxiing toward one end of it. They unload a shipment of cocaine. The cop opening the crates and unpacking the bricks is black. Next to him, another black cop is tossing the bricks into a fire barrel, like the kind the homeless use to keep warm on winter nights. But these cops aren't bums. They're DEA agents, neatly dressed, government employees. The man turns away from the window and points out to the chief that all his men are black. They're more motivated, says the chief. And then he says: you can go now. When the man leaves, the chief smiles, but his smile quickly turns into a scowl. At that moment Fate rose and went to the men's room, where he vomited up the rest of the lamb in his stomach. Then he left and went back to his mother's.

Before he went in, he knocked at the neighbor's door. A woman more or less his own age opened the door. She was wearing glasses and her hair was up in a green African turban. He explained who he was and inquired after the neighbor. The woman looked him in the eye and asked him in. The living room looked like his mother's. Even the furniture was similar. In the room he saw six women and three men. Some were standing or leaning in the kitchen doorway, but most were sitting down.

"I'm Rosalind," said the woman in the turban. "Your mother and mine were very close friends."

Fate nodded. Sobs came from the back of the apartment. One of the women got up and went into the bedroom. When she opened the door the sobs got louder, but when the door closed the sound vanished.

"It's my sister," Rosalind said wearily. "Would you like some coffee?"

Fate said yes. When the woman went into the kitchen, one of the men who was standing came over and asked whether he wanted to see Miss Holly. He nodded. The man led him to the bedroom but remained outside, on the other side of the door. The neighbor lady's body was laid out on the bed, and beside it he saw a woman on her knees, praying. Sitting in a rocking chair next to the window was the girl in jeans and the black dress with yellow flowers. Her eyes were red and she looked at him as if she'd never seen him before.

When he came out he sat on the edge of a couch occupied by women speaking in monosyllables. When Rosalind put a cup of coffee in his hands he asked when her mother had died. This afternoon, said Rosalind in a calm voice. What did she die of? She was old, said Rosalind with a smile. When he got home, Fate realized he was still holding the coffee cup. For an instant he thought about going back to the neighbor's apartment and returning it, but then he thought it would be better to leave it for the next day. He couldn't drink the coffee. He set it next to the videotapes and the urn containing his mother's ashes, then he turned on the TV and turned off the lights and stretched out on the couch. He muted the sound.

•

The next morning, when he opened his eyes, the first thing he saw was a cartoon. Rats were streaming through a city, silently squealing.

He grabbed the remote control and changed channels. When he found the news, he turned on the sound, though not very loud, and got up. He washed his face and neck and when he dried himself he realized that the towel, hanging on the towel rack, was almost certainly the last towel his mother had used. He smelled it but didn't detect any familiar scent. In the bathroom cabinet there were various bottles of pills and some jars of moisturizing or anti-inflammatory cream. He called in to work and asked to speak to his editor. The only person there was the girl at the next desk and he talked to her. He told her he wasn't coming into the magazine because he planned to leave in a few hours for Detroit. She said she already knew and she wished him good luck.

"I'll be back in three days, maybe four," he said.

Then he hung up, smoothed his shirt, put on his jacket, looked at himself in the mirror by the door, and tried and failed to pull himself together. It was time to get back to work. He stood with his hand on the doorknob, wondering whether he should take the urn with the ashes home with him. I'll do it when I get back, he thought, and he opened the door.

•

He was home just long enough to put the Barry Seaman file, a few shirts, a few pairs of socks, and some underwear in a bag. He sat in a chair and realized he was a nervous wreck. He tried to relax. When he went outside, it was raining. When had it started to rain? All the taxis that went by had fares. He slung the bag over his shoulder and began to walk along the curb. At last a taxi stopped. When he was about to close the door he heard something like a shot. He asked the taxi driver whether he'd heard it. The taxi driver was Hispanic and spoke very bad English.

"Every day you hear more fantastic things in New York," the driver said.

"What do you mean, fantastic?" he asked.

"Exactly what I say, fantastic," said the taxi driver.

After a while Fate fell asleep. Every now and then he opened his eyes and watched buildings go by where no one seemed to live, or gray streets slicked with rain. Then he closed his eyes and went back to sleep. He woke up when the taxi driver asked him what terminal he wanted.

"I'm going to Detroit," he said, and he went back to sleep.

The two people sitting in front of him were discussing ghosts. Fate couldn't see their faces, but he imagined them as older, maybe sixty or seventy. He asked for an orange juice. The stewardess was blond, about forty, and she had a mark on her neck covered with a white scarf that had slipped as she bustled up and down assisting passengers. The man in the seat next to him was black and was drinking from a bottle of water. Fate opened his bag and took out the Seaman file. Instead of ghosts, now the passengers in front of him were talking about a person they called Bobby. This Bobby lived in Jackson Tree, Michigan, and had a cabin on Lake Huron. One time this Bobby had gone out in a boat and capsized. He managed to cling to a log that was floating nearby and waited for morning. But as night went on, the water kept getting colder and Bobby was freezing and started to lose his strength. He felt weaker and weaker, and even though he did his best to tie himself to the log with his belt, he couldn't no matter how hard he tried. It may sound easy, but in real life it's hard to tie your own body to a floating log. So he gave up hope, turned his thoughts to his loved ones (here they mentioned someone called Jig, which might have been the name of a friend or a dog or a pet frog he had), and clung to the branch as tightly as he could. Then he saw a light in the sky. He thought it was a helicopter coming to find him, which was foolish, and he started to shout. But then it occurred to him that helicopters clatter and the light he saw wasn't clattering. A few seconds later he realized it was an airplane. A great big plane about to crash right where he was floating, clinging to that log. Suddenly all his tiredness vanished. He saw the plane pass just overhead. It was in flames. Maybe a thousand feet from where he was, the plane plunged into the lake. He heard two explosions, possibly more. He felt the urge to get closer to the site of the disaster and that's what he did, very slowly, because it was hard to steer the log. The plane had split in half and only one part was still floating. Before Bobby got there he watched it sinking slowly down into the waters of the lake, which had gone dark again. A little while later the rescue helicopters arrived. The only person they found was Bobby and they felt cheated when he told them he hadn't been on the plane, that he'd capsized his boat when he was fishing. Still, he was famous for a while, said the person telling the story.

"And does he still live in Jackson Tree?" asked the other man.

"No, I think he lives in Colorado now," was the response.

Then they started to talk about sports. The man next to Fate finished his water and belched discreetly, covering his mouth with his hand.

"Lies," he said softly.

"What?" asked Fate.

"Lies, lies," said the man.

Right, said Fate, and he turned away and stared out the window at the clouds that looked like cathedrals or maybe just little toy churches abandoned in a labyrinthine marble quarry one hundred times bigger than the Grand Canyon.

•

In Detroit, Fate rented a car, and after he checked a map from the car rental agency, he headed to the neighborhood where Barry Seaman lived.

Seaman wasn't home, but a boy told him he was almost always at Pete's Bar, not far from there. The neighborhood looked like a neighborhood of Ford and General Motors retirees. As he walked he looked at the buildings, five and six stories high, and all he saw were old people sitting on the stoops or leaning out the windows smoking. Every so often he passed a group of boys hanging out on the corner or girls jumping rope. The parked cars weren't nice cars or new cars, but they looked cared for.

The bar was next to a vacant lot full of weeds and wildflowers growing over the ruins of the building that had once stood there. On the side of a neighboring building he saw a mural that struck him as odd. It was circular, like a clock, and where the numbers should have been there were scenes of people working in the factories of Detroit. Twelve scenes representing twelve stages in the production chain. In each scene, there was one recurring character: a black teenager, or a long-limbed, scrawny black man-child, or a man clinging to childhood, dressed in clothes that changed from scene to scene but that were invariably too small for him. He had apparently been assigned the role of clown, intended to make people laugh, although a closer look made it clear that he wasn't there only to make people laugh. The mural looked like the work of a lunatic. The last painting of a lunatic. In the middle of the clock, where all the scenes converged, there was a word painted in letters that looked like they were made of gelatin: *fear*.

Fate went into the bar. He took a stool and asked the man behind the bar who had painted the mural outside. The bartender, a heavy black man in his sixties with a scar, said he didn't know.

"Probably some kid from the neighborhood," he muttered.

Fate ordered a beer and cast a glance around the bar. He didn't see anyone who might have been Seaman. Beer in hand, he asked loudly whether anyone knew Barry Seaman.

"Who wants to know?" asked a short guy in a Pistons T-shirt and a sky-blue tweed jacket.

"Oscar Fate," said Fate, "of the magazine *Black Dawn*, from New York."

The bartender came over and asked whether he was really a reporter. I'm a reporter. For *Black Dawn*.

"Man," said the short guy without getting up from his table, "that's a fucked-up name for a magazine." His two fellow cardplayers laughed. "Personally I'm sick of all these dawns," said the short guy. "Why don't the brothers in New York do something with the sunset for once, that's the best time of day, at least in this goddamn neighborhood."

"When I get back I'll tell them. I just write stories," he said.

"Barry Seaman didn't come in today," said an old man who was sitting at the bar, like Fate.

"I think he's sick," said another.

"That's right, I did hear something like that," said the old man at the bar.

"I'll wait for him awhile," said Fate, and he finished his beer.

The bartender settled across from him and told him that in his day he'd been a fighter.

"My last fight was in Athens, in South Carolina. I fought a white boy. Who do you think won?" he asked.

Fate looked him in the eye, frowned noncommittally, and ordered another beer.

"It was four months since I saw my manager. I just went around with my trainer, this old man called Johnny Bird, we went from one town to another in South Carolina, North Carolina, sleeping in these shitty-ass motels. He was wobbly and so was I, you know what I'm saying, me because I'd got hit so much and old Bird because by then he was eighty at least. That's right, eighty, maybe he was eighty-three. We used to argue about that before we went to sleep, with the lights out. Bird said he'd just hit eighty. I said he was eighty-three. They fixed the fight. The promoter told me to go down in the fifth. And to let myself get knocked around some in the fourth. For that, they'd give me double what they'd promised, which wasn't much. I told Bird about it that night, eating supper. It don't matter none to me, he said. I don't give a damn. The problem is, most times these people don't pay their bills. So it's up to you. That's what he said."

•

On the way back to Seaman's house Fate felt a little dizzy. An enormous moon was rising over the roofs. Near the entrance to a building a man came up to him and said something that either he didn't understand or that struck him as unacceptable. I'm Barry Seaman's friend, motherfucker, said Fate as he tried to grab the man by the lapels of his leather jacket.

"Relax," said the man. "Easy, brother."

Inside the doorway he saw four pairs of yellow eyes shining in the dark, and in the dangling hand of the man he was gripping he saw the fleeting reflection of the moon.

"Get out of here or I'll kill you," he said.

"Relax, brother, let me go first," said the man.

Fate let go of him and looked for the moon over the roofs ahead. He followed it. As he walked he heard noises on the side streets, steps, running, as if part of the neighborhood had just woken up. Next to Seaman's building he made out his rental car. He examined it. Nothing had happened to it. Then he rang the buzzer and an irritated voice asked what he wanted. Fate identified himself and said he'd been sent from *Black Dawn*. Over the intercom he heard a little laugh of satisfaction. Come in, said the voice. Fate crawled up the stairs. At some point he understood he wasn't well. Seaman was waiting for him on the landing.

"I need to use the bathroom," said Fate.

"Jesus," said Seaman.

The living room was small and modest and he saw books strewn everywhere and also posters taped to the walls and little photographs scattered along the shelves and the table and on top of the TV.

"The second door," said Seaman.

Fate went in and began to vomit.

•

When he woke up he saw Seaman writing with a pen. Next to him were four thick books and several folders full of papers. Seaman wore glasses when he wrote. Fate noticed that three of the four books were dictionaries and the fourth was a huge tome called *The Abridged French Encyclopedia*, which he'd never heard of, in college or ever. The sun was coming in the window. He threw off the blanket and sat up on the couch. He asked Seaman what had happened. The old man looked at him over his glasses and offered him a cup of coffee. Seaman was six feet tall, at least, but he stood slightly stooped, which made him seem smaller. He made a living giving lectures, which tended to be badly paid, since he was hired most often by educational organizations operating in the ghetto and sometimes by small progressive colleges with tiny budgets. Years ago he had published a book called *Eating Ribs with Barry Seaman*, in which he collected all the recipes he knew for ribs, mostly grilled or barbecued, adding strange or notable facts about the places where he'd learned each recipe, who had taught it to him, and under what circumstances. The best part of the book had to do with the ribs and mashed potatoes or applesauce he'd made in prison: how he'd got hold of the ingredients and how he'd cooked them in a place where cooking, like so many other things, was forbidden. The book wasn't a bestseller, but it put Seaman back in circulation and he appeared on a few morning shows, cooking some of his famous recipes live. Now he had fallen into obscurity again, but he kept giving lectures and traveling the country, sometimes in exchange for a return ticket and three hundred dollars.

Next to the table where he wrote and where the two of them sat to have coffee, there was a black-and-white poster of two young men in black jackets and black berets and dark glasses. Fate shivered, not because of the poster but because he felt so sick, and after the first swallow of coffee he asked whether one of the boys was Seaman. That's right, said Seaman. Fate asked which one. Seaman smiled. He didn't have a single tooth.

"Hard to tell, isn't it?"

"I don't know, I don't feel very well, if I felt better I'm sure I could figure it out," said Fate.

"The one on the right, the shorter one," said Seaman.

"Who's the other one?" asked Fate.

"Are you sure you don't know?"

Fate looked at the poster again for a while.

"It's Marius Newell," he said.

"That's right," said Seaman.

•

Seaman put on a jacket. Then he went into the bedroom and when he came out he was wearing a narrow-brimmed dark green hat. He picked his dentures out of a glass in the dark bathroom and fit them in carefully. Fate watched him from the living room. He rinsed his mouth with a red liquid, spat in the sink, rinsed again, and said he was ready.

They left in the rental car for Rebecca Holmes Park, some twenty blocks away. Since they had time to kill, they stopped the car on the edge of the park and spent a while talking as they stretched their legs. Rebecca Holmes Park was big and in the middle, surrounded by a half-collapsed fence, was a playground called Temple A. Hoffman Memorial Playground, where they didn't see any children playing. In fact, the playground was completely empty, except for a couple of rats that took off when they saw Seaman and Fate. Next to a cluster of oaks stood a vaguely Oriental-looking gazebo, like a miniature Russian Orthodox church. Hip-hop sounded from the other side of the gazebo.

"I hate this shit," said Seaman, "make sure you get that in your article."

"Why?" asked Fate.

They headed toward the gazebo and next to it they saw the dried-up bed of a pond. A pair of Nike sneakers had left frozen tracks in the dry mud. Fate thought about dinosaurs and felt sick again. They walked around the gazebo. On the other side, on the ground next to some shrubs, they saw a boom box, the source of the music. There was no one nearby. Seaman said he didn't like rap because the only out it offered was suicide. But not even meaningful suicide. I know, I know, he said. It's hard to imagine meaningful suicide. It isn't a common thing. Although I've seen or been near two meaningful suicides. At least I think I have. I could be wrong, he said.

"How does rap lead to suicide?" asked Fate.

Seaman didn't answer and led him on a shortcut through the trees, which brought them out into an open space. On the pavement three girls were jumping rope. The song they were singing seemed highly unusual. There was something about a woman whose legs and arms and tongue had been amputated. There was something about the Chicago sewers and the sanitation boss or a city worker called Sebastian D'Onofrio, and then came a refrain, repeating Chi-Chi-Chi-Chicago. There was something about the pull of the moon. Then the woman grew wooden legs and wire arms and a tongue made of braided grasses and plants. Completely disoriented, Fate asked where his car was, and the old man said it was on the other side of the park. They crossed the street, talking about sports. They walked one hundred yards and went into a church.

•

There, from the pulpit, Seaman spoke about his life. The Reverend Ronald K. Foster introduced him, in a way that made it clear Seaman had been there before. I'm going to address five subjects, said Seaman, no more and no less. The first subject is DANGER. The second, MONEY. The third, FOOD. The fourth, STARS. The fifth and last, USEFULNESS. People smiled and some nodded their heads in approval, as if to say all right, as if to inform the speaker they had nothing better to do than listen to him. In a corner Fate saw five boys in black jackets and black berets and dark glasses, none of them older than twenty. They were watching Seaman with impassive faces, ready to applaud him or jeer. On the stage the old man paced back and forth, his back hunched, as if he had suddenly forgotten his speech. Unexpectedly, at a sign from the preacher, the choir sang a gospel hymn. The hymn was about Moses and the captivity of the people of Israel in Egypt. The preacher himself accompanied them on the piano. Then Seaman returned to center stage and raised a hand (he had his eyes closed), and in a few seconds the choir's singing ceased and the church was silent.

•

DANGER. Despite what the congregation (or most of it) expected, Seaman began by talking about his childhood in California. He said that for those who hadn't been to California, what it was most like was an enchanted island. The spitting image. Just like in the movies, but better. People live in houses, not apartment buildings, he said, and then he embarked on a comparison of houses (one-story, at most two-story), and four- or five-story buildings where the elevator is broken one day and out of order the next. The only way buildings compared favorably to houses was in terms of proximity. A neighborhood of buildings makes distances shorter, he said. Everything is closer. You can go walking to buy groceries or you can walk to your local tavern (here he winked at Reverend Foster), or the local church you belong to, or a museum. In other words, you don't need to drive. You don't even need a car. And here he recited a list of statistics on fatal car accidents in a county of Detroit and a county of Los Angeles. And that's even considering that cars are made in Detroit, he said, not Los Angeles. He raised a finger, felt for something in the pocket of his jacket, and brought out an inhaler. Everyone waited in silence. The two spurts of the inhaler could be heard all the way to the farthest corner of the church. Pardon me, he said. Then he said he had learned to drive at thirteen. I don't drive anymore, he said, but I learned at thirteen and it's not something I am proud of. At that point he stared out into the room, at a vague spot in the middle of the sanctuary, and said he had been one of the founders of the Black Panthers. Marius Newell and I, he said, to be precise. After that, the speech subtly drifted from its course. It was as if the doors of the church had opened, wrote Fate in his notebook, and the ghost of Newell had come in. But just then, as if to avoid a certain awkwardness, Seaman began to talk not about Newell but about Newell's mother, Anne Jordan Newell. He described her appearance (pleasing), her work (she had a job at a factory that made irrigation systems), her faith (she went to church every Sunday), her industriousness (she kept the house as neat as a pin), her kindness (she always had a smile for everyone), her common sense (she gave good advice, wise advice, without forcing it on anyone). A mother is a precious thing, concluded Seaman. Marius and I founded the Panthers. We worked whatever jobs we could get and we bought shotguns and handguns for the people's self-defense. But a mother is worth more than the Black Revolution. That I can promise you. In my long and eventful life, I've seen many things. I was in Algeria and I was in China and in several prisons in the United States. A mother is a precious thing. This I say here and I'll say anywhere, anytime, he said in a hoarse voice. He excused himself again and turned toward the altar, then he turned back to face the audience. As you all know, he said, Marius Newell was killed. A black man like you and like me killed him one night in Santa Cruz, California. I told him, Marius, don't go back to California, there are too many cops there, cops out to get us. But he didn't listen. He liked California. He liked to go to the rocky beaches on a Sunday and breathe the smell of the Pacific. When we were both in prison, I got postcards from him in which he told me he'd dreamed he was breathing that air. Which is strange, because I haven't met many black folks who took to the sea the way he did. Maybe none, definitely none in California. But I know what he was talking about, I know what he meant. As it happens, I have a theory about this, about why we don't like the sea. We do like it. Just not as much as other folks. But that's for another occasion. Marius told me things had changed in California. There were many more black police now, for example. It was true. It had changed in that way. But in other ways it was still the same. And yet there was no denying that some things had changed. And Marius recognized that and he knew we deserved part of the credit. The Panthers had helped bring the change. With our grain of sand or our dump truck. We had contributed. So had his mother and all the other black mothers who wept at night and saw visions of the gates of hell when they should have been asleep. So he decided he'd go back to California and live the rest of his life there, in peace, out of harm's way, and maybe he'd start a family. He always said he would call his first son Frank, after a friend who lost his life in Soledad Prison. Truth is, he would've had to have at least thirty children to pay tribute to all the friends who'd been taken from him. Or ten, and give each of them three names. Or five, and give them each six. But as it happened he didn't have any children because one night, as he was walking down the street in Santa Cruz, a black man killed him. They say it was for money. They say Marius owed him money and that was why he was killed, but I find that hard to believe. I think someone hired that man to kill him. At the time, Marius was fighting the drug trade in town and someone didn't like that. Maybe. I was still in prison so I don't really know. I have my theories, too many of them. All I know is that Marius died in Santa Cruz, where he had gone to spend a few days. He didn't live there and it's hard to imagine the killer lived there. The killer followed Marius, is what I'm saying. And the only reason I can think of why Marius was in Santa Cruz is the ocean. Marius went to see the Pacific Ocean, went to smell it. And the killer tracked him down to Santa Cruz. And you all know what happened next. Oftentimes I think about Marius. More than I want to, to tell you the truth. I see him on the beach in California. A beach in Big Sur, maybe, or in Monterey north of Fisherman's Wharf, up Highway 1. He's standing at a lookout point, looking away. It's winter, off-season. The Panthers are young, none of us even twenty-five. We're all armed, but we've left our weapons in the car, and you can see the deep dissatisfaction on our faces. The sea roars. Then I go up to Marius and I say let's get out of here now. And at that moment Marius turns and he looks at me. He's smiling. He's beyond it all. And he waves his hand toward the sea, because he's incapable of expressing what he feels in words. And then I'm afraid, even though it's my brother there beside me, and I think: the danger is the sea.

•

MONEY. In a word, Seaman believed that money was necessary, but not as necessary as some people claimed. He talked about what he called "economic relativism." At Folsom Prison, he said, a cigarette was worth one-twentieth of a little jar of strawberry jam. Meanwhile, at Soledad, a cigarette was worth one-thirtieth of a jar. And at Walla-Walla, a cigarette was worth the same as a jar of jam, for one thing because the prisoners at Walla-Walla—who knows why, maybe because of some brainwashing against food, maybe because they were hooked on that nicotine—would have nothing to do with anything that was sweet, and all they wanted was to breathe that smoke into their lungs. Money, said Seaman, was ultimately a mystery, and as an uneducated man, he was hardly the right person to try to explain it. Still, he had two things to say. The first was that he didn't approve of the way poor people spent their money, especially poor African Americans. It makes my blood boil, he said, when I see a pimp cruising around the neighborhood in a limousine or a Lincoln Continental. I can't stand it. When poor people make money, they should behave with greater dignity, he said. When poor people make money, they should help their neighbors. When poor people make money, they should send their children to college and adopt an orphan, or more than one. When poor people make money, they should admit publicly to having made only half as much. They shouldn't even tell their children how much they really have, because then their children will want the whole inheritance and won't be willing to share it with their adopted siblings. When poor people make money, they should establish secret funds, not just to help the black people rotting in this country's prisons, but to start small businesses like laundries, bars, video stores, the profits to be fully reinvested in the community. Scholarships. Never mind if the scholarship students come to a bad end. Never mind if the scholarship students end up killing themselves because they listened to too much rap, or killing their white teacher and five classmates in a rage. The road to wealth is sown with false starts and failures that should in no way discourage the poor who make good or our neighbors with new-found riches. We have to give it our all. We have to squeeze water from the rocks, and from the desert too. But we can never forget that money remains a problem to be solved, Seaman said.

·

FOOD. As you all know, said Seaman, pork chops saved my life. First I was a Panther and I faced down the police in California and then I traveled all over the world and then I lived for years on the tab of the U.S. government. When they let me out I was nobody. The Panthers no longer existed. In the minds of some, we were old terrorists. In the minds of others, we were a vague memory of sixties blackness, we were picturesque. Marius Newell had died in Santa Cruz. Some comrades had died in prison and others had made public apologies and started new lives. Now there weren't just black cops. There were black people in public office, black mayors, black businessmen, famous black lawyers, black TV and movie stars, and the Panthers were a hindrance. So when they let me out there was nothing left, or next to nothing, the smoldering remains of a nightmare we had plunged into as youths and that as grown men we were leaving behind now, practically old men, you could say, with no future ahead of us, because during the long years in prison we'd forgotten what we knew and we'd learned nothing, nothing but cruelty from the guards and sadism from our fellow inmates. That was my situation. So those first months out on parole were sad and gray. Sometimes I would sit at the window for hours watching the lights blink on a nameless street, just smoking. I won't lie to you, terrible thoughts crossed my mind more than once. Only one person helped me selflessly: my older sister, God rest her soul. She invited me to stay at her house in Detroit, which was small, but for me it was as if a princess in Europe had offered me her castle for a resting place. My days were all alike, but they had something that today, in hindsight, I don't hesitate to call happiness. Back then I saw only two people regularly: my sister, who was the world's most good-hearted human being, and my parole officer, a fat man who used to pour me a shot of whiskey in his office and he'd say: tell me, Barry, how could you be so bad? Sometimes I thought he said it to get me going. Sometimes I thought: this man is on the payroll of the California police and he wants to get me going and then he'll shoot me in the gut. Tell me about your b——, Barry, he would say, referring to my manly attributes, or: tell me about the guys you killed. Talk, Barry. Talk. And he would open his desk drawer, where I knew he kept his gun, and wait. And what could I do? Well, I would say, I didn't meet Chairman Mao, but I did meet Lin Piao, and later on he wanted to kill Chairman Mao and he was killed in a plane crash when he was trying to get away to Russia. A little man, wise as a serpent. Do you remember Lin Piao? And Lou would say he had never heard of Lin Piao in his life. Well, Lou, I would say, he was something like a Chinese cabinet member or like the Chinese secretary of state. And in those days we didn't have a whole lot of Americans in China, I can tell you. You could say we paved the way for Kissinger and Nixon. And Lou and I could go on like that for three hours, him asking me to tell him about the guys I'd shot in the back, and me talking about the politicians I'd met and the countries I'd seen. Until I was finally able to get rid of him, with a little Christian patience, and I've never seen him since. Lou probably died of cirrhosis. And my life went on, with the same uncertainties and the same feeling of impermanence. Then, one day I realized there was one thing I hadn't forgotten. I hadn't forgotten how to cook. I hadn't forgotten my pork chops. With the help of my sister, who was one of God's angels and who loved to talk about food, I started writing down all the recipes I remembered, my mother's recipes, the ones I'd made in prison, the ones I'd made on Saturdays at home on the roof for my sister, though she didn't care for meat. And when I'd finished the book I went to New York and took it to some publishers and one of them was interested and you all know the rest. The book put me back in the public eye. I learned to combine cooking with history. I learned to combine cooking with the thankfulness and confusion I felt at the kindness of so many people, from my late sister to countless others. And let me explain something. When I say confusion, I also mean awe. In other words, the sense of wonderment at a marvelous thing, like the lilies that bloom and die in a single day, or azaleas, or forget-me-nots. But I also realized this wasn't enough. I couldn't live forever on my recipes for ribs, my famous recipes. Ribs were not the answer. You have to change. You have to turn yourself around and change. You have to know how to look even if you don't know what you're looking for. So those of you who are interested can take out pencil and paper now, because I'm going to read you a new recipe. It's for *duck à l'orange*. This is not something you want to eat every day, because it isn't cheap and it will take you an hour and a half, maybe more, to make, but every two months or when a birthday comes around, it isn't bad. These are the ingredients, for four: a four-pound duck, two tablespoons of butter, four cloves of garlic, two cups of broth, a few sprigs of herbs, a tablespoon of tomato paste, four oranges, four tablespoons of sugar, three tablespoons of brandy, black pepper, oil, and salt. Then Seaman explained the preparation, step by step, and when he had finished explaining he said that duck made a fine meal, and that was all.

•

STARS. He said that people knew many different kinds of stars or thought they knew many different kinds of stars. He talked about the stars you see at night, say when you're driving from Des Moines to Lincoln on Route 80 and the car breaks down, the way they do, maybe it's the oil or the radiator, maybe it's a flat tire, and you get out and get the jack and the spare tire out of the trunk and change the tire, maybe half an hour, at most, and when you're done you look up and see the sky full of stars. The Milky Way. He talked about star athletes. That's a different kind of star, he said, and he compared them to movie stars, though as he said, the life of an athlete is generally much shorter. A star athlete might last fifteen years at best, whereas a movie star could go on for forty or fifty years if he or she started young. Meanwhile, any star you could see from the side of Route 80, on the way from Des Moines to Lincoln, would live for probably millions of years. Either that or it might have been dead for millions of years, and the traveler who gazed up at it would never know. It might be a live star or it might be a dead star. Sometimes, depending on your point of view, he said, it doesn't matter, since the stars you see at night exist in the realm of semblance. They are semblances, the same way dreams are semblances. So the traveler on Route 80 with a flat tire doesn't know whether what he's staring up at in the vast night are stars or whether they're dreams. In a way, he said, the traveler is also part of a dream, a dream that breaks away from another dream like one drop of water breaking away from a bigger drop of water that we call a wave. Having reached this point, Seaman warned that stars were one thing, meteors another. Meteors have nothing to do with stars, he said. Meteors, especially if they're on a direct collision course with the earth, have nothing to do with stars or dreams, though they might have something to do with the notion of breaking away, a kind of breaking away in reverse. Then he talked about starfish, he said he didn't know how, but each time Marius Newell walked along a beach in California he came upon a starfish. But he also said that the starfish you find on the beach are usually dead, corpses tossed up by the waves, with exceptions, of course. Newell, he said, could always tell the dead starfish from the ones that were still alive. I don't know how he did it, but he told them apart. And he left the dead on the beach and returned the living to the sea, tossing them near the rocks to give them a chance. Except once, when he brought a starfish home and put it in a tank, with some of that Pacific brine. This was in the early days of the Panthers, when we spent our time directing traffic in the community so cars wouldn't speed through and kill the children. A couple of stoplights would have come in handy, but the city wouldn't help us. So that was one of the first of the Panthers' roles, as traffic cops. And meanwhile Marius Newell saw to his starfish. Naturally, before too long he realized that he needed a pump for his tank. One night he went out with Seaman and little Nelson Sánchez to steal one. None of them was armed. They went to a store that specialized in the sale of rare fish in Colchester Sun, a white neighborhood, and they went in through the back door. When Marius had the pump in his hands, there came a man with a shotgun. I thought that was the end of us, said Seaman, but then Marius said: don't shoot, don't shoot, it's for my starfish. The man with the gun didn't move. We stepped back. He stepped forward. We stopped. He stopped. We took another step back. He came after us. At last we got to the car that little Nelson was driving and the man stopped less than ten feet away. When Nelson started the car the man lifted the shotgun to his shoulder and he took aim. Step on it, I said. No, said Marius. Go slow. The car rolled out toward the main street and the man came walking after us, his gun raised. Now you can hit it, said Marius, and when little Nelson stepped on the gas the man stood still, shrinking until I saw him disappear in the rearview mirror. Of course, the pump didn't do Marius any good, and a week or two later, for all the care he'd lavished on that starfish, it died and ended up in the trash. Really, when you talk about stars you're speaking figuratively. That's metaphor. Call someone a movie star. You've used a metaphor. Say: the sky is full of stars. More metaphors. If somebody takes a hard right to the chin and goes down, you say he's seeing stars. Another metaphor. Metaphors are our way of losing ourselves in semblances or treading water in a sea of seeming. In that sense a metaphor is like a life jacket. And remember, there are life jackets that float and others that sink to the bottom like lead. Best not to forget it. But really, there's just one star and that star isn't semblance, it isn't metaphor, it doesn't come from any dream or any nightmare. We have it right outside. It's the sun. The sun, I am sorry to say, is our only star. When I was young I saw a science fiction movie. A rocket ship drifts off course and heads toward the sun. First, the astronauts start to get headaches. Then they're all dripping sweat and they take off their spacesuits and even so they can't stop sweating and before long they're dehydrated. The sun's gravity keeps pulling them ceaselessly in. The sun begins to melt the hull of the ship. Sitting in his seat, the viewer can't help feeling hot, too hot to bear. Now I've forgotten how it ends. At the last minute they get saved, I seem to recall, and they correct the course of that rocket ship and turn it around toward the earth, and the huge sun is left behind, a frenzied star in the reaches of space.

•

USEFULNESS. But the sun has its uses, as any fool knows, said Seaman. From up close it's hell, but from far away you'd have to be a vampire not to see how useful it is, how beautiful. Then he began to talk about things that were useful back in the day, things once generally appreciated but now distrusted instead, like smiles. In the fifties, for example, he said, a smile opened doors for you. I don't know if it could get you places, but it could definitely open doors. Now nobody trusts a smile. Before, if you were a salesman and you went in somewhere, you'd better have a big smile on your face. It was the same thing no matter whether you were a waiter or a businessman, a secretary, a doctor, a scriptwriter, a gardener. The only folks who never smiled were cops and prison guards. That hasn't changed. But everybody else, they all did their best to smile. It was a golden age for dentists in America. Black folks, of course, were always smiling. White folks smiled. Asian folks. Hispanic folks. Now, as we know, our worst enemy might be hiding behind a smile. Or to put it another way, we don't trust anybody, least of all people who smile, since we know they want something from us. Still, American television is full of smiles and more and more perfect-looking teeth. Do these people want us to trust them? No. Do they want us to think they're good people, that they'd never hurt a fly? No again. The truth is they don't want anything from us. They just want to show us their teeth, their smiles, and admiration is all they ask for in return. Admiration. They want us to look at them, that's all. Their perfect teeth, their perfect bodies, their perfect manners, as if they were constantly breaking away from the sun and they were little pieces of fire, little pieces of blazing hell, here on this planet simply to be worshipped. When I was little, said Seaman, I don't remember children wearing braces. Today I've hardly met a child who doesn't wear them. Useless things are forced upon us, and it isn't because they improve our quality of life but because they're the fashion or markers of class, and fashionable people and high-class people require admiration and worship. Naturally, fashions don't last, one year, four at most, and then they pass through every stage of decay. But markers of class rot only when the corpse that was tagged with them rots. Then he began to talk about useful things the body needs. First, a balanced diet. I see lots of fat people in this church, he said. I suspect few of you eat green vegetables. Maybe now is the time for a recipe. The name of the recipe is: Brussels Sprouts with Lemon. Take note, please. Four servings calls for: two pounds of brussels sprouts, juice and zest of one lemon, one onion, one sprig of parsley, three tablespoons of butter, black pepper, and salt. You make it like so. One: Clean sprouts well and remove outer leaves. Finely chop onion and parsley. Two: In a pot of salted boiling water, cook sprouts for twenty minutes, or until tender. Then drain well and set aside. Three: Melt butter in frying pan and lightly sauté onion, add zest and juice of lemon and salt and pepper to taste. Four: Add brussels sprouts, toss with sauce, reheat for a few minutes, sprinkle with parsley, and serve with lemon wedges on the side. So good you'll be licking your fingers, said Seaman. No cholesterol, good for the liver, good for the blood pressure, very healthy. Then he dictated recipes for Endive and Shrimp Salad and Broccoli Salad and then he said that man couldn't live on healthy food alone. You have to read books, he said. Not watch so much TV. The experts say TV doesn't hurt the eyes. I'm not so sure. It won't do your eyes any good, and cell phones are still a mystery. Maybe they cause cancer, as some scientists say. I'm not saying they do or they don't, but there you have it. What I'm saying is, you have to read books. The preacher knows I'm telling you the truth. Read books by black writers. But don't stop there. This is my real contribution tonight. Reading is never a waste of time. I read in jail. That's where I started to read. I read a lot. I went through books like they were barbecue. In prison they turn the lights out early. You get in bed and hear sounds. Footsteps. People yelling. As if instead of being in California, the prison was inside the planet Mercury, the planet closest to the sun. You feel cold and hot at the same time and that's a clear sign you're lonely or sick. You try to think about other things, sure, nice things, but sometimes you just can't do it. Sometimes a guard at the nearest desk turns on a lamp and light from that lamp shines through the bars of your cell. This happened to me any number of times. The light from a lamp set in the wrong place, or from the fluorescent bulbs in the corridor above or the next corridor over. Then I would pick up my book and hold it in the light and get to reading. It wasn't easy, because the letters and the paragraphs seemed frenzied or spooked in that unpredictable, underground world. But I read and read anyway, sometimes so fast that even I was surprised, and sometimes very slowly, as if each sentence or word were something good for my whole body, not just my brain. And I could read like that for hours, not caring whether I was tired and not dwelling on the inarguable fact that I was in prison because I had stood up for my brothers, most of whom couldn't care less whether I rotted or not. I knew I was doing something useful. That was all that counted. I was doing something useful as the guards marched back and forth or greeted each other at the change of shift with friendly words that sounded like obscenities to my ear and that, thinking about it now, might actually have been obscene. I was doing something useful. Something useful no matter how you look at it. Reading is like thinking, like praying, like talking to a friend, like expressing your ideas, like listening to other people's ideas, like listening to music (oh yes), like looking at the view, like taking a walk on the beach. And you, who are so kind, now you must be asking: what did you read, Barry? I read everything. But I especially remember a certain book I read at one of the most desperate moments of my life and it brought me peace again. What book do I mean? What book do I mean? Well, it was a book called *An Abridged Digest of the Complete Works of Voltaire*, and I promise you that is one useful book, or at least it was of great use to me.

•

That night, after he dropped Seaman off at home, Fate slept at the hotel where the magazine had booked him a room from New York. The receptionist told him that he'd been expected the day before and handed him a message from his editor asking how everything had gone. He called the magazine from his room, knowing no one would be there, and left a message vaguely explaining his meeting with the old man.

He showered and got in bed. He turned on the TV, looking for porn. He found a movie in which a German woman was making love with two black men. The German woman was speaking German and so were the black men. Were there black people in Germany, too? he wondered. Then he got bored and switched to a free channel. He saw part of a trashy show on which a hugely fat woman in her early forties had to sit and listen to her husband, a hugely fat man in his midthirties, and her husband's new girlfriend, a slightly less fat woman in her early thirties, insult her. The man, he thought, was clearly a faggot. The show was shot in Florida. Everyone was in short sleeves, except for the host, who was wearing a white blazer, khaki pants, a gray-green shirt, and an ivory tie. At moments, the host looked uncomfortable. The fat man gestured and bobbed like a rapper, egged on by his slightly less fat girlfriend. The fat man's wife, meanwhile, was quiet, gazing at the audience until, without a word, she started to cry.

This must be the end, thought Fate. But the show or this segment of the show didn't end there. At the sight of his wife in tears, the fat man stepped up his verbal attack. Among the things he called her Fate thought he heard the word *fat*. He also told her that he wasn't going to let her keep ruining his life. I don't belong to you, he said. His slightly less fat girlfriend said: he doesn't belong to you, why don't you get that through your head? After a while, the seated woman reacted. She got up and said she'd heard enough. She didn't say it to her husband or to her husband's girlfriend but directly to the host. He told her to pull herself together and take her turn saying what she needed to say. I was tricked into coming on this show, said the woman, still in tears. No one's tricked into coming here, said the host. Don't be a coward, listen to what he has to say to you, said the fat man's girlfriend. Listen to what I have to say to you, said the fat man, circling her. The woman raised her hand to fend him off and left the set. The girlfriend took a seat. After a while, the fat man sat down, too. The host, who was sitting in the audience, asked the fat man what he did for a living. I'm unemployed now, but I used to be a security guard, he said. Fate changed the channel. He took a little bottle of Tennessee Bull bourbon from the minibar. After the first swallow he felt like throwing up. He put the cap back on the bottle and returned it to the minibar. After a while he fell asleep with the TV on.

•

While Fate was sleeping, there was a report on an American who had disappeared in Santa Teresa, in the state of Sonora in the north of Mexico. The reporter, Dick Medina, was a Chicano, and he talked about the long list of women killed in Santa Teresa, many of whom ended up in the common grave at the cemetery because no one claimed their bodies. Medina was talking in the desert. Behind him was a highway and off in the distance was a rise that Medina gestured toward at some point in the broadcast, saying it was Arizona. The wind ruffled the reporter's smooth black hair. He was wearing a short-sleeved shirt. Then came a shot of some assembly plants and Medina's voice-over saying that unemployment was almost nonexistent along that stretch of the border. People standing in line on a narrow sidewalk. Pickup trucks covered in a fine dust the brown color of baby shit. Hollows in the ground, like World War I bomb craters, that gradually gave way to dumping sites. The smiling face of some kid who couldn't have been more than twenty, thin and dark-skinned, with prominent cheekbones, whom Medina identified in a voice-over as a *pollero* or *coyote* or person who leads illegal immigrants over the border. Medina said a name. The name of a girl. Then there was a shot of the streets of an Arizona town where the girl was from. Houses with scorched yards and dirty silver-colored chicken-wire fences. The sad face of the mother. Exhausted with crying. The face of the father, a tall man with broad shoulders who stared into the camera saying nothing. Behind the two of them were the shadowy figures of three teenage girls. Our other three daughters, said the mother in accented English. The three girls, the oldest no more than fifteen, went running into the dark of the house.

•

As this report was showing on TV, Fate dreamed of a man he'd written a story about, the first story he'd had published in *Black Dawn*, after three other pieces were rejected. He was an old black man, much older than Seaman, who lived in Brooklyn and was a member of the Communist Party. When Fate met him there wasn't a single Communist left in Brooklyn, but the man was keeping his cell operative. What was his name? Antonio Ulises Jones, although the kids in the neighborhood called him Scottsboro Boy. They also called him Old Freak or Bones or Skin, but they usually called him Scottsboro Boy, among other reasons because Antonio Jones often talked about what had happened in Scottsboro, about the Scottsboro trials, about the blacks who were almost lynched in Scottsboro, people no one in his Brooklyn neighborhood remembered.

When Fate met him, purely by chance, Antonio Jones must have been eighty years old and he lived in a two-room apartment in one of the poorest parts of Brooklyn. In the living room there were a table and more than fifteen chairs, those old folding wooden bar stools with long legs and low backs. On the wall there was a photograph of a huge man, well over six feet tall, dressed like a worker of the period, receiving a diploma from a boy who looked straight into the camera and smiled, showing perfect, gleaming white teeth. The face of the giant worker, in its way, also resembled a child's face.

"That's me," Antonio Jones told Fate the first time Fate visited him, "and the big man is Robert Martillo Smith, a Brooklyn city maintenance worker, a specialist at going down into the sewers and wrestling with thirty-foot alligators."

In the three conversations they had, Fate asked Jones many questions, some intended to prick the old man's conscience. He asked about Stalin, and Antonio Jones answered that Stalin was a son of a bitch. He asked about Lenin, and Antonio Jones answered that Lenin was a son of a bitch. He asked about Marx, and Antonio Jones said now he was talking, that was where he should have started: Marx was a wonderful man. After that, Antonio Jones began to speak of Marx in glowing terms. There was only one thing he didn't like about Marx: his temper. This he blamed on poverty, because according to Jones, poverty didn't cause only illness and resentment, it caused bad temper. Fate's next question was what he thought about the fall of the Berlin Wall and the resulting collapse of the real-world Socialist regimes. It was foreseeable, I predicted it ten years before it happened, was Antonio Jones's response. Then, out of the blue, he began to sing the "Internationale." He opened the window and in a deep voice that took Fate by surprise, he intoned the first few lines: Arise, you prisoners of starvation! Arise, you wretched of the earth! When he had finished singing he asked Fate whether it didn't strike him as an anthem made especially for black people. I don't know, said Fate, I never thought of it that way. Later, Jones gave him an off-the-cuff accounting of the Communists of Brooklyn. During World War II, there were more than a thousand. After the war, the number rose to thirteen hundred. At the start of McCarthyism, there were only about seven hundred, and when it ended there were scarcely two hundred Communists in Brooklyn. In the sixties there were just half as many and by the seventies there were no more than thirty Communists scattered in five hardy cells. At the end of the seventies, there were ten left. By the beginning of the eighties, there were only four. During the eighties, two of the four who were left died of cancer and one vanished without saying anything to anyone. Maybe he just went on a trip and died on the way there or the way back, mused Antonio Jones. Whatever it was, he never showed up again, not at headquarters or at his apartment or at the bars where he was a regular. Maybe he went to live with his daughter in Florida. He was Jewish and he had a daughter there. The fact of the matter is that by 1987 there was only one left. And here I still am, he said. Why? asked Fate. Antonio Jones hesitated for a few seconds, considering his answer. Then he looked Fate in the eye and said:

"Because someone has to keep the cell operative."

Jones's eyes were small and black as coal, and his eyelids were heavy with folds. He had hardly any eyelashes. His eyebrows were sparse, and sometimes, when he and Fate went out to take walks around the neighborhood, he put on big sunglasses and picked up a cane, which he left by the door when they got back. He could go whole days without eating. Once you get to be a certain age, he said, food is no good. He wasn't in contact with any other Communists in the United States or abroad, except for a retired UCLA professor, Dr. Minski, with whom he corresponded occasionally. Until fifteen years ago I belonged to the Third International, and Minski convinced me to join the Fourth, he said. Then he said:

"Son, I'm going to give you a book that will be of great use to you."

Fate thought it would be *The Communist Manifesto*, maybe because in the living room, piled in corners and under chairs, he had seen several copies published by Antonio Jones himself—who knew where he'd gotten the money or how he'd fast-talked the printers—but when the old man put the book in his hands he saw with surprise that it wasn't the *Manifesto* but a fat volume titled *The Slave Trade* by someone called Hugh Thomas, whose name he had never heard before. At first he refused to take it.

"It's an expensive book and this must be your only copy," he said.

Jones's answer was that he shouldn't worry, that it had cost him only cunning, not money, by which Fate deduced that Jones had stolen the book, though this also struck him as unlikely, since the old man wasn't in any shape for such things, though he might conceivably have an accomplice at the bookstore where he pocketed his finds, a young black man who turned a blind eye when Jones slipped a book under his jacket.

Flipping through the book in his apartment hours later, he realized that the author was white. A white Englishman who had also been a professor at Sandhurst, the Royal Military Academy, which for Fate made him more or less the equivalent of a drill sergeant, an English motherfucking sergeant in short pants, so he put the book aside and didn't read it. People responded to the interview with Antonio Ulises Jones. To most of his colleagues, Fate noted, the story was little more than a venture into the African-American picturesque. A loony preacher, a loony ex–jazz musician, the loony last member of the Brooklyn Communist Party (Fourth International). Sociological curiosities. But they liked it and soon afterward he became a staff writer. He never saw Antonio Jones again, just as in all likelihood he would never see Barry Seaman again.

When he woke up it was still dark.

•

Before he left Detroit he went to the only decent bookstore in the city and bought *The Slave Trade* by Hugh Thomas, the former professor at Sandhurst. Then he headed down Woodward Avenue and checked out the downtown. He had a cup of coffee and toast for breakfast at a Greektown diner. When he said he didn't want anything else, the waitress, a blond woman in her forties, asked him if he was sick. He said he had an upset stomach. Then the waitress took away the cup of coffee she'd poured him and told him she had something better for him. A little while later she came back with a tea brewed from anise and an herb called boldo that Fate had never tasted and at first he was reluctant to try it.

"This is what you need, not coffee," said the waitress.

She was a tall, thin woman, with very large breasts and nice hips. She was wearing a black skirt and a white blouse and flat-heeled shoes. For a while neither of them said anything, both waiting expectantly, until Fate shrugged and took a sip of the tea. Then the waitress smiled and went to wait on other customers.

•

At the hotel, as he was about to pay his bill, he discovered he had a phone message from New York. A voice he didn't recognize asked him to get in touch with his editor or the editor of the sports section as soon as possible. He made the call from the lobby. He talked to the girl at the next desk and she told him to hold on while she tried to find the editor. After a while an unfamiliar voice came on. The speaker introduced himself as Jeff Roberts, editor of the sports section, and he began to talk to Fate about a boxing match. Count Pickett is fighting, he said, and we don't have anybody to cover the event. The editor called him Oscar as if they had known each other for years, and he talked on and on about Count Pickett, a promising Harlem light heavyweight.

"So what does this have to do with me?" asked Fate.

"Well, Oscar," said the sports editor, "you know Jimmy Lowell died and we still haven't found anyone to replace him."

Fate thought the fight must be in Detroit or Chicago and it didn't strike him as a bad idea to spend a few days away from New York.

"You want me to write up the fight?"

"That's right, kid," said Roberts, "say five pages, a short profile of Pickett, the match, and some local color."

"Where is the fight?"

"In Mexico," said the sports editor, "and keep in mind that we give a bigger travel allowance than they do in your section."

•

With his suitcase packed, Fate headed to Seaman's apartment for the last time. He found the old man reading and taking notes. From the kitchen came the smell of spices and frying onion and garlic.

"I'm leaving," he said. "I just stopped to say goodbye."

Seaman asked if he could give him something to eat first.

"No, I don't have time," said Fate.

They embraced and Fate headed down the stairs, taking them in threes as if he were dashing for the street, like a boy heading out for a free afternoon with his friends. As he drove toward the Detroit–Wayne County airport, he thought about Seaman's strange books, *The Abridged French Encyclopedia* and the one he hadn't seen but that Seaman had claimed to have read in prison, *The Abridged Digest of the Complete Works of Voltaire*, which made him laugh out loud.

•

At the airport he bought a ticket to Tucson. While he was waiting, leaning on the counter at a coffee place, he remembered the dream he'd had the night before about Antonio Jones, who had been dead for several years now. As before, he asked himself what Jones could have died of, and the one answer that occurred to him was old age. One day, walking down some street in Brooklyn, Antonio Jones had felt tired, sat down on the sidewalk, and a second later stopped existing. Maybe it happened that way for my mother, thought Fate, but deep down he knew otherwise. When the airplane took off from Detroit a storm had begun to break over the city.

Fate opened the book by the white man who had been a professor at Sandhurst and started to read it on page 361. It said: *Beyond the delta of the Niger, the coast of Africa at last begins to turn south again and there, in the Cameroons, in the late eighteenth century, Liverpool merchants from England pioneered a new branch of the slave trade. Further on, and well to the south, the River Gabon, just north of Cape Lopez, was also coming into full activity as a slave region in the 1780s. This area seemed to the Reverend John Newton to possess "the most humane and moral people I ever met with in Africa," perhaps "because they were the people who had least intercourse with Europe at that time." But off the coast the Dutch had for a long time used the island of Corisco (the word in Portuguese means "flash of lightning") as a trading center, though not specifically for slaves.* Then he saw an illustration—there were quite a few in the book—showing a Portuguese fort on the Gold Coast, called Elmina, captured by the Danes in 1637. For three hundred and fifty years Elmina was a center of the slave trade. Over the fort, and over a small nearby fort built at the top of a hill, flew a flag that Fate couldn't identify. What kingdom did it belong to? he wondered before his eyes closed and he fell asleep with the book on his lap.

•

At the Tucson airport he rented a car, bought a road map, and drove south out of the city. He planned to stop at the first roadside diner he came to, because his appetite seemed to have sharpened in the dry desert air. Two Camaros of the same model and the same color passed him, honking. He thought they must be in a race. The cars probably had souped-up engines, and their bodies shone in the Arizona sun. He passed a little ranch that sold oranges, but he didn't stop. The ranch was about three hundred feet from the highway, and the orange stand, an old cart with an awning and big wooden wheels, stood by the side of the road, tended by two Mexican kids. A few miles down the road he saw a place called Cochise's Corner and he parked in a big lot, next to a gas station. The two Camaros were parked next to a flag with a red stripe on top and a black stripe on the bottom. In the middle was a white circle emblazoned with the words Chiricahua Auto Club. For an instant he thought the Camaro drivers must be two Indians, but then the idea struck him as absurd. He sat in a corner of the restaurant next to a window, where he could keep an eye on his car. There were two men at the next table. One was tall and young and looked like a teacher of computer science. He had an easy smile and sometimes he clapped his hands to his face in what might have been astonishment or horror, or anything at all. Fate couldn't see the other man's face, but he was clearly quite a bit older than his companion. His neck was thick, his hair was white, and he wore glasses. Whether he was talking or listening he remained impassive, without gesturing or moving.

•

The girl who came to wait on him was Mexican. He ordered coffee and scanned the menu for a few minutes. He asked whether they had club sandwiches. The waitress shook her head. A steak, said Fate. With salsa? asked the waitress. What's in the salsa? asked Fate. Chile, tomato, onion, and cilantro. And we put some spices in, too. All right, he said, I'll try it. When the waitress left he looked around the restaurant. At one table he saw two Indians, one an adult and the other a teenager, maybe father and son. At another he saw two white men with a Mexican woman. The men were exactly alike, identical twins of about fifty. The Mexican woman must have been forty-five or so, and it was clear the twins were crazy about her. They're the Camaro owners, thought Fate. He also realized that no one in the whole restaurant was black except for him.

•

The young man at the next table said something about inspiration. All Fate heard was: you've been an inspiration to us. The white-haired man said it was really nothing. The young man raised his hands to his face and said something about willpower, about the power to hold a gaze. Then he removed his hands from his face and with shining eyes he said: I don't mean a natural gaze, a gaze from the natural realm, I mean a gaze in the abstract. The white-haired man said: of course. When you caught Jurevich, said the young man, and then his voice was drowned out by the deafening roar of a diesel engine. A semi was parking in the lot. The waitress brought Fate's coffee and the steak with salsa. The young man was still talking about the person called Jurevich who'd been caught by the white-haired man.

"It wasn't hard," said the white-haired man.

"A killer who's sloppy," said the young man, and he raised his hand to his mouth as if he were about to sneeze.

"No," said the white-haired man, "a careful killer."

"Oh, I thought he was sloppy," said the young man.

"No, no, he was careful," said the white-haired man.

"Which is worse?" asked the young man.

Fate cut a piece of meat. It was thick and tender and it tasted good. The salsa was tasty, especially once you got used to the heat.

"The sloppy ones are worse," said the white-haired man. "It's harder to establish a pattern of behavior."

"But can it it be established?" asked the young man.

"Given the means and the time, you can do anything," said the white-haired man.

Fate beckoned for the waitress. The Mexican woman rested her head on the shoulder of one of the twins and the other twin smiled as if this were a common occurrence. Fate imagined that she was married to the twin who had his arm around her, but that their marriage hadn't extinguished the other brother's love or dashed his hopes. The Indian father asked for the check. Meanwhile, the young Indian had pulled out a comic book from somewhere and was reading it. Out in the lot Fate saw the truck driver who had just parked his truck. He was on his way back from the gas station bathroom and he was combing his blond hair with a tiny comb. The waitress asked him what he wanted. Another coffee and a big glass of water.

"We've gotten used to death," he heard the young man say.

"It's always been that way," said the white-haired man, "always."

•

In the nineteenth century, toward the middle or the end of the nineteenth century, said the white-haired man, society tended to filter death
through the fabric of words. Reading news stories from back then you
might get the idea that there was hardly any crime, or that a single murder could throw a whole country into tumult. We didn't want death in
the home, or in our dreams and fantasies, and yet it was a fact that terrible crimes were committed, mutilations, all kinds of rape, even serial
killings. Of course, most of the serial killers were never caught. Take the
most famous case of the day. No one knew who Jack the Ripper was.
Everything was passed through the filter of words, everything trimmed to
fit our fear. What does a child do when he's afraid? He closes his eyes.
What does a child do when he's about to be raped and murdered? He
closes his eyes. And he screams, too, but first he closes his eyes. Words
served that purpose. And the funny thing is, the archetypes of human
madness and cruelty weren't invented by the men of our day but by our
forebears. The Greeks, you might say, invented evil, the Greeks saw the
evil inside us all, but testimonies or proofs of this evil no longer move us.
They strike us as futile, senseless. You could say the same about madness. It was the Greeks who showed us the range of possibilities and yet
now they mean nothing to us. Everything changes, you say. Of course
everything changes, but not the archetypes of crime, not any more than
human nature changes. Maybe it's because polite society was so small
back then. I'm talking about the nineteenth century, eighteenth century,
seventeenth century. No doubt about it, society was small. Most human
beings existed on the outer fringes of society. In the seventeenth century,
for example, at least twenty percent of the merchandise on every slave
ship died. By that I mean the dark-skinned people who were being trans-
ported for sale, to Virginia, say. And that didn't get anyone upset or make
headlines in the Virginia papers or make anyone go out and call for the
ship captain to be hanged. But if a plantation owner went crazy and
killed his neighbor and then went galloping back home, dismounted,
and promptly killed his wife, two deaths in total, Virginia society spent
the next six months in fear, and the legend of the murderer on horseback
might linger for generations. Or look at the French. During the Paris
Commune of 1871, thousands of people were killed and no one batted
an eye. Around the same time a knife sharpener killed his wife and his
elderly mother and then he was shot and killed by the police. The story
didn't just make all the French newspapers, it was written up in papers

across Europe, and even got a mention in the New York *Examiner*. How come? The ones killed in the Commune weren't part of society, the dark-skinned people who died on the ship weren't part of society, whereas the woman killed in a French provincial capital and the murderer on horse-back in Virginia were. What happened to them could be written, you might say, it was legible. That said, words back then were mostly used in the art of avoidance, not of revelation. Maybe they revealed something all the same. I couldn't tell you.

•

The young man covered his face with his hands.

"This isn't your first trip to Mexico," he said, uncovering his face and smiling a catlike smile.

"No," said the white-haired man. "I was there for a while a few years ago and I tried to help, but the situation was impossible."

"And why did you come back this time?"

"To have a look, I guess," said the white-haired man. "I was staying at a friend's house, a friend I made last time. The Mexicans are a hos-pitable people."

"It wasn't an official trip?"

"Oh, no," said the white-haired man.

"And what's your unofficial opinion about what's going on there?"

"I have several opinions, Edward, and I'd prefer that none of them be published without my consent."

The young man covered his face with his hands and said:

"Professor Kessler, my lips are sealed."

"All right, then," said the white-haired man. "I'll tell you three things I'm sure of: (a) everyone living in that city is outside of society, and everyone, I mean everyone, is like the ancient Christians in the Roman circus; (b) the crimes have different signatures; (c) the city seems to be booming, it seems to be moving ahead in some ineffable way, but the best thing would be for every last one of the people there to head out into the desert some night and cross the border."

When the sun began to set in a blaze of red, and the twins, the Indi-ans, and the men at the next table had been gone for a long time, Fate decided to ask for the check. A chubby, dark-skinned girl who wasn't the waitress he'd had before brought it and asked whether everything had been to his liking.

"Everything," said Fate, as he felt in his pocket for money.

Then he went back to watching the sunset. He thought about his mother, about his mother's neighbor, about the magazine, about the streets of New York, all with an unspeakable sadness and weariness. He opened the book by the former Sandhurst professor and read a paragraph at random. *Many captains of slave ships looked on their task as, as a rule, complete, when they had delivered their slaves to the West Indies. But it was often impossible to realize the proceeds of the sale of slaves fast enough to provide the ship concerned with a return cargo of sugar. Merchants and captains could not be certain of the prices which they would receive at home for goods taken on their own account. Planters might take several years to pay for the slaves. Sometimes the European merchant preferred to have remittances from the West Indies in bills of exchange than to have sugar, indigo, cotton, or ginger in exchange for the slaves, because the prices of these goods in London were unpredictable or low.* What pretty names, he thought. Indigo, sugar, ginger, cotton. The reddish flowers of the indigo bush. The dark blue paste, with copper glints. A woman painted indigo, washing herself in the shower.

When he got up, the chubby waitress came over and asked him where he was headed. To Mexico, said Fate.

"I guessed that," said the waitress, "but where in Mexico?"

Leaning on the counter, a cook smoked a cigarette and watched them, waiting for his answer.

"To Santa Teresa," said Fate.

"It isn't a very nice place," said the waitress, "but it's big and there are lots of clubs and places to have fun."

Fate looked at the ground, smiling, and realized that the desert sunset had tinted the tiles a soft red.

"I'm a reporter," he said.

"You're going to write about the crimes," said the cook.

"I don't know what you're talking about. I'm going to cover the boxing match this Saturday," said Fate.

"Who's fighting?" asked the cook.

"Count Pickett, the New York light heavyweight."

"I used to follow the fights," said the cook. "I'd bet and check out the boxing digests, but one day I made up my mind to give it up. Now I don't know the names. Do you want a drink? It's on the house."

Fate sat at the counter and asked for a glass of water. The cook smiled and said he knew for a fact all reporters drank.

"I do, too," said Fate, "but I think there's something wrong with my stomach."

After bringing him a glass of water the cook wanted to know who was up against Count Pickett.

"I don't remember the name," said Fate. "I have it written down somewhere, a Mexican, I think."

"Strange," said the cook. "There're never any good Mexican light heavyweights. Once every twenty years you get a heavyweight, who usually winds up crazy or shot dead, but never a light heavyweight."

"I could be wrong, maybe it's not a Mexican," admitted Fate.

"Maybe he's Cuban or Colombian," said the cook, "although the Colombians don't have a tradition of light heavyweights either."

Fate drank the water and got up and stretched. It's time for me to go, he said, though in fact he was happy at the restaurant.

"How far is it to Santa Teresa?" he asked.

"That depends," said the cook. "Sometimes there are lots of trucks at the border and you can spend half an hour waiting. Say three hours from here to Santa Teresa and then half an hour or forty-five minutes at the border, four hours all together."

"From here to Santa Teresa it's only an hour and a half," said the waitress.

The cook looked at her and said that depended on the car and how well the driver knew the terrain.

"Have you ever driven in the desert?"

"No," said Fate.

"Well, it isn't easy. It looks easy. It looks like the simplest thing in the world, but there's nothing simple about it," said the cook.

"You're right about that," said the waitress, "especially at night, driving at night in the desert scares me."

"Make a mistake, take a wrong turn, and you're liable to go thirty miles in the wrong direction," said the cook.

"Maybe I should go now while it's still light out," said Fate.

"It won't do you much good," said the cook, "it'll be dark in five minutes. Sunsets in the desert seem like they'll never end, until suddenly, before you know it, they're done. It's like someone just turned out the lights," said the cook.

Fate asked for another glass of water and went to drink it by the window. Don't you want something else to eat before you go? he heard the cook say. He didn't answer. The desert began to disappear.

•

He drove for two hours along dark roads, with the radio on, listening to a Phoenix jazz station. He passed places where there were houses and restaurants and yards with white flowers and crookedly parked cars, but there were no lights on in the houses, as if the inhabitants had died that very night and a breath of blood still lingered in the air. He made out the shapes of hills silhouetted against the moon and the shapes of low clouds sitting motionless or speeding west at a given moment as if driven by a sudden, fitful wind that lifted dust clouds, clouds adorned in fabulous human garb by the car's headlights or the shadows created by the headlights, as if the dust clouds were tramps or ghosts looming alongside the road.

He got lost twice. Once he was tempted to turn back, toward the restaurant or Tucson. The other time he came to a town called Patagonia where a boy at the gas station told him the easiest way to get to Santa Teresa. On his way out of Patagonia he saw a horse. When the headlights swept over it the horse lifted its head and looked at him. Fate stopped the car and waited. The horse was black and after a moment it moved and vanished into the dark. He passed a mesa, or what he took to be a mesa. It was huge, completely flat on top, and from one end of the base to the other it must have been at least three miles long. There was a gully next to the road. He got out of the car, leaving the lights on, and urinated at length, breathing the cool night air. Then the road sloped down into a kind of valley that at first glimpse struck him as gigantic. In the farthest corner of the valley he thought he saw a glow. But it could have been anything. A convoy of trucks moving very slowly, the first lights of a town. Or maybe just his desire to escape the darkness, which in some way reminded him of his childhood and adolescence. At some point in between childhood and adolescence, he thought, he had dreamed of this landscape or one like it, less dark, less desertlike. He was in a bus with his mother and one of his mother's sisters and they were taking a short trip, from New York to a town near New York. He was next to the window and the view never changed, just buildings and highways, until suddenly they were in the country. At that exact moment, or maybe earlier, the sun had begun to set and he watched the trees, a small wood, though in his eyes it looked bigger. And then he thought he saw a man walking along the edge of the little wood. In great strides, as if he didn't want night to overtake him. He wondered who the man was. The only way he could tell it was a man and not a shadow was because he wore a shirt and swung his arms as he walked. The man's loneliness was so great, Fate remembered, that he wanted to look away and cling to his mother, but instead he kept his eyes open until the bus was out of the woods, and buildings, factories, and warehouses once again lined the sides of the road.

The valley he was crossing was lonelier now, and darker. He saw himself striding along the roadside. He shivered. Then he remembered the urn holding his mother's ashes and the neighbor's cup that he hadn't returned, the coffee infinitely cold now, and his mother's videotapes that no one would ever watch again. He thought about stopping the car and waiting until the sun came up. He knew without being told that for a black man to sleep in a rental car parked on the shoulder wasn't the best idea in Arizona. He changed stations. A voice in Spanish began to tell the story of a singer from Gómez Palacio who had returned to his city in the state of Durango just to commit suicide. Then he heard a woman's voice singing *rancheras*. For a while, as he drove through the valley, he listened. Then he tried to go back to the jazz station in Phoenix and couldn't find it.

•

On the American side of the border stood a town called Adobe. It had once been an adobe factory, but now it was a collection of houses and appliance stores, almost all strung along a long main street. At the end of the street you came out into a brightly lit empty lot and immediately after that was the American border post.

The customs officer asked for his passport and Fate handed it to him. With the passport was his press ID. The customs officer asked if he was coming to write about the killings.

"No," said Fate, "I'm going to cover the fight on Saturday."

"What fight?" asked the customs officer.

"Count Pickett, the light heavyweight from New York."

"Never heard of him," said the officer.

"He's going to be world champ," said Fate.

"I hope you're right," said the officer.

Then Fate advanced three hundred feet to the Mexican border and he had to get out of the car and open his suitcase, then show his car papers, his passport, and his press ID. He was asked to fill out some forms. The faces of the Mexican policemen were numb with exhaustion. From the window of the customshouse he saw the long, high fence that divided the two countries. Four birds were perched on the farthest stretch of the fence, their heads buried in their feathers. It's cold, said Fate. Very cold, said the Mexican official, who was studying the form Fate had just filled out.

"The birds. They're cold."

The official looked in the direction Fate was pointing.

"They're turkey buzzards, they're always cold at this time of night," he said.

●

Fate got a room at a motel called Las Brisas, in the northern part of Santa Teresa. Every so often, trucks passed along the highway, headed to Arizona. Sometimes they stopped on the other side of the highway, next to the gas pumps, and then they set off again or their drivers got out and had something to eat at the service station, which was painted sky blue. In the morning there were hardly any big trucks, just cars and pickups. Fate was so tired that he didn't even notice what time it was when he fell asleep.

When he woke up he went out to talk to the motel clerk and asked him for a map of the city. The clerk was a guy in his midtwenties and he told Fate that they'd never had maps at Las Brisas, at least not since he'd been working there. He asked where Fate wanted to go. Fate said he was a reporter and he was there to cover the Count Pickett fight. Count Pickett versus El Merolino Fernández, said the clerk.

"Lino Fernández," said Fate.

"Here we call him El Merolino," said the clerk with a smile. "So who do you think will win?"

"Pickett," said Fate.

"We'll see, but I bet you're wrong."

Then the clerk ripped out a piece of paper and drew him a map with precise directions to the Arena del Norte boxing stadium, where the fight would be held. The map was much better than Fate expected. The Arena del Norte looked like an old theater from 1900, with a boxing ring set in the middle of it. At one of the offices there, Fate picked up his credentials and asked where Pickett was staying. They told him the American fighter hadn't come to town yet. Among the reporters he met were a couple of men who spoke English and who planned to interview Fernández. Fate asked whether he could go along with them and the reporters shrugged their shoulders and said it was fine with them.

When they got to the hotel where Fernández was giving the press conference, the fighter was talking to a group of Mexican reporters. The Americans asked him in English whether he thought he could beat Pickett. Fernández understood the question and said yes. The Americans asked him whether he had ever seen Pickett fight. Fernández didn't understand the question and one of the Mexican reporters translated.

"The important thing is to trust your own strength," said Fernández, and the American reporters wrote his answer in their notebooks.

"Do you know Pickett's record?" they asked him.

Fernández waited for the question to be translated, then he said that kind of thing didn't interest him. The American reporters snickered, then asked him for his own record. Thirty fights, said Fernández. Twenty-five wins. Eighteen of them knockouts. Three losses. Two draws. Not bad, said one of the reporters, and he went on asking questions.

•

Most of the reporters were staying at the Hotel Sonora Resort, in the center of Santa Teresa. When Fate told them he was staying at a motel on the edge of town, they said he should check out and try to get a room at the Sonora Resort. Fate stopped by the hotel, where he got the sense that he'd stepped into a convention of Mexican sportswriters. Most of the Mexican reporters spoke English and they were much friendlier than the American reporters he'd met, or so it seemed at first. At the bar, some were placing bets on the fight and as a group they seemed generally cheerful and laid-back, but in the end Fate decided to stay at his motel.

From a phone at the Sonora Resort, he made a collect call to the magazine and asked to speak to the sports editor. The woman he talked to said no one was there.

"The offices are empty," she said.

She had a hoarse, nasal voice and she didn't talk like a New York secretary but like a country person who has just come from the cemetery. This woman has firsthand knowledge of the planet of the dead, thought Fate, and she doesn't know what she's saying anymore.

"I'll call back later," he said before he hung up.

•

Fate's car was following the car of the Mexican reporters who wanted to interview Merolino Fernández. The Mexican fighter had set up camp at a ranch on the edge of Santa Teresa, and without the help of the reporters Fate could never have found it. They drove through a neighborhood on the edge of town along a web of unpaved, unlit streets. At moments, after passing fields and vacant lots where the garbage of the poor piled up, it seemed as if they were about to come out into the open countryside, but then another neighborhood would appear, this time older, with adobe houses surrounded by shacks built of cardboard, of corrugated tin, of old packing crates, shacks that provided shelter from the sun and the occasional showers, that seemed petrified by the passage of time. Here not only the weeds were different but even the flies seemed to belong to a different species. Then a dirt track came into sight, camouflaged by the darkening horizon. It ran parallel to a ditch and was bordered by dusty trees. The first fences appeared. The road grew narrower. This used to be a cart track, thought Fate. In fact, he could see the wheel ruts, but maybe they were just the tracks of old cattle trucks.

The ranch where Merolino Fernández was staying was a cluster of three low, long buildings around a courtyard of earth as dry and hard as cement, where someone had set up a flimsy-looking ring. When they got to the ring it was empty and the only person in the courtyard was a man sleeping on a wicker chaise who woke at the sound of the engines. The man was big and heavy and his face was covered in scars. The Mexican reporters knew him and they began to talk to him. His name was Víctor García and he had a tattoo on his right shoulder that Fate thought was interesting. A naked man, seen from behind, was kneeling in the vestibule of a church. Around him at least ten angels in female form came flying out of the darkness, like butterflies summoned by his prayers. Everything else was darkness and vague shapes. The tattoo, although it was technically accomplished, looked as if it had been done in prison by a tattoo artist who for all his skill lacked tools and inks, but the scene it depicted was unsettling. When Fate asked the reporters who the man was, they answered that he was one of Merolino's sparring partners. Then, as if someone had been observing them from the window, a woman came out into the courtyard with a tray of soft drinks and cold beers.

After a while, the trainer of the Mexican fighter showed up in a white shirt and white sweater and asked whether they'd rather interview Merolino before or after the training session. Whatever you want, López, said one of the reporters. Have they brought you anything to eat? asked the trainer as he sat down within reach of the soft drinks and beer. The reporters shook their heads, and the trainer, without getting up from his seat, sent García to the kitchen to bring some snacks. Before García returned they saw Merolino appear along one of the paths that vanished into the desert, followed by a black guy dressed in sweatpants who tried to speak Spanish but could only curse. They didn't greet anyone as they walked into the courtyard, and they headed to a cement watering trough where they used a bucket to wash their faces and torsos. Only then did they come to say hello, not bothering to dry themselves or put on the tops of their sweat suits.

The black guy was from Oceanside, California, or at least he had been born there and had later grown up in Los Angeles, and his name was Omar Abdul. He worked as Merolino's sparring partner and he told Fate he was thinking of staying in Mexico to live for a while.

"What'll you do after the fight?" asked Fate.

"Get along as best I can," said Omar, "like we do, right?"

"Where will you get the money?"

"Anywhere," said Omar, "this country is cheap."

Every few minutes, for no reason, Omar would smile. He had a nice smile, set off with a goatee and a fancy little mustache. But every few minutes he would scowl, too, and then the goatee and the little mustache took on a menacing look, a look of supreme and ominous indifference. When Fate asked whether he was a professional or had been in any matches, he answered that he'd "fought," without deigning to explain further. When Fate asked him about Merolino Fernández's chances of winning, he said you never knew until the bell.

As the fighters dressed, Fate took a stroll around the courtyard and surveyed his surroundings.

"What you looking at?" Omar Abdul said to him.

"The landscape," he said, "it's one sad landscape."

Next to him, the fighter scanned the horizon and then he said:

"That's just how it is here. It's always sad at this time of day. It's a goddamn landscape for women."

"It's getting dark," said Fate.

"There's still light enough to spar," said Omar Abdul.

"What do you do at night, when you're done training?"

"All of us?" asked Omar Abdul.

"Yeah, the whole team or whatever you call it."

"We eat, we watch TV, then Mr. López goes to bed and Merolino goes to bed and the rest of us can go to bed too or watch more TV or head over into town, if you know what I'm saying," he said with a smile that might have meant anything.

"How old are you?" Fate asked suddenly.

"Twenty-two," said Omar Abdul.

•

When Merolino climbed into the ring the sun was sinking in the west and the trainer turned on the lights, which were fed by an independent generator that supplied the house with electricity. In a corner, García stood motionless with his head bowed. He had changed and put on knee-length black boxing shorts. He seemed to be asleep. Only when the lights came on did he raise his head and look at López for a few seconds, as if waiting for a signal. One of the reporters, who never stopped smiling, rang a bell, and García assumed a defensive stance and moved into the center of the ring. Merolino was wearing a safety helmet and he circled García, who threw a couple of left jabs, no more, trying to land a hit or two. Fate asked one of the reporters whether sparring partners usually wore safety helmets.

"Usually," said the reporter.

"So why isn't he wearing one?" asked Fate.

"Because no matter how much anybody hits him they won't do any damage," said the reporter. "Do you see what I mean? He doesn't feel anything, he's out of it."

In the third round García left the ring and Omar Abdul stepped up. The kid was bare chested but he hadn't taken off his warm-up pants. His movements were much quicker than those of the Mexican fighter, and he dodged away easily when Merolino tried to corner him, although it was clear that the fighter and his sparring partner had no intention of hurting each other. Every so often they would talk, while still moving, and laugh.

"You off in Costa Rica?" Omar Abdul asked him. "Come on, baby, open your eyes."

Fate asked the reporter what the fighter was saying.

"Nothing," said the reporter, "all the son of a bitch knows are curse words."

After three rounds the trainer stopped the fight and disappeared into the house, followed by Merolino.

"The masseur is waiting for them," said the reporter.

"Who is the masseur?" asked Fate.

"We haven't seen him, I think he never comes out into the yard, he's a blind guy, you know, he was born blind, and he spends all day in the kitchen eating, or in the bathroom shitting, or lying on the floor in his room reading books for blind people, in that blind people's language, what's it called?"

"Braille," said the other reporter.

Fate imagined the masseur reading in a dark room and a shudder passed through him. It must be something like happiness, he thought. At the watering trough, García dumped a bucket of cold water on Omar Abdul's back. The fighter from California winked at Fate.

"What did you think?" he asked.

"Not bad," said Fate, to be nice, "but I get the feeling Pickett's in better condition."

"Pickett's a punk," said Omar Abdul.

"Do you know him?"

"I've seen him fight on TV a couple times. Motherfucker doesn't know how to move."

"Well, I guess I've never actually seen him," said Fate.

Omar Abdul stared at him in astonishment.

"You've never seen Pickett fight?" he asked.

"No, the truth is the boxing guy at my magazine died last week and since we didn't have anyone else, they sent me."

"Put your money on Merolino," said Omar Abdul after a moment of silence.

"Good luck," said Fate before he left.

The ride back seemed shorter. For a while he followed the rear lights of the reporters' car, until he saw them park outside a bar when they were back on the paved streets of Santa Teresa. He pulled up next to them and asked what the plan was. We're getting something to eat, said one of the reporters. Although he wasn't hungry, Fate agreed to come for a beer. One of the reporters, Chucho Flores, worked for a local paper and radio station. The other one, Ángel Martínez Mesa, who had rung the bell when they were at the ranch, worked for a Mexico City sports paper. Martínez Mesa was short and must have been around fifty. Chucho Flores was only a little shorter than Fate. He was thirty-five and he was always smiling. The relationship between Flores and Martínez Mesa, Fate sensed, was that of grateful disciple and largely indifferent master. And yet Martínez Mesa's indifference seemed less a matter of arrogance or any sense of superiority than of exhaustion, an exhaustion that showed even in his disheveled clothing, a stained suit and scuffed shoes, while his disciple wore a designer suit and designer tie and gold cuff links and possibly saw himself as a man of style. As the Mexicans ate grilled meat with fried potatoes, Fate thought about García's tattoo. Then he compared the loneliness of the ranch to the loneliness of his mother's apartment. He thought about her ashes, which were still there. He thought about the dead neighbor. He thought about Barry Seaman's neighborhood. And everywhere his memory alighted as the Mexicans ate seemed bleak.

●

After they dropped Martínez Mesa off at the Sonora Resort, Chucho Flores insisted on going out for a last drink. There were several reporters at the bar, among them a few Americans Fate would've liked to talk to, but Chucho Flores had other plans. They went to a bar on a narrow street in the center of Santa Teresa, a bar with walls painted fluorescent colors and a zigzagging bar. They ordered whiskey and orange juice. The bartender knew Chucho Flores. The man looked more like the owner than a bartender, thought Fate. His movements were brusque and commanding, even when he began to dry glasses with the apron tied around his waist. And yet he wasn't very old, twenty-five at most, and Chucho Flores, who was busy talking to Fate about New York and reporting in New York, didn't pay him much attention.

"I'd like to go live there," confessed Chucho Flores, "and work for some Hispanic radio station."

"There are lots of them," said Fate.

"I know, I know," said Chucho Flores, as if he'd already done plenty of research, and then he mentioned names of two stations that broadcast in Spanish, stations Fate had never heard of before.

"So what's the name of your magazine?" asked Chucho Flores.

Fate told him, and after thinking awhile, Chucho Flores shook his head.

"I don't know it," he said, "is it big?"

"No, it isn't big," said Fate, "it's a Harlem magazine, if that means anything to you."

"No," said Chucho Flores, "it doesn't."

"It's a magazine where the owners are African American and the editor is African American and almost all the reporters are African American," said Fate.

"Really?" asked Chucho Flores. "Can you do objective reporting that way?"

It was then that Fate realized Chucho Flores was a little drunk. He thought about what he'd just said. In fact, he didn't really have any basis to claim that *almost* all the reporters were black. He had seen only African Americans at the office, although of course he didn't know the correspondents. Maybe there was some Chicano in California, he thought. Or maybe in Texas. But it also seemed likely that there was *no one* in Texas, because otherwise why send him from Detroit and not give the job to the person in Texas or California?

Some girls came up to say hello to Chucho Flores. They were dressed for a night out, in high heels and club clothes. One of them had bleached blond hair and the other one was very dark, quieter and shy. The blonde said hello to the bartender and he nodded back, as if he knew her well and didn't trust her. Chucho Flores introduced Fate as a famous sportswriter from New York. Fate chose that moment to tell the Mexican that he wasn't really a sports reporter, he covered political and social issues, which Chucho Flores found very interesting. After a while another man showed up and was introduced by Chucho Flores as the biggest film buff south of the Arizona border. His name was Charly Cruz, and with a big smile he told Fate not to believe a word Chucho Flores had said. He owned a video store and in his line of work he had to watch lots of movies, but that was all, I'm no expert, he said.

"How many stores do you have?" Chucho Flores asked him. "Go on, tell my friend Fate."

"Three," said Charly Cruz.

"The dude is loaded," said Chucho Flores.

The girl with bleached blond hair was Rosa Méndez, and according to Chucho Flores, she had been his girlfriend. She had also been Charly Cruz's girlfriend and now she was dating the owner of a dance hall.

"That's Rosita," said Charly Cruz, "that's just the way she is."

"What way is that?" Fate asked.

In not very good English the girl answered that she liked to have fun. Life is short, she said, and then she was quiet, looking back and forth between Fate and Chucho Flores, as if reflecting on what she'd just said.

"Rosita is a little bit of a philosopher, too," said Charly Cruz.

Fate nodded his head. Two other girls came up to them. They were even younger and they knew only Chucho Flores and the bartender. Fate calculated that neither of them could be over eighteen. Charly Cruz asked him if he liked Spike Lee. Yes, said Fate, although he didn't really.

"He seems Mexican," said Charly Cruz.

"Maybe," said Fate. "That's an interesting way to look at it."

"And what about Woody Allen?"

"I like him," said Fate.

"He seems Mexican too, but Mexican from Mexico City or Cuernavaca," said Charly Cruz.

"Mexican from Cancún," said Chucho Flores.

Fate laughed, although he had no idea what they were talking about. He guessed they were making fun of him.

"What about Robert Rodriguez?"

"I like him," said Fate.

"That shithead is one of ours," said Chucho Flores.

"I have a movie on video by Robert Rodriguez," said Charly Cruz, "a movie hardly anyone has ever seen."

"*El Mariachi?*" asked Fate.

"No, everybody's seen that one. An earlier one, from when Robert Rodriguez was a nobody. When he was just a piss-poor Chicano motherfucker. A fuckup who took any gig he could get," said Charly Cruz.

"Let's sit down and you can tell us the story," said Chucho Flores.

"Good idea," said Charly Cruz. "I was getting tired of standing."

The story was simple and implausible. Two years before he shot *El Mariachi*, Robert Rodriguez took a trip to Mexico. He spent a few days wandering along the Texas-Chihuahua border and then he went south, to Mexico City, where he spent his time drinking and getting high. He sank so low, said Charly Cruz, that he would go into a *pulquería* before noon and leave only when it was closing and they kicked him out. In the end, he was living in a bordello or a brothel or a whorehouse, where he got to be friends with a whore and her pimp, a guy who went by the name El Perno, which for a pimp was like being called the Penis or the Cock. This Perno guy hit it off with Robert Rodriguez and was a good friend to him. Sometimes he had to drag him up to the room where he slept. Other times he and the whore had to undress him and put him in the shower, because Robert Rodriguez was always passing out. One morning, one of those rare mornings when the future movie director was half sober, the pimp told him he had some friends who wanted to make a movie and asked whether he could shoot it. Robert Rodriguez, as you might imagine, said sure thing, and El Perno took care of the practical details.

The shooting lasted three days, it seems, and Robert Rodriguez was always drunk and high when he got behind the camera. Naturally, his name doesn't appear in the credits. The director is listed as Johnny Swiggerson, which is obviously a joke, but if you know Robert Rodriguez's movies, the way he frames a scene, his takes and overhead shots, his sense of speed, there's no doubt it's his work. The only thing missing is his personal editing style, which makes it clear the film was edited by someone else. But he's the director, that much I'm sure of.

●

Fate wasn't interested in Robert Rodriguez or the story of his first film, first or last, he couldn't care less, and also he was starting to feel like eating some dinner or having a sandwich and then going to bed at the motel and getting some sleep, but still he had to hear scraps of the plot, a story of whores who gave wise advice or maybe they were just whores with hearts of gold, especially a whore called Justina, who, for reasons that escaped him but weren't too hard to figure out, was acquainted with some vampires in Mexico City who roamed at night disguised as policemen. He ignored the rest of the story. As he and the dark-haired girl who had come with Rosita Méndez were kissing, he heard something about pyramids, Aztec vampires, a book written in blood, the inspiration for *From Dusk Till Dawn*, the recurring nightmare of Robert Rodriguez. The girl with dark hair didn't know how to kiss. Before he left he gave Chucho Flores the phone number of the motel where he was staying and then he stumbled out to where he had parked the car.

As he was opening the car door he heard someone ask if he felt all right. He took a deep breath and turned around. Chucho Flores was ten feet away with the knot of his tie loosened and his arm around Rosa Méndez. Rosa was looking at Fate as if he were some kind of exotic specimen, what kind? he didn't know, but he didn't like the look in her eye.

"I'm fine," he said, "there's no problem."

"Do you want me to drive you to your motel?" asked Chucho Flores.

Rosa Méndez smiled more broadly. It occurred to him that Chucho Flores might be gay.

"No need," he said, "I can handle it."

Chucho Flores let go of Rosa Méndez and took a step in his direction. Fate got into the car and started the engine, looking away from them. Goodbye, amigo, he heard the Mexican say, his voice somehow muted. Rosa Méndez had her hands on her hips in what struck him as a completely artificial pose, and she wasn't looking at him or his car as he drove away but at her companion, who stood motionless, as if the night air had frozen him.

●

There was a new kid at the front desk of the motel, and Fate asked him whether he could get something to eat. The boy said they didn't have a kitchen but he could buy cookies or a candy bar from the machine out front. Outside, trucks passed by now and then heading north and south, and across the road were the lights of the service station. Fate headed that way. When he was crossing the road, a car almost hit him. For a moment he thought it was because he was drunk, but then he told himself that before he crossed, drunk or not, he had looked both ways and he hadn't seen any lights on the road. So where had the car come from? The service station was brightly lit and almost empty. Behind the counter, a fifteen-year-old girl was reading a magazine. It looked to Fate as if she had a very small head. Next to the register was a woman, maybe twenty years old, who watched him as he went over to a machine that sold hot dogs.

"You have to pay first," said the woman in Spanish.

"I don't understand," said Fate, "I'm American."

The woman repeated what she had said in English.

"Two hot dogs and a beer," said Fate.

The woman took a pen out of the pocket of her uniform and wrote down the amount of money Fate had to give her.

"Dollars or pesos?" asked Fate.

"Pesos," said the woman.

Fate left some money next to the cash register and went to get a beer out of the refrigerator case and then he held up two fingers to show the small-headed teenager how many hot dogs he wanted. The girl brought him the hot dogs and Fate asked her how the condiments machine worked.

"Push the button for the one you want," said the teenager in English.

Fate put ketchup, mustard, and something that looked like guacamole on one of the hot dogs and ate it right there.

"Nice," he said.

"Good," said the girl.

Then he repeated the operation with the other hot dog and went to the register to get his change. He took some coins and went back over to where the teenager was and tipped her.

"Gracias, señorita," he said in Spanish.

Then he went out with his beer and hot dog. As he waited by the highway for three trucks to go by on their way from Santa Teresa to Arizona, he remembered what he'd said to the cashier. I'm American. Why didn't I say I was African American? Because I'm in a foreign country? But can I really consider myself to be in a foreign country when I could go walking back to my own country right now if I wanted, and it wouldn't even take very long? Does this mean that in some places I'm American and in some places I'm African American and in other places, by logical extension, I'm nobody?

•

When he got up he called the editor of the sports section at the magazine and told him Pickett wasn't in Santa Teresa.

"That's no surprise," said the editor of the sports section, "he's probably at some ranch outside Vegas."

"So how the hell am I supposed to interview him?" asked Fate. "You want me to go to Vegas?"

"Interview? You don't need any fucking interview, all we need is somebody to cover the fight, you know, the atmosphere, the mood in the ring, the shape Pickett's in, the impression he makes on the Mexicans."

"The mise-en-scène," said Fate.

"Mise-what?" asked the editor of the sports section.

"Shit, man, the atmosphere," said Fate.

"In plain English," said the editor of the sports section, "like you're telling a story at a bar and all your friends are there and people are gathered around to listen to what you have to say."

"I hear you," said Fate, "I'll get it to you the day after tomorrow."

"If there's anything you don't understand, don't worry about it, we'll edit it here so it sounds like you spent your whole life ringside."

"All right, I hear you," said Fate.

•

When he stepped onto the landing outside his room he saw three blond kids, almost albinos, playing with a white ball, a red bucket, and some red plastic shovels. The oldest must have been five and the youngest three. It wasn't a safe place for children to play. If they weren't careful they might try to cross the road and be run over by a truck. He looked around: sitting on a wooden bench in the shade, a very blond woman in sunglasses was watching them. He waved to her. She glanced at him for a second and jerked her chin as if she couldn't take her eyes off the kids.

Fate went down the stairs and got in his car. The heat inside was unbearable and he opened both windows. Without knowing why, he thought about his mother again, the way she had watched him when he was a boy. When he started the car one of the albino children got up and stared at him. Fate smiled at him and waved. The boy dropped his ball and stood to attention like a soldier. As the car turned out of the motel parking lot, the boy lifted his right hand to his visor and stood that way until Fate's car disappeared to the south.

As he was driving he thought about his mother again. He saw her walking, saw her from behind, saw the back of her head as she watched a TV show, heard her laugh, saw her washing dishes in the sink. Her face, however, was always in shadows, as if in some way she were already dead or as if she were telling him, in actions instead of words, that faces weren't important in this life or the next. There weren't any reporters at the Sonora Resort, and he had to ask the clerk how to get to the Arena del Norte. When he got to the stadium he noticed some kind of commotion. He asked a shoeshine man who had set up shop in one of the corridors what was going on and the shoeshine man said that the American fighter had arrived.

He found Count Pickett in the ring, dressed in a suit and tie and flashing a broad, confident smile. The photographers were shooting pictures and the reporters around the ring called to him by his first name and barked questions. When'll you be up for the championship? Is it true Jesse Brentwood is scared of you? What did you get to come to Santa Teresa? Is it true you eloped in Las Vegas? Pickett's manager was standing next to him. He was a short, fat little man and he was the one who answered most of the questions. The Mexican reporters addressed him in Spanish and called him by name, Sol, Mr. Sol, and Mr. Sol answered them in Spanish and sometimes he called the Mexican reporters by name too. An American reporter, a big guy with a square face, asked whether bringing Pickett to fight in Santa Teresa was politically correct.

"What do you mean politically correct?" asked the manager.

The reporter was about to answer, but the manager cut him off.

"Boxing," he said, "is a sport, and sports, like art, are beyond politics. Let's not mix sports and politics, Ralph."

"So what you're saying is," said the reporter called Ralph, "you aren't worried about bringing Count Pickett to Santa Teresa."

"Count Pickett isn't afraid of anybody," said the manager.

"There's no man alive who can beat me," said Count Pickett.

"Well, Count's a man, that's for sure. So I guess the question ought to be: has he brought any women with him?" asked Ralph.

A Mexican reporter at the other end of the ring got up and told him to go fuck himself. Somebody not far from Fate shouted that he'd better not talk shit about Mexicans if he didn't want to get his ass kicked.

"Shut your mouth, man, or I'll shut it for you."

Ralph seemed not to hear what they were saying and he stood there calmly, waiting for the manager's answer. Some American reporters who were in a corner of the ring, near the photographers, gave the manager a questioning look. The manager cleared his throat and then he said:

"We don't have any women with us, Ralph, you know we never travel with women."

"Not even Mrs. Alversohn?"

The manager laughed and so did some of the reporters.

"You know very well my wife doesn't like boxing, Ralph," said the manager.

•

"What the hell were they talking about?" Fate asked Chucho Flores as they were eating breakfast at a bar near the Arena del Norte.

"About the women who've been killed," said Chucho Flores glumly. "The numbers are up," he said. "Every so often the numbers go up and it's news again and the reporters talk about it. People talk about it too, and the story grows like a snowball until the sun comes out and the whole damn ball melts and everybody forgets about it and goes back to work."

"They go back to work?" asked Fate.

"The fucking killings are like a strike, amigo, a brutal fucking strike."

The comparison of the killings to a strike was odd. But Fate nodded his head and didn't say anything.

"This is a big city, a real city," said Chucho Flores. "We have everything. Factories, maquiladoras, one of the lowest unemployment rates in Mexico, a cocaine cartel, a constant flow of workers from other cities, Central American immigrants, an urban infrastructure that can't support the level of demographic growth. We have plenty of money and poverty, we have imagination and bureaucracy, we have violence and the desire to work in peace. There's just one thing we haven't got," said Chucho Flores.

Oil, thought Fate, but he didn't say it.

"What don't you have?" he asked.

"Time," said Chucho Flores. "We haven't got any fucking time."

Time for what? thought Fate. Time for this shithole, equal parts lost cemetery and garbage dump, to turn into a kind of Detroit? For a while they didn't talk. Chucho Flores took out a pencil and notebook and started to draw women's faces. He did it very quickly, completely absorbed in the effort, and also, it seemed to Fate, with some talent, as if before he'd become a sportswriter Chucho Flores had studied drawing and spent many hours sketching from life. None of his women were smiling. Some had their eyes closed. Others were old and had their heads turned as if they were waiting for something or someone to call their names. None of them was pretty.

"You're good," said Fate as Chucho Flores started on his seventh portrait.

"It's nothing," said Chucho Flores.

Then, more than anything because it embarrassed him to keep talking about how well the Mexican could draw, Fate asked about the dead women.

"Most of them are workers at the maquiladoras. Young girls with long hair. But that isn't necessarily the mark of the killer. In Santa Teresa almost all the girls have long hair," said Chucho Flores.

"Is there a single killer?" asked Fate.

"That's what they say," said Chucho Flores, still drawing. "A few people have been arrested. Some cases have been solved. But according to the legend, there's just one killer and he'll never be caught."

"How many women have been killed?"

"I don't know," said Chucho Flores, "lots, more than two hundred."

Fate watched as the Mexican began to sketch his ninth portrait.

"That's a lot for one person," he said.

"That's right, amigo. Too many. Even for a Mexican killer."

"And how are they killed?" asked Fate.

"Nobody's sure. They disappear. They vanish into thin air, here one minute, gone the next. And after a while their bodies turn up in the desert."

•

As they were driving to the Sonora Resort, where he planned to check his e-mail, it occurred to Fate that it would be much more interesting to write a story about the women who were being killed than about the Pickett-Fernández fight. That was what he wrote to his editor. He asked if he could stay in the city for another week and asked them to send a photographer. Then he went out to have a drink at the bar, joining some American reporters. They were talking about the fight and all of them agreed that Fernández wouldn't last more than four rounds. One of them told the story of the Mexican fighter Hércules Carreño. Carreño was almost six and a half feet tall, unusually tall for Mexico, where people tend to be short. And he was strong, too. He worked unloading sacks at a market or butcher's, and someone convinced him to try boxing. He got a late start. He might have been twenty-five. But in Mexico heavyweights are few and far between, and he won all his fights. This is a country with good bantamweights, good flyweights, good featherweights, even the occasional welterweight, but no heavyweights or light heavyweights. It has to do with tradition and nutrition. Morphology. Now Mexico has a president who's taller than the president of the United States. This is the first time it's ever happened. Gradually, the presidents here are getting taller. It used to be unthinkable. A Mexican president would come up to the American president's shoulder, at most. Sometimes the Mexican president's head would be barely an inch or two above our president's belly button. That's just how it was. But now the Mexican upper class is changing. They're getting richer and they go looking for wives north of the border. That's what you call *improving the race*. A short Mexican sends his short son to college in California. The kid has money and does whatever he wants and that impresses some girls. There's no place on earth with more dumb girls per square foot than a college in California. Bottom line: the kid gets himself a degree and a wife, who moves to Mexico with him. So then the short Mexican grandkids aren't so short anymore, they're medium, and meanwhile their skin's getting lighter too. These grandkids, when the time comes, set off on the same journey of initiation as their father. American college, American wife, taller and taller kids. What this means is that the Mexican upper class, of its own accord, is doing what the Spaniards did, but backward. The Spaniards, who were hot-blooded and didn't think too far ahead, mixed with the Indian women, raped them, forced them to practice their religion, and thought that meant they were turning the country white. Those Spaniards believed in a mongrel whiteness. But they overestimated their semen and that was their mistake. You just can't rape that many people. It's mathematically impossible. It's too hard on the body. You get tired. Plus, they were raping from the bottom up, when what would've made more sense would be raping from the top down. They might have gotten some results if they'd been capable of raping their own mongrel children and then their mongrel grandchildren and even their bastard great-grandchildren. But who's going to go out raping people when you're seventy and you can hardly stand on your own two feet? You can see the results all around you. The semen of those Spaniards, who thought they were titans, just got lost in the amorphous mass of thousands of Indians. The first mongrels, the ones with fifty-fifty blood, took charge of the country, those were your ministers, your soldiers, your shopkeepers, your founders of new cities. And they kept on raping, but it didn't yield the same fruits, since the Indian women they were raping gave birth to mestizos with a smaller percentage of white blood. And so on. Until we come to this fighter, Hércules Carreño, who started out winning, either because his rivals were even worse than he was or because the matches were fixed, which got some Mexicans to boast about having a real heavyweight champion, and one fine day Hércules Carreño was taken to the United States, and they matched him with a drunken Irishman and then a black guy who'd been smoking pot and then a fat Russian, and he beat them all, and it filled the Mexicans with happiness and pride: now their champion had hit the big time. And then they set up a fight against Arthur Ashley, in Los Angeles. Any of you guys see that fight? I did. They called Arthur Ashley the Sadist. That's the fight where he got the name. Poor Hércules Carreño was wiped right off the map. From round one you could tell it was going to be a massacre. The Sadist took his time, he was in no hurry, picking the perfect spots to land his hooks, turning each round into a monograph, round three on the subject of the face, round four on the liver. In the end, it was all Hércules Carreño could do to hang in till round eight. After that you could still see him fighting in third-rate rings. He almost always went down in round two. Then he tried to get work as a bouncer, but he was in such a fog he couldn't hold down a job for more than a week. He never went back to Mexico. Maybe he'd forgotten he was Mexican. The Mexicans, of course, forgot him. They say he started to beg on the streets and that one day he died under a bridge. The pride of the Mexican heavyweights, said the reporter.

The others laughed and then they all assumed expressions of penitence. Twenty seconds of silence to remember the unfortunate Carreño. The faces, suddenly solemn, made Fate think of a masked ball. For a brief instant he couldn't breathe, he saw his mother's empty apartment, he had a premonition of two people making love in a miserable room, all at the same time, a moment defined by the word *climacteric*. What are you, flacking for the Klan? Fate asked the reporter who had told the story. Watch out, looks like we got ourselves another touchy jig, said the reporter. Fate tried to lunge at him and get a punch in (though a slap in the face would've been better), but he was blocked by the reporters surrounding the man. He's just fucking around, he heard someone say. We're all American here. There's nobody here from the Klan. At least I don't think so. Then he heard more laughter. When he calmed down and went to sit by himself in a corner of the bar, one of the reporters who'd been listening to the story of Hércules Carreño came up to him and held out his hand.

"Chuck Campbell, *Sport Magazine*, Chicago."

Fate shook the reporter's hand and told him his name and the name of the magazine he worked for.

"I heard your sports guy was killed," said Campbell.

"That's right," said Fate.

"Woman trouble, I bet," said Campbell.

"I don't know," said Fate.

"I knew Jimmy Lowell," said Campbell, "at least we saw each other forty times or so, which is more than some men see a mistress, or even a wife. He was a good person. He liked his beer and he liked his dinner. A hardworking man, he used to say, has to eat, and the food has to be good. Sometimes we flew together. I can't sleep on planes. Jimmy Lowell would sleep through the whole flight, only time he'd wake up was to eat or tell some story. The truth is, he didn't really give a shit about boxing, his sport was baseball, but for you guys he covered everything, even tennis. He never had a bad word for anybody. He respected people and people respected him. Wouldn't you say?"

"I never met Lowell in my life," said Fate.

"Don't let yourself get upset by what you just heard," said Campbell. "Sports is a boring beat and guys shoot off their mouths without thinking about it, they make up stories just to have something different to talk about. Sometimes we say stupid things without meaning to. The guy who told the story about that Mexican fighter, he isn't a bad guy. Compared to the others, he's pretty decent, has an open mind. It's just that every so often, to pass the time, we act like assholes. But we don't mean anything by it," said Campbell.

"It's not a problem," said Fate.

"How many rounds you think it'll take Count Pickett to win?"

"I don't know," said Fate, "I saw Merolino Fernández training at his place yesterday and he didn't look like a loser to me."

"He'll go down before the third," said Campbell.

Another reporter asked where Fernández was staying.

"Not far from the city," said Fate, "although I don't actually know, I didn't go alone, some Mexicans took me."

•

When Fate checked his e-mail again, he found a reply from his editor. There was no interest in the story he'd pitched, or no budget. His editor suggested that Fate limit himself to completing the assignment from the sports editor and then return immediately. Fate spoke to a clerk at the Sonora Resort and asked to place a call to New York.

While he waited he thought about other pitches the magazine had turned down. The most recent had been about a political group in Harlem, the Mohammedan Brotherhood. He'd met them during a pro-Palestine demonstration. The turnout was mixed, groups of Arabs, New York lefties, new antiglobalization activists. But the Mohammedan

Brotherhood caught his attention because they were marching under a big poster of Osama bin Laden. They were all black and they were all wearing black leather jackets and black berets and sunglasses, which gave them a vague resemblance to the Panthers, except that the Panthers had been teenagers and the ones who weren't teenagers had a youthful look, an aura of youthfulness and tragedy, whereas the members of the Mohammedan Brotherhood were grown men, broad shouldered with huge biceps, people who spent hours and hours at the gym, lifting weights, people born to be bodyguards, but whose bodyguards? true human tanks whose very presence was intimidating, although there were no more than twenty at the demonstration, possibly fewer, but somehow the poster of bin Laden had a magnifying effect, first and foremost because it was less than six months since the attack on the World Trade Center and walking around with bin Laden, even just in effigy, was an extreme provocation. Of course, Fate wasn't the only one who took notice of the small, defiant presence of the Brotherhood: the television cameras followed them, their spokesman was interviewed, and the photographers from several papers documented the attendance of the group, which looked as if it was asking to be crushed.

Fate observed them from a distance. He watched them talk to the television crews and some local radio reporters, he watched them yell slogans, he watched them march through the crowd, and he followed them. Before the demonstration began to break up, the members of the Mohammedan Brotherhood exited in a planned maneuver. A couple of vans were waiting for them on a corner. Only then did Fate realize that there were no more than fifteen of them. They ran. He ran after them. He explained that he wanted to interview them for his magazine. They talked next to the vans, on a side street. The one who seemed to be the leader, a tall, fat guy with a shaved head, asked him what magazine he worked for. Fate told him and the man smirked.

"No one reads that shit today," he said.

"It's a magazine for brothers," said Fate.

"It's a motherfucking sellout," said the man, still smiling. "It's played."

"I don't think so," said Fate.

A Chinese kitchen worker came out to leave some garbage bags. An Arab watched them from the corner. Strange, remote faces, thought Fate, as the man who seemed to be the leader gave him a time, a date, a place in the Bronx where they would see each other in a few days.

Fate kept the appointment. Three members of the Brotherhood and a black van were waiting for him. They drove to a basement near Baychester. The fat guy with the shaved head was waiting for them there. He said to call him Khalil. The others didn't give their names. Khalil talked about the Holy War. Explain what the hell you mean by Holy War, said Fate. The Holy War speaks for us when our mouths are parched, said Khalil. The Holy War is the language of the mute, of those who've lost the power of speech, of those who never knew how to speak. Why do you march against Israel? asked Fate. The Jew is keeping us down, said Khalil. You won't see a Jew in the Klan, said Fate. That's what the Jews want us to think. In fact, the Klan is everywhere. In Tel Aviv, in London, in Washington. Many leaders of the Klan are Jews, said Khalil. It's always been that way. Hollywood is full of Klan leaders. Who? asked Fate. Khalil warned him that what he was about to say was off the record.

"The Jew tycoons have good Jew lawyers," he said.

Who? asked Fate. Khalil named three movie directors and two actors. Then Fate had an inspiration. He asked: is Woody Allen a member of the Klan? He is, said Khalil, look at his movies, have you ever seen a black man in them? Not many, said Fate. Not one, said Khalil. Why were you carrying a poster of bin Laden? asked Fate. Because Osama bin Laden was the first to understand the nature of the fight we face today. Then they talked about bin Laden's innocence and Pearl Harbor and about how convenient the attack on the Twin Towers had been for some people. Stockbrokers, said Khalil, people with incriminating papers hidden in their offices, people who sell arms and needed something like that to happen. According to you, said Fate, Mohamed Atta was an undercover agent for the CIA or the FBI. What happened to Mohamed Atta's body? Khalil asked. Who can be sure Mohamed Atta was on one of those planes? I'll tell you what I think. I think Atta is dead. He died under torture, or he was shot in the back of the head. Then I think they chopped him into little pieces and ground his bones down until they looked like chicken bones. After that they put the little bones and cutlets in a box, filled it with cement, and dropped it in some Florida swamp. And they did the same thing to the men he was with.

So who flew the planes? asked Fate. Klan lunatics, nameless inmates from mental hospitals in the Midwest, volunteers brainwashed to face suicide. Thousands of people disappear in this country every year and nobody tries to find them. Then they talked about the Romans and the Roman circus and the first Christians who were eaten by lions. But the lions will choke on our black flesh, he said.

●

The next day Fate met them at a Harlem club and there he was introduced to Ibrahim, a man of average height with a scarred face, who set about describing to him in great detail all the charitable work the Brotherhood did in the neighborhood. They ate together at a diner next door to the club. The diner was run by a woman. A boy helped her, and in the kitchen there was an old man who never stopped singing. In the afternoon Khalil joined them and Fate asked the two men where they'd met. In prison, they said. Prison is where black brothers meet. They talked about the other Muslim groups in Harlem. Ibrahim and Khalil didn't think very highly of them, but they tried to be fair and maintain a dialogue with them. Sooner or later the good Muslims would end up finding their way to the Mohammedan Brotherhood.

Before he left, Fate told them that they would probably never be forgiven for having marched under the effigy of Osama bin Laden. Ibrahim and Khalil laughed. He thought they looked like two black stones quaking with laughter.

"They'll probably never *forget* it," said Ibrahim.

"Now they know who they're dealing with," said Khalil.

●

His editor told him to forget writing a story about the Brotherhood.

"Those guys, how many of them are there?" he asked.

"Twenty, more or less," said Fate.

"Twenty niggers," said his editor. "At least five of them must be FBI."

"Maybe more," said Fate.

"What makes them interesting to us?" asked his editor.

"Stupidity," said Fate. "The endless variety of ways we destroy ourselves."

"Have you become a masochist, Oscar?" asked his editor.

"Could be," said Fate.

"You need to get more pussy," said the editor. "Get out more, listen to music, make friends, talk to them."

"I've thought about it," said Fate.

"Thought about what?"

"About getting more pussy," said Fate.

"That isn't the kind of thing you think about, it's the kind of thing you do," said the editor.

"First you have to think about it," said Fate. Then he added: "Can I do the story?"

The editor shook his head.

"Forget about it," he said. "Sell it to a philosophy quarterly or an urban anthropology journal, or write a fucking script if you want and let Spike Lee shoot the motherfucker, but it's not going to run in any magazine of mine."

"All right," said Fate.

"Motherfuckers marched with a poster of bin Laden," said his editor.

"It takes balls," said Fate.

"Balls of steel, plus you have to be a complete goddamn moron."

"You know some undercover cop came up with it," said Fate.

"Makes no difference," said the editor, "whoever came up with it, it's a sign."

"A sign of what?" asked Fate.

"That we're living on a planet of lunatics," said the editor.

•

When his editor came to the phone, Fate explained what was going on in Santa Teresa. He gave a synopsis of the story he wanted to write. He talked about the women being killed, about the possibility that all the crimes had been committed by one or two people, which made them the biggest serial killings in history, he talked about drug trafficking and the border, about police corruption and the city's boundless growth, he promised that all he wanted was another week to get all the material needed and then he'd come back to New York and in five days he'd file the story.

"Oscar," said his editor, "you're there to cover a goddamn boxing match."

"This is more important," said Fate, "the fight is just a little story. What I'm proposing is so much more."

"What are you proposing?"

"A sketch of the industrial landscape in the third world," said Fate, "a piece of *reportage* about the current situation in Mexico, a panorama of the border, a serious crime story, for fuck's sake."

"*Reportage?*" asked his editor. "Is that French, nigger? Since when do you speak French?"

"I don't speak French," said Fate, "but I know what fucking *reportage* is."

"I know what fucking *reportage* is, too," said the editor, "and I also know *merci* and *au revoir* and *faire l'amour,* which is the same as *coucher avec moi.* And I think that you, nigger, want to *coucher avec moi,* but you've forgot the *voulez-vous,* which in this case ought to have been your first move. You hear me? You say *voulez-vous* or you can get the fuck out."

"It's a great story," said Fate.

"How many black men are involved in this shit?" asked the editor.

"Black men? Say what?" asked Fate.

"How many niggers have ropes around their neck?" asked the editor.

"How should I know? I'm talking about a great story," said Fate, "not some riot in the ghetto."

"So in other words, there are no black men," said the editor.

"No black men, but more than two hundred Mexican women killed," said Fate.

"How're Pickett's odds?" asked the editor.

"Take Count Pickett and stick him up your black ass," said Fate.

"You seen the other guy?" asked the editor.

"You can stick Count Pickett up your black faggot ass," said Fate, "and ask him to watch it for you because when I get back to New York I'm going to kick the shit out of you."

"You do your job and hold on to your receipts, nigger," said the editor.

Fate hung up.

Next to him, smiling at him, was a woman in jeans and a leather jacket. She was wearing sunglasses and she had a nice bag and a camera slung over her shoulder. She looked like a tourist.

"Are you interested in the Santa Teresa killings?" she asked.

Fate looked at her and it took him a moment to realize that she had listened to his phone conversation.

"My name's Guadalupe Roncal," said the woman, holding out her hand.

He shook it. It was a delicate hand.

"I'm a reporter," said Guadalupe Roncal when Fate let go of her hand.

"But I'm not here to cover the fight. Boxing doesn't interest me, though I know some women find it sexy. To be honest, it's always struck me as vulgar and pointless. How about you? Do you like to watch two grown men hit each other?"

Fate shrugged his shoulders.

"You won't tell? Fine, I'm not one to judge what you like to watch. Actually, I don't like any sports. Not boxing, for the reasons I mentioned, or soccer, or basketball, not even track and field. So you may wonder what I'm doing in a hotel full of sports reporters instead of someplace quieter, somewhere I wouldn't have to hear all these pathetic stories of great forgotten fights every time I come down to the bar. I'll tell you if you come sit at my table and let me buy you a drink."

As he followed her it occurred to him that he might be in the company of a crazy person or maybe a hooker, but Guadalupe Roncal didn't look like a crazy person or a hooker, although Fate didn't really know what Mexican crazy people or hookers looked like. For that matter, she didn't look like a reporter. They sat at an outside table, with a view of a building under construction, a building more than ten stories high. Another hotel, the woman informed him with indifference. Some workmen leaning on beams or sitting on piles of bricks were looking at them, or so Fate thought, although it was impossible to say for sure because the figures moving around the unfinished building were so small.

"As I said already, I'm a reporter," said Guadalupe Roncal. "I work for one of the big Mexico City newspapers. And I'm staying at this hotel out of fear."

"Fear of what?" asked Fate.

"Fear of everything. When you work on something that involves the killings of women in Santa Teresa, you end up scared of everything. Scared you'll be beaten up. Scared of being kidnapped. Scared of torture. Of course, the fear lessens with experience. But I don't have experience. No experience whatsoever. I'm cursed by a lack of experience. You might even say I'm here undercover, as an undercover reporter, if there is such a thing. I know everything about the killings. But I'm not really an expert on the subject. What I mean is, until a week ago this wasn't my subject. I wasn't up on it, I hadn't written anything about it, and suddenly, out of the blue, the file landed on my desk and I was in charge of the investigation. Do you want to know why?"

Fate nodded.

"Because I'm a woman and women can't turn down assignments. Of course, I already knew what had happened to my predecessor. Everybody at the paper knew it. The case got a lot of attention. You might even have heard about it." Fate shook his head. "He was killed, of course. He got in too deep and they killed him. Not here, in Santa Teresa, but in Mexico City. The police said it was a robbery that went wrong. You want to know how it happened? He got in a taxi. The taxi drove off. Then it stopped at a corner and two strangers got in. For a while they drove around to different cash machines, maxing out my predecessor's credit card, then they headed somewhere on the edge of the city and stabbed him. He wasn't the first reporter to be killed for what he wrote. Going through his papers I found information on two others. A woman, a radio correspondent, who was kidnapped in Mexico City, and a Chicano who worked for an Arizona paper called *La Raza*, who disappeared. The two of them were investigating the killings of women in Santa Teresa. I'd met the radio correspondent at journalism school. We were never friends. We might've exchanged a few words at most. But I think I'd met her. Before they killed her they raped her and tortured her."

"Here, in Santa Teresa?" asked Fate.

"No, man, in Mexico City. The arm of the killers is long, very long," said Guadalupe Roncal in a dreamy voice. "I used to work for the city section. I almost never got a byline. I was a complete unknown. When my predecessor was killed, two of the big bosses at the paper came to see me. They invited me out to lunch. Of course, I thought I'd done something wrong. Or that one of them wanted to sleep with me. I knew who they were, but I had never talked to either of them. It was a nice lunch. They were proper and polite, I was quick and careful. It would've been better if I hadn't made such a good impression. Then we went back to the paper and they told me to follow them, they had something important to discuss with me. We went into one of their offices. The first thing they did was ask me if I'd like a raise. By that point I had figured out that something strange was going on and I was tempted to say no, but I said yes, and then they pulled out a piece of paper and named a figure, which was exactly what I was making as a city reporter, and then they looked straight at me and named another figure, which was like offering me a forty percent raise. I almost jumped for joy. Then they handed me the file my predecessor had put together and told me that from then on I would work solely and exclusively on the story of the women who'd been killed in Santa Teresa. I realized that if I said no I'd lose everything. It came out almost as a whisper when I asked why me. Because you're smart, Lupita, said one of them. Because no one knows you, said the other."

The woman gave a long sigh. Fate smiled in understanding. They ordered another whiskey and another beer. The workmen on the building under construction had disappeared. I'm drinking too much, said the woman.

"Since I read my predecessor's file, I've been drinking lots of whiskey, much more than I used to, and I drink vodka and tequila, too, and now I've discovered this Sonoran drink called *bacanora*, and I drink that, too," said Guadalupe Roncal. "And every day I'm more afraid and sometimes I can't help being a nervous wreck. You've probably heard that Mexicans never get scared." She laughed. "It's a lie. We get scared all right, we just know how to hide it. When I got to Santa Teresa, for example, I was so scared I thought I was going to die. On the flight here from Hermosillo I wouldn't have minded if the plane crashed. At least it's a quick death, or so they say. Luckily someone I work with in Mexico City had given me the address of this hotel. He told me he was going to be at the Sonora Resort to cover the fight and that no one could hurt me here around all these sportswriters. So here I am. The problem is that when the fight is over I can't leave with the reporters and I'll have to stay a few more days in Santa Teresa."

"Why?" asked Fate.

"I have to interview the chief suspect in the killings. He's from the United States, too."

"I had no idea," said Fate.

"How were you going to write about the crimes if you didn't know that?" asked Guadalupe Roncal.

"I thought I'd do some research. On the phone just now I was asking for more time."

"My predecessor was the one who knew most about all of this. It took him seven years to get a general sense of what was going on. Life is unbearably sad, don't you think?"

Guadalupe Roncal massaged both temples, as if suddenly she felt a migraine coming on. She whispered something Fate couldn't hear, and then she tried to flag the waiter but they were the only two at the outside tables. When she realized, she shivered.

"I have to go visit him in prison," she said. "The chief suspect—your countryman—has been in prison for years."

"So how can he be the chief suspect?" asked Fate. "I thought the crimes were still being committed."

"Mysteries of Mexico," said Guadalupe Roncal. "Do you want to come along? Would you like to come with me and interview him? The truth is I'd feel better if a man came with me, which goes against my beliefs as a feminist. Do you have anything against feminists? It's hard to be a feminist in Mexico. Not if you have money, maybe, but if you're middle class, it's hard. At first it isn't, of course, at first it's easy, in college it's easy, for example, but as the years go by it gets harder and harder. Mexican men, I can tell you, find feminism charming only in young women. But we age quickly here. We're built to age quickly. Thank goodness I'm still young."

"You're pretty young," said Fate.

"But I'm scared. And I need company. This morning I drove past the Santa Teresa prison and I almost had a panic attack."

"Is it that bad?"

"It's like a dream," said Guadalupe Roncal. "It looks like something alive."

"Alive?"

"I don't know how to explain it. More alive than an apartment building, for example. Much more alive. Don't be shocked by what I'm about to say, but it looks like a woman who's been hacked to pieces. Who's been hacked to pieces but is still alive. And the prisoners are living *inside* this woman."

"I understand," said Fate.

"No, I don't think you do, but it doesn't matter. You're interested, so I'm offering you the chance to meet the chief suspect in the killings in exchange for your company and protection. I think that seems fair and equitable. Do we have a deal?"

"It is fair," said Fate. "And very kind of you. What I don't understand is what you're afraid of. No one can hurt you in prison. In theory, anyhow, prisoners can't hurt anyone. They only hurt each other."

"You've never seen a picture of the chief suspect."

"No," said Fate.

Guadalupe Roncal looked up at the sky and smiled.

"I must seem crazy," she said, "or like a hooker. But I'm neither. I'm just nervous and lately I've been drinking too much. Do you think I want to get you in bed?"

"No. I believe what you've told me."

"Among my poor predecessor's papers there were several photographs. A few of the suspect. Three, to be precise. All three taken in prison. In two of them, the gringo—sorry, I didn't mean that to be offensive—is sitting and looking at the camera, probably in a visitor's room. He has very blond hair and very blue eyes. Eyes so blue he looks blind. In the third picture he's standing up, looking to the side. He's hugely tall and thin, very thin, but not feeble looking at all. He has the face of a dreamer. I don't know if that makes sense. He doesn't look uncomfortable. He's in prison, but I don't get the sense he's uncomfortable. He doesn't seem calm or relaxed, either. And he doesn't seem angry. He has the face of a dreamer, but of a dreamer who's dreaming at great speed. A dreamer whose dreams are far out ahead of our dreams. And that scares me. Do you understand?"

"I can't say I do," said Fate. "But you can count on me to go with you to interview him."

"All right, then," said Guadalupe Roncal. "I'll be waiting for you the day after tomorrow, at the entrance to the hotel, at ten. Does that sound good?"

"Ten in the morning. I'll be there," said Fate.

"Ten a.m. Okay," said Guadalupe Roncal. Then she shook his hand and walked off. Her gait was unsteady, Fate noticed.

·

He spent the rest of the day drinking with Campbell in the bar at the Sonora Resort. They complained about sportswriting, a dead-end profession that never got anyone a Pulitzer and that most people thought involved little more than showing up at games. Then they began to reminisce about their college years, Fate's at New York University, Campbell's at a college in Sioux City.

"In those days all I cared about was baseball and ethics," said Campbell.

For a second Fate imagined Campbell on his knees in the corner of a dark room, clutching a Bible and weeping. But then Campbell started to talk about women, about a bar in a place called Smithland, a kind of country inn near the Little Sioux River. First you got to Smithland and then you went a few miles east and there, under some trees, was the bar and the bar girls, whose clients were mostly farmers and a few students who came by car from Sioux City.

"We always did the same thing," said Campbell, "first we fucked the girls, then we went outside and played baseball until we were exhausted, and then, when it started to get dark, we would get drunk and sing cowboy songs on the porch."

When Fate was a student at NYU, he never got drunk or slept with prostitutes (in fact, he had never in his life been with a woman he had to pay). His free time was spent working and reading. Once a week, on Saturdays, he went to a creative writing workshop and for a while, not long, just a few months, he imagined that maybe he could make a living writing fiction, until the writer who led the workshop told him he'd do better to focus on journalism.

But that wasn't what he told Campbell.

When it began to get dark, Chucho Flores came in to find him. Fate noticed that Chucho Flores didn't invite Campbell along. He didn't know why, but this made him happy, though it made him unhappy too. For a while they drove aimlessly around Santa Teresa, at least that was how it seemed to Fate, as if Chucho Flores had something to tell him and couldn't find the right moment. The city lights at night changed the Mexican's face. The muscles under his skin grew tense. An ugly profile, thought Fate. Only then did he realize that at some point he would have to go back to the Sonora Resort, because that was where he'd parked his car.

"Let's not go too far," he said.

"Are you hungry?" the Mexican asked him. Fate said he was. The Mexican laughed and put on music. Fate heard an accordion and some far-off shouts, not of sorrow or joy, but of pure energy, self-sufficient and self-consuming. Chucho Flores smiled and his smile remained stamped on his face as he kept driving, not looking at Fate, facing forward, as if he'd been fitted with a steel neck brace, as the wails came closer and closer to the microphones and the voices of people who Fate imagined as savage beasts began to sing or kept howling, less than at first, and shouting *viva* for no clear reason.

"What is this?" asked Fate.

"Sonoran jazz," said Chucho Flores.

•

When he got back to the motel it was four in the morning. Over the course of the night he had gotten drunk and then sobered up and then gotten drunk again, and now, outside his room, he was sober again, as if instead of drinking real alcohol Mexicans drank water with short-term hypnotic effects. For a while, sitting on the trunk of his car, he watched the trucks going by on the highway. The night was cool and full of stars. He thought about his mother and what she must have thought about at night in Harlem, not looking out the window to see the few stars shining in the sky, sitting in front of the TV or washing dishes in the kitchen with laughter coming from the TV, black people and white people laughing, telling jokes that she might have thought were funny, although probably she didn't even pay much attention to what was being said, busy washing the dishes she had just used and the pot she had just used and the fork and spoon she had just used, peaceful in a way that seemed to go beyond simple peacefulness, thought Fate, or maybe not, maybe her peacefulness was just peacefulness and a hint of weariness, peacefulness and banked embers, peacefulness and tranquillity and sleepiness, which is ultimately (sleepiness, that is) the wellspring and also the last refuge of peacefulness. But then peacefulness isn't just peacefulness, thought Fate. Or what we think of as peacefulness is wrong and peacefulness or the realms of peacefulness are really no more than a gauge of movement, an accelerator or a brake, depending.

•

The next day he got up at two in the afternoon. The first thing he remembered was that before he went to bed he'd felt sick and thrown up. He checked on both sides of the bed and then he went into the bathroom but he couldn't find a single trace of vomit. Still, while he was sleeping he had woken up twice and both times he had smelled vomit: a foul odor that emanated from every corner of the room. He had been too tired to get up and had opened the windows and gone back to sleep.

Now the smell was gone and there was no sign that he had vomited the night before. He showered and then he got dressed, thinking that after the fight that night he would head straight back to Tucson, where he would try to catch a red-eye to New York. He wouldn't keep his appointment with Guadalupe Roncal. Why interview a suspected serial killer if he couldn't write about it? He thought about calling and making a reservation from the motel, but at the last minute he decided to do it later, from one of the phones at the Arena del Norte or the Sonora Resort. Then he packed his suitcase and went to the desk to check out. You don't have to leave now, the clerk told him, I'll charge you the same price to keep the room until midnight. Fate thanked him and put the key back in his pocket, but he didn't take his suitcase out of the car.

"Who do you think will win?" the clerk asked him.

"I don't know. Anything could happen in a fight like this," said Fate, as if he'd been a sportswriter all his life.

The sky was a deep blue, broken only by a few cylindrical clouds floating in the east and moving toward the city.

"They look like tubes," said Fate from the open door of the lobby.

"They're cirrus clouds," said the clerk. "By the time they reach the heights of Santa Teresa they'll have disappeared."

"It's funny," said Fate, still standing in the doorway, "*cirrus* means hard, it comes from the Greek *skirrhós*, which means hard, and it refers to tumors, hard tumors, but those clouds don't look hard at all."

"No," said the clerk, "they're clouds in the top layer of the atmosphere, and if they drop or rise a little, just a tiny bit, they disappear."

•

There was no one at the Arena del Norte. The main door was closed. On the walls were some posters, already faded, advertising the Fernández-Pickett fight. Some had been torn down and others had been covered by new posters pasted up by unknown hands, posters advertising concerts, folk dances, and even a circus calling itself Circo Internacional.

Fate walked around the building. He ran into a woman who was pushing a juice cart. The woman had long black hair and was wearing an ankle-length skirt. Among the jugs of water and buckets of ice the heads of two children bobbed. When she got to the corner the woman stopped and began to set up a kind of parasol with metal tubes. The children got off the cart and sat on the pavement, against the wall. For a while Fate stood watching them and the utterly deserted street. When he walked on, another cart appeared from around the opposite corner and Fate stopped again. The man who was pushing the new cart waved to the woman. She barely nodded in recognition and began to take huge glass jars out of the side of her cart, setting them on a makeshift counter. The man who had just arrived was selling corn, and steam rose from his cart. Fate discovered a back door and looked for a bell, but there was no bell of any kind so he had to knock. The children had gone up to the corn vendor, who got two cobs, spread them with thick cream, sprinkled them with cheese and then chile powder, and handed them to the children. As he waited, Fate imagined that the man with the corn was the children's father and that he was on bad terms with the mother, the juice woman, in fact maybe they were divorced and they saw each other only when they ran into each other on the job. But that couldn't possibly be the case, he thought. Then he knocked again and no one came to let him in.

●

At the bar at the Sonora Resort he found almost all of the reporters who were covering the fight. He saw Campbell talking to a man who looked Mexican and walked toward them, but before he reached them he realized that Campbell was working and decided not to interrupt. He saw Chucho Flores by the bar and waved from across the room. Chucho Flores was with three men who looked like ex-fighters and his wave back seemed halfhearted. Fate found an empty table outside and sat down. For a while he watched people get up from their tables and greet each other with long hugs or shout back and forth, and he watched the bustle of photographers shooting pictures, arranging and rearranging groups to their liking, and the procession of Santa Teresa notables, faces that weren't familiar to him at all, well-dressed young women, tall men in cowboy boots and Armani suits, young men with bright eyes and stiff jaws who didn't talk and just shook their heads yes or no, until he got tired of waiting for the waiter to bring him a drink and he elbowed his way out without looking back, not caring that two or three rude remarks were dropped behind him, remarks in Spanish that he didn't understand and that wouldn't have given him reason to stay even if he had understood them.

●

He ate at a restaurant in the eastern part of the city, on a cool patio under a vine-covered arbor. At the back of the patio, on the dirt floor next to a chain-link fence, there were three foosball tables. For a few minutes he looked at the menu, not understanding anything. Then he tried to explain what he wanted with gestures, but the woman who was waiting on him just smiled and shrugged her shoulders. After a while a man came over, but the English he spoke was even more unintelligible. The only word Fate understood was bread. And beer.

Then the man vanished and he was left alone. He got up and went over to the edge of the arbor, next to the foosball tables. One team was dressed in white T-shirts and green shorts and had black hair and very light-colored skin. The other team was in red, with black shorts, and all the players had full beards. The strangest thing, though, was that the players on the red team had tiny horns on their foreheads. The other two tables were exactly the same.

He could see hills on the horizon. The hills were dark yellow and black. Past the hills, he guessed, was the dessert. He felt the urge to leave and drive into the hills, but when he got back to his table the woman had brought him a beer and a very thick kind of sandwich. He took a bite and it was good. The taste was strange, spicy. Out of curiosity, he lifted the piece of bread on top: the sandwich was full of all kinds of things. He took a long drink of beer and stretched in his chair. Through the vine leaves he saw a bee, perched motionless. Two slender rays of sun fell vertically on the dirt floor. When the man came back he asked how to get to the hills. The man laughed. He spoke a few words Fate didn't understand and then he said not pretty, several times.

"Not pretty?"

"Not pretty," said the man, and he laughed again.

Then he took Fate by the arm and dragged him into a room that served as kitchen and that looked very tidy to Fate, each thing in its place, not a spot of grease on the white-tiled wall, and he pointed to the garbage can.

"Hills not pretty?" asked Fate.

The man laughed again.

"Hills are garbage?"

The man couldn't stop laughing. He had a bird tattoed on his left forearm. Not a bird in flight, like most tattoos of birds, but a bird perched on a branch, a little bird, possibly a swallow.

"Hills a garbage dump?"

The man laughed even more and nodded his head.

•

At seven that night Fate showed his press pass and went into the Arena del Norte. There were crowds outside and vendors selling food, soft drinks, and boxing souvenirs. Inside, the second-tier fights had already started. A bantamweight Mexican was fighting another bantamweight Mexican with only a few people watching. Others were buying sodas, talking, greeting each other. Ringside, he saw two television cameras. One of them seemed to be recording what was happening in the main aisle. The other cameraman was sitting on a bench, trying to get a snack cake out of its plastic wrapping. He headed down one of the covered side passageways. He saw people placing bets, two short men each with an arm around a tall woman in a tight dress, men smoking or drinking beer, men with loosened ties making signs with their fingers, as if they were playing a children's game. Above the awning that covered the passageway were the cheap seats and there the noise was even louder. He decided to go check out the dressing rooms and the pressroom. The only people in the pressroom were two Mexican reporters who stared at him like dying men. Both were seated and their shirts were damp with sweat. At the entrance to Merolino Fernández's dressing room he saw Omar Abdul. He said hello but the fighter pretended not to recognize him and kept talking to some Mexicans. The people outside the door were talking about blood, or so Fate thought he understood.

"What are you talking about?" he asked them.

"Bullfighting," one of the Mexicans said in English.

As he was leaving he heard someone call his name. Mr. Fate. He turned around and was met with Omar Abdul's broad smile.

"Don't you say hello to your friends, man?"

From up close he could see that both of the fighter's cheekbones were bruised.

"I guess Merolino's been working out," he said.

"Hazards of the trade," said Omar Abdul.

"Can I see the boss?"

Omar Abdul looked over his shoulder, through the door to the dressing room, and then he shook his head.

"If I let you in, brother, I'd have to let in all these other punks."

"Are they reporters?"

"Some of them are reporters, but most of them just want their picture taken with Merolino, want to kiss his hand, kiss his ass."

"How you doing?"

"Can't complain, can't really complain," said Omar Abdul.

"What do you plan to do after the fight?"

"Celebrate, I guess," said Omar Abdul.

"No, I don't mean tonight, but after it's all over," said Fate.

Omar Abdul smiled. A cocky, teasing smile. A Cheshire cat smile, as if instead of being perched on a tree branch, the Cheshire cat were out in an open field in a storm. The smile of a young black man, thought Fate, but also a very American smile.

"I don't know," he said, "look for work, hang out in Sinaloa on the beach, we'll see."

"Good luck," said Fate.

As he was walking away he heard Omar say: Count Pickett is the one who's going to need luck tonight. When he got back to the hall two different fighters were in the ring and there were hardly any empty seats left. He headed down the main aisle to the press pit. There was a fat man in his seat who looked at him, not understanding what he was saying. Fate showed him his ticket and the man got up and searched his pockets until he found his own ticket. The two of them had the same seat number. Fate smiled and the fat man smiled. Just then one of the fighters landed a hook that knocked his opponent down and most of the audience stood up and roared.

"What should we do?" Fate asked the fat man. The fat man shrugged and kept his eyes on the referee as the countdown proceeded. The fallen fighter got up and the audience roared again.

Fate raised a hand, with his palm toward the fat man, and retreated. When he was back in the main aisle, he heard someone calling him. He looked all around but he couldn't see anyone. Fate, Oscar Fate, the voice shouted. The fighter who had just gotten up threw his arms around his opponent. His opponent tried to get out of the clinch by aiming a flurry of blows at the first fighter's stomach and backing away. Here, Fate, here, the voice shouted. The referee broke up the clinch. The fighter who had just gotten up made a move as if to attack but danced slowly backward waiting for the bell. His opponent backed away, too. The first fighter was wearing white shorts and his face was covered in blood. The second fighter was wearing black, purple, and red striped shorts and looked surprised that the other fighter wasn't still on the ground. Oscar, Oscar, we're over here, shouted the voice. When the bell rang, the referee headed for the corner of the fighter in white shorts and motioned for a doctor to come up. The doctor, or whatever he was, examined the boxer's eyebrow and said the fight could go on.

Fate turned around and tried to find the people who were calling him. Most of the fans had gotten up from their seats and he couldn't see anybody. When the next round began, the fighter in striped shorts went on the offensive, looking for a knockout. For the first few seconds the other fighter stood his ground, but then he threw his arms around the fighter in striped shorts. The referee separated them several times. The shoulder of the fighter with striped shorts was stained with the other fighter's blood. Fate walked slowly toward the ringside seats. He saw Campbell reading a basketball magazine, he saw another American reporter coolly taking notes. One of the cameramen had set his camera up on a tripod, and the lighting boy next to him chewed gum and every so often checked out the legs of a girl in the first row.

He heard his name again and turned around. He thought he saw a blond woman motioning to him. The fighter in the white shorts fell again. His mouth guard popped out and flew across the ring, falling right next to Fate. For a moment Fate thought about bending down and picking it up, but then he was disgusted by the idea and didn't move, watching the sprawled body of the fighter and listening to the referee's count. Then, before the referee got to nine, the fighter stood again. He's going to fight without a mouth guard, thought Fate, and then he bent down and felt for the mouth guard but he couldn't find it. Who took it? he thought. I haven't moved and I haven't seen anybody else move, so who the fuck took the mouth guard?

•

When the fight was over, a song played over the loudspeakers that Fate recognized as one Chucho Flores had called Sonoran jazz. The fans in the cheap seats howled in delight and then they started to sing along. Three thousand Mexicans up in the gallery of the arena singing the same song in unison. Fate tried to get a look at them, but the lights, focused on the ring, left the upper part of the hall in darkness. The tone, he thought, was solemn and defiant, the battle hymn of a lost war sung in the dark. In the solemnity there was only desperation and death, but in the defiance there was a hint of corrosive humor, a humor that existed only in relation to itself and in dreams, no matter whether the dreams were long or short. Sonoran jazz. In the seats below, some people were singing along, but not many. Most were talking or drinking beer. He saw a boy in a white shirt and black pants run down the aisle. He saw the man who sold beer walk up the aisle singing to himself. A woman with her hands on her hips laughed at what a short man with a little mustache was saying. The short man was shouting but his voice was barely audible. A group of men seemed to converse just by clenching their jaws (and their jaws expressed only scorn or indifference). A man stared at the floor and talked to himself and smiled. Everyone seemed happy. Just then, as if he'd had a revelation, Fate understood that almost everybody at the arena thought Merolino Fernández would win the fight. What made them so sure? For a moment he thought he knew, but the knowledge slipped like water through his fingers. All for the best, he thought, because the fleeting shadow of the idea (another stupid idea) might destroy him on the spot.

•

Then, at last, he saw them. Chucho Flores was motioning him to come sit with them. He recognized the blond girl next to him. He'd seen her before, but now she was much more nicely dressed. He bought a beer and made his way through the crowd. The blond girl gave him a kiss on the cheek. She told him her name, which he'd already forgotten: Rosa Méndez. Chucho Flores introduced him to the other two: a man he'd never seen before, Juan Corona, who was probably another reporter, and an extremely beautiful girl, Rosa Amalfitano. This is Charly Cruz, the video king, you know him, said Chucho Flores. Charly Cruz shook Fate's hand. He was the only one still sitting, oblivious to what was going on around him. They were all very well dressed, as if after the fight they planned to attend a gala. One of the seats was empty and Fate sat down once they had moved their coats and jackets. He asked whether they were waiting for someone.

"We were expecting a friend," Chucho Flores said into his ear, "but she seems to have stood us up at the last minute."

"If she comes, it's no problem," said Fate, "I'll get up and go."

"No, man, you're with us now," said Chucho Flores.

Corona asked him what part of the United States he was from. New York, said Fate. And what do you do? I'm a reporter. After that, Corona's English was exhausted, and he didn't ask anything else.

"You're the first black man I've ever met," said Rosa Méndez.

Charly Cruz translated. Fate smiled. Rosa Méndez smiled too.

"I like Denzel Washington," she said.

Charly Cruz translated and Fate smiled again.

"I've never been friends with a black man," said Rosa Méndez, "I've seen them on TV and walking around sometimes, but there aren't many black people in the city."

That's Rosita for you, said Charly Cruz, a good person, a little bit naïve. Fate didn't understand what he meant by a little bit naïve.

"The truth is, there aren't many black people in Mexico," said Rosa Méndez. "Just a few in Veracruz. Have you ever been to Veracruz?"

Charly Cruz translated. He said that Rosita wanted to know whether he'd ever been to Veracruz. No, I've never been there, said Fate.

"Me neither. I was there on the way somewhere else, when I was fifteen," said Rosa Méndez, "but I've forgotten everything about it. It's like something bad happened to me in Veracruz and my brain erased it. Do you know what I mean?"

This time it was Rosa Amalfitano who translated. She didn't smile like Charly Cruz but just translated what the other woman said in complete seriousness.

"Sure," said Fate, though he didn't understand at all.

Rosa Méndez looked him in the eye and he couldn't have said whether she was making small talk or sharing an intimate secret with him.

"Something must have happened to me there," said Rosa Méndez, "because I really don't remember a thing. I know I was there—not for long, maybe three days or only two—but I don't have a single memory of the city. Has anything like that ever happened to you?"

It probably has, Fate thought, but instead of admitting it he asked whether she liked boxing. Rosa Amalfitano translated the question and Rosa Méndez said that sometimes it was exciting, but only sometimes, especially when the fighter was handsome.

"And what about you?" he asked the girl who spoke English.

"I don't care either way," said Rosa Amalfitano, "this is the first time I've come to something like this."

"The first time?" asked Fate, forgetting that he wasn't a boxing expert either.

Rosa Amalfitano smiled and nodded. Then she lit a cigarette and Fate chose that moment to look in the other direction, and his eyes met the eyes of Chucho Flores. Chucho Flores was looking at him as if he'd never seen him before. Pretty girl, said Charly Cruz next to him. Fate remarked that it was hot. A drop of perspiration was rolling down Rosa Méndez's right temple. She was wearing a low-cut dress revealing large

breasts and a cream-colored bra. Let's drink to Merolino, said Rosa
Méndez. Charly Cruz, Fate, and Rosa Méndez clinked bottles. Rosa
Amalfitano lifted a paper cup, probably full of water or vodka or tequila.
Fate thought about asking her which it was, but right away he realized it
was a bad idea. You didn't ask women like Rosa Amalfitano that kind of
question. Chucho Flores and Corona were the only two members of the
group still standing, as if they hadn't yet lost hope of seeing the missing
girl appear. Rosa Méndez asked him whether he liked Santa Teresa a lot
or too much. Rosa Amalfitano translated. Fate didn't understand the
question. Rosa Amalfitano smiled. Fate thought she smiled like a goddess. The beer tasted worse than before, bitter and warm. He was
tempted to ask to take a sip from her cup, but that, he knew, was something he'd never do.

"A lot or too much? Which is the right answer?"

"Too much, I think," said Rosa Amalfitano.

"Too much, then," said Fate.

"Have you been to see a bullfight?" asked Rosa Méndez.

"No," said Fate.

"What about a soccer game? A baseball game? Have you been to see
our basketball team play?"

"Your friend is very interested in sports," said Fate.

"Not really," said Rosa Amalfitano, "she's just trying to make conversation."

So she's just making conversation? thought Fate. All right, then she's
trying to play dumb or act natural. No, she's just trying to be nice, he
thought, but he could feel there was more to it.

"I haven't gone to see any of those things," said Fate.

"Aren't you a sportswriter?" asked Rosa Méndez.

Oh, thought Fate, she isn't trying to play dumb or act natural, she's
not even trying to be nice, she thinks I'm a sportswriter and so these
things must interest me.

"I'm an accidental sportswriter," said Fate, and then he told the two
Rosas and Charly Cruz the story of the real sportswriter and his death,
and how he'd been sent to cover the Pickett-Fernández fight.

"So what do you write about, then?" asked Charly Cruz.

"Politics," said Fate. "Political things that affect the African-American
community. Social things."

"That must be very interesting," said Rosa Méndez.

Fate watched Rosa Amalfitano's lips as she translated. He felt happy to be there.

•

The fight was short. First Count Pickett came out. Polite applause, some boos. Then Merolino Fernández came out. Thundering applause. In the first round, they sized each other up. In the second, Pickett went on the offensive and knocked his opponent out in less than a minute. Merolino Fernández's body didn't even move where it lay on the canvas. His seconds hauled him into his corner and when he didn't recover the medics came in and took him off to the hospital. Count Pickett raised an arm, without much enthusiasm, and left surrounded by his people. The fans began to empty out of the arena.

•

They ate at a place called El Rey del Taco. At the entrance there was a neon sign: a kid wearing a big crown mounted on a burro that regularly kicked up its hind legs and tried to throw him. The boy never fell, although in one hand he was holding a taco and in the other a kind of scepter that could also serve as a riding crop. The inside was decorated like a McDonald's, but in an unsettling way. The chairs were straw, not plastic. The tables were wooden. The floor was covered in big green tiles, some of them printed with desert landscapes and episodes from the life of El Rey del Taco. From the ceiling hung piñatas featuring more adventures of the boy king, always accompanied by the burro. Some of the scenes depicted were charmingly ordinary: the boy, the burro, and a one-eyed old woman, or the boy, the burro, and a well, or the boy, the burro, and a pot of beans. Other scenes were set firmly in the realm of the fantastic: in some the boy and the burro fell down a ravine, in others, the boy and the burro were tied to a funeral pyre, and there was even one in which the boy threatened to shoot his burro, holding a gun to its head. It was as if El Rey del Taco weren't the name of a restaurant but a character in a comic book Fate happened never to have heard of. Still, the feeling of being in a McDonald's persisted. Maybe the waitresses and waiters, very young and dressed in military uniforms (Chucho Flores told him they were dressed up as *federales*), helped create the impression. This was certainly no victorious army. The young waiters radiated exhaustion, although they smiled at the customers. Some of them seemed lost in the desert that was El Rey del Taco. Others, fifteen-year-olds or fourteen-year-olds, tried in vain to joke with some of the diners, men on their own or in pairs who looked like government workers or cops, men who eyed them grimly, in no mood for jokes. Some of the girls had tears in their eyes, and they seemed unreal, faces glimpsed in a dream.

"This place is like hell," he said to Rosa Amalfitano.

"You're right," she said, looking at him sympathetically, "but the food isn't bad."

"I've lost my appetite," said Fate.

"As soon as they put a plate of tacos in front of you it'll come back," said Rosa Amalfitano.

"I hope you're right," said Fate.

•

They had come to the restaurant in three separate cars. Rosa Amalfitano was riding with Chucho Flores. Charly Cruz and Rosa Méndez were riding with silent Corona. Fate drove alone, following the other two cars closely, and more than once, when they seemed to be driving in endless circles around the city, he thought about honking his horn and abandoning the convoy—there was something absurd and childish about it, though he couldn't say exactly what—and heading for the Sonora Resort to write his story about the brief fight he'd just witnessed. Maybe Campbell would still be there and could explain whatever it was he'd missed. Although it's not as if there was anything to understand, if you thought about it. Pickett knew how to fight and Fernández didn't, it was that simple. Or maybe it would be better to skip the Sonora Resort and just drive straight to the border, to Tucson, where he was sure to find a cybercafé at the airport, and write his story, exhausted and without thinking about what he was writing, and then fly to New York, where everything would take on the consistency of reality again.

But instead Fate followed the convoy of cars driving around and around an alien city, with the faint suspicion that the only object of all that driving was to wear him down and get rid of him, although they'd been the ones to ask him along, they'd been the ones who'd said come eat with us and then you can leave for the United States, a last supper in Mexico, speaking without conviction or sincerity, trapped by the formulas of hospitality, a Mexican rite, to which he should have responded by thanking them (effusively!) and then driving away down a nearly empty street with his dignity intact.

But he accepted the invitation. Good idea, he said, I'm hungry. Let's all go get some dinner. As if it was the most natural thing in the world. And although he saw the expression in Chucho Flores's eyes change, and the way Corona was looking at him, even more coldly than Chucho, as if trying to scare him off with his stare or blaming him for the defeat of the Mexican fighter, he insisted on going to eat something typical, my last night in Mexico, what do you say we get some *Mexican* food? Only Charly Cruz seemed amused by the idea that he would stick around with them for dinner, Charly Cruz and the two girls, although in different ways, in keeping with their different personalities, although it was also possible, thought Fate, that the girls were just plain happy, whereas Charly Cruz found himself presented with unexpected possibilities in a landscape that up until then had seemed fixed and devoid of surprise.

•

Why am I here, eating tacos and drinking beer with some Mexicans I hardly know? thought Fate. The answer, he knew, was simple. I'm here for her. They were all speaking Spanish. Only Charly Cruz addressed him in English. Charly Cruz liked to talk about film and he liked to talk in English. His English was fast, as if he were trying to imitate a college student, and full of mistakes. He mentioned the name of a Los Angeles director, Barry Guardini, whom he'd met personally, but Fate had never seen any of Guardini's movies. Then he started to talk about DVDs. He said that in the future everything would be on DVD, or something like DVDs but better, and there'd be no such thing as movie theaters.

The only movie theaters that were worth anything, said Charly Cruz, were the old ones, remember them? those huge theaters where your heart leaped when they turned out the lights. Those places were great, they were real movie theaters, more like churches than anything else, high ceilings, red curtains, pillars, aisles with worn carpeting, box seats, orchestra seats, balcony seats, theaters built at a time when going to the movies was still a religious experience, routine but religious, theaters that were gradually demolished to build banks or supermarkets or multiplexes. Today, said Charly Cruz, there are only a few left, today all movie theaters are multiplexes, with small screens, less space, comfortable seats. Seven of these smaller multiplex theaters would fit into one of the old theaters, the real ones. Or ten. Or even fifteen. And there's no sense of the *abyss* anymore, there's no *vertigo* before the movie begins, no one feels *alone* inside a multiplex. Then, Fate remembered, he began to talk about the end of the *sacred*.

The end had begun somewhere, Charly Cruz didn't care where, maybe in the churches, when the priests stopped celebrating the Mass in Latin, or in families, when the fathers (terrified, believe me, brother) left the mothers. Soon the end of the sacred came to the movies. The big theaters were torn down and up went the hideous boxes called multiplexes, practical, functional. The cathedrals were felled by the wrecking balls of demolition teams. Then the VCR came along. A TV set isn't the same as a movie screen. Your living room isn't the same as the old endless rows of seats. But look carefully and you'll see it's the closest thing to it. In the first place, because with videos you can watch a movie *all by yourself.* You close the windows and you turn on the TV. You pop in the video and you sit in a chair. First off: do it alone. No matter how big or small your house is, it feels bigger with no one else there. Second: be prepared. In other words, rent the movie, buy the drinks you want, the snacks you want, decide what time you're going to sit down in front of the TV. Third: don't answer the phone, ignore the doorbell, be ready to spend an hour and a half or two hours or an hour and forty-five minutes in complete and utter solitude. Fourth: have the remote control within reach in case you want to see a scene more than once. And that's it. After that it all depends on the movie and on you. If things work out, and sometimes they don't, you're back in the presence of the *sacred*. You burrow your head into your own chest and open your eyes and watch, pronounced Charly Cruz.

•

What's sacred to me? thought Fate. The vague pain I feel at the passing of my mother? An understanding of what can't be fixed? Or the kind of pang in the stomach I feel when I look at this woman? And why do I feel a pang, if that's what it is, when she looks at me and not when her friend looks at me? Because her friend is nowhere near as beautiful, thought Fate. Which seems to suggest that what's sacred to me is beauty, a pretty girl with perfect features. And what if all of a sudden the most beautiful actress in Hollywood appeared in the middle of this big, repulsive restaurant, would I still feel a pang each time my eyes surreptitiously met this girl's or would the sudden appearance of a superior beauty, a beauty enhanced by recognition, relieve the pang, diminish her beauty to ordinary levels, the beauty of a slightly odd girl out to have a good time on a weekend night with three slightly peculiar men and a woman who basically seems like a hooker? And who am I to think that Rosita Méndez seems like a hooker? thought Fate. Do I really know enough about Mexican hookers to be able to recognize them at a glance? Do I know anything about innocence or pain? Do I know anything about women? I like to watch videos, thought Fate. I also like to go to the movies. I like to sleep with women. Right now I don't have a steady girl-friend, but I know what it's like to have one. Do I see the *sacred* any-where? All I register is practical experiences, thought Fate. An emptiness to be filled, a hunger to be satisfied, people to talk to so I can finish my article and get paid. And why do I think the men Rosa Amalfitano is out with are *peculiar*? What's peculiar about them? And why am I so sure that if a Hollywood actress appeared all of a sudden Rosa Amalfitano's beauty would fade? What if it didn't? What if it sped up? And what if everything began to accelerate from the instant a Hollywood actress crossed the threshold of El Rey del Taco?

•

Later, he remembered vaguely, they were at a few clubs, maybe three. Actually, it might have been four. No: three. But they were also at a fourth place, which wasn't exactly a club or a private house either. The music was loud. One of the clubs, not the first one, had a patio. From the patio, where they stacked boxes of soft drinks and beer, you could see the sky. A black sky like the bottom of the sea. At some point Fate threw up. Then he laughed because something on the patio struck him as funny. What? He didn't know. Something that was moving or crawling along the chain-link fence. Maybe a sheet of newspaper. When he went back inside he saw Corona kissing Rosa Méndez. Corona's right hand was squeezing one of her breasts. When he passed them, Rosa Méndez opened her eyes and looked at him as if she didn't recognize him. Charly Cruz was leaning on the bar talking to the bartender. Fate asked him where Rosa Amalfitano was. Charly Cruz shrugged. He repeated the question. Charly Cruz looked him in the eyes and said she might be in the ladies' room.

"Where is the ladies' room?" asked Fate.

"Upstairs," said Charly Cruz.

Fate went up the only stairs he could find: a metal staircase that wobbled a little, as if the base were loose. It seemed to him like the staircase on an old-time boat. The staircase ended in a green-carpeted hallway. At the end of the hallway there was an open door. Music was playing. The light that came from the room was green, too. Standing in the middle of the hallway was a skinny kid, who looked at him and then moved toward him. Fate thought he was going to be attacked and he prepared himself mentally to take the first punch. But the kid let him pass and then went down the stairs. His face was very serious, Fate remembered. Then he kept walking until he came to a room where he saw Chucho Flores talking on a cell phone. Next to him, sitting at a desk, was a man in his forties, dressed in a checkered shirt and a bolo tie, who stared at Fate and gestured inquiringly. Chucho Flores caught the gesture and glanced toward the door.

"Come on in, Fate," he said.

The lamp hanging from the ceiling was green. Next to a window, sitting in an armchair, was Rosa Amalfitano. She had her legs crossed and she was smoking. When Fate came through the door she lifted her eyes and looked at him.

"We're doing some business here," said Chucho Flores.

Fate leaned against the wall, feeling short of breath. It's the green color, he thought.

"I see," he said.

Rosa Amalfitano seemed to be high.

•

Fate thought he remembered that someone, at some point, announced it was someone's birthday that night, the birthday of a person who wasn't with them but whom Chucho Flores and Charly Cruz apparently knew. As he drank tequila a woman started to sing "Happy Birthday" in English. Then three men (was Chucho Flores one of them?) started to sing the Mexican birthday song "Las Mañanitas." Many voices joined in. Next to him, standing at the bar, was Rosa Amalfitano. She wasn't singing, but she translated the words of the song. Fate asked her what the connection was between King David and birthdays.

"I don't know," said Rosa. "I'm not Mexican, I'm Spanish."

Fate thought about Spain. He was going to ask her what part of Spain

317

she was from when he saw a man hit a woman in a corner of the room. The first blow made the woman's head snap violently and the second blow knocked her down. Without thinking, Fate tried to move toward them, but someone grabbed his arm. When he turned to see who it was, no one was there. In the opposite corner of the club the man who had hit the woman stepped next to where she was huddled on the ground and kicked her in the stomach. A few feet away from him he saw Rosa Méndez smiling happily. Next to her was Corona, who was looking in a different direction with the usual serious expression on his face. Corona's arm was around Rosa Méndez's shoulders. Every so often she would lift Corona's hand to her mouth and bite his finger. Sometimes Rosa Méndez's teeth bit too hard and then Corona's brow furrowed slightly.

•

At the last place they went Fate saw Omar Abdul and Merolino's other sparring partner. They were drinking alone in a corner of the bar and he went over to say hello. The fighter named García barely nodded in recognition. Omar Abdul, however, gave him a broad smile. Fate asked them how Merolino Fernández was doing.

"Fine, just fine," said Oscar Abdul. "He's at the ranch."

Before Fate said goodbye, Omar Abdul asked him why he hadn't left yet.

"I like this city," said Fate, to say something.

"Brother, this city is a shithole," said Omar Abdul.

"Well, there are some beautiful women here," said Fate.

"The women here aren't worth shit," said Omar Abdul.

"Then you should go back to California," said Fate.

Omar Abdul looked him in the eye and nodded several times.

"I wish I was a goddamn reporter," he said, "you people don't miss a thing."

Fate pulled out some money and beckoned to the bartender. Whatever my friends are having, it's on me, he said. The bartender took the money and looked at the fighters.

"Two more mezcals," said Omar Abdul.

When Fate went back to his table, Chucho Flores asked him whether the fighters were his friends.

"They aren't fighters," said Fate, "they're Merolino's sparring partners."

"García was a fairly well-known fighter in Sonora," said Chucho Flores. "He wasn't very good, but he could stand there and take it better than anybody else."

Fate looked toward the end of the bar. Omar Abdul and García were still there, silent, staring at the rows of bottles.

"One night he went crazy and killed his sister," said Chucho Flores. "His lawyer argued temporary insanity and all he did was eight years in the prison at Hermosillo. When he got out he didn't want to box anymore. For a while he was with the Arizona Pentecostalists. But God never gave him the gift of speech and one day he stopped preaching the Word and started working the door at some clubs. Until López, Merolino's trainer, showed up, and hired him as a sparring partner."

"A couple of fuckups," said Corona.

"Yes," said Fate, "judging by the fight, a couple of fuckups."

•

Then, and this he did remember clearly, they ended up at Charly Cruz's house. He remembered because of the videos. Specifically, the video that was supposed to be by Robert Rodriguez. Charly Cruz's house was big, as solid as a two-story bunker—that he also remembered clearly—and it cast its shadow over a vacant lot. There was no yard, but there was a garage for four or maybe five cars. At some point during the night, although this was much less clear, a fourth man had joined the convoy. The fourth man didn't talk much but he kept smiling for no reason and he seemed nice. He was dark-skinned and he had a mustache. And he rode with Fate, in his car, sitting next to him, smiling at every word Fate said. Every so often he looked behind them and every so often he checked his watch. But he didn't say a single word.

"Can't you talk?" Fate asked him in English after several attempts to start a conversation. "Cat got your tongue? Motherfucker, why do you keep looking at your watch?" And the man invariably smiled and nodded.

Charly Cruz's car led the way, followed by Chucho Flores's car. Sometimes Fate could see the shapes of Chucho and Rosa Amalfitano. Usually when they stopped at a stoplight. Sometimes the two shapes were very close together, as if they were kissing. Other times all he saw was the shape of the driver. At one point he tried to pull up alongside Chucho Flores's car, but he couldn't.

"What time is it?" he asked the man with the mustache, and the man shrugged his shoulders.

In Charly Cruz's garage there was a mural painted on one of the cement walls. The mural was six feet tall and maybe ten feet long and showed the Virgin of Guadalupe in the middle of a lush landscape of rivers and forests and gold mines and silver mines and oil rigs and giant cornfields and wheat fields and vast meadows where cattle grazed. The Virgin had her arms spread wide, as if offering all of these riches in exchange for nothing. But despite being drunk, Fate noticed right away there was something wrong about her face. One of the Virgin's eyes was open and the other eye was closed.

•

The house had many rooms. Some were used just for storage and were stacked full of videos and DVDs from Charly Cruz's video stores or his private collection. The living room was on the first floor. Two armchairs and two leather sofas and a wooden table and a TV. The armchairs were good but old. The floor was yellow tile edged with black and it was dirty. Not even a couple of multicolored Indian rugs could hide it. A full-length mirror hung on one wall. On the other wall there was a poster for a Mexican movie from the 1950s, framed and protected behind glass. Charly Cruz said it was the original poster for a very rare film, of which almost all the copies had been lost. Bottles of liquor were kept in a glass cabinet. Next to the living room was an apparently unused room where there was a latest-generation music system and a cardboard box full of CDs. Rosa Méndez knelt next to the box and began to dig through it.

"Women go crazy for music," Charly Cruz said into Fate's ear, "I go crazy for movies."

The nearness of Charly Cruz startled Fate. Only then did he realize that the room had no windows and it struck him as odd that anyone would choose it for the living room, especially since the house was so big and there had to be lots of rooms with more light. When the music started, Corona and Chucho Flores each took a girl by the arm and left the living room. The man with the mustache sat in an armchair and looked at his watch. Charly Cruz asked Fate whether he was interested in seeing the Robert Rodriguez movie. Fate nodded. The man with the mustache, because of the angle of his chair, couldn't see the movie without craning his neck exaggeratedly, but he showed no curiosity at all. He just sat there looking at them and every so often looking at the ceiling.

The movie, according to Charlie Cruz, was half an hour long at most.

An old woman with a heavily made-up face looked into the camera. After a while she began to whisper incomprehensible words and weep. She looked like a whore who'd retired and, Fate thought at times, was facing death. Then a thin, dark-skinned young woman with big breasts took off her clothes while seated on a bed. Out of the darkness came three men who first whispered in her ear and then fucked her. At first the woman resisted. She looked straight at the camera and said something in Spanish that Fate didn't understand. Then she faked an orgasm and started to scream. After that, the men, who until that moment had been taking turns, joined in all together, the first penetrating her vagina, the second her anus, and the third sticking his cock in her mouth. The effect was of a perpetual-motion machine. The spectator could see that the machine was going to explode at some point, but it was impossible to say what the explosion would be like and when it would happen. And then the woman came for real. An unforeseen orgasm that she was the last to expect. The woman's movements, constrained by the weight of the three men, accelerated. Her eyes were fixed on the camera, which in turn zoomed in on her face. Her eyes said something, although they spoke in an unidentifiable language. For an instant, everything about her seemed to shine, her breasts gleamed, her chin glistened, half hidden by the shoulder of one of the men, her teeth took on a supernatural whiteness. Then the flesh seemed to melt from her bones and drop to the floor of the anonymous brothel or vanish into thin air, leaving just a skeleton, no eyes, no lips, a death's-head laughing suddenly at everything. Then there was a street in a big Mexican city at dusk, probably Mexico City, a street swept by rain, cars parked along the curb, stores with their metal gates lowered, people walking fast so as not to be soaked. A puddle of rainwater. Water washing clean a car coated in a thick layer of dust. The lighted-up windows of government buildings. A bus stop next to a small park. The branches of a sick tree stretching vainly toward nothing. The face of the old whore, who smiles at the camera now as if to say: did I do it right? did I look good? is everybody happy? A redbrick staircase comes into view. A linoleum floor. The same rain, but filmed from inside a room. A plastic table with nicked edges. Glasses and a jar of Nescafé. A frying pan with the remains of scrambled eggs. A hallway. The body of a half-dressed woman sprawled on the floor. A door. A room in complete disarray. Two men sleeping in the same bed. A mirror. The camera zooms in on the mirror. The tape ends.

"Where's Rosa?" asked Fate when the movie ended.

"There's a second tape," said Charly Cruz.

"Where's Rosa?"

"In some room," said Charly Cruz, "sucking Chucho's dick."

Then he got up and went out of the room, and when he came back he had the remaining tape in his hand. As he rewound the video, Fate said he had to use the bathroom.

"End of the hall, fourth door," said Charly Cruz. "But you don't want to use the bathroom, you want to look for Rosa, you lying gringo."

Fate laughed.

"Well, maybe Chucho needs some help," he said as if he were asleep and drunk at the same time.

When he got up, the man with the mustache started. Charly Cruz said something to him in Spanish and he settled comfortably back in the armchair. Fate walked along the hallway, counting doors. When he got to the third door he heard a noise from the floor above. He paused. The noise stopped. The bathroom was big and looked like something straight out of a design magazine. The walls and floor were white marble. At least four people could fit into the bathtub, which was circular. Next to the bathtub was a big oak box in the shape of a coffin. A coffin from which the head would protrude, and that Fate would have said was a sauna, if the box weren't so narrow. The toilet was black marble. Next to it was a bidet and next to the bidet was a marble protuberance a foot and a half high whose purpose Fate was unable to discern. By a stretch of the imagination, you might say it looked like a chair or a saddle. But he couldn't imagine anyone sitting there, not in a normal position. Maybe it was used to hold towels for the bidet. As he urinated, he gazed at the wooden box and the marble sculpture. For an instant he thought both things were alive. Behind him was a mirror that covered the whole wall and made the bathroom seem bigger than it was. Looking to the left, Fate saw the wooden coffin, and turning his head to the right, he saw the protuberant marble fixture. At one point he looked behind him and saw his own back, standing in front of the toilet, flanked by the coffin and the useless-seeming saddle. The sense of unreality that dogged him that night was heightened.

He climbed the stairs trying not to make a sound. In the living room Charly Cruz and the man with the mustache were talking in Spanish. Charly Cruz's voice was soothing. The voice of the man with the mustache was squeaky, as if his vocal cords were atrophied. The noise he'd heard in the hallway repeated itself. The stairs ended in a room with a big window behind the dark brown plastic slats of a venetian blind. Fate went down another hallway. He opened a door. Rosa Méndez was lying facedown on a military-looking bed. She was dressed and had high heels on, but she seemed to be asleep or to have passed out. The room was furnished with only a bed and chair. The floor, unlike the floor downstairs, was carpeted, so his steps made almost no sound. He went over to the girl and turned her head. Rosa Méndez smiled without opening her eyes. This hallway led to another. Fate could see light coming from under one of the doors. He heard Chucho Flores and Corona arguing, but he didn't know what they were arguing about. He thought they both wanted to fuck Rosa Amalfitano. Then he thought maybe they were arguing about him. Corona sounded truly angry. He opened the door without knocking and the two men turned around at once, their faces stamped with a mixture of surprise and sleepiness. Now I have to try to be what I am, thought Fate, a black guy from Harlem, a terrifying Harlem motherfucker. Almost immediately he realized that neither of the Mexicans was impressed.

"Where's Rosa?" he asked.

Chucho Flores managed to point to a corner of the room that Fate hadn't seen. I've lived this scene before, thought Fate. Rosa was sitting in an armchair, with her legs crossed, snorting cocaine.

"Let's go," he said.

He didn't order her or plead with her. He just asked her to come with him, but he put all his soul into the words. Rosa smiled at him sympathetically, but she didn't seem to understand. He heard Chucho Flores say in English: get out of here, amigo, wait for us downstairs. Fate held out his hand to the girl. Rosa got up and took it. Her hand felt warm, its temperature evoking other scenarios but also evoking or encompassing their current sordid circumstances. When he took it he became conscious of the coldness of his own hand. I've been dying all this time, he thought. I'm as cold as ice. If she hadn't taken my hand I would've died right here and they would've had to send my body back to New York.

●

As they left the room he felt Corona grab his arm and saw him lift his free hand, which seemed to be holding a blunt instrument. He turned around and dealt Corona an uppercut to the chin, in the style of Count Pickett. Like Merolino Fernández earlier, Corona dropped to the floor without a sound. Only then did Fate realize Corona was holding a gun. He took it away from him and asked Chucho Flores what he planned to do.

"I'm not jealous, amigo," said Chucho Flores with his hands raised at chest height so that Fate could see he wasn't carrying a weapon.

Rosa Amalfitano looked at Corona's gun as if it were a sex-shop contraption.

"Let's go," he heard her say.

"Who's the guy downstairs?" asked Fate.

"Charly, your friend Charly Cruz," said Chucho Flores, smiling.

"No, you son of a bitch, the other one, the one with the mustache."

"A friend of Charly's," said Chucho Flores.

"Is there another way out of this goddamn house?"

Chucho Flores shrugged.

"Listen, man, aren't you taking this too far?" he asked.

"Yes, there's a back door," said Rosa Amalfitano.

Fate looked at Corona's fallen body and seemed to reflect for a few seconds.

"The car is in the garage," he said, "we can't leave without it."

"Then you'll have to go out the front door," said Chucho Flores.

"What about him?" asked Rosa Amalfitano, pointing to Corona, "is he dead?"

Fate looked again at the limp body on the floor. He could have stared for hours.

"Let's go," he said in a decisive voice.

They went down the stairs, passed through an enormous kitchen that smelled of neglect, as if it had been a long time since anyone cooked there, crossed a hallway with a view of a courtyard where there was a pickup truck covered by a black tarp, and then walked entirely in the dark until they reached the door that led down to the garage. When Fate turned on the lights, two big fluorescent tubes hanging from the ceiling, he took another look at the mural of the Virgin of Guadalupe. When he moved to open the garage door he realized that the Virgin's single open eye seemed to follow him wherever he went. He put Chucho Flores in the front passenger seat and Rosa got in the back. As they drove out of the garage he caught a glimpse of the man with the mustache. He had appeared at the top of the stairs and was looking around for them with the expression of a startled adolescent.

They left Charly Cruz's house behind and turned down unpaved streets. Without realizing it, they crossed an empty stretch that gave off a strong smell of weeds and rotting food. Fate stopped the car, cleaned the gun with a handkerchief, and threw it into the lot.

"What a pretty night," murmured Chucho Flores.

Neither Rosa nor Fate said anything.

•

They left Chucho Flores at a bus stop on a deserted and brightly lit street. Rosa got in the front seat, giving Chucho Flores a parting slap in the face. Then they headed down a labyrinth of streets that neither Rosa nor Fate recognized, until they came out onto another street that led straight to the center of the city.

"I think I've been an idiot," said Fate.

"I was the idiot," said Rosa.

"No, I was," said Fate.

They started to laugh, and after circling the city center a few times, they let themselves be caught up in the stream of cars with Mexican and American license plates heading out of the city.

"Where are we going?" asked Fate. "Where do you live?"

She said she didn't want to go home yet. They passed Fate's motel, and for a few seconds he didn't know whether to keep going to the border or stay there. Half a mile farther down the road he turned around and headed south again, toward the motel. The clerk recognized him. He asked how the fight had gone.

"Merolino lost," said Fate.

"Of course," said the clerk.

Fate asked whether his room was still vacant. The clerk said it was. Fate stuck his hand in his pocket and pulled out the key to the room, which he had kept.

"That's right," he said.

He paid for another night and then he went out. Rosa was waiting for him in the car.

"You can stay here for a while," said Fate, "and whenever you say I'll take you home."

Rosa nodded and they went in. The bed was made and the sheets were clean. The two windows were open a crack. Maybe the cleaning person had noticed a trace of vomit smell, thought Fate. But the room smelled fine. Rosa turned on the TV and sat in a chair.

"I've been watching you," she said.

"I'm flattered," said Fate.

"Why did you clean the gun before you got rid of it?" asked Rosa.

"You never know," said Fate, "but I'd rather not go around leaving fingerprints on firearms."

Then Rosa focused her attention on the TV show, a Mexican talk show that was essentially just an old woman talking. She had long white hair. Sometimes she smiled and you could tell she was a nice, harmless little old lady, but most of the time she had a grave expression on her face, as if she were addressing matters of great importance. Of course, he didn't understand a thing she said. Then Rosa got up from the chair, turned off the TV, and asked whether she could take a shower. Fate nodded. When Rosa went into the bathroom and closed the door he began to think about everything that had happened that night and his stomach hurt. He felt a wave of heat rise to his face. He sat on the bed, covered his face with his hands, and thought of what an idiot he'd been.

•

When she came out of the bathroom, Rosa told him that she had been Chucho Flores's girlfriend, or something like that. She was lonely in Santa Teresa and one day she met Rosa Méndez at Charly Cruz's video store, where she went to rent movies. She couldn't say why, but she liked Rosa Méndez from the moment she met her. During the day, according to Rosa Méndez, she worked at a supermarket and at night she worked as a waitress at a restaurant. She liked movies and she loved thrillers. Maybe what Rosa Amalfitano liked about Rosa Méndez was her perpetual cheerfulness and also her bleached-blond hair, which contrasted strongly with her dark skin.

One day Rosa Méndez introduced her to Charly Cruz, the owner of the video store, whom she'd seen only a few times, and Charly Cruz struck her as a relaxed person, someone who took things easy, and sometimes he loaned her movies or didn't charge her for the movies she rented. Often she would spend whole afternoons at the video store, talking to them or helping Charly Cruz unpack new shipments of movies.

One night, when the store was about to close, she met Chucho Flores. That same night Chucho Flores took them all out to dinner and later he gave her a ride home, although when she invited him in he said he'd rather pass, because he didn't want to bother her father. But she gave him her phone number and Chucho Flores called the next day and asked her out to the movies. When Rosa got to the theater, Chucho Flores was there with Rosa Méndez and her date, an older man around fifty who said he was in the real estate business and who treated Chucho like a nephew. After the movie they had dinner at a fancy restaurant and later Chucho Flores dropped her off at home, claiming that the next day he had to get up early because he was going to Hermosillo to interview someone for the radio.

Around that time, Rosa Amalfitano saw Rosa Méndez not just at Charly Cruz's video store but also at her place in Colonia Madero, in an apartment on the fourth floor of an old five-story building with no elevator, for which Rosa Méndez paid lots of money. At first, Rosa Méndez had shared the apartment with two friends, so the rent wasn't too bad. But one friend left to try her luck in Mexico City and she had a fight with the other friend, and after that she lived alone. Rosa Méndez liked to live alone, even though she had to work a second job to afford it. Sometimes Rosa Amalfitano would spend hours at Rosa Méndez's apartment, not talking, lying on the couch drinking *agua fresca* and listening to her friend's stories. Sometimes they talked about men. Here, as elsewhere, Rosa Méndez's experience was richer and more varied than Rosa Amalfitano's. She was twenty-four and she'd had, in her own words, four lovers who'd changed her in some way. The first was when she was fifteen, a guy who worked at a maquiladora and left her to go to the United States. She remembered him fondly, but of all her lovers he was the one who'd left the least mark on her. When she said this Rosa Amalfitano laughed and Rosa Méndez laughed too without knowing exactly why.

"You sound like a *bolero*," Rosa Amalfitano told her.

"Oh, so that's it," answered Rosa Méndez, "well, *boleros* are true, *mana*, the words of the songs come from deep inside all of us and they're always right."

"No," said Rosa Amalfitano, "they *seem* right, they *seem* authentic, but they're actually full of shit."

At this point, Rosa Méndez would give up arguing. Tacitly she acknowledged that her friend, who was in college, after all, knew more about these things than she did. The boyfriend who'd left for the United States, she explained again, was the one who'd left the least mark on her but also the one she missed the most. How was that possible? She didn't know. The other ones, the ones who came later, were different. And that was all. One day Rosa Méndez told Rosa Amalfitano what it felt like to make love with a policeman.

"It's the best," she said.

"Why, what difference does it make?" her friend wanted to know.

"It's hard to explain, *mana*," said Rosa Méndez, "but it's like fucking a man who isn't exactly a man. It's like becoming a little girl again, if that makes sense. It's like being fucked by a rock. A mountain. You know you'll be there, on your knees, until the mountain says it's over. And that in the end you'll be full."

"Full of what?" asked Rosa Amalfitano, "full of semen?"

"No, *mana*, don't be disgusting, full of something else, it's like you're fucking a mountain but you're fucking *inside* a cave, know what I mean?"

"In a cave?" asked Rosa Amalfitano.

"That's right," said Rosa Méndez.

"In other words it's like being fucked by a mountain in a cave inside the mountain itself," said Rosa Amalfitano.

"Exactly," said Rosa Méndez.

And then she said:

"I love how you say *follar* for fuck; people from Spain talk so pretty."

"You're weird, you know," said Rosa Amalfitano.

"I always have been, ever since I was little," said Rosa Méndez.

And she added:

"Want me to tell you something else?"

"What?" asked Rosa Amalfitano.

"I've fucked *narcos*. I swear. Do you want to know what it feels like? Well, it feels like being fucked by the air. That's exactly how it feels."

"So fucking a policeman is like being fucked by a mountain and fucking a *narco* is like being fucked by the air."

"Yes," said Rosa Méndez, "but not the air we breathe or the air we feel when we go outside, but the desert air, a blast of air, air that doesn't taste the same as the air here and doesn't smell like nature or the country, air that smells the way it smells, that has its own smell, a smell you can't explain, it's just air, pure air, so much air that sometimes it's hard to breathe and you feel like you're going to suffocate."

"So," concluded Rosa Amalfitano, "if a policeman fucks you it's like being fucked by a mountain inside the mountain itself, and if a *narco* fucks you it's like being fucked by the desert air."

"That's right, *mana*, if a *narco* fucks you it's always out in the open."

Around that time, Rosa Amalfitano started to officially date Chucho Flores. He was the first Mexican she slept with. At the university there had been two or three boys who tried to flirt with her, but nothing happened. She did go to bed with Chucho Flores, though. The courtship period wasn't long, but it lasted longer than Rosa expected. When he came back from Hermosillo, Chucho Flores brought her a pearl necklace. Alone, in front of the mirror, Rosa tried it on, and although the necklace had a certain appeal (and had probably cost a lot), she couldn't imagine ever wearing it. Rosa had a long, beautiful neck, but that necklace required a different kind of wardrobe. Other gifts followed: sometimes, as they walked along the streets where the fashionable stores were, Chucho Flores would stop in front of a window and point out something she should try on, telling her that if she liked it he'd buy it for her. Usually Rosa would try on the thing he'd suggested and then she'd try on other things and in the end she'd end up with something to her taste. Chucho Flores also gave her art books, since he'd once heard her talk about painting, and about painters whose works she'd seen in famous European museums. Other times he gave her CDs, mostly of classical music, although sometimes, like a tour guide with an eye for local color, he mixed in music from the north of Mexico or Mexican folk music, which later, alone at home, Rosa listened to distractedly as she washed the dishes or loaded the dirty clothes in the washing machine.

At night they would go out to eat at nice restaurants, where they invariably ran into men and, less often, women, who knew Chucho Flores, and to whom Chucho Flores introduced her as his friend, Miss Rosa Amalfitano, daughter of the philosophy professor Óscar Amalfitano, my friend Rosa, Miss Amalfitano, immediately prompting a paean to her beauty and elegance, and then commentary on Spain and Barcelona, a city they had all visited as tourists, every one of them, the distinguished citizens of Santa Teresa, and for which they had nothing but words of praise and admiration. One night, instead of driving her home, Chucho Flores asked her if she wanted to go for a ride with him. Rosa expected he would take her to his apartment, but they headed west out of Santa

Teresa, and after driving for half an hour along a lonely highway they came to a motel where Chucho Flores got a room. The motel was in the middle of the desert, just before a slight rise, and alongside the highway there was only gray brush, sometimes with its wind-scoured roots exposed. The room was big and in the bathroom there was a Jacuzzi like a small pool. The bed was round and the mirrors on the walls and part of the ceiling made it seem bigger. The carpet on the floor was thick, almost like a cushion. Instead of a minibar there was a small real bar stocked with all kinds of liquor and soft drinks. When Rosa asked him why he'd brought her to a place like this, the kind of place rich men brought their whores, Chucho Flores thought for a while and then he said it was for the mirrors. He sounded apologetic. Then he undressed her and they fucked on the bed and on the carpet.

At first, Chucho Flores was more gentle than anything else, more concerned about his partner's satisfaction than his own. Finally Rosa came and then Chucho Flores stopped fucking and took a little metal box out of his jacket. Rosa thought it would be cocaine, but instead of white powder the box held tiny yellow pills. Chucho Flores took out two pills and swallowed them with a little bit of whiskey. For a while they talked, lying in bed, until he got on top of her again. This time he wasn't gentle at all. Surprised, Rosa didn't protest or say anything. It seemed as if Chucho Flores would put her in every possible position, and some of them—this Rosa realized later—she liked. When the sun came up they stopped fucking and left the motel.

There were other cars in the courtyard parking lot, shielded from the highway by a redbrick wall. The air was cool and dry and had a faintly musky smell. The motel and everything around it seemed sealed in a pocket of silence. As they walked through the parking lot to the car they heard a rooster crow. The noise of the car doors opening, the engine starting, and the tires crunching the gravel seemed to Rosa like the sound of a drum. No trucks went by on the highway.

•

After that, things with Chucho Flores got stranger and stranger. There were days when it seemed he couldn't live without her, and other days when he treated her like his slave. Some nights they slept at his apartment and when she woke up in the morning he'd be gone, because there were times he got up very early to do a live radio show called *Good Morning, Sonora*, or *Good Morning, Friends*, she wasn't sure because she never heard it from the beginning, a show for truck drivers crossing the border in either direction and bus drivers carrying workers to the factories and anyone who had to get up early in Santa Teresa. When Rosa got up she made herself breakfast, usually a glass of orange juice and a piece of toast or a cookie, and then she washed the plate, the glass, the juicer, and left. Other times she stayed for a while, looking out the windows at the sprawl of the city under the cobalt-blue sky, and then she made the bed and wandered around the apartment, with nothing to do except think about her life and the strange Mexican she was involved with. She wondered whether he loved her, whether what he felt for her was love, whether she loved him herself, or whether she was just attracted to him, whether she felt anything for him at all, and whether this was all she could expect from being with another person.

Some afternoons they got in his car and sped east to a mountain overlook from which Santa Teresa was visible in the distance, the first lights of the city, the enormous black parachute that dropped gradually over the desert. Each time they went, after silently watching day change to night, Chucho Flores would unzip his pants and push her head down to his crotch. Then Rosa would take his penis in her mouth, barely sucking it until it got hard, and then she would begin to run her tongue over it. When Chucho Flores was about to come, she could tell by the pressure of his hand on her head, forcing her down. Rosa would stop moving her tongue and be still, as if having his whole penis in her mouth had choked her, until she felt the spurt of semen in her throat, and even then she didn't move, although she could hear her lover's moans and his exclamations, often bizarre, because he liked to say crude things and swear as he came, not at her but at unspecified people, ghosts who appeared for just a moment and were as quickly lost in the night. Then, with a salty, bitter taste still in her mouth, she would light a cigarette as Chucho Flores took a folded cigarette paper out of his silver cigarette case, tipping the cocaine it held onto the inner lid of the case, the outside of which was engraved with bucolic ranching motifs, and then, in no hurry, he would cut three lines with one of his credit cards and snort them with a business card, one that read Chucho Flores, reporter and radio correspondent, and then the address of the radio station.

One of those evenings, without having been asked (since Chucho had never once offered to share his coke with her), Rosa told him to leave her the last line as she wiped a few drops of semen from her lips with the palm of her hand. Chucho Flores asked whether she was sure, and then, with a gesture of indifference but also of deference, he handed her the cigarette case and a fresh business card. Rosa snorted all the cocaine that was left and then lay back in her seat and looked up at the black clouds, indistinguishable from the black sky.

That night, when she got home, she went out into the yard and saw her father talking to the book that for some time had been hanging from the clothesline in the backyard. Then, before her father noticed she was there, she shut herself in her room to read a novel and think about her relationship with the Mexican.

•

Of course, the Mexican and her father had met. Chucho Flores came away from this meeting with a positive feeling, although Rosa thought he was lying, since it didn't make sense for a person to like anyone who looked at him the way her father had looked at Chucho Flores. That night Amalfitano asked the Mexican three questions. The first was what he thought of hexagons. The second was whether he knew how to construct a hexagon. The third was what he thought about the killings of women in Santa Teresa. Chucho Flores's reply to the first question was that he didn't think anything. The second question he answered with an honest no. In response to the third question, he said that it was regrettable, but the police were catching the killers one by one. Rosa's father didn't ask any more questions and sat motionless in his chair as his daughter walked Chucho Flores to the door. When Rosa came back in, and before the sound of her boyfriend's car engine had faded in the distance, Óscar Amalfitano told his daughter to be careful, he had a bad feeling about that man, offering no further explanation.

"So what you mean is," said Rosa from the kitchen, laughing, "I should dump him."

"Dump him," said Óscar Amalfitano.

"Oh, Dad, you just keep getting crazier," said Rosa.

"It's true," said Óscar Amalfitano.

"So what are we going to do? What can we do?"

"You: leave that ignorant, lying piece of shit. Me: I don't know, maybe when we get back to Europe I'll check into the Clínico for an electroshock treatment."

•

The second time Chucho Flores and Óscar Amalfitano met face-to-face, Chucho Flores had come to drop Rosa off at home, along with Charly Cruz and Rosa Méndez. Actually, Óscar Amalfitano should have been at the university teaching classes, but that afternoon he had pleaded illness and come home much earlier than usual. It was a brief encounter, since Rosa made sure her friends left as soon as possible, but her father happened to be unusually sociable, and a conversation was struck up between him and Charly Cruz, which if not pleasant at least wasn't boring, and in fact, as the days went by, in Rosa's memory the conversation between her father and Charly began to take on sharper outlines, as if time, in the classic embodiment of an old man, were blowing incessantly on a flat gray stone covered in dust, until the black grooves of the letters carved into the stone were perfectly legible.

Everything began, Rosa guessed—since at the time she was in the kitchen, not the living room, pouring four glasses of mango juice— with one of the mischievous questions her father often sprang on guests, her guests, of course, not his own guests, or maybe it all began with some declaration of principles by innocent Rosa Méndez, since her voice seemed to dominate the conversation in the living room in the first few moments. Maybe Rosa Méndez was talking about how much she loved movies and then Óscar Amalfitano asked her if she knew what apparent movement was. But inevitably it was Charly Cruz, not Rosa Méndez, who answered, saying that apparent movement was the illusion of movement caused by the persistence of images on the retina.

"Exactly," said Óscar Amalfitano, "images linger on the retina for a fraction of a second."

And then, brushing aside Rosa Méndez, who might have said wow, because her ignorance was great but so was her capacity for astonishment and her desire to learn, her father asked Charly Cruz directly if he knew who had discovered this thing, this persistence of the image, and Charly Cruz said he didn't remember the name, but he was sure it had been a Frenchman. To which her father replied:

"That's right, a Frenchman by the name of Professor Plateau."

Who, once the principle had been discovered, launched himself ferociously into experiments with different devices he built himself, with the object of creating the effect of movement from the rapid succession of fixed images. Then the zoetrope was born.

"Do you know what that is?" asked Óscar Amalfitano.

"I had one when I was a boy," said Charly Cruz. "And I had a magic disk, too."

"A magic disk," said Óscar Amalfitano. "Interesting. Do you remember it? Could you describe it to me?"

"I could make one for you right now," said Charly Cruz, "all I need is a piece of cardboard, two colored pencils, and a piece of string, if I'm not mistaken."

"Oh no, oh no, oh no, no need for that," said Óscar Amalfitano. "A good description is enough for me. In a way, we all have millions of magic disks floating or spinning in our brains."

"Oh, really?" said Charly Cruz.

"Wow," said Rosa Méndez.

"Well, there was a little old drunk, laughing. That was the picture on one side of the disk. And on the other side was a picture of a prison cell, or the bars of a cell. When you spun the disk the laughing drunk looked like he was behind bars."

"Which isn't really a laughing matter, is it?" said Óscar Amalfitano.

"No, it isn't," said Charly Cruz with a sigh.

"Still, the drunk (by the way, why do you call him a little old drunk and not just a drunk?) was laughing, maybe because *he* knew he wasn't in jail."

For a few seconds, remembered Rosa, Charly Cruz's gaze altered, as if he were trying to see where her father was going with all this. Charly Cruz, as we've already said, was a relaxed man, and for those few seconds, although his poise and natural calm were unshaken, something did happen behind his face, as if the lens through which he was observing her father, Rosa remembered, had stopped working and he was proceeding, *calmly*, to change it, an operation that took less than a fraction of a second, but during which his gaze was necessarily left naked or empty, *vacant*, in any case, since one lens was being removed and another inserted, and both operations couldn't be carried out simultaneously, and for that fraction of a second, which Rosa remembered as if she had invented it herself, Charly Cruz's face was empty or it emptied, and the speed at which this happened was startling, say the speed of light, to put it in exaggerated but nevertheless roughly accurate terms, and the emptying of the face was complete, hair and teeth included, although to say hair and teeth in the presence of that blankness was like saying nothing, all of Charly Cruz's features emptied, his wrinkles, his veins, his pores, everything left defenseless, everything acquiring a dimension to which the only response, remembered Rosa, could be vertigo and nausea, although it wasn't.

"The *little old drunk* is laughing because he thinks he's free, but he's really in prison," said Óscar Amalfitano, "that's what makes it funny, but in fact the prison is drawn on the other side of the disk, which means one could also say that the *little old drunk* is laughing because we think he's in prison, not realizing that the prison is on one side and the *little old drunk* is on the other, and that's reality, no matter how much we spin the disk and it looks to us as if the *little old drunk* is behind bars. In fact, we could even guess what the *little old drunk* is laughing about: he's laughing at our credulity, you might even say at our eyes."

•

A little later something happened that upset Rosa quite a bit. She was on her way back from the university, walking along, and suddenly she heard someone calling her name. A boy her age, a classmate, pulled up at the curb and offered her a ride home. Instead of getting in the car, she said she'd rather go have a soda at a nearby coffee shop that had air-conditioning. The boy offered to take her and Rosa accepted. She got in the car and gave him directions. The coffee shop was new and spacious, in the shape of an L, American–style with rows of tables and big windows that let in the sun. For a while they talked about random things. Then the boy said he had to go and he got up. They kissed each other goodbye on the cheek and Rosa asked the waitress to bring her a cup of coffee. Then she opened a book on Mexican painting in the twentieth century and began to read a chapter on Paalen. At that time of day, the coffee shop was half empty. Voices could be heard coming from the kitchen, a woman giving another woman advice, the steps of the waitress who came by every so often to offer more coffee to the few customers scattered around the big space. Suddenly someone she hadn't heard approach her said: you whore. The voice startled her and she looked up, thinking it was a bad joke or that she'd been mistaken for someone else. Standing there was Chucho Flores. Flustered, all she could do was tell him to sit down, but Chucho Flores, his lips barely moving, told her to get up and follow him. She asked him where he planned to go. Home, said Chucho Flores. He was sweating and his face was flushed. Rosa told him she wasn't going anywhere. Then Chucho Flores asked her who the boy was who had kissed her.

"A classmate," said Rosa, and she noticed that Chucho Flores's hands were shaking.

"You whore," he said again.

And then he began to mutter something that Rosa couldn't understand at first, but after a moment she realized he was repeating the same words over and over again: you whore, uttered with teeth clenched, as if saying it cost him a huge effort.

"Let's go," shouted Chucho Flores.

"I'm not going anywhere with you," said Rosa, and she looked around to see whether anyone had noticed the scene they were making. But no one was looking at them and she felt better.

"Have you slept with him?" asked Chucho Flores.

For a few seconds Rosa didn't know what he was talking about. The air-conditioning seemed too cold. She wanted to go outside and stand in the sun. If she'd brought a sweater or a vest she would've put it on.

"You're the only person I sleep with," she said, trying to soothe him.

"Lies," shouted Chucho Flores.

The waitress appeared at the other end of the room and came toward them, but she changed her mind halfway and went to stand at the counter.

"Don't be ridiculous, please," Rosa said, and she fixed her gaze on the Paalen article but all she saw were black ants and then black spiders on a bed of salt. The ants were battling the spiders.

"Let's go home," she heard Chucho Flores say. She felt cold.

When she looked up she saw he was about to cry.

"You're my only love," said Chucho Flores. "I'd give everything for you. I'd die for you."

For a few seconds she didn't know what to say. Maybe the time has come to end things, she thought.

"I'm nothing without you," said Chucho Flores. "You're all I have. All I need. You're all I've ever dreamed of. If I lost you I would die."

The waitress watched them from behind the counter. Some twenty tables away, a man was drinking coffee and reading the paper. He was wearing a short-sleeved shirt and a tie. The sun seemed to vibrate against the windows.

"Sit down, please," said Rosa.

Chucho Flores pulled out the chair he was leaning on and sat down. Immediately he covered his face with his hands and Rosa thought he was going to shout again or cry. What a spectacle, she thought.

"Do you want something to drink?"

Chucho Flores nodded.

"Coffee," he whispered without moving his hands from his face.

Rosa turned to the waitress and beckoned to her.

"Two coffees," she said.

"Yes, miss," said the waitress.

"The guy you saw me with is just a friend. Not even a friend: a classmate. The kiss he gave me was on the cheek. It's normal," said Rosa. "It's something people do."

Chucho Flores laughed and shook his head from side to side without moving his hands from his face.

"Of course, of course," he said. "It's normal, I know. I'm sorry."

The waitress came back with the coffeepot and a cup for Chucho Flores. First she filled Rosa's cup and then the other cup. As she moved away, her eyes met Rosa's and she made a sign, or that was what Rosa thought later. A sign with her eyebrows. She arched them. Or maybe she moved her lips. A word articulated in silence. She couldn't remember. But the waitress was trying to tell her something.

"Drink your coffee," said Rosa.

"I will," said Chucho Flores, but he didn't move, his hands still over his face.

Another man had come in and sat next to the door. The waitress was standing at his table and they were talking. The man was wearing a baggy denim jacket and a black sweatshirt. He was thin and probably no older than twenty-five. Rosa looked at him and the man noticed that she was looking at him, but he ignored her and drank his soda, not returning her gaze.

•

"Three days later I met you," said Rosa.

"Why did you come to the fight?" asked Fate. "Do you like boxing?"

"No, I already told you it was the first time I'd been, but it was Rosa who convinced me to come."

"The other Rosa," said Fate.

"Yes, Rosita Méndez," said Rosa.

"But after the fight you were going to make love with Chucho Flores," said Fate.

"No," said Rosa. "I took his cocaine, but I had no intention of going to bed with him. I can't stand jealous men, but I was willing to be his friend. We had talked about it on the phone and he seemed to understand. But I did think he was acting strange. In the car, looking for a restaurant, he wanted me to give him a blow job. He said: blow me one last time. Or maybe he didn't say it like that, in those words, but that was more or less what he meant. I asked him if he'd gone crazy and he laughed. I laughed, too. It all seemed like a joke. For two days he'd been calling me and when it wasn't him it was Rosita Méndez calling and giving me messages from him. She said I shouldn't break up with him. She said he was a good catch. But I told her I considered our relationship or whatever it was over."

"He understood things were over between you," said Fate.

"We had talked on the phone, I'd explained that I don't like jealous men, I'm not a jealous person," said Rosa, "I can't stand jealousy."

"He thought he'd lost you," said Fate.

"Probably," said Rosa, "or he wouldn't have asked me to give him a blow job. I never would've done it, especially not in the middle of town, even if it was dark out."

"But he didn't seem sad," said Fate, "or at least I didn't get that impression."

"No, he seemed happy," said Rosa. "He was always a happy man."

"Yes, that's what I thought," said Fate, "a happy man looking to have a good time with his girlfriend and his friends."

"He was high," said Rosa, "he kept taking pills."

"He didn't seem high to me," said Fate, "he seemed a little strange, as if he had something too big in his head. And as if he didn't know what to do with it, even though it would blow up on him in the end."

"So is that why you stayed?" asked Rosa.

"Maybe," said Fate, "I don't really know, I should be in the United States right now or writing my article, but here I am, in a motel, talking to you. I don't understand it."

"Did you want to go to bed with my friend Rosita?" asked Rosa.

"No," said Fate. "Not at all."

"Did you stay for me?" asked Rosa.

"I don't know," said Fate.

They both yawned.

"Have you fallen in love with me?" asked Rosa with disarming naturalness.

"Maybe," said Fate.

•

When Rosa fell asleep he took off her high-heeled shoes and covered her with a blanket. He turned off the lights and for a while he stood looking out through the blinds at the parking lot and the highway lights. Then he put on his jacket and quietly left the room. At the desk, the clerk was watching TV and he smiled at Fate when he saw him come in. They talked for a while about Mexican and American TV shows. The clerk said that American shows were better made but Mexican shows were funnier. Fate asked if he had cable. The clerk said cable was only for rich people or faggots. Real life was on the free channels, and that was where you had to look for it. Fate asked if he thought anything was really free in the end, and the clerk started to laugh and said he knew where Fate was heading but he wasn't about to be convinced. Fate said he wasn't trying to convince him of anything, and then he asked whether he had a computer he could use to send an e-mail. The clerk shook his head and looked through a pile of papers on the desk until he found the card of a Santa Teresa cybercafé.

"It's open all night," he said, which surprised Fate, because even in New York he'd never heard of cybercafés that stayed open twenty-four hours.

The card for the Santa Teresa cybercafé was a deep red, so red that it was hard to read what was printed on it. On the back, in a lighter red, was a map that showed exactly where the café was located. He asked the receptionist to translate the name of the place. The clerk laughed and said it was called Fire, Walk With Me.

"It sounds like the title of a David Lynch film," said Fate.

The clerk shrugged and said that all of Mexico was a collage of diverse and wide-ranging homages.

"Every single thing in this country is an homage to everything in the world, even the things that haven't happened yet," he said.

After he told Fate how to get to the cybercafé, they talked for a while about Lynch's films. The clerk had seen all of them. Fate had seen only three or four. According to the clerk, Lynch's greatest achievement was

the TV series *Twin Peaks*. Fate liked *The Elephant Man* best, maybe because he'd often felt like the elephant man himself, wanting to be like
other people but at the same time knowing he was different. When the
clerk asked him whether he'd heard that Michael Jackson had bought or
tried to buy the skeleton of the elephant man, Fate shrugged and said
that Michael Jackson was sick. I don't think so, said the clerk, watching
something presumably important that was happening on TV just then.

"In my opinion," he said with his eyes fixed on the TV Fate couldn't
see, "Michael knows things the rest of us don't."

"We all know things we think nobody else knows," said Fate.

Then he said good night, put the cybercafé card in his pocket, and
went back to his room.

•

For a long time Fate stood with the lights out, looking through the blinds
at the gravel lot and the incessant lights of the trucks going by on the
highway. He thought about Chucho Flores and Charly Cruz. Once again
he saw the shadow that Charly Cruz's house cast over the vacant lot next
door. He heard Chucho Flores's laugh and he saw Rosa Méndez
stretched out on the bed in a bare, narrow room like a monk's cell. He
thought about Corona, Corona's gaze, the way Corona had looked at
him. He thought about the man with the mustache who had joined
them at the last minute and who didn't speak, and then he remembered
the man's voice when they were fleeing, as shrill as a bird's. When he
was tired of standing he pulled a chair over to the window and kept
watching. Sometimes he thought about his mother's apartment and he
remembered concrete courtyards where children shouted and played. If
he closed his eyes he could see a white dress lifted by the wind on the
streets of Harlem as invincible laughter spilled down the walls, running
along the sidewalks, cool and warm as the white dress. He felt sleep
trickling in his ears or rising from his chest. But he didn't want to close
his eyes and instead he kept scanning the lot, the two streetlights in
front of the motel, the shadows dispersed by the flashes of car lights like
comet tails in the dark.

Sometimes he turned his head and glanced at Rosa sleeping. But the
third or fourth time he realized he didn't need to turn and look. It simply
wasn't necessary. For a second he thought he would never be sleepy
again. Suddenly, as he was following the wake of the taillights of two

trucks that seemed to be in a race, the telephone rang. When he answered he heard the clerk's voice and he knew immediately that this was what he'd been waiting for.

"Mr. Fate," said the clerk, "someone just called to ask if you were staying here."

He asked who had called.

"A policeman, Mr. Fate," said the clerk.

"A policeman? A Mexican policeman?"

"I just talked to him. He wanted to know if you were a guest here."

"And what did you tell him?" asked Fate.

"The truth, that you were here, but that you'd left," said the clerk.

"Thanks," said Fate, and he hung up.

He woke up Rosa and told her to put on her shoes. He packed the few things he had unpacked and put the suitcase in the trunk of his car. Outside it was cold. When he went back into the room Rosa was combing her hair in the bathroom, and Fate told her they didn't have time for that. They got in the car and drove to the motel reception. The clerk was standing there polishing his Coke-bottle glasses with the tail of his shirt. Fate took out a fifty-dollar bill and slid it across the counter.

"If they come, tell them I went home," he said.

"They'll come," said the clerk.

As they turned onto the highway, he asked Rosa whether she was carrying her passport.

"Of course not," said Rosa.

"The police are looking for me," said Fate, and he told her what the clerk had said.

"Why are you so sure it's the police?" asked Rosa. "It could be Corona, or Chucho."

"You're right," said Fate, "maybe it's Charly Cruz or maybe it's Rosita Méndez putting on a man's voice, but I'd rather not wait to find out."

•

They drove around the block to see whether anyone was lying in wait for them, but everything was calm (the calm of quicksilver or the calm that heralds border dawns), and the second time around they parked the car under a tree in front of a neighbor's house. For a while they sat there, alert to any sign, any movement. When they crossed the street they were careful to stay away from the streetlights. Then they hopped over the fence and headed straight for the backyard. As Rosa searched for her keys, Fate saw the geometry book hanging from the clothesline. Without thinking, he went over and touched it with the tip of his fingers. Then, not because he cared but to defuse the tension, he asked Rosa what *Testamento geométrico* meant and Rosa translated it for him without comment.

"It's odd that someone would hang a book out like a shirt," he whispered.

"It was my father's idea."

The house, although shared by father and daughter, had a clearly feminine air. It smelled of incense and blond tobacco. Rosa turned on a lamp and for a time they sat back in armchairs draped in multicolored Mexican blankets, neither one speaking a word. Then Rosa made coffee, and while she was in the kitchen, Fate saw Óscar Amalfitano appear in the doorway, barefoot, his hair uncombed, dressed in a very wrinkled white shirt and jeans, as if he'd slept in his clothes. For a moment the two of them looked at each other, wordless, as if they were asleep and their dreams had converged on common ground, a place where sound was alien. Fate got up and introduced himself. Amalfitano asked whether he spoke Spanish. Fate apologized and smiled and Amalfitano repeated the question in English.

"I'm a friend of your daughter's," said Fate, "she asked me in."

From the kitchen came Rosa's voice, telling her father in Spanish not to worry, that he was a reporter from New York. Then she asked him if he wanted coffee too and Amalfitano said yes without taking his eyes off the stranger. When Rosa appeared with a tray, three cups of coffee, a little pitcher of milk, and the sugar bowl, her father asked her what was going on. Nothing right now, I think, said Rosa, but some strange things happened earlier. Amalfitano looked down then and studied his bare feet. He added milk and sugar to his coffee and asked his daughter to explain everything. Rosa looked at Fate and translated what her father had just said. Fate smiled and sat down again in his chair. He took a cup of coffee and began to sip it as Rosa proceeded to tell her father, in Spanish, what had happened that night, from the boxing match to the moment when she had to leave the American's motel. When Rosa finished her story the sun was beginning to come up, and Amalfitano, who had interrupted his daughter only a very few times asking questions and pressing for explanations, suggested that they call the motel and ask the clerk whether the police had shown up or not. Rosa translated her father's suggestion, and more out of politeness than because he thought it would do any good, Fate called the number of the motel. No one answered. Óscar Amalfitano got up from his chair and went over to the window. The street was silent. You'd both better go, he said. Rosa looked at him without saying a word.

"Can you get her to the United States and then take her to an airport and put her on a plane to Barcelona?"

Fate said he could. Óscar Amalfitano left the window and disappeared into his room. When he came back he handed Rosa a roll of bills. It isn't much but it'll be enough for your ticket and the first few days in Barcelona. I don't want to go, Papa, said Rosa. Yes, yes, I know that, said Amalfitano, and he made her take the money. Where's your passport? Go get it. Pack a suitcase. But hurry, he said, and then he went back to his post at the window. Behind the Spirit that belonged to the neighbors across the street, he saw the black Peregrino he was looking for. He sighed. Fate set his coffee on a table and went over to the window.

"I'd like to know what's going on," said Fate. His voice was hoarse.

"Get my daughter out of this city and then forget everything. Or no, don't forget anything, just take her away."

At that moment Fate remembered his appointment with Guadalupe Roncal.

"Does it have to do with the killings?" he asked. "Do you think this Chucho Flores is mixed up in that?"

"They're all mixed up in it," said Amalfitano.

A tall young man in jeans and a denim jacket got out of the Peregrino and lit a cigarette. Rosa looked over her father's shoulder.

"Who is it?" she asked.

"Haven't you ever seen him before?"

"No, I don't think so."

"He's a cop," said Amalfitano.

Then he took his daughter by the hand and pulled her into her room. They closed the door. Fate guessed they were saying their goodbyes and he looked out the window again. The man in the Peregrino was smoking, leaning on the hood of his car. Every so often he looked up at the sky, which was gradually growing brighter. He seemed relaxed, in no hurry, at ease, happy to be watching another sunrise in Santa Teresa. A man came out of one of the neighboring houses and started his car. The man in the

Peregrino tossed the end of his cigarette on the sidewalk and got in his car. He never once looked toward the house. When Rosa came out of her room she was carrying a small suitcase.

"How will we leave?" Fate wanted to know.

"By the door," said Amalfitano.

Then Fate saw, as if it were a movie he didn't entirely understand but that in a strange way took him back to his mother's death, how Amalfitano kissed and hugged his daughter and then strode purposefully outside. First Fate watched him walk through the front yard, then he watched him open the peeling wooden gate, then he watched him cross the street, barefoot, his hair uncombed, to the black Peregrino. When he got there the man rolled down the window and they talked for a while, Amalfitano in the street and the man in his car. They know each other, thought Fate, this isn't the first time they've talked.

"It's time, let's go," said Rosa.

Fate followed her. They crossed the yard and the street and their bodies cast extremely fine shadows that every five seconds were shaken by a tremor, as if the sun were spinning backward. When he got in the car Fate thought he heard a laugh behind him and he turned around, but all he saw was Amalfitano and the young man still talking in the same position as before.

●

It didn't take Guadalupe Roncal and Rosa Amalfitano more than a minute to share their respective woes. The reporter offered to drive with them to Tucson. Rosa said there was no need to go overboard. They deliberated for a while. As they spoke in Spanish, Fate looked out the window, but everything was normal around the Sonora Resort. All the reporters were gone, no one was talking about boxing matches, the waiters seemed to have stirred from a long lethargy and were less friendly, as if waking put them out of sorts. Rosa called her father from the hotel. Fate watched her head toward the reception desk with Guadalupe Roncal, and while he was waiting for them to come back he smoked a cigarette and took some notes for the story he still hadn't filed. In the light of day the previous night's events seemed unreal, invested with childish gravity. As his thoughts drifted, Fate saw Merolino's two sparring partners, Omar Abdul and García. He imagined them taking a bus to the coast. He saw them get off the bus, he saw them take a few steps through the scrub. The oneiric wind whipped grains of sand that stuck to their faces. A golden bath. So peaceful, thought Fate. How simple it all is. Then he saw the bus and he imagined it black, like a huge hearse. He saw Abdul's arrogant smile, Garcia's impassive face, his strange tattoos, and he heard the sudden sound of dishes breaking, not many of them, or a crash of boxes falling, and only then did Fate realize that he was asleep and looked around for the waiter, to ask for another coffee, but he didn't see anyone. Guadalupe Roncal and Rosa Amalfitano were still on the phone.

•

"They're good people, friendly, hospitable. Mexicans are hardworking, they're hugely curious about everything, they care about people, they're brave and generous, their sadness isn't destructive, it's life giving," said Rosa Amalfitano as they crossed the border into the United States.

"Will you miss them?" asked Fate.

"I'll miss my father and I'll miss the people," said Rosa.

•

When they were in the car on the way to the Santa Teresa prison, Rosa said no one had answered the phone at her father's. After she called Amalfitano several times, Rosa had called Rosa Méndez's house, and there was no one there either. I think Rosa's dead, she said. Fate shook his head as if he couldn't believe it.

"We're still alive," he said.

"We're alive because we haven't seen anything and we don't know anything," said Rosa.

The reporter's car was ahead of them. It was a yellow Little Nemo. Guadalupe Roncal drove carefully, although every once in a while she stopped, as if she didn't quite remember the way. Fate thought it might be better to stop following her and head straight for the border. When he suggested it, Rosa was strongly opposed. He asked her whether she had friends in the city. Rosa said no, she didn't really have any friends. Chucho Flores and Rosa Méndez and Charly Cruz, but he wouldn't call them friends, would he?

"No, those aren't friends," said Fate.

•

They saw a Mexican flag flying in the desert, on the other side of the fence. One of the border police on the American side scrutinized Fate and Rosa. He wondered what a white girl, and a pretty white girl at that, was doing with a black man. Fate held his gaze. Reporter? asked the officer. Fate nodded. A big fish, thought the officer. Every night he must knock her around. Spanish? Rosa smiled at the officer. A shadow of frustration crossed the officer's face. When they pulled away the flag disappeared and all they could see was the fence and warehouses surrounded by walls.

"The problem is bad luck," said Rosa.

Fate didn't hear her.

•

As they were waiting in a windowless room, Fate felt his penis getting harder and harder. For a moment he thought he hadn't had an erection since his mother's death, but then he rejected the idea, it couldn't have been that long, he thought, but it could have, the irremediable was possible, the unsalvageable was possible, so why couldn't the blood flow to his cock have stopped for what really was a fairly short period of time? Rosa Amalfitano looked at him. Guadalupe Roncal was busy with her notes and her tape recorder, sitting in a chair bolted to the floor. Every once in a while the everyday sounds of the prison reached them. Shouted names, muted music, footsteps receding in the distance. Fate sat on a wooden bench and yawned. He thought he would fall asleep. He imagined Rosa's legs on his shoulders. He saw his room at the motel again and wondered whether or not they'd made love. Of course not, he said to himself. Then he heard shouts, as if a bachelor party were being held in one of the prison chambers. He thought about the killings. He heard distant laughter. Roars. He heard Guadalupe Roncal say something to Rosa and he heard Rosa answer. Sleep overtook him and he saw himself peacefully sleeping on the sofa in his mother's apartment in Harlem, with the TV on. I'll sleep for half an hour, he said to himself, and then I'll get back to work. I have to write the fight story. I have to drive all night. When the sun comes up everything will be over.

•

After they crossed the border, the few tourists they saw on the streets of El Adobe seemed to be sleepwalking. A woman in her seventies, in a flowered dress and Nike sneakers, was kneeling down to examine some Indian rugs. She looked like an athlete from the 1940s. Three children holding hands watched some objects displayed in a shop window. The objects were moving almost imperceptibly, and Fate couldn't tell whether they were animals or machines. Outside a bar some men in cowboy hats who looked like Chicanos were gesticulating and pointing in opposite directions. At the end of the street there were some wooden sheds and metal containers on the pavement and beyond them was the desert. All of this is like somebody else's dream, thought Fate. Next to him, Rosa's head rested delicately on the seat and her big eyes were fixed on some point on the horizon. Fate looked at her knees, which struck him as perfect, and then her hips and then her shoulders and her collarbones, which seemed to have a life of their own, a dark, suspended life that gave signs of itself only now and then. Then he concentrated on driving. The highway out of El Adobe headed into a kind of swirl of shades of ocher.

"I wonder how Guadalupe Roncal is doing," said Rosa in a dreamy voice.

"By now she must be flying home," said Fate.

"Strange," said Rosa.

•

Rosa's voice woke him.

"Listen," she said.

Fate opened his eyes but he didn't hear anything. Guadalupe Roncal had gotten up and she was standing next to them now, her eyes very wide, as if her worst nightmares had come true. Fate went over to the door and opened it. One of his legs had fallen asleep and he couldn't quite manage to wake up yet. He saw a hallway and at the end of the hallway he saw a rough cement staircase, as if the builders had left it half finished. The hallway was dimly lit.

"Don't leave," Rosa said to him.

"Let's get out of this trap," said Guadalupe Roncal.

A prison official appeared at the end of the hallway and headed toward them. Fate showed his press ID. The official nodded without looking at the ID and he smiled at Guadalupe Roncal, who remained standing in the doorway. Then the official closed the door and said something about a storm. Rosa translated into Fate's ear. A sandstorm or a rainstorm or an electric storm. High clouds dropping down from the mountains, clouds that wouldn't burst over Santa Teresa but that cast a pall on the landscape. A miserable morning. The inmates always get nervous, said the official. He was a young man, with a skimpy mustache, maybe a little bit soft around the middle for his age, and you could tell he didn't like his job. They're bringing the killer now.

●

You have to listen to women. You should never ignore a woman's fears. It was something like that, remembered Fate, that his mother or her neighbor, the deceased Miss Holly, used to say when both of them were young and he was a boy. For an instant he imagined a set of scales, like the scales of Blind Justice, except that instead of two platters, there were two bottles, or something like two bottles. The bottle on the left was clear and full of desert sand. There were several holes in it through which the sand escaped. The bottle on the right was full of acid. There were no holes in it, but the acid was eating away at the bottle from the inside. On the way to Tucson, Fate didn't recognize any of the things he'd seen a few days before, when he'd traveled the same road in the opposite direction. What used to be my right is my left, and there are no points of reference. Everything is erased. Toward noon they stopped at a diner on the highway. A group of Mexicans who looked like jobless migrant workers watched them from the counter. They were drinking bottled water and local sodas, the names and logos odd to Fate. New businesses that would soon fail. The food was bad. Rosa was sleepy and when they got back to the car she fell asleep. Fate remembered the words of Guadalupe Roncal. No one pays attention to these killings, but the secret of the world is hidden in them. Did Guadalupe Roncal say that, or was it Rosa? At moments, the highway was like a river. The suspected killer said it, thought Fate. The giant fucking albino who appeared along with the black cloud.

●

When Fate heard footsteps approaching he thought they were the footsteps of a giant. Guadalupe Roncal must have thought something similar, because she seemed about to faint, but instead of fainting, she clung to the prison official's hand and then his lapel. Rather than pull away, he put his arm around her shoulders. Fate felt Rosa's body next to him. He heard voices. As if the inmates were egging someone on. He heard laughter and calls to order, and then the black clouds from the east passed over the prison and the air seemed to darken. The footsteps came closer. He heard laughter and pleas. Suddenly a voice began to sing a song. It sounded like a woodcutter chopping down trees. The voice wasn't singing in English. At first Fate couldn't figure out what the language was, until Rosa, beside him, said it was German. The voice grew louder. It occurred to Fate that he might still be dreaming. The trees fell one by one. I'm a giant lost in the middle of a burned forest. But someone will come to rescue me. Rosa translated the suspect's string of curses for him. A polyglot woodcutter, thought Fate, who speaks English as well as he speaks Spanish and who sings in German. I'm a giant lost in the middle of a charred forest. And yet only I know where I'm going, only I know my destiny. And then the footsteps and the laughter could be heard once more, and the goading and words of encouragement of the inmates and the guards escorting the giant. And then an enormous and very blond man came into the visitors' room, ducked his head, as if he were afraid of knocking it on the ceiling, and smiled as if he had just done something naughty, singing the German song about the lost woodcutter and fixing them all with an intelligent and mocking gaze. Then the guard accompanying him asked Guadalupe Roncal if she would prefer that he be handcuffed to the chair and Guadalupe Roncal shook her head and the guard gave the tall man a little pat on the shoulder and left and the official who was standing with Fate and the women went out too, though not before saying something into Guadalupe Roncal's ear, and they were left alone.

"Good morning," said the giant in Spanish. He sat down and stretched his legs under the table so that his feet stuck out the other side.

He was wearing black tennis shoes and white socks. Guadalupe Roncal took a step back.

"Ask whatever you want," said the giant.

Guadalupe Roncal raised her hand to her mouth, as if she were inhaling a toxic gas, and she couldn't think what to ask.